Darcy and Elizabeth

THE FACES OF LOVE

A *Pride and Prejudice* Variation

Arthel Cake

This novel is a work of fiction. Any resemblance to any person, living or dead, by name or character-ization, is purely coincidental, unless the character is identified as an historical person.

ISBN: 154101748X
ISBN 13: 9781541017481
Library of Congress Control Number: 2016920573
CreateSpace Independent Publishing Platform
North Charleston, South Carolina

To my beloved sister, Cheryl—my Cassandra—who has offered nothing but support and encouragement to follow my dream. And to our dear Helene, for all the years of friendship.

Also a humble thank-you to Miss Jane Austen, who gave us two of the most unforgettable characters in English literature.

Table of Contents

Chapter 1	1
Chapter 2	14
Chapter 3	27
Chapter 4	41
Chapter 5	54
Chapter 6	72
Chapter 7	86
Chapter 8	96
Chapter 9	116
Chapter 10	134
Chapter 11	148
Chapter 12	165
Chapter 13	181
Chapter 14	189
Chapter 15	202
Chapter 16	218
Chapter 17	235
Chapter 18	249

Chapter 1

The fine March rain dripped from the brim of Fitzwilliam Darcy's hat, ran down the several capes of his greatcoat, darkened the highly polished leather of his Hessian boots, and ran away in rivulets from the headstone before him, at the base of which lay a single red rose. The stone was of a modest size, Derbyshire granite, beautifully scrolled around the name and dates. Such short dates. She had been barely twenty-seven. Strange, he mused. One year ago today he had stood in the thin sunshine of early spring, which cast soft shadows into the new grave where his wife's coffin rested, and thrown a handful of dark soil onto the wooden lid. The humped black earth in the burial ground of Pemberley Chapel had now sunk back to join the rest of the churchyard and was covered with new grass. *Dust to dust, ashes to ashes,* Darcy thought, *In sure and certain hope of the Resurrection....*

The gentle voice of the old vicar whispered in his ear. Darcy no longer felt sorrow for a life ended, only pity for a life wasted. He straightened his shoulders, said a short prayer, and turned away. He wore a blue frock coat for the first time in a year, a sign that formal mourning was over. For a year since her death, he had worn only black; he had owed her that much, the visible evidence of grief. As he walked the mile to Pemberley along the sleek gravel of the pathway, Darcy saw her face once more, whiter than the pillows on which her dark head rested. Even her lips were colorless, the bones pressed sharply against the skin. One thin hand lay limp on the coverlet; the other hand he held in both of his for whatever comfort he might offer.

Her breath come in little gasps. Darcy had begun to count the seconds between the sounds. At first it had been only a few, but in the last hour, the intervals had grown longer, until the last count was nearly a full minute. He felt her hand move slightly in his and leaned forward. Her soft gray eyes, sunk in lavender shadows, opened, and she smiled.

"Dear Fitzwilliam." He had to bend over her to hear the faint words. "These last two years have been the happiest of my life since my father died. I thank you for that and for all your care." Pauses broke the words as she gathered the little strength remaining to her.

"You know there is no need to thank me," he replied. Her hand was very cold in his warm fingers. "You are very dear to me."

"I did not love you, you know?" she went on more slowly still. "You were escape., The only way I knew out of that hell. I have come to love you. I only wish I could have given you a child."

He stroked her hand gently. "It does not matter. Do not think of it. Rest."

She seemed to gain strength from some inner reserve, turning her head to him. "My mother…"

"I sent her word you were ill. She may be on her way here now."

She moved her head in slow negation. "She will not come. My mother has always hated me. I do not understand why, but there is a reason beyond Rosings."

Darcy stroked her hand tenderly. "It is of no consequence. Please, rest, my dear wife."

Her eyes grew dim. Whatever strength she had summoned failed her. "I will rest now."

She closed her eyes. He felt her body relax and then stiffen. Her breath made a small sucking sound. Her hand tightened on his and then went limp. Darcy felt for the pulse in her throat, even though he knew she was gone. He heard the door to her dressing room open behind him and then a cry of distress as her maid realized what had occurred. Darcy folded his wife's hands on her breast, covered her face with the linen sheet, and straightened. He hoped with all his heart that Anne de Bourgh Darcy was finally at peace.

Early leaves hung limp from the trees along the path, dripping onto the dark earth with its sparse new grass as Darcy returned to Pemberley House the way he had come. The green smell of renewal was in the chill breeze, blowing from fields already sprouting for summer harvest. The wooded ridge behind the manor house rose against a gauzy mist to the gray sky. It was time, Darcy knew, to think of the future.

After a quarter hour, he turned off the path and approached the house across the west-sloping lawn. The rain had ceased, but masses of dark clouds stood over the distant peaks climbing into a pale sky. At that moment, he saw the carriage just pulling around the far side of the house toward the stables, and his mouth tightened to a thin line. Increasing his long stride, Darcy reached the front steps and entered the hexagonal entrance hall as a footman hurried forward to take his wet outerwear.

"Where is she?"

"In the drawing room, sir."

Darcy crossed the tiled floor with its diagonal pattern of black and white squares and strode into the drawing room. It was a large room, elegant and comfortable, with polished furnishings and well-padded seating arranged for conversation. Vases of roses from the glass house scented the air. Tall windows with mirrors and tables between them looked out on the extensive gardens. A fire blazed beneath the white Adam mantelpiece, lighting the heavy form standing before it. Lady Catherine de Bourgh eyed her nephew and son-in-law with her customary expression of hauteur. She was tall, like all the Fitzwilliamsand carried herself stiffly erect. Her skin was sallow. Her once-blond hair, perfectly coiffed, showed extensive gray. She wore a black traveling ensemble. A dark-gray pelisse lined with ermine was thrown carelessly across a nearby sofa. The lines of lifelong self-importance drew her face into a perpetually arrogant facade that did not change as she regarded Darcy.

"The housekeeper said you had gone to the churchyard. In the rain. I do not know why, as I see you have obviously eschewed mourning."

Her tone expressed her disapproval and a shade of contempt. Lady Catherine's voice was sharp in spite of its cultured accents. In some inexplicable way, it was coarse. Darcy moved to take the warmth of the fire as she went to the sofa, ignoring her comment. He was used to Lady Catherine's ploys to control a conversation.

"What do you want, Aunt?"

"Not 'Mother'? No, never that. Dear Anne was the only mother you will ever acknowledge. My little sister. My daughter's namesake."

A servant tapped on the door, and when Darcy called her in, she set a tea tray on a table before the sofa. She looked to Darcy, who waved her away with an easy gesture. The maid curtsied and left them, closing the heavy paneled door behind her. Lady Catherine sat down and poured herself a cup of tea before Darcy could offer the courtesy. He continued to stand before the fire, so still he might have been a statue painted to resemble life.

His aunt sipped the tea, set the cup down, and looked at him with speculation. Her pale eyes bored into his, without effect. She smiled, nearly a sneer, and folded her heavy hands in her lap. In youth, Lady Catherine Fitzwilliam had been an attractive if imposing woman. Time had revealed the truth beneath the facade; she looked what she had become—a stark, unfeeling parody of womanhood.

"You must wonder why I have made the trip here, since I have not been welcome for such a long time." When Darcy did not answer, Lady Catherine went on. "I have business to discuss with you, Darcy."

"You did not come when I sent word Anne was dying. You did not come when the funeral was held, for the shoulder feast. I would have made no problem if you had wished to attend the funeral service. You only visited Anne when you thought you might gain some advantage, and your constant complaints and criticism made Anne so ill. I barred you from the house for her sake."

"She was weak," Lady Catherine said flatly. "Just like her father. I tried to make her strong, but it was useless. Her only real purpose was to marry you and join our two families and fortunes."

Darcy's face paled. He gazed at his aunt with disgust. "You abused her; you kept her a virtual prisoner. You bullied and belittled her until she begged me to marry her and take her away from your control. Even my uncle, your own brother, added his voice for the marriage for her sake. You were never a mother to her. She meant nothing to you when she was alive and less now she has died. What possible 'business' can we have to discuss?"

Lady Catherine rose, faced Darcy, and drew herself up. She made an impressive figure, but Darcy was unmoved. A sudden image of Anne filled his mind. She stood by the windows across this room staring out at the gardens. A day gown of sprigged white muslin hung loosely on her thin body; she appeaeed as insubstantial as a ghost. "My mother always hated me. I know it to be true, although I never discovered the reason. Perhaps because she and my father never got along well, and he loved me. I do not know, but I know I am right."

His aunt's voice intruded into his memory, bringing him back sharply to the present. "I want Rosings. I have a right to it. The estate should have been mine when Sir Lewis died, but the fool willed it to Anne. Anne! She was nine years old and barely able to walk from her chambers to the drawing room without Mrs. Jenkinson's arm. I am the one who has kept Rosings the great estate it is. When you married, you removed the steward I chose and put in your own steward to lord it over me, but that will stop. You will give me Rosings, or I will find a way to take it from you!"

Darcy watched her. Amazement and fury warred for control of his emotions. The air fairly crackled with the force of wills between them. He fought for calm, waiting until he controlled his voice to respond. "I removed your steward because he was stealing from the estate. Anne's estate. When I married Anne, *at your behest*, her property became mine, including Rosings." As his anger receded under the force of control, a disquiet he could not explain formed in his mind. "Why do you want Rosings now? Why not approach me when Anne died?"

"Would it have made a difference?" Lady Catherine's voice was still scornful, but Darcy detected an undertone of caution.

He said, "No. You have, by Sir Lewis's will, lifelong occupation of the dower house with a suitable income to maintain it, as well as a trust from your marriage settlement administered by Lord Henry, which gives you an independent income."

"Dower house!" Scorn dripped from her words. "Am I—I, Lady Catherine de Bourgh—to live in the dower house like a poor relation? How dare you?"

"I dare, as you put it, for Anne's sake. You will never have what was hers by right and law. If you have any thought of legal proceedings, I can tell you that Anne also made a will. It was drawn up by my solicitor and has been registered at Doctors' Commons. There are several small bequests and a pension for Mrs.

Jenkinson, for her faithful service. Everything else, with the exception of your occupation of the dower house, Anne left to me."

"A will." Lady Catherine barely whispered the words. Two red spots sprang up on her angled cheeks. Her face, never lovely, twisted until Darcy wondered if she was on the verge of an apoplectic seizure. "You made her——"

"I made her do nothing." Darcy's words were thin ice over a white heat. "I had nothing to gain. It was for her own peace of mind." He came away from the fireplace at last to confront her. "And now I will tell you what is to occur. I have no intention of ever occupying the property. Therefore, as soon as I determine what I wish to do with Rosings, you will remove from the manor to the dower house. You may take your personal property and any staff members who wish to remove with you. I have already written my solicitor and my steward to implement my intentions at the proper time. And that, I believe, concludes your business with me—and your visit. Do not visit again, Lady Catherine." He rang for the butler. "Not here or at any other of my properties. I never want to see you again."

Lady Catherine picked up her pelisse and flung it over her shoulders. Her face was the color of candle wax her lips compressed until they disappeared into the heavy lines from nose to mouth. She turned as the butler tapped on the door. There was pure loathing in her eyes and a light of animal cunning Darcy found strangely disturbing.

"I swear to you, Darcy. I swear, if you do not give me Rosings, I will see you never have a day's peace until you do!"

Mr. Niles entered at Darcy's summons. "Please see Lady Catherine to her coach, Mr. Niles. She will not be staying."

She pushed past the butler, and Darcy closed his eyes for a moment. He knew this was not the end of her demand, but there was nothing she could do about his control of the estate or his decision. Still, unease remained in the back of his mind. Prevented from having her own way, Lady Catherine was a formidable opponent. Darcy had no doubt she meant to press her case. He knew his uncle Lord Matlock would support him, but that was no certainty Lady Catherine could be prevented from causing trouble. With a shake of his shoulders, Darcy pushed the thought aside and went on to his study to take up estate business. There was nothing he could do about her actions at that point, and managing an estate as large as Pemberley, in addition to Rosings and several smaller estates he owned, was a full-time occupation.

"I have invited my very good friend, Mr. Fitzwilliam Darcy, to join me for the shooting," Mr. Bingley said to the room in general.

Bingley and his younger sister, Caroline, sat in the drawing room at Longbourn with the Bennet ladies, on whom they had called. Bingley had taken the chair where he had become accustomed to sit next to Miss Jane Bennet's seat at the end of the settee. Mr. Bingley's pleasant countenance became even more pleasant as he gazed at the eldest Bennet daughter with a smile.

The appellation most commonly applied to the young man was "amiable," and it was an excellent representation of his temperament. Pleasant and easygoing, Bingley made friends easily and kept them well, so that his circle of acquaintances was constantly expanding. His sister Caroline, on the other hand, was his exact opposite. She was taller than average with a fine figure and red-blond hair which was too elaborately coiffed for a morning visit. Her silk gown was also too elaborate; it was of high fashion however in a fuchsia that did her hair and complexion no favors. She might have been attractive except for her air of bored superiority. She adored the *haut ton* and took on their pretentions and attitudes like a second skin. At present, Caroline found her company beneath her and did not care who knew it.

Mrs. Bennet, seated across from Bingley, pricked up her ears as she frowned slightly and attempted to remember something. She had grown plump with middle age, but the traces of youthful beauty were still visible in her large blue eyes and the soft gold of her hair, which had scarcely grayed. Having attained the age when most ladies were at least circumspect, if not wise, without ever having an original thought, she was still able to see an advantage to her unmarried daughters with the keenness of a hunting bird. She said in her rather high-pitched voice, "I believe I know the name. I have seen it betimes in the society news in my husband's newspaper. Not recently, though."

Although she was loath to admit it, Mrs. Bennet followed the gossip of the *ton* with nearly the same avidity as her sister, Mrs. Phillips. Bingley hesitated before continuing. Darcy hated the gossipmongers and society hangers-on and hated even more having his name bandied about in the papers. He tolerated society for his sister's sake, and that would only be until she should come out and enter society herself in a year or two.

Bingley's sister Caroline was not so reticent. With her usual air of instructing the peasants, she said, "Mr. Darcy moves in the highest circles. His uncle is the Earl of Matlock."

"Really?" Mrs. Bennet raised her eyebrows.

She disliked Miss Bingley nearly as much as Miss Bingley disliked her, but her sights were set on the brother as a very fine match for Jane, and she was careful not to antagonize his sister.

"Mr. Darcy has not been in society since his marriage nearly…oh, four years ago," Bingley put in quickly.

"Is Mrs. Darcy coming with him?" Mrs. Bennet inquired.

"I am afraid she passed over a year ago."

"He must be old," Lydia, the youngest daughter of the house, said suddenly with a sly grimace.

Her next older sister, Catherine, put a hand over her mouth to stifle a giggle. Where boisterous Lydia went, delicate Kitty followed.

Her mother looked at her with indulgent reproof, while Jane and her next youngest sister, Elizabeth, seated next to her, frowned at the rudeness. Mary, the middle sister, opened her mouth to offer one of her moral strictures, saw her mother's face, and said nothing. She had heard "Be quiet, Mary" so many times. Mrs. Bennet rarely needed to say it.

"He is not yet thirty," Bingley informed them. He would not discuss Darcy's private business, but some things were common knowledge. "Mrs. Darcy suffered from an affliction of the heart."

"How sad," Jane commented.

Mrs. Bennet said with elaborate casualness, "Had they children?"

"Sadly, no."

"He will be seeking a wife, then. Men of consequence require heirs."

Her attempt at sagacity brought a brief sneer to Miss Bingley's lips. "I am sure," Miss Bingley cut in rather sharply, "he will remarry when he is ready."

"A woman of the nobility, no doubt," Elizabeth commented, looking up from the handkerchief she was embroidering. Jane glanced at her and saw the sparkle in her eyes. "Someone of his own wealth and station in life."

Miss Bingley looked poisonous. "Mr. Darcy may marry where he chooses," she said coldly. "He has a most beautiful estate in Derbyshire, Pemberley, where we have often visited. I always tell Charles that when he buys an estate he must model it on Pemberley. It is magnificent. Perfect. The gardens are a wonder, and the house is a treasure—everything is so beautiful. And the late Mrs. Darcy brought her own estate of Rosings in Kent to the marriage."

"Then certainly he will want a wife to enhance the grandeur of his two estates," Elizabeth said sedately.

Mrs. Bennet looked thoughtful and then said with an undertone of distaste, "We also are expecting a guest. My husband's second cousin, Mr. Collins, is coming for a visit. He is a minister with a living in Kent, Hunsford, on the Rosings estate. It is a strange coincidence. Is it not?"

Her listeners agreed conventionally that it was, and Mr. Bingley said, "His living is now in Darcy's gift. They have probably met. Do you know Mr. Collins well?"

"No." Mrs. Bennet's voice was rather flat. "Mr. Bennet's grandfather and his sister were estranged, and Mr. Bennet abided by his father's disinclination to pursue the acquaintance. Longbourn, as you may know, is entailed away from the female line. When we lose Mr. Bennet, Mr. Collins will inherit the estate."

"I do not approve of entails," Mr. Bingley said. "Although, when I have an estate of my own, I may feel differently. So you have not met Mr. Collins?"

"The visit is in the way of an olive branch, as I understand it," Mrs. Bennet replied with a sniff. "I suppose, as a pastor, Mr. Collins feels obliged to mend the rift in the family. I do not know what other purpose he might have in announcing a visit, unless it is to view what shall one day be his." Her tone revealed she would much rather he stayed at home.

"I am sure," Jane said tactfully, "that Mr. Collins's intentions are good, as befits a man of the cloth." Before either her mother or Miss Bingley could comment, she changed the subject. "Will you and Miss Bingley be attending tomorrow evening's assembly ball in Meryton, Mr. Bingley?"

"Yes, we shall. I have already purchased the tickets." Bingley carefully did not look at Caroline. "Our other sister, Louisa, and her husband, Mr. Hurst, are joining us and will also attend. Mr. Darcy will come as well if he arrives in time and I can convince him to come with us. I am looking forward to it."

"I am sure we are all looking forward to the entertainment," Miss Bingley added with just a touch of acid in her carefully modulated voice.

Elizabeth glanced at her, a small smile turning up the corners of her lips. "I am sure it will be nothing so grand as you are used to, Miss Bingley," she said. "Just a country ball. But those can be quite entertaining."

Lady Catherine de Bourgh sat stiffly on a chair covered in silk brocade in the drawing room of Matlock House. Her unlovely face was drawn into lines of anger that rendered it even less attractive. Amid the delicate lemon, lavender, and dove gray of the room, her dark clothing, although fashionable, gave her the look of a crow in a spring garden. Lord Matlock sat opposite her and was as upright as she; his tense shoulders and stony countenance gave the impression of a man facing an enemy rather than a relative. Lady Catherine's pale eyes flashed. She stared at her younger brother, and her wide, rather thin mouth drew down. "You will not support me in this, Henry? You encouraged the match. You pressured Darcy to wed Anne."

"No one pressures Darcy," Lord Henry Fitzwilliam, Earl of Matlock, stated flatly. "And I encouraged the match, as you put it, for Anne's sake, not for your mistaken ideas about dynastic unions."

Lord Henry had listened with hard-won patience to his elder sister's long, embittered list of complaints, recriminations, demands, and invectives. He should, he thought, be used to it by now, but her latest outpouring was beginning to wear away at his self-control.

"Rosings," Lady Catherine snapped yet again, "should never have been Anne's. It was my due. Sir Lewis had no right to leave it to an invalid!"

"No right?" Lord Henry's tone was taking on a harshness he could not quite master. He was known in the House of Lords for his ability to remain calm in the face of his bitterest enemy's vituperation; Catherine was another matter. "He had *every* right. You knew when you married him that not only was his own property his to dispose of but yours as well. He chose to leave Rosings to Anne as security for her future, which he obviously did not trust to you."

"When I was forced to marry him, you mean!" Lady Catherine seemed to swell in her chair. "I am the one who has managed Rosings for fifteen years. I took care of Anne, saw to her endless illnesses, and forwarded a marriage that any woman of standing would have given her soul to achieve."

"And bullied and abused her. Yes, I know, Catherine. I have my sources, including Anne herself. She begged me to speak to Darcy about the marriage, although she told me frankly she had no desire to marry anyone. She was desperate to get away, and Darcy was safe. She also told me she knew she was unlikely to survive more than a few years, leaving Darcy free to marry again. She loved him in her own way, and I believe he loved her in some fashion, perhaps more as a guardian than a husband. Darcy is very protective of those he loves or feels responsible for."

"I suppose," Lady Catherine sneered, "you knew about her will also?"

"I knew she made one, with Darcy's agreement. I did not know the contents. It is of no consequence. The will was unnecessary. Rosings became Darcy's the day they wed. He allowed you to continue on as chatelaine while Anne lived. If he now wishes to lease or even to sell the estate, that is his right."

"His right? His right! What about *my* rights? Am I to be shunted off like a nobody to the dower house while strangers take over Rosings? Are you such a fool that you believe I will stand by and see that happen? I would sooner burn it to the ground!"

Lord Henry stood, holding his elder sister's eyes. "I do not suggest you attempt it," he said very coldly. "Arson is a capital crime, and it is one, in this case, I believe Darcy would not hesitate to prosecute, even if it meant disgrace for the family. A decision I would fully concur with, whatever its effects on our name."

He hoped she believed him, for he was not certain his opinion was untrue. Lady Catherine rose. She was pale with fury, but she knew better than to press her brother too hard. Not a subtle woman, she was still possessed of the sort of cunning that understood the limits of those with whom it dealt.

"I see. Very well. I shall know what to do, Henry. You may depend upon it."

"I sincerely hope that action will be to remove to the dower house as Darcy has ordered and to cause no more trouble to this family."

She left him abruptly with no word of farewell. Lord Henry looked unseeingly around the cool serenity of the drawing room. The pale light coming in from undraped French-style windows shone on gleaming walnut and rosewood, gentle landscapes, and Sèvres vases full of late flowers. He rubbed his forehead. His sister had never been a contented woman. Even in childhood, she was always dissatisfied, always wanted more possessions, more deference from friends and family, greater admiration. It did not help that their younger sister, Anne, was both beautiful and kind, winning the love Catherine had sought in vain by marrying a man who loved her deeply and devotedly.

Pretty enough as a girl and with a dowry of forty thousand pounds, Lady Catherine desired a marriage of great consequence and turned down the few suitors who overlooked her shrewish nature until she was of an age to be considered "on the shelf." That was when their father arranged her marriage to a baronet some years older than his daughter. A man of stature but small fortune, Sir Lewis de Bourgh survived the wedding by ten years, dying when his only child was nine.

Lady Madeleine Fitzwilliam came in quietly and crossed to her husband's side. "Was she very difficult?"

Lord Henry turned to her automatically and took the hand she laid lightly on his arm, holding it in his. Immediately he felt calm begin to wash away his sister's influence. "More so than usual, if that can be believed. I shall write Darcy, but I do not know what either of us can do, unless she acts in some outrageous way."

"Wait, my dear," Lady Matlock murmured. She disliked her sister-in-law, more for the effect she had on the family than for her personal attacks. "And hope she sees reason."

"Reason and Catherine are not only antagonists; they are deadly enemies," her husband said wearily.

He smiled at her and left the room, but his wife saw he was deeply troubled. She wondered with a sigh how much more strife her sister-in-law would cause before some resolution was reached.

Chapter 2

The assembly rooms in the little market town of Meryton were already warm and stuffy enough for Elizabeth to wish the windows could be cracked open. She sat with her best friend, Charlotte Lucas, observing people she had known all her life, while she waited with some anticipation for Mr. Bingley's party to arrive. The chairs and sofas situated around the walls were occupied by mothers with their daughters in tow, while the gentlemen circulated, engaging in conversation with their friends and neighbors. Others made their way, as Mr. Hurst would do, to a cardroom set up in the rear of the building.

There was a small dais for the musicians at one end of the dance floor where four men were sawing away at their instruments in the hope of arriving at a mutually satisfactory sound. The refreshment table was well stocked with claret, Madeira, and brandy for the gentlemen, as well as sherry and wine punch in which the ladies might partake. For those ladies who did not care for alcoholic beverages, there was a lemonade that rarely fulfilled even its faint promise. Tea and coffee would be served later in the evening, accompanied by various pastries and savories. Unlike private balls, supper was not included in the evening's events.

"Do you suppose Mr. Darcy will accompany them?" Charlotte Lucas asked her friend.

They sat together away from the others for privacy. Charlotte was older than Elizabeth by five years and was teetering on the edge of spinsterhood. She was neither pretty nor unattractive; her face and figure had a solid plainness that did not attract the young men of the district. Elizabeth had begun to wonder if her Uncle and Aunt Gardiner might be induced to invite Charlotte for a visit when next Elizabeth traveled to see them in London. There were unmarried male associates and friends of the Gardiners in the city. Surely a solid business-man would be more likely to find Charlotte's practical nature and quiet strength appealing.

Roused from her thoughts by Charlotte's question, Elizabeth said, "He is said to be unsocial. And he was widowed over a year ago. Mr. Bingley and his sisters and brother-in-law ought to be arriving at any time though, so we shall find out shortly."

As if in response to her words, the doors opened, and Bingley entered with his party. His pleasant face was made more pleasant by a broad smile. An auburn-haired woman several years older than him followed on the arm of a solid, square-faced man. *The elder sister and husband*, Elizabeth thought. The lady had a pleasant face, much like her brother's, softened by an aura of femininity with none of her younger sister's disdain. Last came Caroline Bingley on the arm of a very tall, well-built man in impeccable evening dress. The look of triumph on her face was not echoed by her escort, who kept his eyes straight ahead.

Elizabeth watched the ladies of Mr. Bingley's party without one whit of envy. She only felt admiration for the fashionable cut and luscious apricot silk of Mrs. Hurst's gown. Miss Bingley rather caused her dismay at the display of bosom and bad taste in her choice of mustard-yellow satin with what appeared to be an excessive amount of expensive lace. Her own gown, Elizabeth noted, was two seasons old. She was to have had a new one this year, but her mother, as usual, had given in to Lydia's ceaseless whining, and her favorite was displaying herself this evening not in a modest white but a garish pink. Jane's gown was new, not because she had taken advantage of precedence; quite the opposite. She had insisted Elizabeth have a new ball gown, and Elizabeth had insisted as strongly that she was the last of the sisters, bar Mary, who cared about what she wore.

"I do not have a gentleman with five thousand pounds a year hanging on my every word. I saw some lovely Brussels lace at Michaelson's. I have more than enough for that, and a length of the green ribbon we looked at. I shall wear my beryl and silver clips and pendant and look quite the fashion plate."

Charlotte leaned to her friend in the general hush and then hubbub of the new arrivals, lowering her voice so Elizabeth alone heard her. "My goodness, what a handsome man. Like a prince from a fairy tale."

"In the toils of the wicked witch," Elizabeth muttered, and Charlotte suppressed a giggle.

The inhabitants of the room, who by now knew Mr. Bingley well and universally liked him, began to whisper. Exasperated, Elizabeth glanced around and saw her mother bend toward Jane, who was seated next to her; she saw Jane's face pale even more than its natural color. There was a predatory gleam in Mrs. Bennet's eye. Mr. Bingley headed straight for the Bennet women and their guest, Mr. Collins, bowed to Jane and her mother, and spoke to them in his friendly fashion. He was introduced to the newcomer and shook hands with his usual easy manners. Jane replied briefly, causing her mother's face to tighten momentarily before she put on what Elizabeth thought of as her "company" smile.

As Elizabeth watched the pantomime, Mr. Darcy detached his arm from Miss Bingley's grip with a murmured word and glanced around the room. Charlotte had just made a trenchant comment about the elevation of Miss Bingley's nose putting her in danger of tripping over something. Elizabeth was smiling an amused, satirical smile, an unconscious replica of her father's habitual expression. As she did, for a heartbeat, two, Darcy's eyes met hers. Elizabeth felt heat rise in her cheeks, and she lowered her head. When she risked a glance at him, Mr. Darcy had joined Bingley and was greeting the ladies and Mr. Collins, whose bow he acknowledged with a small bow of his own. As soon as he could detach Bingley, Darcy spoke quietly to him, much to Miss Bingley's obvious displeasure.

"Who is that young woman seated next to the pillar? The one in the white ball gown."

Bingley followed Darcy's nod. He said brightly, "Oh, that is Miss Elizabeth Bennet, Miss Bennet's next youngest sister. Would you like me to introduce you?"

The words that formed in Darcy's brain were, "No, I thank you." The words that emerged from his lips were, "Yes, I should."

Beaming, Bingley led the way to where Elizabeth and Charlotte were seated. They were no longer conversing. They rose as the gentlemen approached, and Bingley made the introductions. Darcy bowed formally to both ladies, who curtsied in return. Miss Elizabeth's ball gown, he noted, was a year or more out of fashion but so simply cut and so masterfully constructed that he found it charming nonetheless. Her hair was a mass of braids and curls the color of burnished ebony, highlighted by silver and beryl hair clips. Her eyes the finest he thought he had ever seen, a rich dark brown flecked with gold and green. A beryl pendant in an antique setting nestled in the hollow of her creamy throat. Only Darcy's lifelong self-discipline gave him the ability to keep countenance.

After the usual opening courtesies, Bingley said, "I would ask you to dance, Miss Elizabeth, but I have already engaged Miss Bennet for the first set. Perhaps you would honor me with the second?"

"I should be delighted, Mr. Bingley," Elizabeth responded.

Darcy hesitated and then said quietly, "You have almost certainly been engaged for the first set yourself, Miss Elizabeth."

"Not yet," she responded lightly.

"Then, will you do me the honor?"

Elizabeth found she could not look away from the dark, intense eyes. "It will be my pleasure, Mr. Darcy."

As he led her to the dance floor to the seesaw tuning of the musicians' instruments, she caught a glimpse of Miss Bingley's face. Despite several young men vying for the newcomer's attention, her eyes spit poison at Elizabeth. It made Elizabeth want to laugh at the silliness of such intense jealousy in as casual a situation as a country ball. The woman certainly had her sights set on becoming the second Mrs. Darcy. How Mr. Darcy felt about it was anyone's guess. He certainly did not seem to show any devotion to his friend's sister, or even any particular interest.

As they took their places for the opening dance, traditionally a minuet, Elizabeth glanced across the room at Charlotte. She usually sat out most of the dances, and Elizabeth saw, to her surprise, that Mr. Collins was speaking to her friend. They had been introduced when the Bennet party arrived, along with her parents, Sir William and Lady Lucas, and other neighbors and friends, but Mr. Collins had exhibited no more than polite acknowledgment. It was a kindness, Elizabeth thought as she faced Mr. Darcy, that she appreciated for her friend's sake, especially when she saw them join the set. Her mother's prejudice notwithstanding, she did not consider the pastor an enemy. The entail was not of his making, and he had given no indication that his visit was to appraise the property, as Mrs. Bennet claimed.

The musicians finished preparations, and the music began. Darcy found Elizabeth to be an excellent dancer. She was light, graceful, and highly accomplished. He had never cared for dancing and did so, when it was unavoidable, only with ladies of his close acquaintance, but like anything else Darcy set out to do, he did it with consummate skill. As they were close enough to speak without raising their voices, he waited for her to make the first conversational sally, a little afraid it would prove to be as trite and conventional as most young women's. Instead, Elizabeth said lightly, "Dear me, I must find a way to ask you your opinion of Hertfordshire without forcing you to admire it. I believe it is quite different from Derbyshire. Perhaps that will do."

"Indeed, Miss Elizabeth. There is little in common between the two landscapes. Derbyshire has mountainous terrain, and Hertfordshire is quite flat by comparison. As to an opinion, I have only just arrived, having not spent time here before, so I hold no opinion."

"Admirably put."

They parted and came back together in the dance, and Darcy said, "Have you lived here all your life?"

"Yes. I was born here shortly after my parents moved from Cheshire."

"They are not native, then?"

"My mother's family had a summer home here. Have you family in Derbyshire, Mr. Darcy?"

"My uncle and aunt have an estate near Matlock. I have three cousins. My sister is currently in London, but she resides at Pemberley, my estate, part of the year."

The minuet parted them again briefly, and as they returned to one another, Elizabeth said with a twinkle in her eyes, "Ah, yes, Miss Bingley was extolling the beauties of your estate, Mr. Darcy. It sounds quite fabulous." To her chagrin, he looked annoyed. She quickly said, "I apologize, Mr. Darcy. My tongue runs away with me at times. I did not mean to be impertinent."

He shook his head. "You were not impertinent, Miss Elizabeth. I fear I am not very good company this evening."

Elizabeth commented softly, "I believe, Mr. Darcy, you are quite uncomfortable with the press of people."

Startled at the accuracy of her observation, he answered without considering. "Why do you say that, Miss Elizabeth?"

"Your manner, chiefly. Most men of my acquaintance tend to become quite easy when they dance. I do not think you feel easy right now."

Darcy's finely cut mouth turned up slightly at the corners. "Do you often venture opinions on your dancing partners' state of mind?"

"I am afraid I enjoy studying my fellow human beings and coming to conclusions about their behavior. Sometimes, I admit, erroneous."

"Surely there can be only a limited opportunity for observation in what is, after all, a fairly small society."

"Oh." Elizabeth tilted her head slightly, a gesture Darcy would come to know well. "People change all the time. There is forever something new to discern."

Darcy did not reply, and Elizabeth was at the point of apologizing again when he said, "I do not feel easy in the presence of large numbers of people, especially those with whom I am not very well acquainted."

Elizabeth considered for a moment and then said without looking at him, "I find that surprising, sir, in a man who exhibits every evidence of self-confidence and worldly experience."

"And I find it surprising, Miss Elizabeth, that a young woman should be so perceptive and at the same time so charming."

Uncertain of his intent, Elizabeth moved the conversation onto a more conventional footing and finished the set in a strange mood for her, wondering what it was about Mr. Darcy that made her want to know him better.

The few people who were not dancing watched them and began to buzz. The phrase "such a handsome couple" circulated until Mrs. Bennet's sister, Mrs. Phillips, called her attention to the two. She stared, frowned, and made the comment that Elizabeth was always putting herself forward.

"Nonsense, Fanny," Mrs. Phillips said with a smile. "I am sure that Mr. Darcy asked *her* to dance, and if she had refused him, she would likely not have been asked by any other for most of the evening. You ought to be happy that a man of his consequence asked any of your girls to dance. And the first set too."

Mrs. Bennet did not reply. She really did not concern herself with Elizabeth's social triumph. She had other plans for her second daughter, although she realized they might change, depending on circumstances. She looked at Jane and Mr. Bingley, their faces bright and their eyes on each other, when Jane's were not modestly downcast. Again she frowned, and then raised her chin with resolve. It would not do. She meant to have a word with Jane when they returned to Longbourn.

Miss Bingley danced the first set with a local landowner's son, a brash young man whose conversation tended to be rural and whose attempted compliments were less well received than he might have expected. When the first set ended, Mr. Darcy saw Elizabeth back to her chair and offered to fetch her a glass of punch or lemonade, which she declined. With a bow, he left her; Charlotte returned at that moment accompanied by Mr. Collins. They all talked briefly, and then Mr. Collins left, and Charlotte and Elizabeth looked at one another with the wordless understanding of lifelong friends.

"The first set, Lizzy," Charlotte said with a twinkle. "My dear, your success is assured."

"Mr. Collins is not a terribly bad dancer," Elizabeth replied, avoiding the comment. "He is well enough off to afford a wife and family and not so very old."

"Really, Lizzy," Charlotte said and laughed. "The man was just being polite. He knows no one here, and I suppose I looked harmless."

Elizabeth made no reply, her eyes briefly following Mr. Darcy as he rejoined his party. Miss Bingley attached herself to Darcy the moment he approached. With an air she meant to sound teasing but which actually revealed her pique, she said, "So, Mr. Darcy, are you enjoying your first venture into Hertfordshire society? You seemed quite taken with Miss Eliza Bennet."

If Caroline saw his jaw tighten, she misinterpreted it.

"I found Miss Elizabeth a more than adequate partner."

"What? Only 'more than adequate'? How dreadful for you, Mr. Darcy. And her conversation, was that more than adequate as well?"

Vexed, Darcy said shortly, "It was most enjoyable."

Bingley came up, glowing, from his dance with Jane. "Well, Darcy," he said with a laugh, "are you regretting your decision to come along tonight?"

"Not at all," Darcy replied, disengaging his arm from Miss Bingley for the second time in half an hour.

"I told you that you would find the Bennet sisters charming. And Miss Bennet, what an angel!"

"Really, Charles," Caroline snapped. Must you go into raptures over every country gawk you meet?"

Bingley's face darkened. "That comment, Caroline," he said shortly, "was uncalled for, unkind, and untrue. You seemed to be enjoying your dance with Mr. Brandley."

"Enduring, you mean." She cast a sideways glance at Mr. Darcy. "I only enjoy really superior dancing. A quadrille or galliard with a *more than adequate* partner. A *minuet*, for heaven's sake! No one in Society would dream of something so old fashioned."

"A minuet is the traditional opening dance of country balls, and not a few private balls as well," her brother said with obvious irritation. Bingley, however, was not a man designed for ill humor. "Are you dancing this set, Darcy?"

Darcy hesitated. Miss Bingley would be impossible if he did not dance one set with her. He bowed to her and said, "Will you give me the pleasure, Miss Bingley?"

With barely concealed triumph, Caroline curtsied. "I should love to, Mr. Darcy."

The evening went swiftly. Elizabeth danced every set with a different partner. All of them were men she knew well and, for the most part, liked. As the dance progressed, Elizabeth saw Mr. Collins sitting next to Charlotte in conversation. She noticed Miss Bingley had captured Mr. Darcy for the second set as she partnered with Mr. Bingley. The master of Netherfield Park was his usual accommodating self, but his eyes strayed constantly to Jane until Elizabeth felt he was really dancing with both of them. She also caught her mother's look once or twice; it did not bode well, Elizabeth told herself. She was almost able to read Mrs. Bennet's mind, and what she saw left her disturbed. She must talk to Jane when they were alone tonight. Jane must not give in to their mother's manipulations. If Mr. Bingley was as attracted to Jane as Elizabeth felt he was, he needed to declare himself. Soon. Very soon.

Darcy leaded fatigue from his journey and retired as soon as the party arrived back at Netherfield Hall. When his man, Martin, left him for the night, he poured himself a small brandy and sat in a deep armchair before the fire in nightshirt and dressing gown, his mind occupied with the events of the evening and of the various concerns that plagued him. Georgiana was safe at Pemberley with her new companion, Mrs. Annesley, a kindly widow of early middle years whom his sister seemed to like and, to some degree, trust. The near-disaster of the summer still haunted Georgiana; he only hoped time would heal the wounds she had suffered. Lord Matlock had written him of Lady Catherine's visit and her threat. Although neither man took the idea of arson seriously, both were certain she was planning some action to get her way. Darcy had no solid plans for Rosings at present, except that it should never fall into Lady Catherine's hands. He owed Anne that much.

Darcy's mind drifted to the assembly ball and Miss Elizabeth Bennet. His imagination saw her in a gown of the latest fashion, dancing in a grand ballroom like the one at Matlock House. Her fine eyes would shine, as would her lovely smile. She had a light, pleasing figure. It was not the current more statuesque vogue, but Darcy preferred it. He had caught a faint, enticing scent of lavender as they danced; Caroline Bingley's perfume was a custom blend of muguet, bergamot, lily, musk, and several other fragrances that she applied far too liberally. Despite an education at one of the best seminaries in London, Caroline Bingley's manner and attitude had a subtle crudeness that made Darcy glad he saw no more of her than he did.

He was, he admitted to himself, taken with Elizabeth Bennet. Was it because she was so very different from Anne? So vibrant, so full of life? Even as he questioned his attraction, Darcy knew it was more than that. There was something in her manner, her expression, and her attitude that he felt on a visceral level. She might have an uncle in trade, as Miss Bingley had been at pains to point out on their way back from the assembly ball, but even if her mother had married above her station, the daughter was a gentlewoman, and her father's family was old country gentry.

Miss Bingley had been particularly trying during the short journey to Netherfield. Despite Darcy's silence, she had shot barbs at the Bennet family toward her sister, expecting an ally in her disparagement. "I was amazed when I saw the Bennet sisters," she said with a sidelong glance at Darcy's profile, "that they were known as the neighborhood beauties. Miss Bennet is a pretty girl, but her sisters are nothing out of the ordinary. And, my dear, did you see Miss Eliza's ball gown? Two seasons old *at least* and refurbished with lace and that *sweet* little green ribbon! I should have died rather than be seen in it."

"It was very fine Brussels lace," Louisa replied with a pointed yawn behind her gloved hand. "That does not come cheap."

Caroline sneered. "Oh, I suppose it cost her father a month's income."

To counteract his sister's snide remarks, Bingley explained what he had learned about the Bennets' history. Mr. Bennet's father, a gentleman farmer, became enmeshed in gaming fever and went through his entire estate within a decade, leaving the Longbourn property as the only asset after his death. Mr. Bennet paid his father's debts with everything he was able to realize from the Cheshire estate and moved his family to the smaller Hertfordshire property. What had befallen the Bennets threatened more than one family in the gentry and nobility, Darcy knew, especially those who did not diversify their holdings.

Enclosure had driven many tenant farmers from the land to the cities. If newer methods of crop production were not employed, especially the four-crop rotation after the Dutch model, revenues were bound to fall, and more tenants would remove from the land. Mines and mills were impacting labor as well. As the use of machinery to produce cloth and other goods expanded, the demand for fuel expanded as well. His own land contained coal deposits not yet explored. Darcy knew that one day, however much he might regret it, Pemberley's survival would depend on something other than farming. He was already making plans for that time.

What the South Sea Company's collapse in the 1720s had begun, the intermittent Continental wars of the following years had continued, with interrupted trade and more taxes to maintain an army on foreign soil. The war with the American colonies resulted in the loss of property and assets for investors in those colonies. The French Revolution and the rise of Napoleon put paid to regular commerce with France and brought a new burden of outlay for the armed forces. As if that were not enough, Darcy thought, the profligate behavior of the age dissipated fortunes, bankrupted estates, and destroyed reputations. Mr. Bennet had made the best of a bad situation. In Darcy's eyes, his father's failure diminished neither the man nor his daughter.

Darcy finished the brandy, set the glass aside, and got into bed, reaching for the book on the bedside table. He had been alone too long, he thought. Although he had no strong desire to remarry, the practical truth was that he needed to get an heir. Only, this time he would choose the woman—not his aunt and not his family. No one else would force a decision on him.

Darcy tried to read, his eyes growing heavier as he turned the pages, until finally, they closed, and he slid into a half-formed dream, totally without his conscious intent. He was walking through the main doors of Pemberley with his new bride on his arm, smiling gaily up at him. Her face was Elizabeth Bennet's.

The carriage ride to Longbourn after the assembly ball was a dither of chatter from Lydia and Kitty, repeated gossip, comments about the doings of various friends, critiques of their acquaintances' gowns, and general silliness. The Netherfield party was much admired for the ladies' fashionable attire and for Mr. Bingley's desire to dance every set and two with Miss Bennet, who blushed prettily at the memory. Mr. Collins listened without comment, his face carefully blank. Elizabeth and Jane were crowded together with Kitty on one seat while Lydia, Mrs. Bennet, and Mr. Collins took up the other. The elder sisters said nothing. Jane wore her usual serene expression, but Elizabeth knew her dearest sister well enough to sense suppressed emotion beneath the habitual calm. When they reached Longbourn, Mr. Collins handed the ladies down and accompanied them indoors, giving Elizabeth no chance to speak to Jane privately. Once inside, Mrs. Bennet sent the younger girls up to bed and drew Jane aside.

"A word with you, my dear," she said, stopping at the door of the drawing room. "Good night, Mr. Collins, Lizzy."

Elizabeth, full of misgivings, knew it was useless to protest, and she said good night, going up to her room. She undressed with the help of the maid the Bennet ladies shared, a patient creature named Annie, carefully put away her jewelry, donned her night shift and robe, and took down her hair. She brushed out the luxurious flood of loose curls, and was braiding it for the night when a tap at her door sent her to open it and pull Jane in. Elizabeth shut the door quietly and led her sister to the bed, sitting beside her. Jane was holding on to control by a very slim thread. When Elizabeth put an arm around her and held her closely, she broke down, tears spilling over her cheeks.

"Oh, Lizzy, how can she? Mama wants me to drop Mr. Bingley and try to attract Mr. Darcy! I cannot. I *will* not! I hardly know the man, and he has shown no interest in me at all. Mr. Bingley is the kindest, most amiable gentleman I have ever met. What would he think of me if I suddenly turned away from him as she wishes and pursued Mr. Darcy? What shall I do?"

Elizabeth took Jane's handkerchief from her sleeve and put it into her hand. "First, try not to cry. Mama may want you to drop Mr. Bingley, but she cannot force you to do so. Also, if he is as attracted to you as I believe he is, he will declare himself, and you will agree to marry him, and that will be the end of it."

"I wish," Jane whispered, laying her bright head on her sister's shoulder. "I wish he would speak! We have been acquainted for barely a month, but he is so diffident, so gentle. If only he would say the words, I would agree in a moment. Last night...," Jane nearly broke down but Elizabeth's strength sustained her, "while we danced, he almost declared himself. He said how much he enjoys my company and how similar our tastes are. At the last moment, though, he must have decided the ball was no place for so serious a matter, and we finished the set in perfect harmony but without any further indication of his regard."

Elizabeth was silent while Jane regained her composure. At last, she said, "If you want a resolution, my love, you will have to precipitate it. The next time he calls, one of us will suggest a walk. Mr. Collins can accompany us as chaperone. Mama will like that. She has been hinting at bringing us together since he arrived. I must say, he has acted with admirable rectitude in the face of such an obvious attack."

"He is a parson, after all," Jane said.

Elizabeth smiled. "And rectitude is his profession, so he will serve admirably. Seriously, dearest, you must find a way to tell Mr. Bingley how you feel. That you find him compatible in every way to your own character. If he means to propose, he will. If not, at least you will know for certain."

"As long as Miss Bingley does not accompany him," Jane said in a voice as close to annoyance as she ever achieved. "I dislike thinking badly of anyone, but she seems determined to separate us. I know we are not wealthy, and Papa's holdings now are small compared to the Cheshire estate, but that is no reason for anyone to look down on us."

"Miss Bingley," Elizabeth said wrinkling her nose, "is a snob. Their own grandfather was a tradesman, and so was their father, until he sold his business interests and invested the money. Mr. Bingley is a gentleman by nature and education, but he has no background of landed wealth. You are quite equal there, my dearest sister, if not more so."

"I should hate to cause a rift between brother and sister," Jane murmured. "Family quarrels are so terrible."

Elizabeth hugged her again. "If I were you, I should worry more about my own happiness than Miss Bingley's. She will survive quite nicely, and her quest for Mr. Darcy will hardly be affected."

"Mr. Darcy?" Jane looked quizzically at her sister. "I did not notice any particular regard for Miss Bingley on his part. He danced the first set with you, Lizzy. Everyone was commenting on it."

"So I gathered from Mama's expression!" Elizabeth laughed. "However, that was a courtesy to Mr. Bingley, I am sure. He danced the second with Miss Bingley, and, I believe, one other with Mrs. Hurst."

"He is a very striking figure," Jane said. "Mr. Bingley puts great store in his counsel and friendship."

"How convenient for Mr. Darcy, to have such an accommodating friend." Elizabeth saw Jane smile and said, "Do not worry, dearest. If things come to a crisis, there is always Papa. He will never force any of us to marry against our will."

Chapter 3

Despite the sisters' plan to provide Mr. Bingley with a chance to declare himself, nature called a temporary halt. Two days of heavy rain ensued, forcing the Bennets to remain indoors, while the mud-choked roads prevented visitors from calling. The third day began with patches of sunlight glazing the leaves of the maples with color and reflecting a thousand prisms of light from the ivy on the old stone wall around the kitchen garden. It was still too wet to venture on a long ramble, but Elizabeth, assessing the grounds over tea and a muffin in the breakfast parlor, thought Longbourn's gardens would do nicely for a walk, if Mr. Bingley should call.

She went to her father's book room with a muffin wrapped in a napkin and knocked lightly. At his call, Elizabeth entered to find him before the fire, a book in hand as usual. She saw the tea tray on the sidebar and the cup beside him on a small table. She placed the muffin next to his cup and took the companion chair.

"I thought you might like some breakfast, and the muffins are particularly good this morning."

Mr. Bennet smiled and set the book aside. "Thank you, Lizzy." He watched his favorite daughter with a raised brow. "You are up early as usual, even after a late night. I hear you were quite a success at the assembly ball."

Elizabeth blushed lightly. "Word of small things travels as fast as word of large ones, if not faster."

"Ah, but dancing the first set with a wealthy gentleman of high social standing is no small matter in a village such as Meryton."

"He is Mr. Bingley's good friend. It was no more than a gesture of courtesy."

"Perhaps. Did you enjoy his company?"

Elizabeth considered. "Yes, in the main. He is not a social man, as Mr. Bingley warned us, but he is well educated and informed, and his conversation is pleasant."

"Then I see no reason to regret the encounter." Mr. Bennet broke off a piece of the muffin and ate it with a swallow of tea. "What of the rest of the evening?"

Elizabeth gave him the amusing précis of the ball that he expected. When she was done and Mr. Bennet had finished his muffin, she still hesitated to leave. After several moments of contemplating her expression, her father said, "You may as well tell me what troubles you, my Lizzy. I doubt it is anything so terrible we cannot find a solution."

Slowly, Elizabeth told her father of her mother's desire for Jane to put aside Mr. Bingley in favor of an attempt to capture Mr. Darcy's affection. If her voice was more bitter than she realized, her father made no mention of it. When she had finished, he ran a hand through his mane of silver hair and was silent for a time. At last he said, "Jane is perfectly safe, Lizzy, as you know. I believe she could not find a better husband than Mr. Bingley, although they are both so easy that every servant will cheat them and so accommodating that friends and relatives will take advantage of them. Still, he is a fine young man, and Jane deserves the happiness I know she would find with him. Do not concern yourself, Lizzy. Your mother may scheme, but that is all she can do."

Elizabeth nodded. "I trust so. Jane is so biddable, it concerns me, but I believe, in this case, she will stand firm."

"Then let us hope Mr. Bingley screws his courage to the sticking place and speaks his mind soon."

Elizabeth rose and leaned to kiss her father's cheek. "Thank you, Papa."

The door closed behind her light step, and Mr. Bennet sighed. From the early days of his marriage, he had realized, to his chagrin, that his wife was amenable to neither reason nor prudence. In the midst of the crisis of his father's death and the estate's dissolution, he had made no effort to curb or control her, and by the time they were settled at Longbourn, with the property to put in order and a new family to consider, Mr. Bennet had accepted the path of least resistance. He stepped in only when her actions became too outrageous for even his detached and scholarly nature to accept. It had been a mistake, he realized, but one he felt it was too late to rectify. With another sigh, he picked up his book and continued to examine the beginnings of the Roman Empire.

The morning after the ball, Darcy managed to avoid Miss Bingley by the simple expedient of rising early, as Caroline Bingley never came downstairs until after ten. When he reached the breakfast parlor, the ladies were nowhere in evidence, and Bingley was lingering over his coffee. He was obviously pleased with himself and the world, despite the rain that streaked the windows. Darcy took a cup of coffee from the footman serving, selected a moderate breakfast from the dishes on offer, and sat down at Bingley's end of the table. Bingley waved the footman away, and he left the two friends alone.

"Did you enjoy yourself last night, Darcy?" Bingley asked.

"Yes, thank you." Darcy sipped his coffee. It was hot, strong, and black, as he liked it.

"You looked very well dancing with Miss Elizabeth."

"You looked very absorbed dancing with Miss Bennet."

A dreamy look crept over Bingley's open face. "Ah, Darcy, she is the most wonderful woman I have ever met. So beautiful, so kind, such an angel."

Darcy studied his friend. He knew Bingley well enough to perceive the difference in his words and attitude from other infatuations. Darcy drank another swallow of his coffee before he said, "Are you serious, Bingley?"

"Yes." Bingley met his friend's questioning look. "Yes, I am."

Darcy nodded. He went on eating and then laid his fork aside. "She is the daughter of a minor country gentleman. Has she a dowry or any notable connections?"

Bingley stiffened. "You have been listening to Caroline."

"Only during the second set last night. She has ambitions to rise in society. She feels that any alliance with a woman of lesser social status will be disastrous."

"For whom?" Bingley asked sharply. "For her? Or for me? Caroline is selfish. She always has been. She wants a grand marriage and thinks that if I do not marry exceedingly well, it will spoil her chances."

"She is probably right," Darcy replied. "Still, it is your choice, not hers."

Bingley put his cup down and laid both hands flat on the immaculate tablecloth. "Miss Bennet's dowry is one thousand pounds. I do not know what Caroline told you, but as I explained, her family is an old one in Cheshire. Her grandfather gambled away the estate, otherwise her father would be a very wealthy man. None of that diminishes the fact she is a gentlewoman, a step above the son of a tradesman."

"I apologize, Bingley," Darcy said quietly. "I was not criticizing Miss Bennet. She is a very beautiful woman and seems to possess a modest and gentle temperament, from what little I observed."

Bingley, somewhat mollified, said, "I will not marry for money, Darcy. Money does not warm a man's heart or his bed. I want a wife I can live with in harmony and affection, and Miss Bennet is perfect for me." He rose and contemplated his friend. "I am going to call on the Bennets as soon as this blasted rain relents. Do you wish to come with me?"

Taken by surprise, Darcy said after a moment's hesitation, "Yes, I should like to."

"Please do not mention it to Caroline," Bingley added with a rueful smile. "I do not feel like another argument. Not today."

Darcy nodded. He finished his breakfast and was going to check the morning post when Miss Bingley waylaid him in the hall. He found it hard to think of Miss Bingley's attempts to gain his attention in any other way. She wore a violent purple morning dress that showed too much bosom and was embellished with every frill and furbelow known to the mantua-maker's art. For a moment, Darcy saw again a white ball gown and deep brown eyes full of laughter and mischief. Then Caroline Bingley drew him into the empty morning room and closed the door, laying a hand on his arm. Darcy retreated and opened the door firmly, placing himself in a position where Miss Bingley would be forced to step around him in order to close it again. She looked up at him with what she believed to be a helpless appeal in her rather sharp-featured face and glanced toward the empty hall before lowering her voice to a near whisper. "I desperately need your assistance, Mr. Darcy."

Darcy, suspecting the source of her problem, kept his voice neutral. "How may I assist you, Miss Bingley?"

"You can speak to Charles. He will listen to you. You can convince him what a terrible mistake he is contemplating!"

"Mistake? Exactly what mistake do you refer to, Miss Bingley?"

She almost stamped her foot. Struggling to control her anger, Caroline said, "He is infatuated with Miss Bennet. He is contemplating marriage. It is a complete disaster! I have told you her mother's father was a tradesman. Her uncle in London owns the business now. Her other uncle is a lawyer here in the village. He has a plot of land he calls an estate and deems himself a gentleman. The prospect of such connections is in every way appalling. Charles is mad!"

Her face had reddened in a very unflattering manner, and her mouth had drawn into a thin line that suddenly reminded Darcy of his aunt Catherine. He drew back a step from her now clutching fingers and said, "I understand her father's family is quite old and has been gentry for generations."

"I suppose one might say that." Caroline sneered. "Poor gentry. The grandfather was a gambler who wasted his entire estate and reduced Mr. Bennet to his present status of 'country gentleman.'"

"The fortunes of a family may be severely damaged by one irresponsible heir, but the family's status is not. Miss Bennet is a gentlewoman, however small her dowry or indifferent her connections."

"What do you think the reaction of the *ton* will be if Charles marries her? Do you want him to become a laughingstock?" Her voice, despite her attempt to modulate it, was growing shrill.

Darcy felt as if the usually cheerful yellows and greens of the morning room had taken on a gray pallor. He drew himself up and reiterated his statement to his friend. "I fail to see how any of this concerns me, Miss Bingley. Charles is of age. He is able to make his own decisions."

"If it ruins me...us? What will our friends in town say to such a misalliance? One thousand pounds dowry. *One thousand*! And no connections but a bumpkin lawyer and an uncle in Cheapside. Charles could marry an heiress if he just opened his eyes and saw what Miss Bennet really is. A fortune hunter who has deceived him into thinking her an innocent!"

Disgusted by both her importuning him to interfere and his own half-realized inclination to do so, Darcy looked at her with barely disguised irritation. Once, he realized, he would have agreed with her. Experience and practical reality had altered his opinion of trade to a degree he would formerly have dismissed out of hand. Although he did not advertise the fact, he owned a one-third interest in a shipping company and a partnership in a cotton mill near Matlock. Darcy was a firm believer in diversity as a necessity of retaining and expanding wealth. And he had no reason to believe that Jane Bennet was anything but the charming young woman she presented to the world.

Darcy said coldly, "You want me to discourage Charles from pursuing a marriage with Miss Bennet?"

"Yes! Oh yes, Mr. Darcy. Please, please help me! Point out to him how terrible such a marriage will be. How our friends will drop us, laugh at us! How everything our father worked for will be lost! How can he even contemplate it? You can convince him. He knows you have his best interests at heart. Talk to him, please!"

She was actually shaking with emotion, Darcy noted. She was tall enough that he had only to dip his head slightly to meet her eyes. "I am sorry, Miss Bingley, but I do not interfere in my friends' lives or give advice they have not requested. I do not know Miss Bennet, but on the surface, she seems a genteel young woman. She is not to blame for her grandfather's actions, nor is her father. Admittedly, a dowry of one thousand pounds is minimal, but Bingley is not in need of money. If he chooses to marry for love, it is his affair."

"Love!" She spat out the word, barely controlling her fury. "He has known her little more than a month. How can he claim to be in love after such a short acquaintance? He falls in love twice a year!"

"Marriage," Darcy informed her, "should put an end to that at least. As for falling in love in so short a time, I have known it to happen in far less. My own parents are said to have known at first meeting they were destined for one another. No, Miss Bingley, I will not interfere because you fear loss of status if your brother marries a gentlewoman of small fortune. He will still have my friendship and support. I expect that will count for something."

"He will ruin us," Caroline said bitterly, tears of frustration and pique forming in her eyes.

"Hardly, Miss Bingley."

Darcy bowed and quit the room, leaving her staring angrily after him, her hands clenched into fists at her sides.

As if her display of temper had resonated in the heavens, half an hour later, it began to rain again. Sheets of water sluiced down the windows and ran in rivulets from the eaves. Any plan to call on the Bennets was shelved for several days to come.

If Mrs. Agnes Younge will contact B. Slade, Esq., 66C Faring Street, London, she will learn something greatly to her advantage.

"There, what d'you think of that?"

With a rattle of newsprint, Mrs. Younge tapped a bony finger on the page. Her companion did not look up but rather, stared at the middle distance thoughtfully. George Wickham had once been a handsome man. Although he was little more than a year younger than Darcy, a decade of progressive dissipation had left him with an unhealthy pallor, yellow-tinged eyeballs with incipient pouches under them, and the beginnings of a paunch. Another five years lived in the same manner would see a blurring of his jawline, sagging skin under his neck, and other unpleasant results. Wickham spoke and dressed like a gentleman and was still attractive enough to draw in an occasional wealthy widow. But as soon as she said one of two magic words, "marriage" or "solicitor", she found herself alone and lacking whatever amount of money Wickham could get away with. With his habits, the game kept him barely solvent. Now he spoke lazily to his companion, folding the racing edition of the paper with the advertisement visible. "Get me a drink, and sit down."

Mrs. Younge, who knew him too well to mistake his tone, fetched a bottle of cheap gin and a less-than-sparkling glass and put them within his reach. She sank into the other chair at the stained table, twisting her hands nervously in her lap.

"Darcy, d'you reckon?"

George Wickham smirked, poured gin into the glass, and drank it in two swallows. He coughed, grimaced, and said, "Darcy? Hell no. If he wanted to find you, he'd never spread it across a common newspaper. He'd just show up at the door one day, and you'd never know how he did it."

"Who then? It sounds like one o'' them lawyers that finds heirs, but I got no one to leave me anything. It's a trap, I tell you!"

"Trap?" Wickham leaned back in his chair, which gave an alarming creak. "What trap? Why? You run a legitimate boardinghouse, at least as far as anyone know. Who cares if all your boarders are women who only work in the evenings? In any case, the runners don't use newspaper ads to catch abbesses, much less receivers of stolen goods." He poured more gin, not so much this time, and sipped it. "I'll see this B. Slade, Esquire, if you like. If it's legitimate, it might be worth our while to follow up. If not, I'll know it."

Mrs. Younge glanced around the small room she used as both kitchen and dining room. The walls were covered with peeling paper; the floor was warped and uneven; the single window looked as if it had been smeared with grease and inadequately wiped clean. Not that the view of broken roofs and ramshackle buildings was worth the effort of cleaning it. Everywhere she looked was dirt and disorder. "If it'll get me out of here," she said bitterly, "I'll take whatever it is."

"Good girl." Wickham reached out and ran a finger along her cheek. "I'll see Mr. Slade this afternoon. Find my blue coat, will you? And see if that lazy slut Bridgie has washed my other cravat. I wouldn't want Mr. Slade to think I was in need of money."

Mrs. Younge gave a bark of laughter. "You? In need of cash? When aren't you?"

"True. So, this may be the answer to both our prayers."

When Wickham left the hansom and walked down Faring Street two hours later, he found it familiar, although he had never been there before. Like many areas bordering the oldest sections of London, it was rapidly sliding down the ragged slope from near respectability to disrepute. Mr. B. Slade had his office on the third floor of a narrow building of crumbling brick, the exterior stained a uniform dull gray by the constant soot in the air from unnumbered coal fires. Mr. Slade himself was small, balding, and obsequious but with a sharp glint in his pale eyes. Wickham did not give his name. He only indicated he was acting for his good friend, Mrs. Younge.

"Is this some sort of inheritance?" he asked as he took the dilapidated chair before an equally rickety desk.

He was not impressed by his surroundings. The room was small with one dingy window on the street and little other furnishings.

"Not to say so, no." Mr. Slade folded his hands on the desktop. "It is rather in the way of payment for services rendered."

"What sort of services?"

Mr. Slade cleared his throat. "My principal wishes to gather some information regarding Mrs. Younge's employment with a certain gentleman last summer. This person is willing to pay handsomely for it but does not wish to come into the picture directly. So I am acting as an agent."

"My friend will not want to get involved in anything resembling blackmail," Wickham told him with a perfectly straight face.

"Oh, my dear sir, I should not either. I take it that this is a family matter. Perhaps a young woman is somewhere in the picture. You understand, I am sure. Not the sort of thing one questions a gentleman about directly. And with what my principal is willing to pay, I am assured there are more than sufficient funds to amply reward cooperation."

Wickham considered. "How handsomely will this pay? The gentleman in question is not without influence, and I doubt he would be pleased by this inquiry into his personal affairs."

"My dear sir, he need never know the source of the information." *So, Mr. Slade mused, the man already knows what this is about. Involved to the hilt, no doubt.*

Wickham sneered. "Oh, he'll know all right. My friend will have to leave the area, perhaps even the country. Travel of that sort does not come cheap."

"Shall we say two hundred pounds earnest money? One thousand pounds when the information is delivered. Three additional, if it is satisfactory."

"Shall we say five hundred earnest? Four thousand when the information is delivered. One can always claim dissatisfaction after the fact."

The two men appraised each other, saw reflections of common proclivities and inclinations, and came to a wordless understanding. Slade had been given some leeway to negotiate, and his own commission was assured. He had seen to that at the beginning. He opened a drawer of the desk that loudly protested the disturbance and took out a cracked leather pocketbook from which he drew out five one-hundred- pound notes. He pushed them across the desk into Wickham's waiting hands.

"Have your friend here tomorrow afternoon at three. I will have a general idea of what my principal wishes to know. Your friend can write it out. She can write, can she not?"

"Certainly."

"She can write out her response, and I will forward it to my principal. I warn you, however, it must be truthful and accurate."

Wickham rose with a vulpine smile. "Oh, we are always truthful and accurate if enough cash is involved. Until tomorrow afternoon."

He put the notes away and left the building. At the next corner, he found a hansom and gave Mrs. Younge's direction. Wickham believed he knew who Slade's principal was. He needed time to think. Inherently a coward, Wickham had never dared to try blackmailing Darcy. He knew his man well enough to be certain that either Darcy or his cousin Colonel Fitzwilliam would come after him with fatal results. Now, the situation had changed. There was another party involved. One Darcy dared not take revenge on. He needed a plan. If he played this hand right, it might just provide him with enough money to escape his creditors and live as a gentleman should.

The Bennet ladies were in the drawing room when Mr. Bingley called on the fourth morning after the assembly ball. Darcy had received an express from London and cried off accompanying his friend. Bingley wondered if the contents were bad news of some sort but refrained from asking. Darcy's face had assumed its master-of-Pemberley expression, and Bingley was loath to intrude on his friend's privacy. In addition, he had plans of his own for the day that sent him away on horseback with a smile on his lips while he whistled a merry tune. When he entered the drive at Longbourn, he grew a bit more reserved, but his pleasant face still bore traces of exceeding good humor. A groom took his horse, and he was admitted to the house by the butler, Mr. Hill who escorted him to the drawing room, where the ladies and Mr. Collins sat in quiet conversation.

When Bingley had greeted all the members of the party, he took a chair by Jane's seat on the end of the settee and entered into general comments on the weather. It was only a matter of a few minutes before this led to Elizabeth suggesting a walk in the gardens, and inviting Mr. Collins to join her. He rose as if he had been awaiting the invitation, encouraged by her mother's voluble approval. The situation gave Elizabeth some qualms, but she and Jane gathered their pelisses, gloves, and bonnets, and the four of them stepped out into pale autumn sunshine.

They kept off the lawns, which were still soaked which made for very bad footing, instead staying on the flagged and cobbled paths between the flower beds and trees. The smells of wet earth, rotting leaves and the green scent of pines carried on a chill breeze were invigorating. Elizabeth let Jane and Mr. Bingley proceed ahead of her and Mr. Collins while she searched for some neutral subject of conversation.

After a few silent minutes, Elizabeth said, "You being rector of Hunsford is quite a coincidence, Mr. Collins, as Mr. Darcy and Mr. Bingley are such good friends."

"Not at all, Miss Elizabeth." Mr. Collins tipped his head a little to one side to regard her. "My grandmother was a native of Kent. When my great-grandmother's estrangement occurred, my great-grandfather moved from Cheshire to the place of her birth in Kent. His eldest son met and married my grandmother. Her father owned a grain mill at Chemhill. He had no sons, so my grandmother inherited, and my grandfather took over the mill. My own father was a second son, so he became a minister, and I followed in his footsteps."

"Did you know Mr. Darcy's aunt, then?"

Mr. Collins shook his head. "No. When I was ordained and the living at Hunsford became vacant, I applied, and Lady Catherine de Bourgh appointed me to the post. I moved into the parsonage, and it was a week before Mr. Darcy's steward informed me that Rosings had passed out of Lady Catherine's hands on the marriage of her daughter. I immediately wrote Mr. Darcy to request an interview at his convenience. He was coming to Rosings in a short time, so rather than have me travel to London or Derbyshire, he met with me at Rosings, and, I am happy to say, he confirmed the living. Not, you see, such a great coincidence after all."

"Indeed not."

They walked on. Elizabeth kept a sharp eye on Jane and Mr. Bingley's progress. She saw the two halt twice and had to slow her steps to keep a distance between the couples. Mr. Collins walked slowly with his hands clasped behind his back. He exuded a very parsonic attitude. The breeze blew his coattails away from his body and tugged at Elizabeth's pelisse and the brim of her bonnet. Mr. Collins seemed to be contemplating some matter he was hesitant to speak of. When Jane and Mr. Bingley suddenly moved off the path into the edge of a small copse and halted, he, too, stopped and turned to face Elizabeth.

"I was glad you suggested this walk, Miss Elizabeth," he said when she turned to look at him. "There is a matter of some personal importance I wish to discuss with you."

Alarmed and caught off guard, Elizabeth dropped her eyes and fought for composure. "I…I am sure it is nothing that requires such privacy, Mr. Collins."

He made a sound like a chuckle which startled her into looking at him. "Rest assured, Miss Elizabeth," he said with a small smile, "I am not going to ask you to marry me. Meaning no insult in the least. You are a lovely young lady but not at all of the temperament to be a parson's wife."

"No insult is taken," Elizabeth stammered. "But I fear I do not understand."

Mr. Collins continued after a moment. "My patroness, if I may call her that, Lady Catherine de Bourgh, insisted it is time I marry, and for once, I agree with her as the notion has been in my mind for some time. She 'suggested' I find a wife among my cousins. This at first seemed logical and even kind, in view of the entail. After a week in the bosom of your family, I am certain that no such alliance is advisable. Miss Bennet," he gestured slightly at Jane and Bingley, "is in the way of making a very advantageous and, I daresay, happy marriage. The younger ladies are too young. I considered Miss Mary for a time, but her piety, although sincere, is dogmatic and not yet tempered by experience. I would feel as if I was taking on a new curate instead of a wife."

"In that case, Mr. Collins," Elizabeth was curious and no longer alarmed by the conversation, "in what way can I be of help to you?"

"Miss Charlotte Lucas is a great friend of yours," he said obliquely.

Elizabeth nodded. "My best friend. You mean…"

Mr. Collins hesitated before saying, "You will, I fear, find my approach to matrimony more rational than romantic. A flaw in the eyes of most young ladies, I am sure. However, my situation in life makes it imperative that I choose well when I marry. Disharmony in any family is regrettable. In a minister's family, it is disastrous."

They had stopped on the path. Elizabeth noted that Jane and Mr. Bingley were standing in close proximity. Mr. Bingley was speaking rapidly and with considerable emotion. Mr. Collins's presence brought her back to her own conversation. "I do understand," Elizabeth assured him, although she agreed that his approach to selecting a wife would not appeal to many women. "I can only say that Miss Lucas is of a more mature and rational nature than any other lady of my acquaintance."

"I am not surprised. On the social occasions when we spoke, I found her suitable in every way. Her beauty is internal but real. She has the calm, practical nature I want in a wife, and I believe she will be capable of affection once we come to know one another better. Also, I am afraid she will be faced with dealing with Lady Catherine's constant oversight, which will require considerable tact."

"How can I be of assistance in this matter?"

"You can perhaps tell me", some color tinged his cheeks, "if Miss Lucas has an inclination to marry. If she has not, and I know some young women prefer to remain single, then I would not want to importune her or have her family pressure her to accept an offer of marriage."

"Miss Lucas has no prejudice against marriage that I am aware of."

Mr. Collins almost sighed with relief. "Then, can you tell me, Miss Elizabeth, if you think she would be amenable to a country parson courting her?"

"I think, Mr. Collins," Elizabeth smiled, torn between diversion at her companion's quandary and her anxiety over Jane, "that you must ask her that question. However, you are quite correct in your assessment of Miss Lucas. She is a wonderful person, and I believe she could be quite content as a parson's wife."

He bowed and turned back to the path as Jane gave a low cry of delight. Mr. Bingley was holding her hands. His face was alight with a happiness that was reflected in Jane's brightly blushing countenance.

"I believe," Mr. Collins said, "one future has just been determined."

Chapter 4

Darcy sat in Bingley's library at Netherfield with a sheet of paper on his knee. The note was from his cousin, Colonel Richard Fitzwilliam. Included with it was a cutting from one of the lesser London papers. Darcy's face was dark with bitter anger as he reread the few words for an uncounted time.

> *Darcy,*
> *The enclosed was in the sporting edition and the evening edition of several papers. Do you know anything about it?*
> *RF*

The cutting was the advertisement for Mrs. Younge.

He was inclined to leave for London as soon as a horse could be saddled, but reason told him he needed more information before he acted. Darcy went to a small writing desk by the window and took out a sheet of paper and a pen. Richard was stationed in London at present, in the process of training new cavalry recruits and waiting for his next assignment. He had resources, and he was an experienced agent for the army. At present, Darcy dared trust no one else. After a moment's consideration, he wrote:

> *Richard,*
> *I know nothing about this. Find out all you can about who placed the advert, and about B. Slade. I can be in town in a matter of hours if necessary.*
> *FD*

An express would reach the colonel by morning at latest. As soon as he replied, Darcy could decide on a plan of action based on whatever information he obtained. He took the sealed letter to Mr. Hastings to be sent out as soon as possible. He had started upstairs when he heard a sharp cry from the drawing room and running footsteps.

Caroline Bingley rushed down the hall and took three stair steps before she saw Darcy. She halted, her faced streaked with furious tears, to glare at him. "He has done it. He has proposed to that…that country gawp, and now we will be ruined!"

Sobbing, she gathered her skirts and rushed on up the stairs to her rooms. Darcy turned back and entered the drawing room to find Bingley pouring himself a brandy. He looked up, poured a second for his friend, and said with a wry, slightly uncertain smile, "You heard that I am engaged?"

"In a manner of speaking." Darcy accepted the glass and raised it. "I wish you happy in every way."

Bingley's expression relaxed. "Thank you. I am happier than I have ever been in my life. Nor do I believe my marriage will be a social disaster, whatever Caroline may say."

"She will come around in time." Darcy sounded distracted. He drank some of the brandy and said slowly, "I may have to leave for town in a day or two on business."

"Nothing of consequence, I hope."

"I do not yet know. It will be handled."

Bingley nodded; he had complete confidence in Darcy's ability to deal with any problem that might arise. As he sipped his drink, he said, "Speaking of social disasters-- or, at least, mismatches -- Mrs. Bennet believes that Mr. Collins will shortly propose to Miss Elizabeth. I can hardly credit it, but they went walking with Miss Bennet and me this afternoon and seemed in close conversation, what little I observed."

Darcy's hand tightened on his glass until he felt the snifter press dangerously into his hand. His heart lurched in his chest, stifling his breath. Bingley was staring at him, alarm written plainly on his open face. "Darcy, are you ill? What is it, man?"

"Nothing," he stammered. "I just...remembered something." He took several deep breaths and finished his brandy in a swallow. "Is it certain, then?"

Bingley shook his head. "No, not at all. Frankly, I cannot imagine Miss Elizabeth as a minister's wife, but if she is inclined toward Mr. Collins, it is really none of my affair. Mrs. Bennet is anxious to marry off her daughters, but now that Miss Bennet and I are betrothed, she will be busy with wedding plans and all the things ladies go through for a marriage, so any other wedding will not be so much on her mind."

But would it be on Elizabeth's mind, Darcy wondered with a devastating heaviness filling him. There was an entail, and this country parson, while a step down for a gentlewoman, was the grandson of a gentleman and not an objectionable mate. Except to Darcy. The idea of the vivacious, cheerful, lovely Miss Elizabeth wed to the stodgy minister was highly objectionable to Darcy. The further realization that Mr. Collins's wife would be forced to deal with Lady Catherine made such a marriage even more questionable. Subconsciously echoing Mr. Collins's statement, he realized it was worse than unsuitable; it was a potential disaster.

Darcy glanced at the mantel clock. It was too late to call today. Bingley undoubtedly meant to spend as much time as possible at Longbourn, and it was perfectly suitable for Darcy to accompany him. He must gauge Miss Elizabeth's feelings for Mr. Collins as soon as he was able, and if there was any hope of turning her from a marriage with the parson, Darcy determined to take it.

"Lizzy, I want a word with you."

Elizabeth heard the warning note in her mother's tone and, with some trepidation, followed her into the empty morning room. Mrs. Bennet shut the door and faced her least favorite daughter, a sharp gleam in her eye. "Well, Lizzy?"

Elizabeth stared at her mother in the best representation of honest innocence she could manage. "What, Mama?"

"Did Mr. Collins propose to you?"

"No!" Elizabeth modified her voice. "No, he did not. Did you expect he was going to?"

"You were talking quite seriously during your walk. I had every reason to think he might be coming to the point at last."

Elizabeth shook her head. "We had a perfectly normal conversation. About people he has met here and his background."

Mrs. Bennet's mouth tightened. She folded her arms in an attitude of officious interrogation. "What did you say to offend him?"

Elizabeth was frankly surprised and considerably vexed. "Mama, I would never purposely offend a guest. Mr. Collins was not in the least offended."

"He obviously enjoys your company, and he has come here to find a wife among you. Jane is betrothed," she did not sound overjoyed at the prospect, "and I can hardly expect you to attract Mr. Darcy. Mr. Collins is your best hope for matrimony, Miss Lizzy, and you had better make an effort to seize it before he changes his mind and goes back to Kent."

Elizabeth almost said, "Do you expect me to propose to him?" However, she guarded her tongue and instead replied quietly, "Mr. Collins must make his own decision regarding whom to marry."

"A little encouragement from you will not be amiss. When your father dies, do not expect to make your home here unless you are Mrs. Collins. We shall all be thrown out to live in the hedgerows."

It was an old, tired, and threadbare threat. "I doubt Mr. Bingley would allow that, Mama," Elizabeth replied, keeping her temper with an effort. "And Papa is in perfectly good health."

"One never knows," Mrs. Bennet said darkly. She bustled to the door and gave Elizabeth a displeased glare. "Think it over carefully, Lizzy. You may never have another chance as good as this one."

Elizabeth went upstairs to change for dinner in a state of mind between irritation and apprehension. She was attempting to brush out her mane of loose curls when a tap at her door brought an ecstatic Jane into the room. Elizabeth put down her brush and rose. Jane enfolded her in her arms, hugging her tightly. "Oh, Lizzy, Mr. Bingley has proposed, and I have accepted, and he is with Papa now, and we are to be married before Christmas!"

"My dearest sister!" Elizabeth disengaged herself enough to see Jane's large blue eyes starred with tears of joy. "I am so very happy for you! No one deserves such felicity more than you do, and Mr. Bingley is perfect for you in every way."

Elizabeth led Jane to the bed, and they sat side by side as they had so many times in the past with their arms around each other. "What did Mama say?"

Jane's expression clouded slightly. "She saw Mr. Bingley go into Papa's book room, and I had no choice but to tell her. I…I think she was not best pleased, but she only said that at least *one* of her daughters was able to find a husband. What could she mean by that?"

Elizabeth said, wryly, "She wants me to make an effort to attach Mr. Collins and elicit a proposal from him." She hesitated and then went on. "You are the only one, dear Jane, whom I would tell this to, but Mr. Collins confided in me today that he wants to marry Charlotte."

Jane's eyes widened, and then her expression grew thoughtful. "Mama will be beside herself when she finds out, but I truly believe he is making a wise choice. Will Charlotte marry him, do you think?"

Elizabeth nodded. "I saw them together at the assembly ball, and she gave every indication of enjoying his company. Apparently, they have had conversation before at one of the parties we attended since he came. You know Charlotte has given up hope of marrying anyone local, and Mr. Collins is a perfectly acceptable match. She has often said to me that she is not romantic by nature, and she wants to marry so she will not be a burden on her family."

"Then it is likely that if he asks her to marry him, she will accept. Oh, Lizzy, what a quandary for you!"

"Not really, dearest. Mama is never pleased with me, no matter what the situation."

She rose and returned to her dressing table. Jane followed, picked up the discarded hairbrush, and began to bring order to the chaos of her sister's hair. "If things become unbearable, you can always live with Mr. Bingley and me," she half-jested.

"Yes, I shall be nanny and governess to your children and grow old with grace."

They laughed at the image, but in her heart, Elizabeth wondered if she had just had a glimpse of her future.

"Well, Mr. Slade?"

Lady Catherine de Bourgh sat enthroned in the drawing room of the de Bourgh town house, her disdainful gaze studying Mr. Slade as if he were something impaled on a pin. As he had not been invited to sit, he stood with both hands clasped nervously in front of him. He was used to dealing with the marginally criminal elements of his particular clientele; it struck him, as he observed the elderly woman before him, that he had never faced a more determined -- or more dangerous -- human being. A lifetime of arrogant dissatisfaction had etched lines from her nose to the drawn-down corners of her thin mouth, and given her hooded eyes the look of a predatory bird. What alarmed Slade most was her total lack of emotion. She was preparing to ruin someone's life without the least qualm or regret.

Slade said in his best professional manner, "I have been contacted by the woman's…gentleman friend. He states that she is agreeable to an arrangement, provided she is well paid. I am to supply her with whatever questions you have, and she will respond to them in writing."

Lady Catherine nodded after a moment. "You have not met her personally?"

"No, my lady. She is reluctant to come directly into contact with anyone, and her friend has her complete confidence."

"According to him." Lady Catherine tapped her fingers on the arm of the large, heavy chair she occupied and fell silent.

It was not a comfortable silence, and as it dragged on, Slade felt perspiration dampen his brow. He let his eyes travel around the room as a distraction. It was full of massive, dark furnishings, upholstered chairs and settees in colors and patterns that had not been fashionable for at least a generation. Thick velvet drapes the color of old blood were barely pulled back enough to let in a bit of daylight; a huge fireplace overmantel was decorated with a crest and scrolls, but only a tiny fire burned in the hearth. It made no headway against the chill of the room. There were no personal items at all, no bric-a-brac, no mementos; only a French gilt clock noisily counting time on the mantel and a single painting he assumed was her country estate, a large modern mansion set in rigidly formal gardens.

"How much does she want?"

The harsh voice spoke so suddenly he startled. Reassuming an expression of confidence, Slade said, "I have paid her five hundred pounds earnest money, with assurance of four thousand more upon receipt of the information."

"After I have reviewed it."

Slade hesitated and then said, "She would not agree to those terms. She is a very cautious woman, and I have the feeling she fears someone else who may be a party to the matter."

Lady Catherine drew breath for an obliterating rejection but did not voice it. Yes, if Mrs. Younge had information about Darcy or Georgiana, she was likely to be afraid of his reaction to her betrayal. It was as much as a confirmation that scandal existed and Mrs. Younge knew about it.

"Very well, Mr. Slade. My question is this. Exactly what occurred at Ramsgate last summer when Mrs. Younge was in residence there? I want the information in minute detail, with nothing left out. With no one protected. Everything she knows, suspects, or guesses. Is that clear enough?"

"Yes, my lady." He sounded humble and more than a bit relieved.

"Bring me her response as soon as you have it. Personally. Now, get out."

Slade bowed and made a hasty exit, taking his overcoat and hat from a footman and opening the front door himself rather than having to linger an unnecessary second in the house. He felt, not unnaturally, that he had made a lucky escape.

Mr. Bingley departed for Longbourn at the earliest hour permissible for a visit. Grass had sprung up beside the road after the rain; it was scattered with wild flowers in a soft array that seemed to echo his mood. Darcy accompanied him. There would be no answer from Richard today, probably not tomorrow either. If there was no communication after that, Darcy meant to go to London and look into the matter himself. His thoughts were torn between the meaning of the advertisement and Miss Elizabeth when Bingley pulled his horse up, and Darcy realized that someone was approaching them along the footpath leading to Meryton.

Mr. Collins halted and bowed to the two men. Darcy touched his hat in acknowledgment, and Bingley made a brief bow in return. Mr. Collins said to Bingley, "You are visiting Longbourn I take it? Miss Bennet is a very fine young lady. You are a very fortunate man. I hope I may soon be as fortunate myself."

Darcy stiffened in the saddle, causing his mount to shift its weight. He changed position in the saddle automatically to compensate. His reply was calm but cool. "You are to be married, Mr. Collins?"

"I have not gotten quite so far as that," Mr. Collins said lightly, "but I have hopes to be betrothed soon."

"I wish you well," Bingley responded. "You are going into Meryton?"

"I have been invited to dine at Lucas Lodge."

"Ah, you will enjoy yourself, I am sure," Bingley replied cheerfully. "Sir William is an excellent host."

"I am sure he is. He has invited the vicar of the church in Meryton as well, he tells me. I hope it will not be exclusively an ecclesiastical conversation. I shall try to see that it is not."

He smiled, preparing to continue on when Darcy said suddenly, "How is my aunt Lady Catherine, Mr. Collins?"

"She was quite well when I saw her several days before I left Kent. She was preparing to remove to London for a short stay."

Darcy's face showed nothing of the icy anger that pulsed through him. Mr. Collins bade the two men good day, and they rode on to Longbourn. Darcy remained silent in his own thoughts, while Bingley was engrossed in excited anticipation of seeing his betrothed. Darcy had to find a way to ascertain Elizabeth Bennet's feelings for the parson. He needed to know whether she felt some attraction to the man, or if marriage to Mr. Collins was strictly a matter of practicality. He had no doubt her mother was pressing her to accept the man. Her lack of regard for her second daughter was quite obvious to a careful observer. Was Elizabeth desperate enough to leave the family home and establish her own that she was considering an offer she must know would be wrong for her in every way?

They reached the house, and a groom hurried to take their horses. Hill admitted them and led the way to the drawing room. Darcy's swift glance at the occupants showed him that Mary was the only one present. She put aside the book she had been reading and rose to curtsy as the gentlemen entered. Mary noted Mr. Bingley's look of disappointment at not seeing Jane with the internal amusement of a lady devoted to the improvement of the mind who felt superior to common passions. Mary was eighteen and believed her life's course already set.

"My mother and sisters are in the morning room," she said. "They are discussing preparations for the wedding. Lydia has gone to visit Maria Lucas. Mr. Hill will have gone to tell them you are here." She rang for tea and seated herself. The gentlemen did likewise. "I was not aware that such a simple ceremony entailed so much concern over so many details. I am sure one could sail around the world with less fuss and bother."

"I suppose one might," Bingley rejoined, "but you must admit that her wedding is a special time in a woman's life. She wants everything to be just right. Do you not anticipate taking care over your own wedding someday?"

Mary looked at him; for a moment, something sad brushed her face. Then she said in a rather superior tone, "I do not anticipate marrying at all. If I should, I will make certain that everything is focused on the religious aspects, not the personal."

Before Bingley could reply, Jane and Elizabeth came in from the hall. They curtsied as the men rose and bowed. Mrs. Hill followed them with a tea tray that she set down carefully on a table before the settee. Jane thanked her and indicated she would pour out herself. Elizabeth seated herself next to her sister, Darcy taking the chair opposite her. Mary returned to her book after accepting a cup from Jane. For a time, the conversation was general, and then Bingley put aside his empty cup and looked at his betrothed. He said quietly, "I wonder if you would consent to walk out for a bit, Miss Bennet. The weather is quite mild, and I should be glad of the exercise, considering how the recent rains have kept everyone indoors. Darcy and Miss Elizabeth can accompany us, if that suits everyone."

The others consented, and Jane and Elizabeth went to fetch their bonnets and shawls. Mrs. Bennet came hastily from the morning room as the four gathered in the hall, her face a little flushed. She observed the party, drew breath, and then seemed to realize there was no imperative reason to keep either daughter indoors.

"I am sorry I was not able to receive you, Mr. Bingley, Mr. Darcy," she said with an air of self-importance, "but there is so much to do, so many plans, lists to make, and details to be attended to. I am really quite beside myself."

Darcy saw Elizabeth's lips tighten and the color come up in both ladies' faces at their mother's rudeness. One never failed to greet guests, even unwanted ones, and that certainly did not apply to Bingley or, Darcy was certain, himself. Her excuse was made to show herself in the light of a woman overwhelmed with responsibilities. It only made her look vulgar, and embarrassed her daughters.

"I am sure you will handle everything beautifully, Mrs. Bennet," Bingley said.

"Thank you, sir. I hope I can arrange a wedding as well as any woman in London society. Will you and Mr. Darcy join us for dinner?"

"Thank you, I would be delighted." Bingley glanced at Darcy, who nodded his acceptance of the invitation.

The two couples went outside as Mrs. Bennet bustled off to the kitchen to consult with the cook. It was cool but mild, as Bingley had indicated. They walked around the house and then, instead of keeping to the gardens, followed the path past the copse and away from the house. On the left, fallow fields not yet ready for planting spread to a distant line of trees and the mellow hills beyond. The area to their right was wooded, mostly with old-growth oaks and beeches. Leaf mold showed dark under a multicolored layer of newly fallen leaves. Dead limbs made twisted humps like gray bones of old animals thrust up out of the earth.

On the left, a stone wall that had obviously been built some years before traced an uneven line between the path and fields. Another dark line of trees marked the boundary of the Lucas property. A few white clouds looked painted on the sky above them.

Elizabeth raised her face to the breeze and breathed in deeply. Darcy wished she could take off her bonnet so her expression was visible. Her entire body gloried in the light and air; this was her element, nature and the outdoors. Darcy knew Pemberley would embrace her as its own, and he was certain she would respond by loving it as he did.

They walked slowly to allow Bingley and Jane some privacy. At length, Darcy said, "You will no doubt miss your sister's company when she weds. I know I shall miss my sister's company when she is married."

Elizabeth, a little surprised that Mr. Darcy had spoken of his feelings, said, "Yes. But Jane will only be at Netherfield, so we will still see much of one another. Is Miss Darcy in society yet?"

"No. She is only sixteen. She will not have her coming out for at least two years."

Deciding to chance an inquiry since Mr. Darcy had begun the subject, she said, "Does Miss Darcy reside with you in London?"

"Not at present. She is staying at Pemberley, my estate in Derbyshire."

Some shadow crossed his face, and Elizabeth wondered if she had annoyed him, but the moment passed; he regarded her with grave reserve. "We saw Mr. Collins as we rode here," he said. "He was on his way to the Lucas'. He seemed in very good humor and hinted that he would soon make an announcement. From what little he said, one can only speculate it is to be of a betrothal."

Elizabeth looked sideways at him, and Darcy felt his breath thicken. She said softly, "Yes, I believe he has gone so far as to decide on a wife. It is usually the man who decides, after all."

Swallowing past the lump in his throat, Darcy said, "He seems a pleasant enough man."

"Yes. Not as ecclesiastical as one might expect. His living is in your gift?"

"It is." Darcy was silent for so long Elizabeth began to search for a subject of conversation to break the impasse. Suddenly he went on, "I understand Mr. Collins came to find a wife among your sisters, because of the entail."

"Yes."

How on earth, Elizabeth wondered with some alarm, had they gotten onto this quite personal line of discourse? It was unlike everything she knew of Mr. Darcy, and was nearing impropriety for her to pursue.

Darcy halted suddenly, forcing Elizabeth to face him. "Miss Elizabeth, I know I have no right to ask this, and you may very properly refuse to reply, but are you attached to Mr. Collins or...or even promised to him?"

Astounded, Elizabeth could not speak. She felt a trembling she could not control. Her face paled, and she kept her eyes lowered. As Darcy began to stammer an apology, she took control of herself, responding with what composure she could manage, "There is no understanding between Mr. Collins and myself, and no...no attachment on either side."

Before Darcy was able to say more, she walked on so hurriedly that she nearly caught up to Bingley and Jane, who strolled in close contact, Jane's arm linked through the crook of Bingley's elbow, his free hand covering her gloved fingers on his arm. Darcy's long stride caught Elizabeth up, but he made no attempt to speak. He only walked sedately at her side. Her thoughts tumbling this way and that, Elizabeth could only wonder at his motive for such a question. Surely he felt no attraction to her, and yet, why question whether she was contemplating marriage to Mr. Collins if he had no personal interest in the answer? It was every way puzzling and not a little unsettling. Elizabeth chanced a glance at him. His eyes were on the ground, his profile presented a clean outline against the shadowy darkness of the woods. Teasing, teasing man!

They continued on for some time, neither one finding a safe topic to explore. As they began to turn back toward Longbourn, Darcy asked, "Do you ever visit London, Miss Elizabeth?"

Glad to have something to say, Elizabeth replied, "I visit with my uncle and aunt Gardiner once or twice a year." She hesitated and then added, "My uncle owns Gardiner Imports."

"I am familiar with the name. My aunt and sister have shopped at his warehouses. He has an excellent reputation."

"He is an excellent man," Elizabeth said. And that, Elizabeth thought with surprising bitterness, would be your only contact -- that your relatives patronize his business. He is in trade, after all.

"I do not have the honor of his acquaintance, but I believe Bingley knows him," Darcy went on. "Will you be going to town when Miss Bennet shops for her trousseau?"

"I...I suppose so."

Elizabeth watched Jane lean a little into Mr. Bingley's shoulder. She heard Darcy's deep voice, quite close to her, say, "Will you allow me to call on you, if your uncle permits? I am sure Bingley will want to see Miss Bennet while she is there."

Elizabeth felt the trembling return. After several agonizing moments when Darcy was afraid she would refuse, she said, "You may call, Mr. Darcy. I am sure my uncle will have no objection."

He thanked her, and they continued to Longbourn without further conversation, neither of them easy enough in their minds to speak of trivialities.

Chapter 5

"He wants to know about Ramsgate?" Mrs. Younge's voice had taken on a shrill note that set Wickham's teeth on edge. "Darcy will go mad if anybody finds out about that!"

"Well he may, but it will be too late by then for him to reach us. We'll have enough money to go anywhere—Italy, the islands, wherever you fancy."

"No, I won't do it! I won't take the chance! Why d'you think I've kept silent all this time? Just so I can wind up dead or in prison? It's not worth the risk!"

She is not in any way a retiring woman, Wickham thought, except where her own skin is involved. He gripped her arm so hard she yelped. He was going to be very glad to finally be rid of her. He bored into her eyes with his own, exerting the control he had built up over years. "You will, my dear. And there is no risk if you do exactly as I say." He shook her. "Do you understand?"

Cowed, she nodded stiffly. Wickham was the immediate threat, one she was fully familiar with. He could be an entertaining companion when he was in funds and plied with drink, but at a low ebb, he had no scruples at all. She feared him, and with good reason.

Wickham released her, went to a sideboard, and retrieved paper, pen, and ink. "This is what you are to do. Write everything out, just as it happened. You can leave out your part in bringing us together if you like. Do not use my name. Say the gentleman gave his name as Winter. I have used it before, so it will do. Is that clear? Then write it out again."

Slowly she nodded, still rubbing her bruised arm. "Why do it twice?"

"Because we are selling them to two different people, my dear. We collect for them twice, and then we disappear. If Slade's employer uses it, there will be no proof a Mr. Winter ever existed. The scandal will be bad enough, even if it cannot be substantiated. That is my little revenge on Darcy and his milksop sister. Let him marry her off then, if he can."

"And who will buy the other one?"

"Darcy, of course. He will believe it's the only one and pay high for it. When we are safely out of the way, let him deal with whatever comes."

She is still frightened, Wickham thought as she began to write, *but more of me than any future retribution from Darcy*. He poured himself a drink and sat in a worn armchair, watching her until she finished the second copy. No more cheap Holland for him. When this was over, he would drink the best wine and the finest whisky. And all of it would be at Darcy's expense. That was the real satisfaction of the plan.

As soon as the ink was sanded, Wickham read over both copies, folded them, sealed them with a little candle wax, and put them away in his coat. I have to go carefully, Wickham thought. He had no way of knowing how swiftly Slade's principal was going to act, and if he or she used the document before Darcy had paid up and they were safely away, the entire enterprise was likely to blow up in their faces. Unless he was able to find out whom Slade was working for.

"I'm going out," he told Mrs. Younge, "to do a little reconnoitering, as the bloody colonel would say."

She watched him leave, not rising from the table. Agnes Younge had no illusions about her sometime lover; Wickham's interest was all for Wickham. He was as likely as not to take the money and abandon her to the wrath of Darcy and probably Slade's employer. She vacillated for another quarter hour before she stood up with a shiver, gathered her bonnet, shawl, and reticule, and left the house in search of a hansom. It was past time to hedge her bets.

The hansom let her out a block from Grosvenor Square. She walked slowly up the sidewalk under the spread of the old elms, past mansions with spotless facades and carefully tended gardens. *Places the likes of which I will never again occupy, not even as a servant,* she thought bitterly. She had had a good thing as Georgiana Darcy's companion. She had been respectable and well paid. *Good as being a housekeeper and less work,* she told herself. Wickham with his schemes had talked her out of it, and now what did she have? A run-down rat's nest full of mollies, enough stolen goods to get her hanged, and a man who would throw her under a dray as soon as warm her bed. She deserved better, and she meant to have better. To hell with George Wickham!

Full of righteous anger and self-pity, Mrs. Younge turned into the driveway of Darcy House, hesitated, and then walked boldly up to the front door. She knocked loudly on the door and stood there until it opened. Mr. Burgess stared at her as if she were something tracked onto the clean steps.

"I want to see Mr. Darcy," she said flatly. "Don't say he's not in. What I got to say to him he'll want to hear. Tell him it's about George Wickham."

To say Mrs. Bennet was upset by Mr. Collins's announcement of his betrothal to Charlotte Lucas would be to deny her the full glory of her displeasure. In order to avoid frostbite, Mr. Collins removed to Lucas Lodge, leaving Elizabeth to bear the brunt of her mother's anger and disappointment. Elizabeth could not occupy the same room as Mrs. Bennet for five minutes without hearing how, if only she had made an effort, she would be the one engaged, not Charlotte. How selfish she had been to let such a chance pass her by. Her mother grew so heated at breakfast one morning that when she reiterated for an uncounted time how when her husband died they would all be thrown out into the hedgerows, Mr. Bennet lowered his newspaper and cut through her diatribe with more asperity than usual. "My dear, you might give my ultimate departure the benefit of the doubt for a year or two."

"Nonetheless," Mrs. Bennet answered in full cry, "Lizzy had no right to think only of her own inclinations and not of her mother and sisters."

"Perhaps," Mr. Bennet rejoined, "Mr. Collins had some involvement in the matter."

"Any man will propose if a woman lets him know she is interested in him. Lizzy knows well enough how to flirt if it suits her. She could have found a way for him to offer for her."

"So, she should have compromised Mr. Collins and, thereby, forced his hand? Not advice I would expect to be given to a young lady."

Mrs. Bennet glared at him and then sniffed loudly. "You know exactly what I mean, Mr. Bennet."

"So I do. My memory still retains its vigor, if the rest of me is failing rapidly."

He returned to his reading with a loud rattle of paper, and Mrs. Bennet fell silent for the moment. Whenever he was present, which was no more often than usual, Mr. Bennet deflected the worst of his wife's recriminations. But in the end, Elizabeth was forced to write her Aunt Gardiner and beg for an early invitation to visit prior to Jane's removal to town to purchase her wedding gown and trousseau.

At Netherfield, Darcy had his own reason for leaving for London. Colonel Fitzwilliam had sent an express that the advertisement put in the papers by B. Slade, Esq., was actually on behalf of some unknown principal. Since it was not Richard's father, and Darcy had never suspected it was the earl, he speculated that Lady Catherine de Bourgh, presently in residence at de Bourgh House, was the instigator of the scheme. He had a man watching Slade's office in the event Mrs. Younge answered the ad in person. If that occurred, the man was to follow her and obtain her direction.

After pacing his room far into the night, Darcy decided to leave Netherfield and return to London. He had a terrible presentiment that if Mrs. Younge was involved, Wickham had to be part of the equation. Darcy felt the anger that George Wickham always engendered. He had spent too many years watching his father gulled by the man's charm, seeing the deterioration from selfish youth to dissipated adult. He had endured a seemingly endless history of paying off Wickham's debts and making provisions for the young women he seduced and bastards he fathered, rather than have innocent people harmed. All of it had taken a deep toll. Darcy wanted nothing more than to find a way to be rid of Wickham forever. Colonel Fitzwilliam had proposed his own way to accomplish that goal, but Darcy was not ready to be a party to what was in effect murder.

Darcy offered only a brief explanation of urgent business to Bingley and left Netherfield Park early the next morning. He contemplated waiting long enough to call on the Bennets and say good-bye to Elizabeth, but Darcy realized it would make little difference at this point. His imperative was to deal with the potential disaster to Georgiana and the family before any other private concerns. If the Ramsgate business became public knowledge, everyone connected with him would suffer.

He had arrived at Darcy House midmorning and was in his study going over the post and waiting for word from Colonel Fitzwilliam when his cousin arrived in person. The men shook hands warmly, and Fitzwilliam took a chair. His usual easy demeanor was replaced by a tension Darcy understood all too well.

"My man at Slade's has seen nothing of any women visitors. He has, however, noted that a man came to see Slade yesterday and was with him a quarter hour. The man was dressed as a gentleman, but Rafford said something about him raised his suspicions. Tall, fair hair worn rather long. Looked like a drinker but not so far gone as to show obvious signs. Does that sound like anyone we know?"

Darcy's face was tight but controlled. "I thought Wickham might have a hand in this. He and Mrs. Younge are probably still together. We have to find out where they are."

"I have sent another man to stay near Rafford. If the unknown man returns, one of them will follow him. I do not think Mrs. Younge will go to Slade herself."

"If Slade leaves," Darcy said slowly, "it might be well to follow him as well. He has to report to his employer sooner or later."

"My thought exactly." The colonel rose and went to the sidebar. He poured out two modest brandies and returned to his chair. "Actually, this job is good for my men. Keeps them in practice now that things have temporarily quieted down on the Continent."

Darcy drank a little of the liquor and set the glass aside. "My main concern is Georgie. She's at Pemberley and safe enough there, but if this goes wrong, I do not know what will happen with her. She has not recovered from Ramsgate. To have it come out…"

"We will stop it," Richard said grimly. "I promise you that. I cannot see why Lady Catherine should want to ruin her own niece or her family, but I have to believe she is the one behind this."

Darcy told him exactly why. Fitzwilliam shook his head. He finished his drink and said slowly, "For everyone's sake, would it not be better to let her have Rosings? She cannot live forever. I only suggest it," he added at Darcy's expression, "because of the continued harassment she is certain to inflict. Dealing with her spite will take up a great deal of time and energy better spent otherwise."

"Apparently the earl cannot control her," Darcy said bitterly, "even as head of your family. And you know Lady Catherine. If I give in to her on this she will find something else she wants, and the persecution will continue."

Fitzwilliam nodded slowly. "You are right. I am afraid she is insatiable. When your marriage to Anne did not give her unlimited access to Pemberley and took away her control over Anne, she was badly disappointed. Aunt Catherine has never taken disappointment well. Witness her marriage to Sir Lewis."

"I do not know how the man survived eleven years. I…."

Mr. Burgess tapped at the door. When he entered at Darcy's summons, he wore a strange expression that warned Darcy something was amiss.

"There is a…a person to see you, Mr. Darcy. Mrs. Younge. She says she has something of importance to relate concerning…Mr. Wickham."

Darcy's expression froze. After several heartbeats, he said, "Give me several minutes and then show her in."

Mr. Burgess bowed and withdrew. Darcy turned to Fitzwilliam. "The library. Leave the door ajar. You will be able to hear everything without being seen."

The colonel returned his glass to the sidebar and was at the connecting door in a moment. Darcy noted that the slim crack in the panel was virtually invisible as a new tap sounded on the study door. When Mr. Burgess opened the door to the study again, it was to usher in Mrs. Younge. Darcy dismissed him with a motion of his hand, and stood watching his caller without a hint of expression. She was obviously ill at ease. Her clothing told him she had fallen on hard times; her face showed her age as it had not done last spring when he and Colonel Fitzwilliam engaged her as a companion for Georgiana.

"Sit down," he said coldly.

She took the chair before the desk, clutching her reticule tightly in her lap with both hands. Darcy resumed his seat behind the polished spread of mahogany, letting his hands rest on the surface. He waited, outwardly calm but inwardly seething. Her eyes passed over the objects before her; the stack of letters and contracts, the silver inkwell, a framed miniature of Georgiana. She licked dry lips, raised her head, and tried to look confident. "I came to see you because I have some information you will want to know."

Darcy noted she was making an effort to sound as educated as she had when in his employ. He decided to chance a shot at a venture. "About Mr. Slade? I already know about that."

"You don't...do not know that George Wickham is involved."

"I suspected it. I already have people working on this matter. I doubt there is anything you can reveal that I cannot find out for myself."

Anger and fear warred in her expression. At length she said, "You do not know that Wickham made me write out everything that happened last summer at Ramsgate, only changing his name to Winter. Two copies; one for Mr. Slade and one for you."

"He expects to collect from both Slade's employer and myself? It sounds like Wickham. And you want me to pay you for the information."

Mrs. Younge sat even straighter. "He's already got five hundred pounds from Slade, and I haven't seen a penny of it! Now George's trying to find out who hired him. If he does, he'll go straight to whoever it is for the money. Four thousand pounds. George would kill his own mother for that much."

"And then try to sell me a worthless document. Yes, it definitely sounds like him. However, your information, while interesting, is not worth anything like the sum you have been promised."

Mrs. Younge twisted her thin hands in her reticule. She swallowed, and her throat worked. At last, her nerve broke. "I want to get away from him!" Her voice sounded shrill in the quiet room. "I have to get out! He'll leave me when he gets his hands on the cash, and then where'll I be? He knows too much. He'll split on me. Oh God! Why did I ever trust the bastard?"

Darcy got up, poured her a half glass of port, and returned to the desk. She drank it in two swallows, but a little color came back into her sallow face. He said quietly, "First, you will tell me, completely and without deception, exactly what it is that Wickham knows about you. If you do so, I will assist you in leaving London and, indeed, England, for some location where Wickham will never find you."

She stared at him, caught between desperate hope and instinctive cynicism. It took her several minutes of internal debate before she realized she had no other choice. Mrs. Younge gave him her direction, the occupation of her "boarders," and information about the stolen goods stored in her attic awaiting removal to the fences who would sell the articles. She told him of Wickham's gambling debts and something even Wickham did not know she knew—that he had given information to a Bow Street investigator about one of his confederates who was wanted for theft. The man, who was named Killan, had been arrested, tried, and hung.

"The runner told one of the girls, and she told me. I daren't let George know, or I don't know what he'd do." She drooped back in the chair. "Is that enough?"

"Quite enough," Darcy said. He called without raising his voice, "Fitzwilliam."

The colonel entered from the library, causing Mrs. Younge to jump to her feet in alarm. Darcy said again more forcefully, "Sit down. Colonel Fitzwilliam is only a witness in the event you should decide to break our agreement." He took out paper and pen and began to write, speaking over the scratch of the nib. "I am making up a statement for you to sign. It details what you have just told me. Colonel Fitzwilliam can witness it. I will pay you two thousand pounds and see that you have passage on a ship to a foreign destination."

Mrs. Younge subsided. She drew a breath, hesitated, then said breathlessly, "Three thousand pounds. You can afford it, and I need to make a new start."

Darcy looked up at her and then glanced at Fitzwilliam, who shrugged. "Two thousand five hundred plus your passage, and not a penny more. Otherwise you can leave and deal with Wickham yourself."

She waited in silence until Darcy finished writing. When she had read over the paper, she signed it, and Fitzwilliam signed as witness. Darcy sanded the document and laid it aside. Mrs. Younge waited. Her face was sullen as if she thought he would now go back on his bargain. Instead, he said, "There is a ship leaving for the Caribbean the day after tomorrow. It is a merchantman but can accommodate several passengers. When I send you word, take your things to the direction on my card, and give it to the captain." He took one of his calling cards and wrote a few words on the back. "He will see you are taken care of, and he will give you a packet containing the money when the ship is at sea. He is a man of honorable reputation. You need have no concern for your safety, but I cannot speak for his crew, so I would advise you to keep the money a secret."

He gave her the card. She glanced at the back and looked up at Darcy with a mixture of relief and fear in her eyes. "If George ever finds out, he'll kill me."

"See that he does not find out, then. I believe that completes any business we have."

She rose and put the card in her reticule. After a moment, she left the study without further comment. Colonel Fitzwilliam opened the door and followed her out. When he returned, Darcy raised an eyebrow at him.

"A little implied threat does no harm with someone like Mrs. Younge," he said. "She's terrified of Wickham, and now she's frightened of me as well. That should keep her quiet." He raised an eyebrow to echo his cousin's. "How do you know about the ship?"

Darcy said, "I own an interest in the company that owns the ship. I keep track of their arrivals and departures." He sat back. "As soon as she is safely on the ship and out of the country, her written story can no longer be repeated. Wickham will come to me first. He will want to be sure I do not find out there is a second copy before he can sell it to Slade."

"How are you going to deal with Wickham?" Fitzwilliam looked as if the name left a nasty taste in his mouth.

"I, too, have my statement from Mrs. Younge. I made sure to indicate that Wickham knew of all her activities and participated in them. Mr. Wickham will not enjoy being arrested for keeping a bawdy house or receiving stolen goods, much less it being known that he informed on a confederate, which resulted in the man's execution. I think I have only to promise that the information will be advertised where it will do the most harm to effect a trade for his copies of Mrs. Younge's story."

"If you cannot," his cousin told him grimly, "I can assure you he will never use them."

When Fitzwilliam had gone, Darcy remained at his desk. The reaction was setting in. He felt an internal tremor compounded of anger, guilt, and frustration.

At that moment, Darcy wanted nothing more than to find Wickham, put his hands around the man's throat, and choke the foul life from his body. The image of his sister as he had left her at Pemberley rose in his mind. Since Ramsgate, she had become a gray wraith, floating through the days without purpose. She would sit in the window seat of her private sitting room, pale and listless, and stare blindly at the autumn gardens. Georgiana no longer regularly practiced the pianoforte, her great passion for music suppressed beneath the weight of remorse and guilt. Wickham had not despoiled her body, but he had despoiled her heart -- a wound so much harder to mend. Darcy did not even know where to start the process of bringing her back from the place she wandered, alone in her pain.

Wickham deserved to die for what he had done to that gentle soul. But Darcy knew even Wickham's death was not the answer. If there was a way to help her, he must find it. He could not bear to think of her going on as she was, and his greatest fear had become that in time, she would not go on. If he was married to a woman of sense and understanding, perhaps she might be able to help his sister. Unbidden, the thought of Elizabeth Bennet came to him. Purposefully, Darcy turned to the papers he must attend to, putting the thought aside. It remained, however, silent and waiting at the edge of consciousness.

Elizabeth's week in London was taken up by pleasant activities. She chose fabrics and patterns for her bridesmaid dress and two other gowns. Her father had allowed her enough for the dress and a new ball gown. As Mr. Bennet refused to be obligated to anyone, even his brother-in-law, Mr. Gardiner charged Elizabeth his cost for the material. This allowed her, at her aunt's insistence, to also have a new evening gown made. Fittings took up more time. In her free hours, she walked in a nearby park with the two oldest Gardiner children and their nanny or went shopping with her aunt. Mrs. Gardiner knew there was an underlying reason for Elizabeth to leave Jane in Hertfordshire at this particular time, but she did not pry. As the time for the others to arrive drew nearer, she noticed Elizabeth seemed more withdrawn; her appetite, always healthy, had also declined.

On the day of the last fitting for the gowns, Mrs. Gardiner took Elizabeth to Gunter's, the famous confectioner's shop in Berkley Square. They had ices, for which the establishment was famous, in the back room, where shoppers could sit and recuperate from their labors. In the warm, pleasant-smelling atmosphere, the two women enjoyed their treats and talked of trivial matters for some minutes before Elizabeth fell suddenly silent.

She said at last, "You have been very kind, Aunt, to not question me about why I needed to come to town early."

"I know if you wish to tell me, you will do so. It is certainly not Jane."

"No, not my dearest Jane. I feel bad about leaving her with all the wedding preparations to be taken on, but I could not bear another day at home."

Mrs. Gardiner reached out and patted Elizabeth's hand where it lay on the immaculate tablecloth. "Fanny?"

Elizabeth nodded. Her voice was so soft her aunt was forced to lean toward her to hear. "Mama wants all of us to marry as well as may be. Mr. Bingley was obviously drawn to Jane, and she to him. But Mama had recently met Mr. Bingley's friend, Mr. Darcy. He is very wealthy, and Mama wanted Jane to…to abandon Mr. Bingley and try to attach Mr. Darcy's affections. Jane refused, for once. I was so proud of her! When Mr. Bingley proposed to Jane we were all so happy for her. They are so perfect for one another. Mama accepted the fact, and I thought everything was settled. But when Mr. Collins—our cousin, the parson—proposed to Charlotte Lucas, Mama blamed me for not securing him." Elizabeth looked around suddenly at the other patrons. "I cannot speak of this here. It is too public."

Mrs. Gardiner nodded. She rose and paid for their refreshments, and the two women returned to the Gardiner coach. In the relative privacy of the rattling vehicle as they set off for Cheapside, Elizabeth told her aunt of Mrs. Bennet's disappointment and resentment against her as well as Mr. Collins. Mrs. Gardiner was not unaware of her sister-in-law's attitude where Elizabeth was concerned. It vexed her, but the matter was an internal family problem over which she had no control or influence.

"Surely, she must know," Mrs. Gardiner said, "that if Mr. Collins wished to marry you, or any of your sisters, he would have offered for you. It was his decision."

"Mama is not very rational when it comes to marrying off a daughter, especially me. I dared not tell her that Mr. Collins told me of his decision to propose to Miss Lucas or that he indicated in a very kindly manner that I was not of a temperament to be a parson's wife."

"And a perceptive man he is," Mrs. Gardiner said approvingly. "You would do your best, but you would be miserable, or at the least, discontented."

Elizabeth looked down at her gloved hands. "That is not quite all."

When she did not continue, Mrs. Gardiner said, "You need not say more, my dear, if it distresses you."

As they neared Cheapside, the traffic around them increased until it made a constant background of rattles and thumps, the clatter of horses' hooves over cobbles, the creak of wood and leather, the jangle of chains, and the heavy rumble of cart wheels like distant thunder. From the roadside, hawkers cried their services and wares; tinkers, ragpickers, milkmaids, vendors of everything from fish to matches. It was the symphony of commerce, the business of doing business that elevated the great city, its port and the country, above its Continental cousins; revolution- and war-shattered France, the continually contentious German states, and Italy, living on the memory past glories.

Elizabeth was silent as the noise filled the cab of the coach. When she spoke, it was still with her eyes on her hands clasped in her lap. "Do you know anything of Mr. Fitzwilliam Darcy?"

Mrs. Gardiner smiled. "Anyone who knows anything of the upper levels of society knows the name. You said he is Mr. Bingley's friend, and you have met him."

"I danced with him at the Meryton assembly. He is visiting Mr. Bingley at Netherfield Park. He called several times in Mr. Bingley's company. He asked me if my uncle Gardiner would allow him to call on me while I am in London."

"I see." Mrs. Gardiner was beginning to have an inkling of some deeper problem than a clash of personalities in Elizabeth's relationship with her mother, but she only said, "I can see no reason why he should object. Mr. Darcy is well known to be an honorable and upright man, unusual traits among the members of the *ton*. What did you think of him?"

Elizabeth considered. "He is very well educated. We had several very pleasant conversations."

"He is said to be very handsome."

"Yes, he is, but he makes nothing of it. I found him…intriguing. I believe him to be a complex man and perhaps a little shy."

Mrs. Gardiner smiled. "I hope he does call. I look forward to meeting him."

"He is already in town," Elizabeth said softly. "Mr. Bingley told us he was called away suddenly on business, the day before I left."

"Does he know you are in London?"

Elizabeth shook her head. The carriage pulled into the driveway of the Gardiner home, and a footman handed the ladies out. As they walked into the house, Mrs. Gardiner noted Elizabeth's heightened color. Curious as to how much had not been said, she wondered if Mr. Darcy were somehow a factor in Elizabeth's problems. It was a question that was to loom large in the coming days.

"Really, Charles, I do not know why you felt it necessary to chase after Jane Bennet when she is in town to buy her wedding gown and trousseau, but since you have, I thought a small dinner party might be a good idea."

Bingley regarded his sister with a flutter of disquiet. She had come into his study after a perfunctory tap at the door in her usual brisk fashion, to propose a celebratory dinner in honor of his engagement. This sudden acceptance of the situation left her brother to wonder at her motive. He knew she was angered by his choice of wife, so her offering to arrange a dinner for Jane was suspect. However, he liked the idea and said so.

"Excellent," Caroline went on. "We can have Louisa and Miles, Mr. Darcy, if he is free, the relatives from Cheapside, of course, and Miss Eliza."

"The Gardiners," Charles replied forbiddingly, "are people of fashion. They are cultured and perfectly acceptable in any society in which they might find themselves."

"I am sure you are right." Caroline brushed aside her brother's words. "And I think we ought to invite the Handelmans. Mr. Handelman is Miles's cousin, and I am sure they will be quite taken with Jane. So, that makes…oh dear, one gentleman short. I shall have to find someone to invite to make up an even number. I am sure someone among our acquaintances will be available. Perhaps Mr. Chesney. He is quite old, but he was Father's friend for years, and he is perfectly amiable."

Charles nodded and returned to his correspondence. Smiling with rather too much satisfaction, Caroline left him. She had someone specific in mind, but she was not about to inform her brother of her selection. Gayne Hobson was young, charming, and well off -- and he had a reputation as a man who liked women a little too well. He would do nicely for Miss Eliza Bennet. Let Darcy see exactly what sort of lady she was. That ought to cool any feelings he might be developing for the country clod.

When she triumphantly related her scheme to her older sister, Louisa Hurst, she found less support than she might have hoped. "Caroline," Louisa sipped her tea and gazed up at her sister with a raised brow, "you know Charles will be livid when he finds out."

"I do not care. It will not be until the night of the dinner, and what can he do then? I intend to show Miss Eliza Bennet for what she is, a scheming hussy with her eye on improving her status at the expense of Mr. Darcy—or any other man with money and position. Mr. Hobson is perfect for the task."

"Mr. Hobson is a gentleman in name only."

Louisa was growing tired of her sister's plotting. It strained the atmosphere of the house needlessly. Charles was committed to marry Jane Bennet, and her personal opinion was that he could have chosen worse.

Caroline smirked. "If Mr. Darcy has any feelings for her, they will not survive the evening, I promise you."

Louisa set her cup on the pretty little marquetry table beside her chair and contemplated Caroline with a shrewd eye. "Never make promises you are not certain you can keep. However, on your head be it."

"I shall succeed," Caroline assured her.

Louisa shrugged.

Unaware of his sister's plotting, Charles called on Darcy to invite him to the dinner and to ask if he wished to accompany him when he visited his fiancée. Bingley found his friend looking grimmer than might be expected. Afraid Darcy had experienced some business reverse, Bingley tried to lighten the mood of the visit. When Darcy found out that Elizabeth Bennet had been in town for nearly a week, his reaction was surprise and then regret.

"I would have called on her if I had known," he told his friend.

"I am sorry, Darcy, but I had no idea you would want to know. She left the day after you did at an invitation from her aunt. Miss Bennet tells me it was to order her dress for the wedding and a new ball gown. In that way when the others arrived, Miss Bennet's wedding gown and trousseau would be the focus."

"When do you call upon the Gardiners?"

Bingley said, "Tomorrow morning."

"We can take my carriage, if you like."

Bingley agreed, and after some further conversation, he left, leaving Darcy to brood over Elizabeth's reason for coming to town early. Surely there were enough modistes in London to make a trousseau, a wedding gown, and two other gowns without a week's preparation. He suspected from certain observations that it might have to do with her mother. Mrs. Bennet seemed to wish her eldest daughter to take precedence over the other sisters. Elizabeth and her elder sister were exceptionally close. She might have come to London early so there would be no conflict as the wedding plans progressed. It was sad, but not so unusual for a mother and daughter to be at odds for one reason or another. His own late wife and her mother were an extreme example.

The memory brought another more urgent matter to mind. He had received a note from Wickham in yesterday's post proposing a meeting at a neutral location. In turn, Darcy sent a message to Richard Fitzwilliam; Darcy had chosen a coffee house in an area near Covent Garden that was marginally disreputable, so Wickham would not suspect a trap. They were to meet at five o'clock that afternoon. Wickham had indicated he had a document of value to the preservation of the Darcy family's reputation and wanted five thousand pounds for it. Darcy's lips drew back in a near snarl. He was almost tempted to allow Colonel Fitzwilliam to deal with the man as he saw fit. Only a lifetime of believing in and adhering to the law stopped him. Wickham would fall foul of the wrong man one day. Sooner, if he tried to use Mrs. Younge's confessional.

Bingley had been gone barely half an hour when Burgess showed Darcy's cousin into the study. The colonel sat before the desk and regarded Darcy with an air of accomplishment. "The ship is halfway down the estuary by now, with Mrs. Younge s safely on board. I found out her captain is an old navy man. He will follow instructions and lock her in her cabin until they are at sea. Not that she is about to swim for it."

Darcy nodded in relief. "We are meeting Wickham at five this evening at Garrett's Coffee House. Can you have your men in place in the event he decides to run?"

"I have already notified three men that I will require their services this afternoon on a training exercise. I will instruct them and then wait until I see Wickham enter the building. You are sure you do not wish me to take this problem out of your life?"

"Not entirely, but let us try to settle it without bloodshed."

Fitzwilliam made a disappointed face and then sobered. "You know this will not stop her."

"Perhaps not, but it will take any threat of exposure from Georgiana. At the moment, that is my only concern."

The colonel rose. "I will get to it, then. See you this evening."

Darcy also stood and held out his hand. "Thank you, Richard."

Fitzwilliam shook his hand. "Any time, Cousin. I am an old hand at hunting weasels."

"Mama has been impossible," Jane told her sister as they sat in Elizabeth's bedroom at the Gardiners' home. "She has been looking at all the fashion plates Lydia and Kitty have, and she wants to deck me out in a wedding gown that will make me look like a half-melted French confection!"

Elizabeth repressed a smile. "Can you not tell her what you want?"

"I have. Numerous times. She just ignores me. It is *my* wedding after all. Why cannot I have the gown *I* want?"

"Because she is Mama." Elizabeth took Jane's hands in both of hers. "Mr. Bingley will not care if you wear a flour sack or two pounds of Brussels lace. Perhaps our aunt can persuade her to modify her ideas."

Jane sighed. "I wish so, but you know what she is like when she decides on something. I can at least choose my own trousseau. She seems to care little about that."

"A trousseau does not reflect on the bride's mother. It is a chiefly a private, not a public, display."

"Would she be happier," Jane murmured with her head bowed, "if Papa had not had to give up the estate in Cheshire?"

Elizabeth hesitated and then said, "I do not know. Possibly she would. I always wonder if she remembers the part of the wedding ceremony that says, 'for better, for worse, for richer, for poorer.'"

"I would not care," Jane said, "if Mr. Bingley lost every penny he has. But if I had been raised with money and all it buys, the luxuries and servants and never having to worry about what anything cost, if I had always had those things and then lost them all, I wonder how I might behave."

"You would always be my wonderful, kind, caring Jane." Elizabeth leaned over and kissed her sister's cheek. Straightening, she said, "What do you think of Miss Bingley's dinner invitation? Do you think it is Mr. Bingley's idea?"

"I do not know. He said nothing about it before we left Hertfordshire. Perhaps she is trying to make amends for her behavior before we became betrothed."

Elizabeth raised an eyebrow. "I will have to see that to believe it. In any event, she has included the Gardiners, so we will have family support if we require it. And Mama will be there, since she has arrived in Town." Elizabeth looked down. "I only wish Papa had come with you."

"So do I, but he said he preferred the peace and quiet of a fortnight without chatter of wedding plans. Lydia and Kitty were disappointed they were not allowed to come, but Mary was satisfied to stay at home, as usual."

"I can imagine what a shopping expedition with Lydia and Kitty would entail." Elizabeth made a comical face. "The entire budget would be spent on the two of them instead of your gown and trousseau."

Jane's smile was genuinely amused. "Oh, surely not. Mama wants my wedding to be the talk of Meryton for a year at least! I might look as if I were encased in icing, but it will be *my* icing."

They laughed at the image, but Elizabeth knew her sister well enough to know she had serious reservations about her mother's idea of a proper wedding gown. She silently resolved to speak to their aunt and to do everything in her power to divert their mother from distressing Jane by imposing her own ideas of fashion on her daughter. It was the most important day of Jane's life. It ought to be hers alone, not Mrs. Bennet's social triumph.

"Let us see if we can scrape some of it off," Elizabeth said lightly. As they separated to dress for dinner, Elizabeth added wryly, "It makes me wonder, should I ever marry, what my wedding will be like."

Jane replied from the doorway, "Well, there is always Gretna Green," and she nimbly dodged the cushion Elizabeth threw at her.

Chapter 6

The Garrett Coffee House was something of a misnomer. Mr. Garrett, the original owner, had died in 1792, leaving the business, then located just off Fleet Street, to his son, who promptly sold it. Five years later, a fire destroyed the original building, along with several others, causing the removal of the name to a new premise near Covent Garden. Over time, the clientele changed, and the coffeehouse became more than a place for sellers, drivers, porters, and carters handling produce at the market. Gradually it turned into a meeting place for questionable characters—molls, minor criminals, and small fish of the London underworld who wished to transact business of a sort that shunned public notice. The main room was not large; a long, dim interior lit by oil lamps along the walls that gave off more smoke than light. Wooden booths, blackened by time and dirt, proceeded along the right-hand side to near the serving counter in the rear, with a few tables and benches placed to the left, leaving a walkway like a tunnel between. It was not a location for any man unable to take care of himself. A man who looked wealthy was in even more danger.

Darcy had dressed very simply in dark clothing with an old overcoat used for driving thrown over them. He carried a stick containing a very sharp sword but no other weapons. Fitzwilliam would undoubtedly be armed, and his men as well. The less show of force the better. Darcy wanted no open conflict if it was avoidable; he was concerned that bystanders, however culpable in other circumstances, should not be accidentally injured. He took a booth near the door where he was able to watch customers enter, and he ordered coffee. The waiter sat a cup of some black fluid in front of him, and Darcy nodded thanks without speaking. He sipped the brew and then pushed the cup aside with a grimace. Whatever it was, it was like no coffee he had ever tasted.

Men came and went, workers from the market, produce sellers, draymen, pimps, even one or two women of obvious employment. Darcy wanted to check his watch but thought better of it. It was too fine to display in this place. He watched the light outside the doorway fade and wondered if Wickham had decided to sell the document to Slade instead, when a familiar figure entered the room, paused to survey the customers warily, and strode to his booth, sliding onto the bench opposite. Wickham raised a hand to the waiter, who brought him a tin mug of gin, plunking it down on the scarred tabletop.

"It will be on my friend's bill," Wickham said smoothly. Darcy nodded and waved the waiter away. Wickham drank, his eyes casually probing the dim corners of the room. Satisfied, he said, "Well, Darcy, we have some business to transact. You've brought a draft for five thousand pounds, I hope."

"What am I paying for?"

Wickham pulled a folded paper out of his coat and laid it on the stained slab of wood turning the paper to face Darcy so he could read it, but keeping hold of the edges. Darcy glanced over it and raised his eyes to the mocking gaze fixed on his face. "Mrs. Younge is a friend of yours, I take it."

"For some years, as you probably guessed after Ramsgate. Someone else is prepared to pay for this. I thought it only fair to give you first refusal."

So engrossed was he in watching Darcy, he had lost track of the rest of the room. Wickham startled violently when Colonel Fitzwilliam sat down beside him and pushed him bodily against the wall with bruising force. "Hello, George," he said quietly. "Fancy seeing you here."

"It's a trap!" Wickham hissed. "Damn you, it won't do you any good to take the paper. I can have another written up by tomorrow."

"Not unless you take a long, cold swim in the Thames," Fitzwilliam informed him mildly.

Wickham blanched, his sallow skin took on a yellowish hue. But it was Darcy he spoke to. "You won't stoop to murder, Darcy. I know you. Pay me, and that will be the end of it, I swear."

"On your honor?" Darcy asked softly. "On the love you had for my father? No, Wickham, I think not. I will have both documents, now, and I will pay you...with this."

Darcy withdrew a similarly folded paper from his coat and held it out as Wickham had done, for his enemy to read. Wickham turned even paler as he reached the last lines. His hands began to tremble, he gripped the edge of the table worn smooth by thousands of sleeves. Sweat prickled his upper lip. "It's a bluff," he said hoarsely. "You can't prove any of it!"

"I need not prove the last charge. A word, a rumor in the right places will be enough for the man's friends to come after you. And if the constables search Mrs. Younge's boardinghouse, will the women there take the blame, or will they tell the law that you were fully aware of what went on?"

"Mrs. Younge owns the place. I just board there...."

Darcy said in a flat voice, "Mrs. Younge is now somewhere at sea. She has enough to make a life for herself wherever she lands. She will not be back, and you will not find her. And if you try to use her information, I will see to it you are exposed as the man who betrayed this Killan to his death. Is that very clear, Wickham?"

Wickham swallowed hard, as if his throat constricted his breathing. He knew full well that even a hint he had sold Killan to the law was a death sentence of its own. Darcy saw the muscles in his shoulders tighten as if he felt the point of a knife between them. After a long pause he said, "All right, all right. I will give you the documents in exchange. But I should get something more out of it."

"Is your rotten life sufficient?" Fitzwilliam asked. "You took an advance from Slade. That ought to be enough for you to leave London. I suggest you do that. And do not think of selling Mr. Slade your own version of the story. Darcy may have scruples where you are concerned, but I do not."

With a muttered blasphemy, Wickham produced the second copy of Mrs. Younge's statement and passed it to Darcy, and snatched up the indictment. He looked from one man to the other; panic began to take hold. At a nod from Darcy, the colonel rose and let Wickham leave the booth. Without watching Wickham's precipitous retreat, he reseated himself and said, "I have a man waiting for him. If he goes to Slade, I will know about it, and I will act on the information."

"Very well."

Darcy folded the papers together after checking that the second was an original and put them away. He took several coins from his waistcoat pocket and laid them on the table. "Come and dine with me. I need something to take the taste of this meeting out of my mouth. Not to mention the coffee."

"With pleasure." Fitzwilliam grinned. "Your cook is a genius, and your cellar would compensate, even if she were not."

"It was kind of Miss Bingley to organize a dinner for the Bennets," Darcy said to his friend as they traveled to Cheapside in his coach the following morning.

"I am glad she is taking the trouble," Bingley replied. "Miss Bennet will be my wife, and Caroline has to adjust to that fact. This is, I hope, the first step."

Darcy looked out the window at the passing buildings. They had nearly reached their destination, but it was not as he might have expected. On reflection, he admitted that because Mr. Gardiner owned a business and lived within sight of his warehouses, this did not mean he did not occupy a well-kept, handsome house on a well-kept, handsome street.

As if reading his friend's thoughts, Bingley said, "My father did business with Mr. Gardiner's father and with the man himself. He was educated at Oxford, as a 'cit' of course, as I was at Cambridge. I do not doubt that he will have his sons educated as gentlemen. One day one of them will buy an estate, as I am doing."

"Times are changing," Darcy said thoughtfully. "I do not know that I agree with all the ways of change, but I firmly believe that one day, although not in our lifetime, the idea of class distinctions will be as obsolete as redingotes and powdered wigs."

Bingley laughed although a trifle hesitantly. "You may be right."

Before he could go on, they pulled into the driveway of the Gardiners' residence, exiting the coach while a footman knocked on the door. A butler answered, took their cards, and led them to the drawing room where the ladies sat. They rose at the gentlemen's entrance, curtsying to the formal bows. Bingley introduced Darcy to Mrs. Gardiner, who welcomed him and indicated the gentlemen should be seated. She rang for tea. Bingley took a chair next to

Jane. Elizabeth, after a swift look at Mr. Darcy's grave face, resumed her seat on the settee next to her aunt and picked up her embroidery. Not for the first time she though the employment at least had the virtue of giving her hands something to do and her eyes somewhere to rest.

"We received Miss Bingley's invitation, and I have sent a reply," Mrs. Gardiner said when they were settled. "We are looking forward to meeting your sister."

Mrs. Bennet, seated across from Jane, grimaced in such a way that Jane blushed, and Elizabeth quickly said, "It will be our first social engagement in London."

"I hope not the last," Bingley responded cheerfully.

"Indeed," Mr. Darcy spoke for the first time. "Have you ever seen a performance of Shakespeare by a professional company, Miss Elizabeth?"

Elizabeth looked up, surprised. "No, unfortunately I have not."

"The Theatre Royal, Drury Lane is hosting a Shakespearian company, with Edmund Kean performing Shylock in *The Merchant of Venice*. I plan to go on Thursday evening. It would give me great pleasure if you and your family and Mr. Bingley would join me."

Elizabeth shot a swift glance at her mother. Mrs. Bennet looked as if she did not know whether to accept the invitation or resent it. Her attitude toward Mr. Darcy baffled Elizabeth. What was there about the man that ruffled Mrs. Bennet so much? She wanted very badly to accept on the moment, but she knew if she spoke, her mother would reject the offer. It was Mrs. Gardiner who saved the situation.

"My husband and I will be very pleased to accept, Mr. Darcy, thank you. I have seen Mr. Kean in a different play, and he is outstanding. His performance of Shylock has been much praised." She looked steadily at Mrs. Bennet and added, "I hope you will agree as well, Sister."

With some reluctance, Mrs. Bennet accepted the invitation. Elizabeth smiled at Darcy, sending his heart rate up several notches. They talked a little about Shakespeare until Mrs. Bennet introduced the subject of wedding clothes and her toil in the matrimonial fields. Mrs. Gardiner deftly moved the conversation to other more general subjects, with partial success. If she was vexed, she was skilled enough not to show it; Elizabeth had more trouble retaining a neutral expression and tone of voice.

After the gentlemen left, Mrs. Bennet said, "I do not know why a gentleman would ask ladies to see a play by Shakespeare when we might all have gone to a pantomime and farce. It is something Mr. Bennet might enjoy, and Lizzy, of course, but I prefer lighter fare."

"They are an excellent Shakespearean company, and Mr. Kean is known as a superb actor," Mrs. Gardiner said mildly. "It will be a wonderful opportunity for my nieces to see the play done as it should be. We can take in a pantomime later in your stay. Perhaps Mr. Gardiner would agree to take us all to Vauxhall Gardens."

"Oh, I should love to go there!" Mrs. Bennet sighed. "After we were first married, Mr. Bennet took me one evening when we were in town. They had just opened for the season. I remember it as if it were yesterday—the lights, the music. We ate in the supper boxes. Such wonderful food. Oh, and the arrack punch. We danced and, later, watched the fireworks display, and the Chinese Tower seemed to burn down, but it was only an illusion. I so enjoyed it!"

"Then I will ask Mr. Gardiner if we may go," Mrs. Gardiner promised.

Appeased, Mrs. Bennet returned to Jane's wedding clothes. Mr. Bennet had been generous about the money for the trousseau and wedding gown, but Mrs. Bennet, as usual, was dissatisfied. Even with Mr. Gardiner supplying fabrics at a considerable discount, she did not like the pattern Jane had chosen, had not found lace that suited her, was certain the gowns would not be ready on time, and generally gave the impression she was the only person in the family with the taste and ability to manage the nuptials properly.

After several repetitions, Mrs. Gardiner put in quietly, "Really, Fanny, you have not yet explored all of the milliners' shops and linen drapers available. We will find what Jane wants in plenty of time, I am sure."

"What Jane wants? If we did what Jane wants, she would be married in a grain sack! I hope I know what a wedding of this importance requires in the way of a gown. Mr. Bingley is a wealthy man. I am sure he expects his bride to be dressed in the latest fashion. I want everyone in Meryton to talk about this wedding for months."

"Oh," Mrs. Gardiner replied softly, "I am sure they will. Talk. You know how people are."

Frowning suddenly, Mrs. Bennet said, "What do you mean, Sister?"

"Only that I am sure there are neighbors who feel…well, envy is such a harsh word. Shall we say they just regret that their own daughters did not secure Mr. Bingley's affection? A too-fashionable wedding gown might lead them to speculate that the Bennets are putting on airs. But gossip is only that, after all. I am sure you know your neighbors better than I."

Elizabeth put her head down and kept stitching. She dared not look at Jane, much less her aunt or mother. Mrs. Bennet's face underwent several changes of expression before she spoke, not the least of which was apprehension. Being the subject of ill-intentioned neighborhood gossip was one of her greatest fears. She knew all too well how rumors and whispers affected a family in a small community.

"Perhaps you are right, Sister," she said finally. "A fashionable gown but not of *quite* the latest mode."

"I think that is a wonderful idea, Mama," Jane put in at last. "Perhaps we can go shopping for lace and other items tomorrow."

It was decided, and the talk turned to other things. Elizabeth thanked her aunt privately that evening for her help. Jane would have been miserable in the concoction Mrs. Bennet had in mind. She then turned her thoughts to tomorrow night's dinner and to Thursday's entertainment, and went to bed happier than she had been for some days.

Mr. Bingley was not as happy. He chanced upon Mr. Hobson at White's and was astonished to find Hobson was to be a dinner guest that night. Caroline shrugged off her brother's pique, as she usually did. She was fully engaged in last-minute preparations and, when confronted, turned a pout on Bingley he had seen too many times before to mistake.

"I needed another gentleman to make up the table, and as it is, I am one short on account of Mrs. Bennet. I can hardly retract the invitation now. In any event, Mr. Hobson is a perfectly suitable gentleman, and it is only for dinner."

"I thought you were to invite Mr. Chesney."

"He is gone to Brighton for the waters." Caroline neglected to inform Bingley she had made sure of Mr. Chesney's location before advancing his name.

"You could think of no one else?"

"Not on short notice. For heaven's sake, Charles, what is wrong with Mr. Hobson? He is wealthy, civilized, and cultured. Why do you dislike him?"

"I do not dislike him exactly," Bingley replied. "It is only that he has a questionable reputation."

"Oh, pooh! Do not be childish. He has accepted, and that is that."

And it was. Bingley had to agree silently that it was too late to find another guest or to rescind Hobson's invitation. He really knew nothing specific to the man's detriment. He was said to keep a mistress, but so did half or more of the male members of the *ton*, married and unmarried. He gambled but not to excess. He was not known as a drinker or for having any worse habits than that. It was all vague, a sort of aura the man carried with him that made some men uncomfortable in his presence.

Darcy arrived early that evening and had a drink with Bingley before the other guests were expected. He was no happier than his host when he found out Mr. Hobson was to be present.

"Caroline invited him to make up another gentleman at dinner," Bingley said apologetically. "I did not know until this morning. Really, I know nothing ill of the man. He just seems to rub people the wrong way."

"How do you know Hobson?" Darcy asked obliquely.

"We have been to several parties and a ball where he was present. Peters-Wayne introduced us. I see him at White's occasionally, but there is no other contact."

"With your wide acquaintance, I wonder why Caroline picked Mr. Hobson?"

"I asked her, but she was not specific. You think she had some particular purpose?"

Darcy shrugged. Privately, he was certain Caroline had invited Hobson for a reason, but until the evening played out, he had no way of discovering what it was. He knew Hobson only slightly, but Darcy was certain he would never allow the man near Georgiana. There were rumors, true or not, that several young ladies who had come too much in contact with the man had withdrawn from society. Darcy hated gossip, but he firmly believed Hobson was too much a man of the world to be allowed access to innocents.

The Gardiners arrived with Mrs. Bennet, Jane, and Elizabeth. Darcy greeted them impassively, noting that Elizabeth seemed to have taken particular pains with her gown and hair. Since women usually dressed to impress other women, he wondered if her object was Miss Bingley. He hardly believed she showed such a fashionable face for him. Her gown of rose silk crepe was cut without frills in the empire style that hugged the body only enough to suggest the figure beneath the fabric. Her dark curls were put up in braids and ringlets with a silver diadem circling her brow; a rose diamond pendant rested at the hollow of her throat. Darcy was still admiring her completely natural beauty when the last guest arrived.

Gayne Hobson wore his blond wavy hair brushed back from a face which just missed being conventionally handsome. His chin was slightly pointed, his nose narrow; he had a wide, thin-lipped mouth that turned up slightly at the corners, giving him a sardonic look. There was about him an indefinable air of impertinence some women found charming. He greeted his hostess and Bingley and was introduced to the Gardiners and Bennets. When he came to Elizabeth, his light-green eyes held hers for several seconds longer than strictly appropriate.

"I am most charmed to make your acquaintance, Miss Elizabeth," he said with a smile.

"And I yours, Mr. Hobson."

Looking at Darcy, Hobson acknowledged his presence with a bow that Darcy reciprocated coolly. They went into the drawing room, and a servant offered a tray of drinks. Elizabeth took a sherry and sat on a sofa next to Jane. She was not there long before Mr. Hobson occupied a chair across from her and engaged her in conversation. Darcy looked at Caroline in time to catch a smirk she swiftly hid. He had no doubt Hobson had been chosen because Caroline Bingley wanted Elizabeth engaged at dinner by someone other than himself. He still had no idea why Hobson, but he determined to watch the man carefully. A dinner was hardly a place for seduction, if that was Hobson's game, but groundwork could be laid for later meetings. And that, Darcy thought grimly, is not going to happen.

Caroline, of course, seated Darcy at her right hand. She was an accomplished hostess, and the courses were excellent in both content and preparation. As the dinner progressed, Darcy heard Elizabeth's sparkling laughter, and his gaze turned to the far end of the table where she sat next to Mr. Hobson. Miss Bingley's voice cut into his thoughts with a jangle that brought him sharply back.

"Miss Eliza Bennet seems to be enjoying Mr. Hobson's company. He is quite charming her, I see. And why not? He is young and attractive and will inherit a fairly large estate one day. Everything a woman of Miss Eliza's station might wish for."

Her knowing smile turned Darcy's stomach. He took a deep breath lest he say something unforgivable to Bingley's sister, replying with what calm he was able. "One is supposed to enjoy one's dinner companion. It is absurd to leap from casual conversation to matrimony on the basis of a chance meeting."

His slight emphasis on the word "chance" brought a swift expression of alarm, which was just as swiftly hidden. Miss Bingley did not pursue the subject, and Darcy was left to wonder just how impressed Elizabeth was with Mr. Hobson. He had no chance to find out, however, as the ladies withdrew after dinner and left the gentlemen to their port and cigars. Hobson entered into a discussion of wine with Mr. Gardiner, Mr. Hurst, and Bingley that progressed to the scarcity of French wines and, thus, to trade in general. Darcy paid little attention, only putting in a comment occasionally out of courtesy. As they were preparing to rejoin the ladies, Hobson approached him, a half smile on his face that stiffened Darcy's spine with dislike. He stared coolly at the man. They were temporarily alone, and Darcy knew Hobson had something to say he did not want the others to overhear.

"Miss Elizabeth is a lovely woman," Hobson observed. "Very bright, witty, thoroughly charming. Under other circumstances, she would make a wonderful mistress." At the look on Darcy's face, Hobson raised a restraining hand. "Before you call me out, Darcy, let me state that I would never make such an offer to Miss Elizabeth. Contrary to general opinion, I do not seduce innocents. If she had money, I might consider offering for her, but alas, that is not possible." He waited a moment as if considering and then continued. "I am leaving for Coldwell tomorrow. My father is gravely ill. I have no doubt that shortly I shall inherit the estate. There has been no land added and no infusion of money since my grandfather's time, and that must be amended. I need a wife with one or both. So, Miss Elizabeth is quite safe from me, and you may pursue her with impunity. If you secure her, you will be a lucky man."

Darcy's face was frozen with anger and outrage. He said in a dangerous voice, "You presume far too much, Hobson."

Hobson shook his head. "You may keep your countenance with the others, but I have seen you look at her, and it is not a look of indifference. Also, and most importantly, I do not like being used in a jealous woman's game. I must thank my hostess," he added ironically, "for a most pleasant evening. Good night."

He walked away, and Darcy did not follow. Hobson's words echoed in his mind with a new resonance.

In the drawing room, the ladies had settled until such time as the gentlemen should rejoin them. Mr. Bingley never lingered long over his port, being abstemious by nature, nor did Mr. Darcy, who was abstemious by training and inclination. With several notable exceptions, he had never overindulged in spirits, and on those occasions, the results had not been worth any pleasure he had derived from the liquor.

In the drawing room, Miss Bingley watched Elizabeth closely to see if she was anxious for the gentlemen to appear. When her scrutiny provided no response, she tried a more direct approach. "Miss Eliza," she said with a satisfied smile, "what is your opinion of Mr. Hobson?"

Elizabeth heard the intent beneath the question and replied lightly, "You set me a difficult task, as I have never seen the gentleman before this evening."

"But you do, I believe, like to define the character of your acquaintances, do you not?"

"At times." Elizabeth sipped her tea. "He speaks well. He has met a number of interesting people. He is very self-confident. How justified his self-confidence might be, I cannot tell on the basis of a single dinner conversation."

"The family estate is in Berkshire," Caroline persisted. "I understand it is fairly large, with a lovely house and grounds. Mr. Hobson will inherit one day. He is an only son."

"That will be very pleasant for him," Elizabeth commented and turned to her aunt with a question about their plans for the next day.

Caroline let the conversation drop. She had made her point. Mr. Hobson was obviously interested. If he needed encouragement, an exaggeration of Elizabeth's interest was easily provided. Caroline did not care whether he pursued her, married her, or simply called her motives into question. Any of them, she was certain, would be enough to end Mr. Darcy's interest in the Bennet chit. She caught her sister's eye and smiled brightly. Louisa shook her head disparagingly.

Darcy remained in the dining room for several minutes after Hobson left to let his anger dissipate. It was Miss Bingley's maneuvering, of course, but he had no doubt Hobson was correct in his speculation. There was no other reason for her to invite a man the Bingleys barely knew to what was essentially a family dinner except to put him with Elizabeth. How successful she had been, Darcy needed to find out.

By the time Darcy reached the drawing room, Hobson was leaving it, accompanied by Bingley. Darcy shook off the residue of emotion and went in, moving to stand at the window while Miss Bingley poured out coffee and tea. *I am in love with Elizabeth Bennet.* The enormity of it overwhelmed him, and for several moments, he simply stared blindly at the frost-decorated panes before him. He had known for some time, he admitted to himself, that he was strongly attracted to her, physically and in other ways. She was what he had never really hoped to find in a genteel lady; a woman of spirit, wit, and intelligence, all of the qualities his own mother had possessed. In addition, Elizabeth had an independence that was in no way headstrong. Her mother might call it impertinence, but it was not. It was a natural expression of a woman who understood her own mind and heart. Darcy could not have designed a wife more perfect than Elizabeth Bennet.

He turned from the window and saw her seated next to her aunt on a sofa, a cup of tea in her delicate hands. A chill slid over Darcy. He was certain of his own feelings, but what of hers? Darcy thought without arrogance that he had everything to recommend him; money, position, an ancient name. He was young and had been assured by many ladies that he was physically attractive. It was, as Caroline Bingley had said, everything Elizabeth might wish for. But Elizabeth was not any young lady. What she wished for in a husband was a mystery, and it was one he must solve before declaring himself.

He took a chair near the sofa and accepted coffee, ignoring Caroline Bingley's simpering smile. The Bennets were to spend a fortnight in town before returning to Hertfordshire. Darcy began to plan how he might spend as much of that time with Elizabeth as possible. The play this week was a beginning. There were other sights and entertainments he might invite her and her family to enjoy. Her aunt was a more than suitable chaperone, and if Bingley and Miss Bennet accompanied them, no one was likely to see his efforts as more than an attempt at hospitality.

Darcy caught Elizabeth's eye and said, "Are you enjoying the evening, Miss Elizabeth?"

"Yes, Mr. Darcy," she replied with a smile. "I am."

"You seemed amused by Mr. Hobson. I hope he was an acceptable dinner companion."

"He is an interesting man," Elizabeth said. "He was telling me about the family home in Berkshire burning down in his grandfather's time and how, when they went to rebuild, his grandmother wanted classical architecture and his grandfather Palladian. The eventual compromise is apparently quite unique."

Darcy breathed a silent sigh of relief. "You prefer Palladian, Miss Elizabeth?"

"Not particularly. I like harmony in a house, whatever its style. What is your home like, Mr. Darcy?"

"Pemberley is built around an original structure from the fifteenth century. It has been renovated, and the style is English baroque. I would very much like you to see it."

Elizabeth tipped her head a little to one side. He knew it for a gesture she employed when her words were not to be taken seriously. "My Aunt and Uncle Gardiner are contemplating a trip to the Peaks next summer and have invited me to go with them. Perhaps I shall see Pemberley then, if it is open to the public."

"It is, but you are always welcome with any of your family as my guests." Afraid he had said too much, Darcy continued quickly. "Is your visit to town fully scheduled?"

Puzzled, Elizabeth considered before she said, "I do not know my mother and aunt's exact plans, but most of the time will be devoted to my sister's wedding gown and trousseau."

"Would you allow me, with a suitable chaperone, to escort you to the British Museum? They have the only known copy of *Beowulf* in existence, as well as the Lindisfarne Gospels. And there is a large collection of Egyptian and other ancient artifacts. I think you would enjoy it."

Fully taken aback, Elizabeth could only stutter her pleasure at the idea. A moment later, she caught her mother's repressive look and hesitated. "I do not know if my mother would approve. I shall have to ask her."

"Tell her," Darcy took his courage in both hands, "that my aunt Lady Matlock will accompany us and possibly my cousin Colonel Fitzwilliam. If she agrees, we can find a day and time that is convenient for all of us."

"Thank you." Elizabeth looked into his dark eyes, her face glowing.

Darcy took that image to bed with him that night after meeting, on his return home, as well as a report of his aunt creating a disturbance at Darcy House. He slept not soundly but well.

Chapter 7

Mr. Burgess heard the commotion from the first floor, immediately recognizing both voices involved. Apprehensive, he hurried to the front hall to find Steves confronting an enraged Lady Catherine de Bourgh, who was attempting to push her way past the big footman and into the house. Her own footman stood on the steps trying unsuccessfully to look invisible. Steves stepped aside as Mr. Burgess approached but not far enough for Lady Catherine to get through the open door.

"My lady." Burgess used his most authoritative tone. "What seems to be the problem?"

"I want Darcy," Lady Catherine all but shouted. "Call him immediately!"

Without yielding ground, Burgess said politely, "Mr. Darcy is out for the evening, my lady. He is not expected home for some time."

"In that case, I will wait."

Burgess prepared for the storm. "I am exceedingly sorry, Lady Catherine, but Mr. Darcy has issued strict instructions that you are not to be admitted to Darcy House. I will be most happy to give him a message when he returns."

"Where is he?"

"Dining out." Mr. Burgess thought that an acceptable answer without offering specifics.

"Where?"

"I cannot say, my lady."

Lady Catherine's face showed a dangerous flush on the cheekbones, and her voice grated as she replied. "You will get out of my way, or I shall summon a constable and have you arrested for attacking a member of the nobility."

"No one will attack you, my lady. This is Mr. Darcy's home, and his word is law on these premises. I cannot disobey his orders."

Lady Catherine gave way to invective that shocked Mr. Burgess, although his face showed nothing of his feelings. When she had vented her anger and frustration, it was apparent she understood that Darcy's servants had every right and, indeed, duty to enforce his commands. She stared at the butler for several seconds and raised her cane as if for emphasis.

"Tell Darcy he may think he has won, but he has not. I shall triumph in the end. I am a Fitzwilliam. We never give up."

She turned on her heel and marched down the steps, her footman hurrying to reach the conveyance and open the door for his mistress. The sound of her carriage wheels on the driveway was like a lullaby to Mr. Burgess. He turned to Steves, who kept his face blank, as any good footman does, wondering if he was about to be dressed down by the butler.

"Mr. Darcy will appreciate your efforts," Mr. Burgess said. "As I do." To Steves's shock, he added, "What a bloody woman!"

In her carriage, Lady Catherine sat rigid on the heavily upholstered seat, while her maid all but cowered on the bench across from her. Slade had not only failed to find Mrs. Younge, but he had also alerted Darcy to the search by putting advertisements in several London papers instead of quietly investigating on his own. She was out his fee and the five hundred pounds she had advanced for information that was never forthcoming. Perhaps there never had been any information about Ramsgate. The man who said he represented Georgiana's former companion might well have been no one at all, just a stranger who convinced Slade he could deliver the true story. There might not, she had to admit, even be a story. Darcy was not above summarily dismissing a servant who was remiss in any way in her duties to his sister.

It had been a mistake to come to Darcy House, she realized as the carriage rattled along the streets toward the de Bourgh town house. Anger at Slade's failure had overruled her good judgment. Darcy's servants were renowned for their loyalty; her position as his aunt, former mother-in-law, and the widow of a baronet was no guarantee of cooperation from any of them. She must find another way to get at him, one he would not suspect. Georgiana was at Pemberley, effectively out of reach and no doubt better protected than even Darcy's usual level of security. She required something closer to home to use as a weapon against him, but what?

Lady Catherine suddenly stared at her maid, whose name was Gracie. Her glare caused the poor woman to shrink back even further into the squab behind her. Her ladyship said in a low voice, "You were always friendly with Molly, Lady Anne's maid, were you not?"

"Y-yes, milady."

"I believe she is still at Pemberley. Do you ever hear from her?"

"She…she writes a note now and then."

"Excellent. The next time she contacts you, I want to know about it. She is close to the family, I understand?"

"Yes, milady. She stayed on at Pemberley as an upstairs maid after…after Lady Anne's passing. She knows about all their doings." It was a slight exaggeration but one Gracie could live with.

Lady Catherine was smiling a very unpleasant smile. "I want you to find out from her everything she can tell you about Mr. Darcy's affairs. Whom he sees, what he does, anything, no matter how trivial. I have developed an interest in my nephew's life. You will obey me in this."

"Yes, milady."

Relieved, the maid nodded vigorously. It was not much to ask of her. She had done far worse to keep her job and stay in Lady Catherine's good graces. Why her employer wanted the information was not her affair. Molly did not gossip about the family, but she did mention things that happened at Pemberley. Hopefully it would be enough to satisfy Lady Catherine. The woman stared down at her hands, clasped tightly in her lap, and thanked her stars that her employer seemed to have calmed and was almost looking cheerful. A dire warning for someone but not, thank God, herself.

That night after their dinner engagement, Mrs. Bennet sat in her nightdress and dressing gown in her bedroom at the Gardiner's, plaiting her hair for the night. Her room was quiet, the household had already gone to bed. As her hands worked automatically, Mrs. Bennet's face reflected the displeasure she felt. She was not pleased with Mr. Darcy's newest invitation, although she could not have said exactly what about it put her out of sorts. It had been issued generally, even if spoken to Lizzy. Perhaps it was the substance of the invitation. What sort of gentleman asked a lady to walk around a dusty museum looking at old books and foreign tat? And what sort of lady was eager to do so? Well, Lizzy, of course, Mrs. Bennet thought. She was just like her father. Interested in anything any real lady would disdain. And there was all of Jane's trousseau yet to be chosen, as well as her wedding dress. She had thought Lizzy wanted to be part of her sister's plans. Selfish as usual.

Still, she did not really want Lizzy's opinions, even if Jane did. What did Lizzy know about fashions? Running about the neighborhood in muddy half boots and old frocks no better than any milkmaid might wear. She was certain her sister Gardiner had chosen the fabric and patterns for Lizzy's new gowns. For an uncounted time, Mrs. Bennet told herself that Lizzy should have been a boy. Then she would have been her father's problem. Everything would have been so much easier—the entail broken, she and her other daughters safe from eviction and poverty. It was all Thomas's fault. He had always cosseted and encouraged Lizzy's tendencies to act like a hoyden. How was she ever to find a husband? The idea of Lizzy at home for the rest of her life made Mrs. Bennet shudder.

Mrs. Bennet rose, removed her dressing gown, and got into bed. She had to agree to the invitation, she supposed. Once the fittings for the gowns were done, Jane might accompany her sister, if only to meet Mr. Darcy's aunt. Any contact with the nobility was to be accepted as a gift from heaven. It was such a pity Jane refused to try to attach Mr. Darcy's affection. Married to the nephew of an earl and a countess. What a triumph for her beautiful daughter that would have been! Well, she sighed, it was not to be.

It was not that she disliked her second daughter, she told herself. It was just that Lizzy was so *different* from her sisters. Even Mary, with her moralizing and her extracts, was biddable, and Kitty caused no trouble. Her Lydia was spirited, full of fun, so like herself as a girl. She just wanted a bit more experience, and without doubt she would marry as well as Jane. Lizzy was a dutiful daughter. She just had a mind of her own, and she was stubborn, like her father. Mrs. Bennet preferred Lydia's sprightliness, if it sometimes tried even her patience with the girl.

A new thought struck her. Mr. Darcy had mentioned his cousin, a Colonel Fitzwilliam. Apparently he was the second son of the earl. He was unlikely to have a fortune, however, he must be comfortably off, and he was an officer in the king's army as well. If he took to Lizzy, there was a new possibility of her marrying as well as she might expect. A soldier might appreciate her character. Most officers liked lively women. And a man used to military discipline would be just what it would take to force her unconventional daughter into the mold of a proper lady and wife. If Lizzy married, Mrs. Bennet realized as she blew out the candle on the night table and settled herself to sleep, her troublesome daughter would move away. As her eyes grew heavy, Mrs. Bennet contemplated life at Longbourn without the constant irritation of Lizzy, and she smiled as she dropped off.

She regained her pique the following day at breakfast when she learned that *The Merchant of Venice* was not about a successful tradesman but a Jewish money-lender and a female attorney. "Just like Shakespeare." She rattled her teacup and glared at Elizabeth as if she had some influence on the Bard's work. "Everyone raves about what a genius he was, but I have never shared the general opinion. His plays are overly complicated and violent. Not fit for ladies to see."

To no one's surprise, she developed a sick headache after dinner and requested her brother extend her apologies for her inability to attend the theater that night. Elizabeth, knowing the headache was a ruse, was not upset by her mother's absence from the theater party. She contemplated her evening gown, laid out on the bed, with satisfaction. The pale yellow flattered her skin and hair, and the gown fit her perfectly. It was last year's, but due to her father's bounty, Elizabeth had purchased new lace, of a higher quality than she might usually have bought, and new buttons, each button painted with a tiny yellow rosebud. The afternoon she spent replacing the trimmings and buttons in antici-pation of an evening's entertainment with her uncle and aunt had taken on the aspect of serendipity since Mr. Darcy's invitation.

She found Mr. Darcy an impressive man. Mr. Darcy in evening dress, as she had seen at the Meryton assembly, was impressive indeed. Elizabeth found she did not want to disappoint him. It was an odd sensation, caring what a man unrelated to her thought of her. The young men of Meryton she had known since childhood. Their opinions were familiar, and she was comfortable with them. Mr. Darcy's opinion of her was unknown; Elizabeth hoped it was favorable. She found his mixture of stern probity and hidden sensitivities strangely compelling. His conversation enlightened and delighted her. There was nothing foolish about him, nothing of the peacock, despite his wealth and status. She thoroughly enjoyed his company, and her anticipation of the evening filled her with excitement.

To her intense appreciation, the evening was everything she had hoped and more. The players were superb, the audience relatively well behaved, and Mr. Darcy attentive and informative. Refreshments had been supplied by the Darcy House cook and served at intermission in the private box by an impeccable footman. Before leaving for Gracechurch Street, plans were made to visit the British Museum the following Tuesday. Mr. Darcy's aunt had a previous engagement, but his cousin Colonel Fitzwilliam was coming with them. Jane and Mr. Bingley were included in the party, and Mrs. Gardiner was able to go as well. Replete with happiness, Elizabeth rode in the Gardiner carriage in silence until her aunt finally spoke. "Well, Lizzy, the evening was quite a success."

"Yes, Aunt. I had such a wonderful time. The actors were amazing. I especially enjoyed the actress who played Portia. I wonder if women will ever actually become lawyers."

"One day, I have no doubt," her uncle put in. "Not in our lifetimes, I fear, but perhaps in another century. Times change, attitudes change. Many women are intelligent enough to learn the law. When the general population accepts that, I believe it will happen."

Jane said to her sister, "You spent much time in conversation with Mr. Darcy during the intermission. Were you discussing the play?"

"Yes. And other things. He was telling me about the Theatre Royal burning down and how they rebuilt it. The original was huge and not convenient for all of the audience members to see the plays. The new one, as we saw, is a little smaller and better designed."

"Nothing of gossip or comments on the players?" Jane teased.

To her dismay, Elizabeth felt herself blushing. "Mr. Darcy does not gossip," she said, keeping her head down.

He had complimented her on her appearance quite properly, but for some reason, his voice sent shivers down her back.

"Well," her aunt added as they turned into Gracechurch Street, "we will see him and Mr. Bingley again tomorrow, I have no doubt, and the trip to the museum is set. He is really being most agreeable."

Her affectionate look at Elizabeth went unnoticed in the half-light of the carriage interior. Yes, Mr. Darcy was being agreeable indeed, and Mrs. Gardiner was a woman of sense and intelligence. She knew attraction when she saw it, even if her niece did not.

Lady Catherine de Bourgh stared at her maid impatiently, her face stony. "Well? What have you found out?"

Gracie held a piece of paper in both hands like a thoroughly inadequate shield. She said in a quaver, "Only a bit, milady. The cook at Darcy House is cousin to the assistant cook at Pemberley, but she only writes her cousin now and then."

"Get on with it," Lady Catherine ordered roughly. "What news?"

"Mr. Darcy's best friend, Mr. Bingley, is getting married to a lady from Hertfordshire. Mr. Darcy will be in town until Mr. Bingley returns to his estate, and then he'll go along and stay until after the wedding."

"Bingley." Lady Catherine sneered. "I know of him. Pretentious upstart with the stink of trade still on him. Darcy takes up with odd friends. Nevertheless, it is a start. Very well, you may go."

Gracie curtsied and scurried from the drawing room. Her ladyship was in a mood the maid had seen before, mean and spiteful. If there were any way she could find other employment, she would be gone in an hour, but her ladyship would refuse to give her a character, or worse, tell lies about her so that no one else would hire her. She had done it to others in the past.

In the drawing room, Lady Catherine sat for a time contemplating the information before she rose and went to an escritoire by the windows. She wrote out a short letter and called a footman to deliver it. Mr. Slade had failed her once.

He dared not fail her again. And he was the sort to be of use in her schemes -- unscrupulous and hungry for money.

She gazed with narrowed eyes at the French gilt clock on the mantel. Darcy was in town for another week or more. Time enough to see what he did and whom he associated with. He was not likely to expect anyone to follow him. Lady Catherine tapped a finger on the mahogany top of the writing desk. If she was unable to attack him directly, perhaps an indirect approach might give her an opening. He had made himself invulnerable to most methods of persuasion, especially legal and financial. Perhaps he was less impregnable on a personal level.

His friend Bingley or his fiancée might offer an opportunity for blackmail. Lady Catherine did not scruple at the term or the actuality. It was just another means to an end. Darcy would go to great lengths to protect a friend. If she was unable to get to him through Georgiana, there were bound to be others he felt an obligation to protect. Darcy was weak in his own fashion, much as Sir Lewis had been. Both men had kept her from using Anne to enhance her own position, the only thing her daughter had ever been good for. She refused to let her nephew take Rosings from her as Sir Lewis had, especially now. For a moment, desperation shook her. Time was against her. She must gain her ends soon; she did not want to contemplate the results of failure.

Lady Catherine rose and rang for the butler. When he appeared, she said, "I am not at home to anyone but a Mr. Slade, who will call later today. When he arrives, show him directly in here."

"Yes, milady." The man bowed deeply and went out.

As he passed through the hall, he ordered the footman to remove the door knocker as a sign they were not receiving callers, except for the one she indicated. He had worked for Lady Catherine for over ten years. He returned to his pantry wondering what sort of devilment was afoot now. He was not reassured when Mr. Slade arrived shortly after dinner was served. He installed the man in the drawing room and went to announce his arrival. Lady Catherine refused to leave the table, and the butler was sent to inform Mr. Slade that her ladyship would be delayed for some minutes.

Mr. Slade took the news philosophically. The room was cold; only a small coal fire burned in the large fireplace. The pale light that crept in through the windows barely illuminated the corners, gleaming dully in dark silk wall hangings, all liberally brocaded with gold. Like a cave, Slade mused uneasily. The overmantel was gray marble elaborately carved with swags of fruits, flowers, and ribbons. On the mantel, a fire-gilded French clock ticked self-importantly. It was all as ostentatiously rich and aesthetically sterile as its owner.

By the time Lady Catherine entered the drawing room, Mr. Slade had helped himself to a glass of Madeira to ward against the chill. Ordinarily her ladyship would have expressed her displeasure at such behavior in no uncertain terms, but she wanted Mr. Slade's help, which gave him a certain leeway. As Lady Catherine ensconced herself in the throne-like chair she preferred, he sat opposite her, his narrow face carefully blank.

"I summoned you, Mr. Slade," she began, "because although you failed in your commission from me, I believe you may still be of some use."

Mr. Slade smelled money. He said with a shade of obsequiousness, "Always happy to be of use, your ladyship."

"So you should be, after taking your fee without producing anything you promised. And five hundred pounds earnest money as well. I could demand you repay me, but I shall not."

"Very kind of your ladyship," Mr. Slade said warily, his apprehension growing. "What is it you need me to do, my lady?"

"I want you to follow Mr. Fitzwilliam Darcy. I will give you his direction and a description, although I daresay he is well enough known in society that you will have no trouble identifying him. I want to know everywhere he goes, everyone he sees for the next few days. If he discovers he is being followed, "she leaned forward and glared into Mr. Slade's eyes, "not only will I not pay you, but I shall take measures to ruin you. I assure you, I have the resources and the connections to do so. Do you understand?"

"Yes, my lady." Mr. Slade believed her threat implicitly, although how successful her "measures" might be was debatable. "I can do that for you. Easy as pie."

"It had better be," she replied grimly. "Report to me in three days, in writing."

Hesitantly he said, "And my fee for the work, my lady?"

Lady Catherine smiled. It was a very unpleasant smile. "What I have already paid you, Mr. Slade. If I am well pleased, I may add a trifle more." She rang for the butler. "Show Mr. Slade out," Lady Catherine ordered, and added coldly, "Three days."

Chapter 8

"Sit down, Lizzy." Mrs. Bennet indicated a chair in the morning room. "I have something to say to you."

Elizabeth had been leaving the breakfast parlor when her mother summoned her into the morning room. Expecting another lecture on something she had done or not done, she sat down, folded her hands in her lap and waited. Mrs. Bennet gathered herself and took a chair opposite her daughter. She noted that Elizabeth had taken some care with her appearance this morning and began to think the interview might not be as difficult as she anticipated.

"You know," she began, "when your father dies, we shall all be on Mr. Bingley's charity. He will do his best for us, but there are the younger girls to think of, and he can only do so much with his own family to provide for."

Elizabeth had an inkling of where the conversation was heading and steeled herself. "I know, Mama." *Oh how well I know!*

"Very well. You also know that, so far, none of the eligible young men in Meryton seem inclined to offer for you, and I do not wonder. What landowner wants a wife who rambles about the country and has no feminine wiles to attract him? You are pretty enough, but you seem determined to end up an old maid, and it will not do. You must marry, Lizzy, and soon."

Elizabeth thought of a good many replies to that but said only, "How am I to do that, Mama? It is the man who proposes."

"Indeed. Since you let Mr. Collins slip through your fingers, there has been precious little opportunity to meet any single men of appropriate status who are looking for a wife. However, a chance may be about to happen." Mrs. Bennet sat straighter. She drew a breath and said shortly, "Mr. Darcy is bringing his cousin Colonel Fitzwilliam with him today. I do not know if the colonel is single, but if he is, you had better exert yourself to be exceptionally pleasant to him. He is the younger son of an earl, and while he is probably not wealthy, he must be comfortably off and of an age to take a wife. One never knows what may happen. His older brother may not have children or may die young. This may be your last chance to marry, Miss Lizzy, and this would be a far better match than any of us might have expected. Be assured, if you do not make the effort, when Mr. Bennet passes, you will be very much on your own."

She rose as a maid tapped at the door to announce the gentlemen's arrival. Elizabeth did not know whether to laugh or cry. She straightened her skirts and followed Mrs. Bennet from the room. She wondered why her mother wanted so badly to be rid of her, or if it was only concern for her future. She did not fit her mother's ideas of how a lady should behave, and she never would. It was true that most men of their acquaintance wanted wives whose only interests were wrapped up in children and domestic skills. Even though she loved children and was well trained in managing a household, Elizabeth, although well liked, was not sought after as a spouse. She knew instinctively that if she played the role of conventional country gentlewoman, sooner or later, it would destroy the essential core of her self. That did not bode well for a marriage.

Mr. Darcy's voice came to her ears as she entered the drawing room. With a surge of gratitude, she saw him standing near her mother and aunt. A man in regimentals stood at his side. Mr. Darcy turned, and Elizabeth faltered at the look in his dark eyes. His companion also turned to her, a smile lighting his pleasant face. He had the Fitzwilliam fairness; his reddish-blond hair was cut shorter than the current fashion, in a military style. His expression was reserved but amiable, his bearing upright. Dark-blue eyes surveyed her with interest.

"Miss Elizabeth Bennet, may I present my cousin, Colonel Fitzwilliam?"

Elizabeth curtsied as the soldier bowed formally but with grace.

"I am delighted to make your acquaintance, Miss Elizabeth," he said. His voice was lighter than Darcy's but with some of the same resonance. "Darcy has spoken of you, but the reality exceeds his words."

Blushing, Elizabeth went to sit on the sofa next to Jane, but her mother was already securing that place. She was left to take a chair with Colonel Fitzwilliam next to her. Mr. Darcy sat across from them, by the end of the sofa near her mother. Mrs. Gardiner had rung for refreshments. There was a natural pause, and Colonel Fitzwilliam turned to Elizabeth with a smile. "My cousin tells me he intends to take us to the British Museum to look at old books and Egyptian artifacts. I can understand his interest. He has always been a reader, but most young ladies would swoon at the prospect."

"I am afraid I am a reader myself," Elizabeth said lightly. "And to think of the hands that produced such a work of art as the Lindisfarne Gospels, the mind that conceived them. It is like reaching over the centuries to touch another life."

"A profound reader, I see," he said.

Elizabeth caught her mother's eye and sighed inwardly. She said, "I see you are a member of the Horse Guards. Are you stationed in London presently?"

"We are in barracks at present. I am staying at my parents' home in Mayfair. Are you in town long, Miss Elizabeth?"

"Another week, at most. My sister is being wed to Mr. Bingley in three weeks, and there are many preparations still to be undertaken at home. You are married, Colonel Fitzwilliam?"

"Alas, no. At present, my career takes precedence over personal considerations." He glanced across at Darcy, who was giving less than half his attention to Mrs. Bennet's prattling, and continued. "Perhaps if I found a lady I felt was suitable, I might well change my mind."

"And what do you deem suitable, Colonel?"

Darcy had begun to frown, although he tried to hide it. Fitzwilliam said, "Oh, someone for whom a soldier's life is acceptable. A woman of spirit and humor. Do you ride, Miss Elizabeth?"

"Badly, I am afraid. I prefer to walk."

"If I were to bring a very gentle old mare for you, we might go riding in Rotten Row one afternoon."

Elizabeth considered him with one eyebrow raised. "How old, and how gentle?"

"Oh, very old. One-hundred-and-two in human years. Her name is Matilda, and she barely goes at a walk, never faster."

"In that case," Elizabeth's mouth turned up at the corners, "I might trust her for one ride, but not more. I would not want to abuse a one-hundred-and-two-year-old horse."

Colonel Fitzwilliam laughed, and Elizabeth joined him. Darcy's brow was darkening as he listened, but Mrs. Bennet looked smug. With another glance at his cousin, Colonel Fitzwilliam sobered and took up another topic. They talked amiably for a half hour, and then Elizabeth, Jane, and Mrs. Gardiner left to get their outerwear.

The three ladies rode with Mr. Bingley in his carriage, while Darcy and Colonel Fitzwilliam went as they had come, in Darcy's town coach. In the relative seclusion of leather and upholstery, Fitzwilliam contemplated his cousin, who still looked troubled.

He said after a time, "How serious is it, Cousin?"

Darcy, who knew Richard was only teasing him by flirting with Elizabeth, looked up. "I want to marry her."

"That serious. Have you spoken to her?"

"Not yet. I need to know her mind, Richard. If she has any inclination for me."

If I were you," Fitzwilliam said, "I would not wait too long. I suppose there is no money?"

"Her dowry is negligible. The father owns a small estate, large enough to provide for his family, but there are four other sisters and an entail."

"Well," Fitzwilliam sat back, "you do not need the money. Unlike me, you can forego marrying an heiress and wed whom you like. If she were wealthy, I might be tempted myself."

His grin kept Darcy from replying as he might have. They reached Montague House in Bloomsbury, the site of the museum, and a caretaker took them on a tour. He answered their questions and explained about the four collections that comprised the basis of the museum's founding, including the royal library of King George II. Elizabeth was enthralled. When their guide left them, Darcy added details about Sir Hans Sloane, whose private collection of "oddities" formed the core of the original museum. The time passed quickly, and after two hours, Jane was becoming fatigued, although she made no complaint.

Recognizing her sister's growing distress, Elizabeth reluctantly requested that they leave. Mr. Bingley instantly agreed, and the gentlemen escorted the ladies back to their carriages.

At the Gardiners' home the gentlemen were invited to stay for dinner. The meal was taken up with a discussion of what the ladies had seen. Elizabeth's eyes glowed as she recounted the antiquities and the books. Darcy felt his chest tighten at the sight of her enthusiasm, the life that animated her face. The colonel was right; he must speak to her and soon, before she returned to Hertfordshire. If she accepted his courtship, he would request her father's consent at the first possible moment. The problem became how was he to approach her privately? She must be given a chance to reply to him without interference from her mother or anyone else.

A plan began to form in his mind. It required his aunt's cooperation. This was something he was satisfied he could secure. He took Colonel Fitzwilliam to the Matlock residence and went in with him. Lady Matlock was just finishing arrangements for a musical evening the following Saturday. Her private sitting room on the second floor of Matlock House was as refined and elegant as the countess herself, decorated in shades of gray-green, silver, and dark rose. Lady Madeleine Fitzwilliam, Countess Matlock, looked up at her nephew from a list she was perusing and smiled. She stood slim and erect, her blond hair liberally combed with gray. Her face was a softer version of Richard's square jaw, open to her favorite nephew.

"You have brought my wandering son home," she said pleasantly.

"Yes, Aunt." Darcy bowed over her hand.

"Help yourself to a brandy, or I can ring for tea if you prefer."

"Nothing I thank you."

Darcy moved restively to the fireplace, a simple plaster surround set with tiles of botanicals painted by Lady Matlock herself. A Constable landscape graced the wall above the mantel. Darcy remembered his aunt purchasing it after the Royal Academy exhibition last spring. She said nothing but put the list aside. Now that he had a private interview with his aunt, Darcy searched for a way to begin.

Lady Matlock studied the tall, elegant form of her favorite nephew and spared him the trouble. "Sit down, my dear, and tell me why you are here. It is not Lady Catherine, is it?"

"Not for some days. I want to ask a favor of you. I wish you to invite two young ladies to your musical evening."

She smiled indulgently. "Well, two will be no problem. Who are they?"

"Their name is Bennet. Miss Bennet is betrothed to my good friend, Mr. Bingley. Miss Elizabeth is her younger sister."

His request that she invite the Bennet sisters was met with delicately raised brows. "Mr. Bingley's fiancée and her sister? I shall issue the invitation, Darcy, if you tell me why you wish it."

"They are gentlewomen who need to be introduced to London society. Is that not reason enough?"

"Normally, it would be, but you are wearing a path in my new Wilton carpet, and that is not reasonable."

Abruptly, Darcy sat down opposite his aunt. She watched him closely but not unkindly. His hands gripped the polished arms of the chair tightly. He started to speak, stopped, and finally said, "I want you to meet Miss Elizabeth Bennet."

"The sister. You are interested in the lady?"

"Yes."

Lady Matlock shook her head. "At last. I certainly want to meet a lady who has caught your eye after all the years I paraded every eligible young lady of the *ton* past you to absolutely no effect."

"She is not like any other woman I have ever met. Her family is old, but she has no fortune or connections. She is intelligent, witty, curious, spirited, everything I might wish for in a wife."

Lady Matlock contemplated her nephew noting his agitation. She said quietly, "Have you given her any indication of your feelings?"

"Not yet. I need somewhere I can speak to her privately, and because we cannot be alone, it is impossible to tell her of my feelings and intentions."

Lady Matlock sat back. "Well, I will invite Miss Bennet and her sister. You are old enough to know your own mind and, I hope, heart. What your uncle will say, I cannot guess."

"With all due respect, my uncle does not control my life." The hard edge his voice had taken on softened. "I think you will like her, Aunt."

Lady Matlock reflected that once Darcy made up his mind, no one but Darcy could change it. However, she only said mildly, "I hope I may. We will know Saturday evening."

Mr. Slade, whatever his attributes or failings, was no fool. He had come in contact with the Lady Catherines of society before, one or two from the quality but most from the milieu he inhabited; brothel keepers, tavern owners, wives of men who subsequently died or disappeared, or whose properties mysteriously burned down. So far he had kept his hands clean. This was not from any sense of ethics or probity, but from a fear of the law and a greater fear of his clients. Mr. Slade's skin was of preeminent concern to Mr. Slade. If Lady Catherine turned on him and told this Mr. Darcy who he was and what he was doing, that skin was in jeopardy.

With this fear and others driving him, Slade did something he rarely engaged in; he used the three days she had allowed to look into Lady Catherine's activities and background. Considering the lady herself, what he found surprised him for as long as it took him to look at it with native cynicism. She was known as a thoroughly unpleasant woman, a domestic tyrant disliked by her tenants and most of her neighbors. Further, she was said to have mistreated her daughter in spite of the young woman's chronic illness. But it was her more recent activities that caused Mr. Slade to shake his head and then smile satirically.

On the afternoon of the third day of his deadline, Mr. Slade presented himself at Darcy House, hat in hand, and asked to see the master. The stuffy butler returned after several minutes and escorted him to Mr. Darcy's study, closing the door softly behind him. The room, well-lit for the usual sanctum, smelled faintly of leather, neat's-foot oil, and brandy. Mr. Darcy sat behind a massive mahogany desk of some antiquity. Mr. Slade saw a dark young man whose face revealed nothing of what the visit might indicate to him. "Mr. Slade. What business do you have with me?"

Slade cleared his voice through a throat gone suddenly dry. "I have some information for you I think you'll find worth your time."

"And money?"

"No, sir, I ain't…am not asking for payment." Slade rocked a bit from one foot to the other. "I find myself in a difficult position. Three days ago I was asked to follow you and report your every move to a client. I…I have not done so."

"There would be little for you to report if you had." Darcy sounded almost bored. He watched the smallish man's mouth twitch and his hands jerk with nerves. "Sit down," he said abruptly, indicating the chair before his desk. "Tell me exactly why you are here."

Mr. Slade collapsed rather than sat. He gripped the chair arms, swallowed, and said, "My client is your…."

"Aunt, Lady Catherine de Bourgh."

It had been a bolt at a venture, but it hit home. Mr. Slade jumped, half rose, and then sank back. "You knew?"

"I guessed. If you have not followed her instructions, why are you here?"

"To bloody get shut of her!" Mr. Slade wiped his mouth on a none-too-clean handkerchief and leaned forward. He said with intensity, "I investigated her doings instead, and I found out quite a bit. That woman's dangerous. If she'll turn on her own flesh and blood, she'll turn on anybody."

Darcy put both hands flat on the desktop, a sign to those who knew him that he was growing impatient. "Why do you not tell me whatever it is you have learned, Mr. Slade?"

Mr. Slade nodded. He drew a breath and said, "Lady Catherine has a lover. She's been feeding him money from the estate for two or three years. He gambles, and he's always short."

"And who is this man?" Darcy kept his voice level with an effort that did not show on his face.

"Rhymes is his name. You probably know he was her steward until he got sacked. He stays here in London most of the time, at her town house, but he visits her estate too. Lately he's been there more than here. It's my guess he was bleeding money off her estate when he worked there, and he's been bleeding money from her ever since."

It had been cleverly done. Darcy had suspected the former steward of malfeasance, but the books showed nothing concrete to prove his theory. Lady

Catherine was a notoriously bad manager, with an inflated opinion of her skills and abilities. She ruled her staff with fear and her tenants by intimidation. Perhaps in her self-inflicted loneliness, the man had preyed on her need for someone, anyone, to care for her. Disgusted, Darcy rose.

"You have given me the information, Mr. Slade. I will not thank you for it, but I can assure you Lady Catherine will not hear from me who supplied it."

He rang for Mr. Burgess to show Mr. Slade out. At the door, Mr. Slade looked back. "You know your own business and your own relatives, but I'd walk careful with that lady. I tell you, Mr. Darcy, a bad woman is worse than a bad man."

When Mr. Slade was gone, Darcy sat motionless for a long time, lost in contemplation. He knew he could not bring himself to use the information as blackmail. It went against the very fabric of the man he was to sink to Lady Catherine's level, whatever the consequences. There had to be a way to make her see reason or, at least, to desist in her persecution. Her mad quest to secure Rosings, no doubt in order to continue supporting her lover, must be stopped, especially now he had found Elizabeth Bennet. Darcy ran his hands through his hair in frustration. How was he to act? What was he to do?

He rose and began to pace, walking to the windows that were darkening now with the early dusk. The garden outside wore the barren look of winter; only the evergreen shrubs and warm colors of chrysanthemums showed life amid the carefully raked gravel paths and mulched flower beds. A red-berry bush made a bright accent in the otherwise drear landscape. It was alive with birds gathering its bounty. Darcy breathed deeply and regularly to calm his mind, and fell back on the logic that was essentially a part of him.

Lady Catherine wanted Rosings. That was the core of the problem. It had been Anne's, and now officially it was his, but Anne had entertained no real love of her home, for it had been little more than a prison to her. Darcy was not about to relinquish the estate. It was a minor but fairly valuable addition to his other holdings; to see it dissipated on a scoundrel was intolerable. What options did that leave?

Darcy returned to his desk, took up pen and paper, and slowly began to write. When he finished, he rang for a footman and had the missive carried to his attorney. He then composed a short note to Lady Catherine that would also be carried to her town house by hand. Darcy poured himself a modest brandy and stood by the fire to review his plans. With some bitterness, he realized it was unlikely he would be able to attend his aunt's musical evening or speak to Elizabeth Bennet before the following week. Perhaps there was another way to make her aware of his feelings for her. It was a dangerous gambit for both of them, if he did not trust her completely he was placing his honor and Georgiana's future in jeopardy.

With a determined expression, Darcy returned to his desk and again took up pen and paper.

The ballroom at Matlock House was large enough, Elizabeth noted, for the morning room and dining room at Longbourn to both fit easily inside it. Chairs had been set out for forty guests, while sofas and settees lined the walls for any overflow. A dais at the end of the room held a pianoforte; four chairs and music stands were set up there as well, which led her to believe the musicians were a quartet, with a singer on the program as well.

Lady Matlock greeted her guests in the large entry hall. She had generously included Mr. Bingley in her invitation to Jane, and he introduced his fiancée and Elizabeth to the countess, with whom he had a slight acquaintance through Darcy. Lady Matlock was gracious to all her guests, but she paid a little more attention to Elizabeth, asking her if she enjoyed Herr Haydn's music, and receiving an intelligent response. They passed into the ballroom, where Colonel Fitzwilliam, in evening dress, immediately approached Elizabeth and bowed with a smile.

"You are looking particularly lovely this evening, Miss Elizabeth."

"Thank you, Colonel." She glanced around the room and saw only people of fashion she did not know. "I thought perhaps Mr. Darcy might be attending tonight."

"He intended to do so, but he was called away at the last minute. He assigned me to guard you from the importunities of any aggressive males who might approach you."

"Does he expect many tonight? I thought music hath charms to soothe the savage breast?"

"That depends entirely on the savage." Colonel Fitzwilliam laughed and offered her his arm.

Mr. Bingley and Jane joined them. Several friends of the Fitzwilliams came up and were introduced, and the time until the performance began passed agreeably. The musicians were indeed a quartet and played extremely well. The latter part of the entertainment brought on Madame Fiorino, a large woman with luxuriant dark hair and deep-set dark eyes, who sang in a powerful coloratura soprano. With an accompanist on the pianoforte, she brought to life several Italian arias and a poignant love ballad.

Elizabeth was thrilled. Her only regret, which she admitted to herself alone, was that Mr. Darcy had missed the concert, although she knew he had undoubtedly heard professional musicians many times. She found she missed his deep, confident voice and his knowledge of the world. His presence would have added a further dimension to her pleasure in the evening. After the music concluded, refreshments were served in the adjoining dining room. Everything from the shining silver and snowy linens to the trays and stands of exceptional pastries, savories, and a selection of superb wines was a revelation of how an earl and his family lived. This is Mr. Darcy's milieu, Elizabeth thought, his place in life. How dared she have even the slightest thought that he might want her to share it?

As she and Jane waited in the hallway for their wraps to be brought, Colonel Fitzwilliam approached her. Elizabeth said lightly, "You may tell Mr. Darcy you performed your guard duty to perfection, Colonel. Not one savage approached me all evening."

"I am always punctilious in my duty, Miss Elizabeth." He stood quite close to her, and Elizabeth wondered with some trepidation if he meant to ask if he might call on her. Instead he pressed a folded paper into her hand. "My cousin asked me to give you this and to extend his abject apologies that he was unable to give it to you himself. I do not know the contents, but I suggest you read it in private when you arrive at your uncle's home."

Knowing full well she should reject any missive from a gentleman not a close relative, Elizabeth hesitated only a second and then put the paper into her pocket. At that moment the footman brought her pelisse and gloves, and with another bow, Colonel Fitzwilliam walked away. On the carriage ride home with Mr. Bingley and Jane, she felt as if the note crackled with her every movement. Guilt and curiosity battled for preeminence, and not unexpectedly, curiosity won.

She went to her room after assuring her aunt and mother the evening had been delightful but fatiguing. Once there, she took out the note and put it in a drawer of the small writing desk by the window before she called her maid to help her undress. Impatient to read the note, Elizabeth sent the maid away as soon as she was able and brushed out her own hair. She was in two minds as to whether she ought to tell her aunt about the note. Mrs. Gardiner was more understanding than Mrs. Bennet, but to receive a missive from Mr. Darcy was an undeniable breach of propriety. Mrs. Gardiner was strict in following the rules of social behavior. She would not approve, and if the incident became known, it could ruin Elizabeth's reputation and, by implication, harm her sister as well. Surely Mr. Darcy was aware of the stricture. It must be something of importance for him to breach such a basic tenet of society.

Taking her candle, Elizabeth went to the writing desk and sat down. She withdrew the folded paper and laid it on the surface, staring at it as if she might read it without opening it. As her fingers brushed over the fine, hand-pressed paper, she knew in her heart Mr. Darcy was incapable of doing anything to harm her. Her chin rose. She unfolded the parchment and spread it out carefully. She saw the Darcy crest embossed at the top before any of the words reached her conscious mind.

She was unfamiliar with Mr. Darcy's handwriting, but the very fine copperplate had to be his. The note was very short, only four lines. Drawing a breath, Elizabeth read:

EB

> *Doubt thou the stars are fire;*
> *Doubt that the sun doth move;*
> *Doubt truth to be a liar;*
> *But never doubt I love.*

FD

Elizabeth felt her hands shaking. The breath stifled in her chest, her heart stuttered until she thought it must stop. He did not...he could not mean it. Even as she denied the truth, it overwhelmed her. The simple piece of paper before her was enough to compromise both her and him. If it somehow became known he had sent it and she accepted it, he would be forced to marry her. He must have unquestioning trust in her to send such an open declaration of his affection, knowing as he surely did the consequences if she informed her father or uncle. He must believe she would understand and never betray his confidence, whatever her feelings for him.

Elizabeth closed her eyes and tried to gather her scattered thoughts. Mr. Darcy must have meant to speak to her but found no opportunity. Thus he had resorted to sending her a missive, the meaning of which she could not possibly misunderstand. Elizabeth closed her eyes and pressed both hands to her temples. What *did* she feel? How was she to answer him, for it was an unmistakable declaration? Elizabeth knew she must not write in return. Such an action only compounded the chance someone might intercept the message. She was fervently grateful that Colonel Fitzwilliam had warned her to read it when alone. The thought of her mother's reaction if she saw the contents made Elizabeth shudder. She would understand only that Mr. Darcy had communicated inappropriately with Elizabeth and insist they wed at once.

Elizabeth rose, refolded the paper, and looked around the room. She must find some place to safely secret the note until she was able to speak to Mr. Darcy. Briefly, Elizabeth thought of burning it, but she could not bring herself to do so. He had to call tomorrow. Whatever had kept him from his aunt's tonight would not keep him away from the Gardiners' for long. She opened the drawer of her night table, took out a small volume of psalms her father had given her, and slipped the note between the pages. Elizabeth blew out her candle and got into bed. For a long time she stared the blank expanse of the canopy over her head.

She remembered the times she had spent in Mr. Darcy's company, in Hertfordshire and in London. Their conversations had been the most enjoyable of her life, except for those with her father. Mr. Darcy sought her opinions and listened to them; he informed her without condescension, agreed or disagreed when they debated, but never used his superior intellect and grasp of logic to make her feel ignorant or foolish. On the contrary, she was always left eager to debate with Mr. Darcy again.

Elizabeth had known from the beginning he was very wealthy, although he made nothing of it. She reflected that her mother was right about one aspect of the matter; Mr. Darcy took her places most young ladies would have avoided if at all possible. He seemed to know what she found interesting and accommodated her. They were both voracious readers. Darcy's choices were more universal than hers: history, philosophy, economics, political theory, science. Much of it had to do, she realized, with his intense commitment to bettering his estate. He loved Shakespeare, as did she. However, while Elizabeth had a love of history instilled by her father, she also read novels and poetry. Her favorite poet was Wordsworth; Mr. Darcy's was Dryden.

All of her reflections seemed to coalesce in those minutes while she lay in bed in the dark room. It was as if her heart whispered that she had found a man she could be happy with, a man who answered her need for both companionship and respect. A man who would not try to make her into someone she was not and never could be.

But never doubt I love.

Dark eyes seemed to look intensely at her from the darkness. How long, Elizabeth wondered, had she known she was falling in love with Mr. Darcy?

Lady Catherine received Darcy in the drawing room of the de Bourgh town house. She sat enthroned as usual in the heavy, high-backed armchair she preferred. When he was seated facing her with an ease he did not feel, she regarded him haughtily for a full minute before speaking. "You asked to see me, Darcy. I did not think we had anything to discuss, unless you have come to your senses."

Ignoring her tone, Darcy said quietly, "We have Mr. Rhymes to discuss, Aunt."

The name struck her visibly despite her attempt to act indifferent. "My former steward. What of him?"

"Let us not dissemble. He is your lover, and he has been for some time."

Lady Catherine's face paled. The rouge on her cheeks stood out against her sallow skin. "That is an infamous lie!"

Darcy's tone was still quiet but relentless. "I did not come here to judge you. Your relations with the man are a fact. He stays here with you when in London and visits Rosings at other times. There is also the fact you have been supporting him."

"I suppose," she replied with an attempt at bravado, "you have suborned my servants."

"No, Aunt. I have sources of my own."

"Do you mean to threaten me with exposure so I will withdraw to the dower house and leave Rosings to you?"

The raw hatred in her face momentarily took Darcy aback. He remembered Mr. Slade's warning and knew the man was right, although the knowledge did not sway him. "No, Aunt. You want Rosings; I am prepared to come to an arrangement with you."

Her small eyes narrowed, still glaring. At last she said, "What arrangement?"

Darcy withdrew a document from his inner coat pocket. "You will remove to the dower house. The estate, including everything in the house, was Anne's. I have no doubt that some of the more valuable items from the inventory that was done when we married are gone, as I know Mr. Rhymes is an unsuccessful gambler." Darcy barely hid the contempt he felt. He went on when Lady Catherine made no comment. "You will be entitled to your personal property. A new inventory will be taken. The contents of the house will be checked at intervals. If anything is removed that is listed on the new inventory, I will have Mr. Rhymes arrested for theft."

Lady Catherine gave an inarticulate cry of anger. "What am I to live on?"

"The interest from the investments Sir Lewis left you, to which I will add one-third of the estate profits each quarter. You cannot touch the principal, but with the additional funds, there is enough for two people to live comfortably. I will continue to pay your staff. I have also set in motion the establishment of an entail, so the house cannot be sold."

"Entailed to your son, no doubt," Lady Catherine's voice shook, "should you ever have one."

"That is not your concern." Darcy was beginning to feel Lady Catherine's enmity as a dark wall between him and an end to the conflict she had instigated. He said with the force of personality he was able to summon at need, "This is your only option if you want to remain at Rosings. I will not have it stripped to satisfy a wastrel and a thief."

"I do not care what you publish," Lady Catherine told him bitterly. "My family abandoned me when my father married me off to Sir Lewis. I have lived with the disdain of my neighbors and the insolence of my tenants all my life. Mr. Rhymes is the only one who understands, the only one who cares. You will not take him from me!"

"I have no intention of doing so." Darcy felt a welling of pity in spite of himself. "If he stays or goes is his decision and yours. I will give you a few days to think about this. If you refuse, nothing will be said about Mr. Rhymes by me or at my instigation."

He bowed and left her, placing the document on the table beside her chair. He wondered as his carriage rolled out of the driveway if she would read it, tear it up, or ignore it. Whatever her actions, Darcy knew in his heart that her antagonism was stronger than ever. He had balked her twice, once by keeping her influence away from Anne and again by refusing to give her Rosings to do with as she liked. Sooner or later, Darcy thought wearily, her hatred, like a snake in deep grass, would rise up to attack him. He only hoped it did not strike anyone else.

Mrs. Bennet turned from the drawing room window and fixed Elizabeth with an accusatory stare. "The gentlemen are arriving, and Colonel Fitzwilliam is not with them. What did you say to him at the musicale, Lizzy?"

Elizabeth looked at her mother in disbelief. "We talked of common things. He asked me about Hertfordshire and told me of Derbyshire, where his father's estate is located. We spoke of music and other trivial matters, all quite pleasantly."

Mrs. Gardiner, who had also been startled by her sister-in-law's words, said, "Really, Fanny, you know Colonel Fitzwilliam is a soldier. His time is not his own. He is probably on duty today."

Somewhat mollified, Mrs. Bennet resumed her seat and fanned herself with her ever-present lace handkerchief. "I suppose so. It is only that he is such an excellent prospect, and Lizzy is so inept at attracting gentlemen's attention. I hate to think of one more prospective husband walking away."

Somewhat alarmed the visitors might overhear Mrs. Bennet, Mrs. Gardiner said rather more loudly than usual, "Yes, the weather has become milder since yesterday. It is quite a nice day for October."

The gentlemen were announced, and the ladies rose to curtsy as they came in. Darcy immediately sought Elizabeth's reaction to his presence. She gave him one swift, unreadable glance and sat down, her needlework in hand. Darcy hesitated, then took a chair next to her end of the sofa. Mrs. Gardiner smiled at him, her gaze warm.

"Miss Elizabeth," Darcy said, "how are you this morning?"

She did not look up, but her color rose. "I am quite well, I thank you, Mr. Darcy."

After a moment, he said, "What are you reading at present?"

"Poetry. I thought I might try Dryden."

Her color deepened, causing Darcy to make a conscious effort not to reach out and take her hand. Bingley was engrossed in conversation with Jane and Mrs. Gardiner. Darcy drew a breath and lowered his voice. "Shakespeare?"

At last, Elizabeth looked at him, and the expression on her lovely face took his breath. "He is my favorite. He seems always to know the ways of the heart."

We have to speak alone, Darcy thought desperately. He had to be certain of her acceptance before he openly declared his suit. Mrs. Bennet's sharp voice tore through his concentration on Elizabeth so suddenly he startled.

"Where is Colonel Fitzwilliam this morning, Mr. Darcy? We expected him to call with you."

Darcy almost stammered. "My cousin is on duty, madam. He sends his regrets. He is not on leave at present, and with the situation in France, he is more often engaged with his regiment than not."

"A soldier must always put duty first," she said sententiously. "Perhaps he will call again when he is able."

"I am sure he would be honored."

Elizabeth had recovered her composure. Tea arrived, and she helped her aunt pass the cups around, effectively stopping any further attempt by Darcy to engage her in conversation. The visit continued for some minutes before there was a tap at the door, and a middle-aged woman stepped in at Mrs. Gardiner's summons. She was neatly dressed in dark gray with a white cap. She curtsied to her mistress, who greeted her with friendly familiarity.

"Yes, Nanny?"

"I am going to take the children to the park, madam, if you have no objection."

"None at all. Thank you, Nanny."

Seizing the opportunity offered, Darcy said, "I believe you like to walk, Miss Elizabeth. Perhaps we could accompany the children to the park?"

Elizabeth cast a swift glance at her mother, who looked momentarily dissatisfied, and then said, "If you would like to go, Lizzy, I see no reason why you should not."

Mrs. Gardiner noted her niece's color and Mr. Darcy's studied casualness, and smiled. "It is only a short distance. A pretty little park for the local residents. I think you will enjoy it."

Elizabeth went for her outerwear. A footman brought Darcy's greatcoat and hat, and they followed Nanny and the two oldest Gardiner children to a park of some three acres. The grounds were fenced with iron palings, but there was an open gate. Graveled paths bordered by shrubs and trees wound through flower beds with only a few late roses showing faded blooms. The breeze touched their faces, cool but not sharp. A few clouds drifted lazily across the sky.

They let Nanny and the children go ahead, walking silently together. Elizabeth's hand rested lightly on Darcy's arm. At the center of the park, a grassy area with a modest fountain in its center afforded a place for the children to run. Darcy stopped short of the edge and turned to Elizabeth, his deep voice caressing her. "I must abjectly apologize for sending you the note and not speaking to you myself, but a family matter arose that could not be put off, and I needed to deal with it personally. I would never have written to you otherwise."

"Colonel Fitzwilliam was very discreet," Elizabeth nearly whispered. "Do not apologize. I...it told me what I never thought to know."

"That I love you, my wonderful Elizabeth?"

His use of her given name sent a sharp frisson through her; a powerful sensation she had never felt before. "It told me my own heart."

Neither of them gave a thought to Nanny and the children. Darcy raised her gloved hand to his lips. They stood very close together, not speaking, as they openly felt the intensity of their emotions for the first time. Elizabeth began to tremble. Darcy wanted nothing more than to take her in his arms, an impulse he barely withstood. "I want you to be my wife, Elizabeth," Darcy said huskily.

"I want to be your wife," she replied, and suddenly looked into his eyes, aware as never before of the strength of his ardor.

He was silent until he was able to control his voice. "I will request a formal courtship from your father, if that is your wish. As for myself, I would marry you as soon as I can obtain a special license."

Elizabeth drew back from him a little, suddenly aware of the hazards that lay ahead, beginning with Mrs. Bennet. She felt his fingers tighten on her hand. How was she to explain to him what she herself did not understand -- her mother's seeming antagonism for Darcy?

"Nothing must be said until you have my father's consent."

Her eyes pleaded for his agreement. Darcy said slowly, "You think he will refuse me?"

"No. I...I do not want my mother to know until Papa agrees and everything is settled."

Something that Darcy had sensed before in Mrs. Bennet's attitude toward him rose in his mind. He determined to explore the matter later, and only said, "It shall be as you ask. I am returning to Hertfordshire next week to stay with Bingley until after the wedding. I will see your father as soon after I arrive as possible."

"Thank you."

Elizabeth smiled, and Darcy had to exert all of his self-control not to kiss her right there in a public park. He was lost indeed.

Their intimacy was abruptly interrupted by the Gardiners' five-year-old son, Edward, who ran up with a child's excitement glowing on his cherubic face. "Cousin Lizbet, Cousin Lizbet, there's a fwog in the fountain!"

Elizabeth immediately stooped to the boy's level. Instinctively her tone took on his enthusiasm. "What sort of frog, Edward?"

"A gween one!"

He seized her hand and tugged, and Elizabeth, not unwilling to ease the potency of her feelings for the time being, followed her small cousin to view his discovery. Darcy watched her go. He had begun on the path to make Elizabeth Bennet his wife. Whatever impediments might arise, nothing, Darcy told himself, not society, not family, no force short of death, was powerful enough to keep them apart.

Chapter 9

"Mrs. Bennet." Mr. Bennet's voice had lost its perennial tone of irony, growing firmer. "Pray allow me to understand you. What possible objection can you have to Lizzy marrying Mr. Darcy? I confess I find it bewildering, considering his position, his wealth, and his character. Indeed, I know nothing of the man on which to base a refusal."

Mrs. Bennet sat facing her husband across the desk in his book room. The surface was piled with books and papers, with the exception of a space in the center, where presently Mr. Bennet's hands rested, clasped together. His wife held her handkerchief tightly in her lap; her fingers tightened on the fabric nervously. Her face was closed in the manner he knew all too well. His wife had never been rebellious or defiant, but her opinions, however wrongheaded, were defended to the last gasp.

"He is too high," she said shortly, her voice rising. "How is Lizzy to enter into a society she has never experienced? She will be his hostess. She must know how to treat his friends and relatives properly, how to act properly, entertain properly. What does Lizzy know of such things? How will she cope with the everyday duties of the wife of a man like that, to run a household, two households, of such size and importance? Lizzy may think she is capable of it, but she is not, despite the fact that I have trained her, as I have all of my daughters, to be good managers. Oh, she will have more fine clothes and jewels and carriages than Jane, but that will not compensate for her deficiencies. She will lose Mr. Darcy's affection in the end. What will become of this brilliant marriage then?"

She sat back in her chair. Her mouth was pinched, two spots of color burned in her cheeks. Mr. Bennet, too, sat back. His wife did not like to have her opinions contradicted, however erroneous they might be. He contemplated her stubborn expression with as much sadness as exasperation. Mr. Bennet had known for some time this conversation must one day happen; he found it no more palatable for its inevitability.

"When Jane accepted Mr. Bingley's proposal, you found no fault with the match, and it was considerably higher than we might ever have expected any of our daughters to wed. True, Mr. Bingley is neither as rich nor as socially prominent as Mr. Darcy, but he is still a man of means whose wife will need to manage both Netherfield Park and his town house. And deal with his sisters, which is no mean feat. If Jane is capable of all that, why do you doubt Lizzy's ability to perform her duties as Mr. Darcy's wife? No, Fanny, I think it is more than that. You have never cared for Lizzy, even as a child. I think you do not want her to have a husband more prominent than Jane's."

"I never cared for her?" Mrs. Bennet stiffened in her chair. "You care for her too much. You have always treated her as if she were somehow better than the other girls, and she has used that to go her own way. She is unmanageable, impertinent, willful, a hoyden, not a true lady. Mr. Darcy will tire of her quickly, I can tell you, unless he is firmer with her than you have ever been!"

"I have never thought Lizzy superior to her sisters in any way but one," Mr. Bennet replied quietly. "Jane is an intelligent woman, and so may our other daughters be, but they lack Lizzy's thirst for knowledge. I refused to ignore that inherent desire to learn that is denied women in our society, and I taught her whatever she wanted to know. That is not the favoritism I see bestowed on Kitty or Lydia. It is an acknowledgment of Lizzy's strength. She is intelligent, intuitive, curious, and far more sensitive than you have ever given her credit for. I saw no reason to hitch a racehorse to a wagon just because the wagon was convenient." He drew a long breath. His wife's expression had not changed, and Mr. Bennet sighed inwardly. "I know the fact that she was not a male plays some part in your feelings toward her, but her gender is neither her fault nor yours. If God did not choose to give us a son, there is no one to blame."

Mrs. Bennet's voice was strained. She twisted her handkerchief in both hands, leaning forward. "And if God does not give Mr. Darcy a son, will he feel that way about it? What does Lizzy know of failure, of sacrifice, of the derision of her neighbors? She will have all that and more to deal with if there is no heir."

Mr. Bennet suppressed the anger he felt rising. He knew it was useless to either reason with or override his wife. He said, as calmly as he was able, "Mr. Darcy adores Lizzy. I do not believe there is anything she might do that could change his feelings. As for his homes, how do you suppose they have been run after the death of his first wife, or during her lifetime, for that matter? She was an invalid. Do you suppose she rose from her sickbed to direct the servants and host balls and soirees? Before he married, and after his mother died, how do you think his estate home and his town house were managed? Lizzy will learn what she must. She is quick and bright. Until then, I am certain the domestic arrangements will continue as they have for some time."

"Yes," Mrs. Bennet said bitterly, "she will no doubt have a host of servants at her beck and call and be able to lord it over all of us. But that will not make her a lady. She would do better to marry someone from her own station in life, as no doubt her sisters will."

Mr. Bennet felt the weight of half a lifetime's frustration and pain settle on him. He was in love with his wife when they married, but over time his love had faded in the harsh light of her constant dissatisfaction, her inability to cope with the loss of the wealth and position he had once been heir to, and her basic lack of understanding. He said, "You were certainly quick enough to foist her off on Mr. Collins, and what a deplorable match that would have been. You even tried to interest this Colonel Fitzwilliam in her, although he seems to have found her no more than a pleasant acquaintance. No, my dear. Lizzy's want of conventional accomplishments is not the problem. Because Lizzy has never met your expectations, she is getting more than she deserves. Or perhaps what you feel you deserved and could not have."

Mrs. Bennet's face paled. She started to rise from her chair then sank back. Her hands still twisted the lace handkerchief in her lap. She said in nearly a whisper, "You did what you had to do, Thomas, to keep us from scandal, but it was such a beautiful house. To see it all taken away was so hard." Her voice failed. She dabbed at her eyes with the misused lace. "And then carrying a child through all of it, and settling here as nothing more than local gentry when they all knew I had married high. They ridiculed me. Not in my hearing but between themselves, until the baby came. Then it was a girl, and everything was so much worse!"

"They do not ridicule you now, Fanny," Mr. Bennet said with a surge of compassion. "You are a respected woman and an integral part of this community. And none of it was Lizzy's fault. She just happened to be born at the wrong time."

"She has always been so *different*."

"She has always treated you with respect and affection. You have treated her chiefly with disrespect and disaffection. It is not fair, but I suppose it is far too late to mend. Be grateful she is marrying well and, if it pleases you, that she will spend much time far from us in Derbyshire. When she presents us with a grandson, you may feel differently." It was more hope than belief. "After all, she is marrying a better man than you did."

Silence stretched for long moments. Outside the window a bird gave one long, sweet, piercing call. "No, Thomas," Mrs. Bennet said at last, quietly. "Mr. Darcy is not a better man than you. I do not know a better man than you." She rose and went to the door. "If you will excuse me, I still have much to do for Jane's wedding."

The door closed behind her. Mr. Bennet sighed. He wondered if her words were true or if they were simply said to allow her a dignified retreat. He sat quite still behind his scattered desk. He knew full well that his wife still held her opinion of the match, but perhaps she was satisfied that there was no preventing it to let the matter drop. He truly hoped so, for all their sakes.

"You have a letter from your brother?"

Mrs. Annesley came into Georgiana Darcy's private sitting room in the cool light of late morning and found her charge sitting in her favorite place, the window seat overlooking part of the magnificent gardens of Pemberley. Even in winter, the gardens produced shrubs and evergreens that kept them from the forlorn barrenness of the season. Georgiana held the paper in her lap, but she had obviously already read it. She was too pale for it to be good news.

The girl looked up blankly, then dropped her eyes again, large, lovely blue eyes of an unusual cerulean color. She was a pale blonde, as her mother had been, with delicate features and a tall, slim frame, too thin for Mrs. Annesley's comfort. Whatever had occurred prior to her employment last summer had badly affected the child. If Georgiana were older, she might think there had been a love affair, but at fifteen and under the ever-watchful eye of her brother, that was out of the question.

"Yes," Georgiana said softly. "I have had a letter from my brother. He…he is to be married."

"What wonderful news!" Mrs. Annesley took a chair near her charge. "Do you know the lady?"

"No. She is from Hertfordshire. Fitzwilliam met her when he was visiting his friend Mr. Bingley. Her name is Elizabeth Bennet."

"When is the wedding to be? Are you not happy to have a sister? You have said you always wanted a sister."

"Yes," Georgiana whispered. Tears formed in her eyes. She took out her handkerchief and dabbed at them.

"Then what is wrong, my dear?" Mrs. Annesley leaned forward and gently touched Georgiana's hand. "Surely your brother would never marry a lady who could not love his sister."

"How can I know that?" Georgiana sounded frightened. "If she finds me wanting, I will be sent away. I could not bear it!"

Mrs. Annesley heard the real panic in the girl's voice. She moved to the window seat and took both of Georgiana's hands in hers. "My dear, never think such a thing. I know the announcement is something of a shock, but your brother loves you dearly. His wife will not displace you in his affections. Loving a wife and loving a sister are two very different things. And why should she find you less than the gentle, caring person you are?"

The girl was crying freely now. Mrs. Annesley handed Georgiana her own handkerchief and put an arm around the bent shoulders, while she murmured soothing words until Georgiana calmed enough to control her emotions. At last, she raised her head still not looking directly at her companion. "You do not know. No one but Fitzwilliam and my cousin Richard know. I am terrified he will tell Miss Bennet, and she will hate me."

Mrs. Annesley recognized the true pain in the girl's voice and manner. She knew saying the wrong thing at that point would be worse than saying nothing at all. However, she felt she must do something to assuage Georgiana's terrible pain. "You need not tell me anything," Mrs. Annesley said slowly. "But anything you do tell me will never go beyond these walls, not even to your brother."

Georgiana nodded once. The light shone like a golden veil on her bowed head. It was several minutes before she was in enough command of her voice and thoughts to speak. "Last summer was very hot in London. I was ill from it, and my companion convinced Fitzwilliam to let me spend the summer in Ramsgate, in my own establishment. It was wonderful by the sea. I was so happy. Then, after a time, we met a man I had known in childhood, a Mr. Wickham. He was my father's godson, and a boyhood friend of my brother. My companion allowed him to visit me, and he...he convinced me he was in love with me." Her voice sank to barely a whisper. "I thought I loved him. He proposed marriage, and I...I accepted. Then he said it would be so romantic to," the girl bent forward as if in physical pain, "to elope. He said he wanted to present me to Fitzwilliam as his bride. I did not know that my brother had long since dropped the man for the best of reasons."

Mrs. Annesley said softly, "But you did not elope, did you?"

"No. Fitzwilliam came unexpectedly to visit and found Mr. Wickham with me. I could not deceive my brother and I told him everything. He sent Mr. Wickham away, and when my 'suitor' left, he did not even say good-bye. He admitted it was my dowey he wanted, and walked out. Fitzwilliam took me back to London. He dismissed my companion. She was working with Mr. Wickham to obtain my dowry. Fitzwilliam found you, dear Mrs. Annesley, and we came to Pemberley. Oh, I was such a fool, such a silly, stupid, green fool! And now it will haunt me the rest of my life that I betrayed my brother's trust. He does not blame me, but I blame myself. If his new wife finds out, what will she think of her new sister?"

"First, my dear," Mrs. Annesley straightened, her tone gentle but firm, "it was not your fault, and your brother is very right not to blame you. The man used you for his own purposes, and you are, by no means, the first, or unfortunately the last, young woman to be so used. You escaped a far worse fate than mistaking the man's intentions. You escaped marrying him, which would truly have ruined your life." Mrs. Annesley rose and rang for tea. When she returned, she said, "It is my belief some things happen for a reason. Your brother's visit saved you from a terrible mistake. It also gave you the opportunity to realize that not all people who profess friendship or even love are sincere. That is most valuable knowledge to have, and it will serve you well as you gain more experience of life. If you wish to recover from your betrayal, you will have to accept we are none of us always wise. Few of us get off so easily in life's trials."

The maid brought tea, and Mrs. Annesley sent her away with polite thanks and took charge of the tea tray herself. She did not say so, but she was convinced Georgiana was ready to begin recovering from the pain inflicted on her spirit by the man she had trusted. If not, she would never have confided the incident to anyone. Mrs. Annesley believed youth springs back, even from a broken heart or broken faith, with far more resilience than at any other age. In time, this experience was likely to save the girl worse hurt when she entered the marriage market and was besieged by certain young men who were hardly less greedy or deceptive than the man at Ramsgate. All of her brother's vigilance would not change that.

Georgiana carefully folded the letter and put it in her pocket. She wiped her eyes and left the wet handkerchief for the maid to take to the laundry. For the first time in months, some of the burden of guilt and shame was lifted from her slim shoulders. She needed to think about what her companion had said and to accept the idea that Fitzwilliam had found a woman he wished to marry. Georgiana had liked their cousin Anne and felt sorry for her illness, not a little because of their aunt Lady Catherine. She ought to be happy for him, not sunk in selfish doubts and fears. She watched Mrs. Annesley pour out the tea and bring her a cup. With a small smile, Georgiana thanked her. She knew her companion understood it was for far more than the tea.

Lady Catherine de Bourgh's maid, Gracie, knocked diffidently on the door of the drawing room and waited for the summons to enter. She held a letter in both hands as if it might somehow protect her from her mistress's displeasure. When she stepped into the stuffy obscura of the room, she saw Lady Catherine sitting in her throne chair, an open newspaper resting on her lap.

"I have a note from Molly, milady." She curtsied and waited for a response; it not at all what she expected.

"My nephew is to be married."

"Yes, milady. Molly just got the news from Mrs. Reynolds when the staff members at Pemberley were told."

"It is in the newspaper," Lady Catherine said, tapping the pages. "To a Miss Elizabeth Bennet of Hertfordshire. Does she know more than that?"

The icy stiffness of Lady Catherine's tone and posture made Gracie tremble. "N-no, milady. Only that she is said to not be wealthy or of the *ton*. The cook told her Mr. Darcy is said to be besotted with her."

"Is he? How fortunate for him."

There was a long silence while Gracie stood stiffly, not sure if she was expected to leave or stay. Lady Catherine's voice, a low monotone, startled her. "Bennet is the name of Mr. Collins's cousins. He was recently in Hertfordshire visiting them. He must have seen Mr. Darcy there. He must have learned something of the Bennets' history. Perhaps he even knows something of Darcy's attachment to this woman, this great love of his."

The pure hatred in her voice was terrifying. Gracie tried not to shiver as cold seeped into her bones. She felt that if she tapped Lady Catherine's arm, she would hear the flat resonance of stone. Lady Catherine fell into a black study. Gracie knew her mistress was no longer aware of her presence, for which she was grateful. The mantel clock clicked loudly in the brown silence of the room. At last, Lady Catherine rose abruptly and threw the newspaper aside. Gracie hastened to clear a path to the door, but Lady Catherine suddenly seemed to realize her maid was still there.

"Pack my trunks," she said sharply. "Tell Mr. Redding to have my carriage prepared for tomorrow morning. We are returning to Rosings."

Elizabeth came downstairs in a far happier mood than she had enjoyed lately. Mr. Darcy had spoken with her father when he came to call that morning and obtained Mr. Bennet's consent to court her. Elizabeth had also spoken with her father. While he was reluctant to lose his favorite child, he understood her feelings far better than she realized. Sadly, he also recognized that she would be far happier with a man who loved her and was able to care for her than in the family home.

With growing pleasure, Elizabeth anticipated Mr. Darcy's visits now they were betrothed. Her mother's odd disapprobation had rendered her more than usually silent, so Elizabeth was able to enjoy her betrothed's conversation without censure or constant interruption. The puzzle of Mrs. Bennet's attitude toward Mr. Darcy nagged at her in quiet moments, but she was determined not to let it dampen her pleasure in her fiancé's company.

As Elizabeth passed her father's book room, her mother's high-pitched voice, rarely modulated, struck her ears. It seemed even shriller than usual. Involuntarily she stopped, and though not intending to eavesdrop, Elizabeth, nonetheless, remained just outside the closed door.

"He is too high." Mrs. Bennet's tone carried clearly. Her voice dropped enough to blur the next words, then, "Lizzy may think she is capable of it… compensate for her deficiencies? She will lose Mr. Darcy's affection…become of this brilliant marriage then?"

Elizabeth felt numbed by the words. Her father's response was too low to hear. She tried to go on, but her mind refused to allow her body to continue. She felt frozen with hurt and anger. Her mother was speaking again. Her voice was still loud enough for her sharp words to penetrate the thick panel.

"I never cared for her? You care for her too much…somehow better than the other girls…she has used that…willful, not a true lady. Mr. Darcy will tire of her!"

Mr. Bennet spoke again, and Elizabeth could still hear nothing of his response. Only the scraping dissonance of her mother's anger. "And if God does not give Mr. Darcy a son, will he feel that way about it?"

Elizabeth became aware of Hill entering the hallway. She had not heard the knock on the door, but his advance set her in motion. She turned past him and made her way blindly up the stairs. She gathered her shawl, bonnet, and gloves, and went out the back of the house, carrying them until she reached a bench in the garden, where she stumbled to a halt. Tears of pain blinded her. All these years, she had been no more to her mother than a burden, disdained because her father loved her and because she had not been a son. Now her mother wanted her to marry someone, anyone except a man of rank and wealth, because Mrs. Bennet felt she was not deserving of such a match.

Elizabeth rocked herself in a paroxysm of sorrow, guilt, and bitter resentment. She heard nothing until warm arms surrounded her to draw her against a firm chest beneath wool and linen. Darcy held her until her tears abated. Elizabeth felt her shawl settled around her shoulders and her arm tucked through the crook of her betrothed's elbow. He led her along the footpath until another broke away toward the woods. In the shelter of pines and barren beech and poplars, he found the rustic seat Elizabeth often used and seated her, sitting close beside her.

Raising her chin, he took out his handkerchief and wiped the tears from her face before kissing her tenderly. "Mr. Hill said you were in some distress when you went out. Can you tell me what has happened?"

Elizabeth picked up the gloves he had dropped into her bonnet when he set it beside her, but Darcy took them from her, replaced them in their temporary receptacle, and pressed the delicate hands to his lips. She shivered, holding tightly to his strong fingers. Could she tell him? She had never felt so alone as at that moment, and yet, he was there, solid and strong, sharing her pain, loving her. Her confusion subsided. Elizabeth lifted her head, breathed in deeply, and met his eyes.

"I am afraid I have committed the domestic sin of listening at doors." Her attempt at humor did not make him smile, and she sighed as she continued. "My parents were having a...heated conversation when I came downstairs. My mother's voice carries. She was objecting to our betrothal."

Darcy frowned. "I know she does not care for me, but why should she disapprove of our marriage?"

"It is not you she disapproves of. It is me." Tears again filled her eyes, and Darcy's grip on her hands tightened. "She has never approved of me. I was not a son. I am too independent. She thinks I...I will fail you as a wife. She thinks there will be no heir, and you will lose all affection for me."

"My God," Darcy whispered. "How she dares! Elizabeth, you must know she is wrong in every particular. You are my life. I could no more cease to love you than cease breathing. She has no right to speak of my feelings when she cannot possibly know them. You do not believe her, do you?"

The anxiety in his voice focused her attention. She shook her head and reached up to stroke his cheek. "No, Mr. Darcy, I do not. I am just shocked to hear spoken what I have long known by instinct. I did not wish to eavesdrop," she added. "I suppose it is my own fault for not continuing on my way."

A breeze stirred the layer of yellow leaves under their feet, revealing the dark loam beneath. An abandoned bird nest lay among the detritus in a tangle of twigs, feathers, and string with a bit of speckled shell clinging to it. The wind tugged loose a tress from Elizabeth's hair, to rest on her creamy neck. Darcy lifted it in his fingers and gently tucked it behind her ear. "In a short time, we will be wed, my dearest, and no one will matter except those who care for us."

Elizabeth nodded. She pressed her head to his shoulder, and they sat that way for long minutes, until she calmed enough to return to the house.

Mr. Collins was working in his garden when he heard the coach approaching along the lane. He hastily wiped his hands on a rag and put on his coat as he walked toward the gate into the road. He just reached it when Lady Catherine's coach drew up, and the doyen of Rosings herself appeared at the window.

"Good morning, my lady." He bowed precisely. "How may I assist you?"

"Come to tea this afternoon, Mr. Collins, and bring Mrs. Collins."

She retreated from the opening, and the coach drove on. Used to such preemptory summons, Mr. Collins went into the house to tell Charlotte that Lady Catherine had returned and ordered them to take tea with her. It was not unusual for them to be asked, or ordered, to tea or dinner at Rosings, but to have such an invitation tendered when Lady Catherine had been away and barely set foot on the property, much less entered the door of her residence, was unusual in the extreme.

"What can she mean by it?" Charlotte asked, not so much alarmed as curious. She knew only Mr. Darcy might dismiss her husband, and that was unlikely.

"I do not know, my dear. It is new to my experience of her ladyship. She certainly wants something, but what I cannot imagine."

The mystery did not solve itself until they were seated in the drawing room of Rosings with tea and cakes, Lady Catherine presiding from her large chair. She was making an attempt at cordiality that set Mr. Collins's teeth on edge. He sipped his tea and gathered his wits for whatever onslaught was to come. After a few minutes of what passed for small talk at these affairs, Lady Catherine set her cup and saucer aside and fixed Mr. Collins with a steady gaze. "You were recently in Hertfordshire, where you met and married your charming wife." She nodded at Charlotte. "Did you see my nephew Mr. Darcy while you were there?"

"Yes, my lady. He was staying in the neighborhood with a friend. I did not spend much time in his company, however."

"Do you know he is engaged to marry a Miss Elizabeth Bennet?"

Mr. Collins glanced at his wife. She said, "My sister, Maria, wrote me that Mr. Darcy and Miss Elizabeth were betrothed. I only received the letter yesterday."

Lady Catherine seemed to be struggling with some internal upheaval. She said at last, "I do not know if you are aware of an estrangement between myself and my nephew."

"No, my lady. And he would hardly speak of it to me."

"No, certainly not." The imperious tone broke through only to be quickly suppressed. "I look on the event of his marriage as an opportunity for a reconciliation, but I need to know more about his fiancée. Surely Mrs. Collins knows the lady? Is she gently bred?"

Charlotte felt a disinclination to answer, but was unable to explain he unease. She said carefully, "We have known each other since childhood, although I am several years older. Her father owns the estate bordering my father's, and they are good friends. Elizabeth Bennet is the best sort of lady; open, forthright, bright, and vivacious."

"Delicate of constitution or mind?"

"I would not say so." *Is Lady Catherine thinking of children*, Charlotte wondered? "She is quite hardy. She has fine sensibilities and some understanding of human nature."

"And her family? Landed gentry, of course, but for how long?"

"Four or five generations," Mr. Collins replied. He had determined not to mention Cheshire or the family's history. "Perhaps more. It is not a large estate, but Mr. Bennet is well enough off to provide a good life for his family."

"Well, my nephew is certainly not in need of money, although a large dowry would normally be expected. And the estate is entailed to you, Mr. Collins, is it not?"

The parson was feeling more and more uneasy. "It is. I do not expect, in this case, money or position enter into the matter."

"Then my nephew was taken with the lady when you were there?"

"I did not see evidence of it other than the usual politeness of a guest in an unfamiliar area. Mr. Bingley, Mr. Darcy's friend, is to marry Miss Elizabeth's older sister. So, of course, they saw a fair amount of each other."

"You can tell me no more about the family, Mrs. Collins? Surely you must know them well."

"They are prominent in the Meryton area, along with a number of other families. There are five sisters. I have always found them most genteel. The Bennets are an honorable family. I…I do not know what else to say."

"As my nephew is a man of impeccable reputation, I would suppose the family of his betrothed has never been touched by scandal?"

"Oh, no, my lady!" Charlotte felt the older woman's eyes bore into her. "They are most respectable people."

Lady Catherine nodded. She seemed content with the response. "You understand my feelings, I am sure. I am almost my nephew's closest relation. His marriage is of considerable interest to me. I would not want his reputation sullied. So, there is nothing that would prevent me from settling matters with my nephew?"

Charlotte hesitated. After a moment, she said, "I am certain Miss Elizabeth would not wish for dissension in her husband's family, if that is your concern."

Lady Catherine seemed to brood over the words, her gaze turned inward. She came back to her guests abruptly. "My daughter was Mr. Darcy's first wife, as you know. I wanted the marriage between Anne and Darcy. Looking back, I see it was a mistake. My daughter was too fragile."

"Yes," Mr. Collins replied. "I was saddened to hear of her death at so young an age."

"It was inevitable," Lady Catherine said. She spoke in such a strange manner that Charlotte shivered. "I trust this time his marriage will last far longer."

Lady Catherine withdrew into her private thoughts once more. Mr. Collins looked at his wife and found the muscles in her neck and shoulders tightened. She liked the interview no more than did he. As he set his cup aside, Lady Catherine came back to the present. She smiled as pleasantly as it was possible for her to do. Charlotte mused that it was the smile of a fox contemplating an unguarded henhouse.

"I thank you for the information, Mr. Collins, Mrs. Collins. I will not keep you from your work longer. I shall know what to do now."

She rose. It was a dismissal. The Collins' were only too happy to oblige. As they walked back to the rectory, Charlotte tried to shake off the apprehension she felt building inside her. She took her husband's hand and found it cold.

"Should I write to Lizzy, William? Lady Catherine's interest is most... unexpected."

Mr. Collins pondered as they walked. Lady Catherine had never before evinced an interest in mending family fences. Her attitude, when crossed, was always obdurate. To offer an olive branch meant she intended to gain the entire tree in return.

Her husband nodded. "Yes, do so. I think," he added, "I shall offer a special prayer for Mr. Darcy and Miss Elizabeth."

Charlotte murmured softly, "Deliver us from evil."

Caroline Bingley huffed into her brother's study with barely a perfunctory tap on the door. "Well, Charles, I hope you have an excellent excuse for calling me here so abruptly."

Bingley gazed upon his sister. She was dressed as usual in an extravagant day dress in a most unusual shade of orange, the inevitable plumes bobbing in her hair. He wondered, not for the first time, how she had totally escaped

Louisa's sense of fashion. "Darcy asked to speak to me this morning. He had some important news to impart."

"News? What news?"

"Sit down, Caroline," Bingley said, not unkindly.

"Why? What is it?"

"I believe it is better if you hear the news sitting down."

Caroline dropped into a chair with the grace of an expensive seminary education. She stared at her brother, hardly mollified, and wondered what news could possibly require her to sit to hear it. "Yes, Charles?"

"I wanted to tell you before you saw it in the society news. Darcy is to be married."

All at once, Caroline stiffened. Her heart began to thump very hard against her stays, and she almost felt giddy. Mr. Darcy had asked Charles for her hand. Finally, after three years, he had come to the conclusion she was the perfect wife for him. Mrs. Fitzwilliam Darcy, mistress of Pemberley. She would have all the servants, expensive gowns, beautiful jewels, carriages, and social acceptance any woman might wish for, and it was all falling over her like a shower of gold.

"Mr. Darcy is…is getting married?"

"To Miss Elizabeth Bennet."

Caroline shook her head. "I…I do not think I heard you clearly. He is…he is marrying…"

"Miss Elizabeth, Jane's sister. My sister as well, in a short time."

"No. No. You must be mistaken. Mr. Darcy and that…that…country bumpkin? NO!"

Caroline jumped to her feet; her face had flushed an unlovely red. Bingley said quietly, "Calm yourself. And mind your language. Miss Elizabeth is a perfectly lovely young woman."

"She is a joke! Is it not bad enough you must marry Miss Too-Good-To-Be-True Bennet? Now Mr. Darcy—*my* Mr. Darcy—has been taken in by that chit Eliza Bennet! She must have forced him to marry her, compromised him…."

"Caroline," Bingley said sharply, "stop it. You are hysterical. Darcy is in love with Miss Elizabeth. It is as simple as that. I have tried to persuade you more than once that Darcy was not partial to you. He has treated you with courtesy and respect but never any sign of affection. If he had wanted to offer for you, he would have done so long since. I am sorry, but there it is. They are betrothed and will be married in due time. If you want to retain Darcy's regard, you will accept it and act accordingly."

His voice was sterner than she had heard it before. He sounded more like their father than her easygoing brother. Caroline stared at him. Her shower of gold had suddenly turned to lead. "I cannot bear it," she cried. "I cannot bear it!"

Charles watched her storm from the room, and sighed. He had witnessed enough of her tantrums to know that eventually she would get over her disappointment. It was her own fault, he acknowledged silently. Darcy had never led her on. It was her own interpretation of his courtesy and her innate ability to deceive herself that had led her to depend on Darcy eventually asking for her hand. Charles shook his head. She had never loved the man, only his wealth, prestige and the material advantages of such a marriage. Yes, she would get over it, once the initial shock dissipated. She had better; Bingley was not about to jeopardize his friendship with Darcy, not especially now that his best friend was also to be his brother. He certainly would not do such a thing to satisfy Caroline's vanity.

Louisa Hurst sat in her boudoir in the suite she and her husband had been assigned at Netherfield Park. At the moment she was leafing through the latest copy of *La Belle Assemblée* and wondering if she could convince Milton she really needed a new ball gown in addition to the two gowns she had already purchased for Charles's wedding. Louisa looked up sharply as her younger sister burst in upon her. Louisa was not as tall as Caroline, but she was possessed of an English-rose complexion, an hourglass figure, and a mass of shining auburn hair. She had been married for five years to Miles Hurst, who lived on the interest from investments and the revenue of his middle-size estate in Berkshire. Louisa was not a romantic; unlike Charles and Caroline, she resembled her late father, a sturdy man with excellent business sense and a no-nonsense approach to life.

Caroline threw herself onto Louisa's favorite chaise longue, sobbing noisily and beating her fists against the delicate silk brocade upholstery. Louisa contemplated her for all of half a minute, put aside her magazine, rose, and took up her smelling salts from the dressing table. She strode to the chaise, opened the tiny bottle, and shoved it under her sister's nose just as Caroline gulped in a breath. The result was a satisfying spasm of choking and coughing that effectively put an end to the histrionics.

"Now." Louisa replaced the bottle and sat down again. "Who has died?"

"I wish *I* were dead," Caroline moaned.

"And miss the wedding festivities? How disloyal of you. Come, what is it now? Has Charles done something even more outrageous than propose to Jane Bennet?"

"No." Caroline sat up, groped for her handkerchief, and blotted her eyes. "Mr. Darcy is going to m-marry Eliza Bennet! I wish I could *kill* her! How she dares even look at him? And now she will be mistress of P-Pemberley, and what will I do? Everyone will know I was thrown aside for a nobody!"

"Thrown aside?" Louisa drawled. Caroline's obsession with Mr. Darcy was beginning to seriously annoy her. "My dear, he never picked you up, much less threw you aside. I admit, I was hopeful for a time, but Mr. Darcy so obviously thought of you only as Charles's sister, I soon put the notion out of mind, as I advised you to do. You would have done well to heed my advice and find someone else to marry. There are men enough in the *ton* who would find you quite a catch, and your dowry is substantial enough to attract a baronet. Why trouble over Mr. Darcy?"

"Because I want *him*."

Louisa picked up her magazine. "Well, you cannot have him. Really, Caro, you have gotten too much of your own way all your life, primarily thanks to you being the youngest and Mama spoiling you. A few disappointments will not kill you. There are things about marriage you cannot know until you are married, and I do not mean what might be called the mechanics of marital relations. The first is that your husband's word is law. Do you really imagine that Mr. Darcy would allow you to do anything you please, or that he would dissipate his fortune to satisfy his wife's slightest whim? Do not be a fool. Marry a man you can manage, or you will regret it."

"Do you 'manage' Mr. Hurst?" Caroline sneered.

"When necessary. Believe it or not, there is a spark of romance in Miles I can enflame if I choose. That is not the point. Stop acting like a child denied a treat, and grow up, Caro, or you will suffer for it."

Caroline glared at her sister. "I could still win him if that miserable little hussy was out of the way."

Louisa sighed. "Very well, Sister, as you like. But do not think of doing anything by way of revenge. I will see to it you are stopped. Without Mr. Darcy, we would have spent out lives pressing our noses to the windows of London society with no hope of entering the premises. We are a tradesman's children. I will not ruin our present opportunities for your childish pique."

"You are heartless," Caroline snapped.

"No, dear, just practical. Use what is available to improve your position in life, and do not cry over spilt milk. I learned that from Father. You would do well to practice it. Now, go wash your face, and think about your future. There are eligible men available, and you are not getting any younger."

Chapter 10

*I*n the end, Elizabeth's father settled the matter of her wedding to Mr. Darcy. Jane went to him ten days before her own nuptials to ask for his help. She knew Elizabeth was unhappy, and it threw a pall over her own joy. She found him in his book room after dinner, while her mother was engulfed in yet another disagreement with their cook over the menu for the wedding breakfast. Mr. Bennet was surprised to see his eldest daughter. Jane rarely invaded his sanctuary, and her grave face softened his habitually ironic approach to his family.

"Well, Jane, have you decided to call off the wedding and become a ribbon merchant?"

She smiled without real appreciation of his jest and sat in the chair before his desk. "No, Papa. I have come to beg a great favor."

Mr. Bennet put aside his book and considered her gravely. "Yes, child?"

"I want Lizzy to be married in the same ceremony as Mr. Bingley and me. I know it is very little time since she was betrothed to Mr. Darcy, but she…she will never come to you herself, and I cannot bear to see her so downhearted. She hides it as best she can, but I see it clearly."

"It has not to do with your mother, does it, Jane?"

Jane studied her hands in her lap. "Mama says nothing most times, but she wears a constant face of disapproval. I do not understand why. Mr. Darcy so obviously loves Lizzy and she him. She could not make a better match." Jane raised her large blue eyes; they glistened with unshed tears. "Oh, Papa, it would make things so much simpler. We have always wanted to be married together, and Mr. Darcy can obtain a special license, so there need be no banns read. You will not have the expense of a second wedding so soon after the first, and Mama need not make additional preparations for an event she…she seems to dislike so much. Lizzy will not even need a wedding dress. Her new ball gown is perfectly lovely and quite suitable."

"And Mr. Darcy, in the charming old phrase, would take her barefoot in her shift. Well, child, I am not sure you have not hit on a solution to your mother's newest self-induced crisis. I will speak to her. And no," he raised a restraining hand, "I will not mention your name."

Jane smiled radiantly. "Thank you, Papa. I know Lizzy will be so pleased."

And so Elizabeth was, although her strongest emotion was relief. Mr. Bennet approached her at once and found her immediately compliant with the suggestion. He called Mrs. Bennet into his book room that evening and approached the matter as if he had already made the decision. Mr. Bennet was not too amazed to see his wife also show relief at the news.

"Yes, that will save a good deal of time and money," she said after giving his words a short consideration, which he knew was mostly for show. "There will be no proper trousseau, but I am sure Mr. Darcy will want to oversee Lizzy's wardrobe and will dress her appropriately from London mantua-makers. Yes, very wise, Mr. Bennet."

"I thought you would approve," he said with more than a touch of his usual irony. "I will speak to Mr. Darcy when he calls tomorrow, and it will all be settled then, I am sure."

Mr. Darcy agreed at once to the new arrangements, relieved and grateful for Mr. Bennet's assistance. He was both glad they could be married so soon and concerned about how Elizabeth felt about their hastened nuptials. He approached her in the drawing room, greeted Jane formally, and bent to speak softly to Elizabeth. "Your father has given me permission to speak to you privately. Is the garden too cold?"

"It is damp today. We can go to the morning room. We should be undisturbed there."

She rose, and Darcy followed her to the room where the family usually gathered when they did not use the drawing room. The drapes had been pulled back at the windows, giving a view of the apple orchard's barren trees in the distance. Rain hung heavy on the near horizon of soft hills. Gray light invaded the room, softening the bright blues and yellows. In the Welsh dresser, a tea service of blue willowware held a rather lonely pride of place among the knickknacks and souvenirs. Mrs. Bennet had retained it from the Cheshire house by telling the auctioneers it was a personal gift from her mother. Someone had taken pity on the distrait young wife, and allowed her to keep it. In truth, it was a wedding present from her brother, Edward Gardiner, and his wife.

They left the door open but retreated far enough that they would not be easily overheard from the hallway. Elizabeth turned to Darcy, raising an eyebrow at his serious mien.

"Papa has told you that Jane and I want to be married in a double ceremony?"

"Yes. I am most agreeable to the plan, but if you would rather wait, I shall accede to your wishes."

"No, Mr. Darcy, I do not want to wait." A brief sadness touched her lovely eyes, and was swiftly gone. "My new ball gown will suit for a wedding dress, and I can obtain a trousseau in London, or wherever Miss Darcy shops when at Pemberley. I am sorry to come to you so poorly prepared, but it is for the best."

Darcy regarded her gravely. "You do not mind not having a wedding day just for yourself?"

"No, Mr. Darcy, I do not. Jane and I want to be married together. We have often spoken of it. As for my mother, do not trouble yourself. She will make every effort to prepare a fine wedding. She is quite good at parties, and there are the neighbors and our friends to impress."

He was certain Elizabeth did not realize the bitterness underlying her words. She smiled up at him, and he ached to take her in his arms. Darcy reached into his vest pocket and produced a small red leather case. "I have something for you, Elizabeth." Her given name on his lips caused a shiver to course through her. Darcy opened the box and took out a ring. "For our betrothal."

He lifted her right hand and slid the ring onto the third finger. Jane had given him one of her own rings with the information that her sister's hands were a size smaller than hers so he was able to have the ring sized to fit. Elizabeth caught her breath. Amid swirls of white gold, small blue-white diamonds sparkled and glittered. She raised her face to him. He was enchanted by its innocent joy. "Oh, Fitzwilliam, it is so beautiful. I have never seen anything so lovely!"

"I have," he replied huskily.

Darcy could no more stop himself from kissing her than hold back a river in spate. He cupped her face in his hands and pressed his lips to hers, moving carefully, not wanting to frighten or startle her. To his surprised gratitude, she tentatively returned the pressure. Darcy drew her closer. Her small hands were trapped between them, pressing his chest. He ran the tip of his tongue over her lips, and they parted for him, allowing him to intensify the kiss. It took all his self-discipline to withdraw from her. His breathing sounded harsh in the still room. He heard her gasping breaths as well. Elizabeth bowed her head on his shoulder, aware only of his presence and his love surrounding her.

"Tuesday week," Darcy murmured into her hair.

Elizabeth nodded. "Tuesday week."

There was still much to do, for both of them. Darcy left for London the following morning in his traveling coach to seek out Colonel Fitzwilliam. He found his cousin at Matlock House and at liberty, as he had taken a fortnight's leave. His cousin readily agreed to go on to Pemberley and escort Georgiana and Mrs. Annesley to Darcy House and then to Netherfield Park in time to meet Elizabeth prior to the ceremony. He acquired the special license necessary for him to marry outside his home parish. He also visited his solicitor to arrange for the finalization of the marriage documents they had already discussed. Darcy sent an express to his sister informing her the wedding had been moved up, and requesting he to be ready to leave when Colonel Fitzwilliam arrived. Finally, he took from his safe box the pieces of his mother's jewelry which had been set aside for his wife. After some consideration, Darcy selected a set of pearl earrings, hair clips, and a double-strand necklace for Elizabeth's wedding present.

Elizabeth, freed of the prospect of another two months of Mrs. Bennet's sour looks and stiff silences, involved herself in the wedding plans even more fully than when it had been only Jane's marriage to consider. She went to the mantua-maker in Meryton who always made the Bennet ladies' gowns and ordered a traveling costume for her trip to London after the wedding, reasoning that a ball gown, even though suitable to be married in, was not suitable for a journey of at least four hours in a coach, with the weather uncertain but likely to be cold.

At Netherfield Park, Mr. Bingley's sisters welcomed Georgiana and her companion effusively. She and Colonel Fitzwilliam were accommodated in the guest wing. Mrs. Annesley was given a room across the hall from her charge. Mrs. Hurst organized a tea for the two Bennet sisters in honor of the double wedding and to introduce Miss Darcy. Normally Caroline acted as her brother's hostess, but she was still sulking, much to Louisa's disgust. Charles did not notice. He was absorbed with his fiancée to the exclusion of anything less cataclysmic than an earthquake.

On the day of the tea, Georgiana sat before her dressing table mirror as her maid finished her hair. Her mind darted from one worry to another; what was Miss Elizabeth like, could she make a good impression on the lady? Georgiana thanked the girl automatically when she finished, her large blue eyes never leaving her image im the mirror. They saw a heart-shaped face with hair the color of new corn arranged in a simple bun surrounded by braids. Ringlets framed her pale countenance. She looked, she thought, as frightened as she felt.

"Which dress, miss?" Millie asked twice before Georgiana responded.

"Oh. The blue or the pink. Which do you think?"

"Both are lovely on you, miss, but I think the pink."

"Very well. And my rose diamond pendant and earrings."

Georgiana did not watch the maid go into her closet to retrieve the gown and jewelry. Her stomach was a hard knot under her ribs. Her temples felt as if a band had tightened around them, and her palms sweat. Thank goodness she could wear lace gloves. Her anxieties were the same as they had been since she received her brother's letter at Pemberley. Would his betrothed like her? Was she to be excluded from their lives as she would have been with Miss Bingley? *Oh, thank God he has not chosen Miss Bingley!* she thought. Her musings continued, *Is Elizabeth Bennet kind? Does she know about last summer? What will she do or say if she finds out?*

"Here you are, miss."

Georgiana startled, half rising from her seat. She stopped the maid's apology and was helped into the pink silk tea gown and the diamond jewelry. She requested her lace gloves, and after fifteen minutes was ready to descend to the drawing room and the ordeal that waited there. She had started for the dressing room door when a light knock halted her.

"Come."

Georgiana expected her brother. Instead, her cousin and co-guardian Colonel Fitzwilliam opened the door and made a courtly bow. "I have come to take you downstairs. Never fear the Bingley dragons when your knight in shining armor is by your side."

Despite her anxiety, Georgiana smiled. "They are not truly dragons, Cousin, but I thank you nonetheless. I expected Fitzwilliam, but you are a fine substitute."

He offered his arm, and they walked along the hall to the main staircase. "Darcy received a letter from Pemberley that required an immediate answer. He asked me to take his place, and I agreed with pleasure." Noting that Georgiana was trembling, he added seriously, "I have been in company with Miss Elizabeth Bennet several times, and she is a delightful young lady. There is nothing pretentious about her. She is a country-bred gentlewoman. She laughs much and has a bright, inquiring mind. You will like her, and she will like you."

Georgiana looked up at him. "I truly hope so, Cousin. I want to like her. After all, until I marry, she will be a great part of my life."

The colonel dropped his voice. "Fitzwilliam loves her very much," he said. "I have no reason to believe she does not love him as well. There is nothing mercenary in her character. Trust me."

Georgiana lowered her head but nodded. "Then it will be well."

Darcy met them at the foot of the stairs, kissed his sister's cheek, and said, "I cannot fathom how grown up you are, Georgie. That is a lovely gown."

"Thank you, Fitzwilliam. I hope it is appropriate."

"Admirably."

He took her hand, and they stood in the entry as Bingley joined them. The sound of a carriage came from the drive. Georgiana tensed, and her brother patted her hand reassuringly. She saw his eyes darken in anticipation of the visitors, or one visitor, at least. Having experienced love, even if for the wrong man, Georgiana knew it when she saw it.

Elizabeth followed Jane through the door; Bingley sprang forward and took his fiancée's hand, turned to introduce her to Georgiana. Elizabeth smiled at the girl, noting how nervous she was. When Darcy introduced them, she impulsively reached out and took Georgiana's hand. "I have so wanted to meet you," she said warmly. "Mr. Darcy has spoken of you often. I feel as if we are already acquainted."

"Thank you, Miss Elizabeth." Georgiana blushed.

Bingley, with Jane on his arm, led the way into the drawing room. Elizabeth walked beside Georgiana and drew the girl out. First she did so with inquiries about her trip from Derbyshire. When they were seated together on a settee in the drawing room, Elizabeth went on to ask Georgiana about her interests. After a few minutes, the gentlemen tactfully left them; Darcy returned to his correspondence, and Bingley and Colonel Fitzwilliam engaged in a game of billiards. Knowing she was absorbed in music, Elizabeth asked Georgiana about her favorite pieces. All the time, Louisa made conversation with Jane, and Caroline sat silently a little outside the group, failing in her attempt to look composed.

Tea was served with candied fruit, delicious little tarts, raisin cake, and other delicacies. Elizabeth praised the cook and told Georgiana that their cook at Longbourn made a crumble with fresh raspberries and clotted cream that was her favorite sweet.

"It sound delicious," Georgiana said, no longer as timid as at first. "Mrs. Adams at Pemberley is a wonderful cook and makes all sorts of cookies at Christmas. We take them to the tenants as part of the holiday baskets. The children look forward to it every year."

"I am used to visiting the tenants on our own estate," Elizabeth said. "I anticipate you introducing me to those at Pemberley. Perhaps we can make the visits together?"

"Oh, that would be delightful." Georgiana's face had lost its usual shy demeanor and was animated. "I have longed for someone to go with me. I never know what to say."

"It is not difficult," Elizabeth told the girl. "You just think of them as people like any others."

"When you are married," Georgiana began; at that moment Caroline Bingley's voice cut like acid through the conversation.

"Indeed, Miss Eliza," she shot a swift glance at her sister, "we have wondered at the precipitous haste of your wedding."

Elizabeth felt Georgiana stiffen beside her and laid a comforting hand on the girl's arm. She said with an edge in her voice, "As our wedding plans please Mr. Darcy and myself, and my sister and Mr. Bingley have no objections, I see no reason why they should be of concern to anyone else."

Louisa looked sharply at Caroline, and Jane's shocked face showed her alarm, but Caroline sneered and ignored both women. "After the brazen way you threw yourself at Mr. Darcy, it would not surprise me if, in a moment of weakness, he fell prey to your enticements. I see no other reason for such a hasty marriage."

"Caroline!" Louisa's voice was a warning, but Caroline no longer heeded it.

Georgiana knew her brother and Miss Elizabeth were being insulted, although the exact nature of the calumny escaped her. Shocked at the open hostility of Miss Bingley's words and manner, she wanted to defend Fitzwilliam and her new friend but did not know how.

Jane stared at Miss Bingley aghast. Although aware of her dislike of both her and Elizabeth, she had never expected an open attack. It was so outrageous that Jane was temporarily at a loss for words. Not only was the woman directing an insult to her beloved sister but, by extension, to her entire family. It was as unforgiveable a social sin as she was able to conceive.

Elizabeth said coldly, "You are beside yourself, Miss Bingley. Whatever your feelings against me may be, you have no right to insult Mr. Darcy or to expose Miss Darcy to your baseless accusations."

"Baseless! You may say so...."

"I do say so. You show yourself to be what you have always accused others of being, without propriety or social grace."

Caroline's face was flushed. Her voice turned harsh, "You are tender of Miss Darcy's sensibilities, but Georgiana had best beware. You will ruin her. You have no elegance, no style, no fashion, and no accomplishments. The *ton* will laugh at you, you will humiliate and ruin Mr. Darcy's standing, and no man of substance will offer for the sister of a...a country cow!"

Georgiana caught her breath, stunned beyond words. She had never heard such language from a lady. She shuddered to think what her brother would say to such vicious abuse. Louisa Hurst, however, had regained her senses and reached her sister before she could say more. Grasping Caroline's arm, she whirled her around and propelled her forcibly into the hallway. Caroline turned on her in fury, but Louisa had spent years dealing with Caroline's tantrums and felt not the slightest intimidation.

"You fool!" she hissed. "You complete and total idiot! How dare you do something so stupid? Do you think Mr. Darcy will not hear of this, not to mention Charles? If Darcy drops us after your little performance in there, you will be the only one to blame. Go to your rooms. Now, this instant! And think about who controls the money in this family!"

Mr. Hastings, the butler, appeared from below-stairs at that moment, and Louisa dropped her sister's arm. "Will you please escort Miss Bingley to her rooms? She is not feeling well. See to it her maid attends to her."

"Yes, madam."

Unflappable in the manner of a good butler, Mr. Hastings bowed to Louisa and stood by, waiting for Caroline to accompany him.

Crying openly, Caroline stumbled toward the main staircase, and Louisa turned back to the drawing room. She wondered if there was any way to mitigate the damage her sister had done. She found Elizabeth speaking quietly and calmly to Georgiana, while Jane stood at her sister's side; shock still showed plainly on the girl's pale face. Louisa rang for fresh tea and turned back to the three women. In spite of her best efforts, her voice shook a little. "I do not know what I can say after Caroline's abominable behavior. I cannot express my humiliation at such a display. She has not been herself of late, but that is no excuse. I can only offer my abject and profuse apologies for this unforgivable scene."

Under Elizabeth's gentle comforting, Georgiana had regained a little of her color, but she still showed the aftereffects of witnessing so much raw emotion—and from a woman who had always presented herself as the epitome of social correctness. Jane sat down in a chair near her sister. Distress darkened er blue eyes. She knew Miss Bingley was jealous of Elizabeth and that she had marked Mr. Darcy as her intended husband, but it was inconceivable to Jane that any civilized lady would stoop to such outrageous behavior in company. Once the betrothal was announced, that, for Jane, would have been the end of it. Whatever private pain Miss Bingley might suffer, she had been very wrong to impose it on Elizabeth and especially on Miss Darcy. It was difficult for Jane to censure anyone, but she felt, at that moment as if she could never again be in company with Caroline Bingley with any ease of spirit.

Elizabeth looked up at Louisa and said quietly, "Thank you, Mrs. Hurst. I believe it is best if this entire incident be put aside. To carry it further will only injure those who least deserve it."

"I agree with Elizabeth," Jane added more calmly than she felt. "Let us not impose this matter on others."

"That is...that is exceedingly kind of you, Miss Elizabeth. Please understand that I do not share my sister's opinion."

"Thank you."

The fresh tea arrived. After urging Georgiana to drink a sweetened cup, Elizabeth suggested Miss Darcy retire to her rooms and rest for a time. Gratefully, Georgiana agreed, and Louisa rang for her maid. In the hallway, Elizabeth spoke softly to the girl and patted her arm. "We will meet under happier circumstances soon," she told Georgiana. "And continue our discussion."

"Yes." Georgiana managed a small smile. "Thank you, Miss Elizabeth."

"Please call me Elizabeth, or Lizzy, as my family does. We are to be sisters, after all."

Georgiana nodded. "And please call me Georgiana, or Georgie, as my family does."

Elizabeth smiled and waited until Millie descended on them like a hen with one chick and shepherded her mistress away. Jane had joined Elizabeth by then, along with Louisa Hurst, who at Jane's request, had sent for their carriage. Darcy came out of the library to find Elizabeth and Jane already in their outerwear. Knowing something was wrong, he walked the two sisters to their carriage, his brow furrowed in concern.

"It is nothing," Elizabeth replied to his inquiry. "Miss Darcy needed to rest for a bit, and there is much to do at Longbourn. Please make our apologies to Mr. Bingley. Will we have the pleasure of seeing you tomorrow?"

"Elizabeth." He kept his voice low. "You will not put me off so easily. I know you too well. What happened?"

With a sigh, Elizabeth said, "Mrs. Hurst may confide in Mr. Bingley, although I advised her not to. Caroline Bingley saw fit to express her dismay at our marriage in rather strong terms. That is all."

"That is more than enough." Darcy's tone was icy with anger. "Why do you want to keep this from me? I have a right to know when my betrothed is injured by anyone."

"I am not harmed by her words," Elizabeth assured him, wondering at the intensity of his wrath. She had no way of knowing how Caroline Bingley's pursuit had vexed him for years. "I might have expected it if I had thought out the matter, but I did not think she would behave so badly in company. However, I do not wish to further distress Miss Darcy or Mr. Bingley with the matter."

"I will have a word with Bingley," Darcy told her. He kissed her hand tenderly, reassuring her that his immediate anger had passed. "Soon we will have no need to see anyone we do not wish to."

"I look forward to the day," Elizabeth said softly.

It was Bingley who went to Darcy, however. He asked his friend to come into his study. With the door shut, he immediately poured two brandies, handed one to Darcy, and drank half the other in two swallows.

"I have just spoken to Louisa." Bingley indicated chairs before the fireplace. "I am appalled at what she has told me. Apparently Caroline accused Miss Elizabeth of seducing you. Oh, not in those words, but the meaning was clear enough. And in front of your sister too. I cannot begin to apologize, Darcy." He ran a hand through his rusty hair, distress clear on his face. "She has had too much of her own way over the years, and I have done nothing to control her. Our mother treated her like a princess. Unfortunately Caroline came to believe she is entitled to anything she wants. I blame myself for not taking a firmer hand with her."

"You are her brother, not her father," Darcy said quietly. "Elizabeth did not want you to feel responsible for the outburst. My main concern is Georgiana. If she has taken no harm from the experience, I am not inclined to pursue it."

Bingley did not look at his friend. "That is uncommonly generous of you, Darcy. If it were Jane who had been subjected to such accusations, I am afraid I would never want to see any of the family again." He set his glass aside and stared at the flames snapping over a crumbling log. "I will have to send her away, but it will be difficult with the wedding in two days. There is no one in town I want her to stay with at the moment, and to send her north on such short notice is impossible. Louisa and Hurst are leaving after the wedding breakfast. They can take her with them. Until then, I suppose I shall confine her to her rooms."

Darcy felt for his friend's dilemma. However, he had no desire for a scene at the wedding. After a moment he said, "You will not want her to attend the ceremony?"

"She has shown she cannot be trusted," Bingley said grimly. "I do not think she will want to be there, considering her outburst today and her opposition to my marrying Miss Bennet."

Slowly, Darcy said, "I may have a solution. Georgiana's companion, Mrs. Annesley, could accompany Miss Bingley to the Hurst town house and remain with her until the Hursts return. She is completely trustworthy and discreet. I will not need my coach until after the wedding. It can easily take Miss Bingley to town tomorrow and be back in time for my use."

Bingley swallowed. He shook his head. "That is magnanimous beyond words, Darcy. It is the perfect solution. But how can I accept after what Caroline did today?"

"It is to my benefit as well," Darcy assured him. "I believe we will both be able to concentrate on our fiancées with no further distractions."

To which sentiment Bingley responded, "Amen."

Darcy returned upstairs a few minutes later to find his sister in the small sitting room attached to her suite. Mrs. Annesley was sitting with her, knitting peacefully, which told him there was no crisis at hand. Georgiana rose from her seat on the chaise longue and hurried to Darcy; he held her close for a moment. The action and her demeanor told him she was disturbed but not deeply so. He had learned to read her moods with better understanding since Ramsgate. It was one of the few advantages of that nearly disastrous incident.

"Are you well, Georgie?"

She raised her head, stepping back. "Yes, Fitzwilliam. You know about Miss Bingley?"

"Yes. I am sorry you were forced to witness such a disgusting display."

"I was quite shocked," she responded, "but Elizabeth -- she asked me to call her Elizabeth -- was wonderful. She did not flinch and did not sink to Miss Bingley's level. If someone spoke to me in that manner, I should have swooned."

"Fortunately, Miss Elizabeth is made of sterner stuff." He touched her cheek with gentle fingers. "If you are not harmed, I am relieved. Miss Bingley will be leaving for London tomorrow morning, and she will not return."

"I am glad," Georgiana whispered. She hesitated and then continued in the same tone, "I was terrified you would marry Miss Bingley."

"I assure you from my heart, dearest, that I would never, *never* have married Miss Bingley."

Georgiana nodded. She moved restlessly, which told Darcy that something was on her mind.

"What is it, Georgie? Tell me, please."

She sighed. "You have told me many times how Mother brought joy into our father's life. I believe that is what a marriage should be. When you married Cousin Anne, it was not a joyous marriage. You took on more responsibilities, more burdens. I know it was not Anne's fault, and you took very tender care of her, but it was not truly a marriage; not such as our parents had. I want you to have that kind of marriage, and I believe you will with Elizabeth."

Darcy hugged his sister. "You are not only growing up, you are growing wise. We shall indeed have a joyous marriage, and you will gain a sister beyond compare." Some emotion in Georgiana's face made Darcy study her closely. "Are you still troubled, Georgie?"

His sister did not raise her eyes, her hands clasped tightly together. She whispered, "I must tell Elizabeth about...about Ramsgate. She has a right to know before she accepts me as a sister. If I wait until after the wedding, she will be justified in feeling that it was kept from her purposely. I do not want that, William. Please say you do not object to me telling Elizabeth about...*him*."

Darcy hugged Georgiana to his side. He fully believed Elizabeth would see the incident for the cruel deception it had been, but he was unable to completely put away a small chill of doubt. Darcy spoke so softly that the words reached only Georgiana. "It is your decision, sweetling."

Georgiana closed her eyes briefly and then straightened her back. "Will you take me to call on her tomorrow?"

"Certainly. You may go with Mr. Bingley and me in the morning."

"Thank you, Brother."

Georgiana returned to her seat. Once this decision was made, she felt a sense of relief.

Darcy said to her companion, "Mrs. Annesley, may I have a word with you?"

She rose immediately. "Certainly, Mr. Darcy."

She followed him in*to the hall, thinking he meant to ask her about Georgiana's state of mind. When he asked her to undertake the trip to London, she was surprised but not unwilling.

"As you know, Mr. Darcy, I intended to visit my sister in Greenwich while Miss Darcy stays with Lord and Lady Matlock. I can easily go there as soon as the Hursts return."

"I will send a note to Mr. Burges. He will see that you reach your sister's home whenever you are ready. Thank you, Mrs. Annesley. I am afraid it will not be pleasant, but you have solved a dilemma for both myself and Mr. Bingley. I am grateful."

She smiled. "I am happy to be of help."

Darcy went to his rooms and wrote a short letter to Mr. Burgess, instructing him to send the carriage to the Hursts' town house for Mrs. Annesley on the day after next and to send her to Greenwich in the carriage with an escort.

Day after tomorrow, Darcy thought fervently. Day after tomorrow.

Chapter 11

When Elizabeth arrived home, she found a letter waiting for her from Charlotte Collins. She took it to her room, not wanting to face another interrogation by her mother, who believed her daughters' personal correspondence was open to her scrutiny. Elizabeth sat on the window seat to read it. Shaken by her experience with Miss Bingley and exhausted from the strain of the atmosphere in the house, she anticipated nothing more than a newsy epistle of life in Kent. Within the first paragraph, Elizabeth discovered how wrong she was.

> *My dear Lizzy,*
>
> *I hope you and your family are all well and happily anticipating Jane's wedding. Mr. Bingley is a pleasant, amiable man and perfectly suited to Jane's calm temperament. I am certain they will have many happy years together. I wanted you to be one of the first to know that Mr. Collins and I are expecting an addition to our family in about five months. If a boy, we will name him Lucas Willoughby Collins, as Willoughby was Mr. Collins's mother's maiden name. If a girl, perhaps Faith.*
>
> *My main reason for writing, dear friend, is to warn you of Lady Catherine's recent behavior. She invited Mr. Collins and me to tea the day she returned from London and quizzed us about the Bennet family and about you in particular, intimating that she wished your marriage to be an opportunity to reconcile with Mr. Darcy. Mr. Collins believes her interest is not as stated. Lady Catherine is not a woman of a conciliatory nature. Any indication that her wishes or desires may be thwarted*

sends her into a rage. I believe her capable of great cruelty if given the
opportunity. I have no doubt Mr. Darcy is well able to deal with his
aunt, but pray take care, my dear, and know that Mr. Collins and I
wish you both only the greatest happiness together.
Your loving friend,
Charlotte Collins

Elizabeth held the letter in both hands. Frustration at this latest threat to her peace, as well as her marriage to Mr. Darcy filled her. Elizabeth felt no personal fear of the woman, but what her influence on Mr. Darcy might be, she was not certain. She debated showing him the letter but decided against it. She would face any problem if one arose. For the moment, Charlotte's warning was only that, a caution against some future threat, but it was one Elizabeth took seriously. She was not about to let it cloud her wedding, however. William loved her; of that she was as sure as of anything in her life. It was enough.

Elizabeth was a little surprised the following morning to see Georgiana accompanying her brother and Mr. Bingley when they called. She was even more discomposed when, after a few minutes of rather stiff conversation, Georgiana quietly asked her if they might take a turn around the garden. As she gathered her outerwear, Elizabeth wondered if the girl's manner and this proposed *tête-à-tête* were because of yesterday. Had Georgiana taken Miss Bingley's accusations seriously? They strolled aimlessly past the dormant rose garden and the mulched beds where bulbs of crocuses and daffodils would be planted for early spring blooming. When the two ladies reached a rustic bench that was one of Elizabeth's favorites, she sat and invited Georgiana to join her.

"What is it you wished to discuss with me, Georgiana?"

The girl's expressive face was set in a mask of determined calm, but Elizabeth sensed the effort it cost her to maintain the facade. Georgiana twisted gloved hands together in her lap, swallowed, and lifted her head. "I have something I must tell you before you and William are married and I become irrevocably a part of your family."

Wisely, Elizabeth did not question or interrupt. She realized that if she broke the narrative, Georgiana might falter, causing unknown harm to their relationship. Elizabeth nodded. She sat close beside the girl without touching her. Georgiana continued to hesitate, then drew a deep breath and let it out in a shuddering exhale.

"Last summer, my former companion convinced William to let me spend time at Ramsgate in my own establishment. The seaside was wonderful, and I enjoyed myself greatly until we met a…a man. I cannot call him a *gentleman* now. I knew him from my childhood. His name is G-George Wickham. He is the son of our father's late steward, and was our father's godson. He and William were children together, friends, almost brothers. I had not seen him in years, and I found him charming. He began by renewing our former acquaintance, and then he moved on to courting me." Here she halted, her face paled until Elizabeth felt some alarm. Swiftly, Georgiana continued. "He said such lovely things to me, painted such a beautiful picture of what our life together was to be. We were to know only happiness and bliss. I believed him. I believed every lying word! I did not know that Father had cast him out for the dissolute way he lived."

Georgiana shivered. At this point, Elizabeth could not help taking the girl's hands in hers. "You did not have reason to doubt him, did you? He presented himself as your father's godson and as an old friend of your brother. He would naturally be accepted at face value. He used that against you."

"Mrs. Younge, my companion, was in league with him. She encouraged the suit. She broke faith with me and with William, but I do not blame her more than myself. I was raised to know right from wrong. Although it went no farther than…than kisses, he wanted more. Then he asked me to elope with him. To leave my family, my dearest brother, my duty to my name, put aside my own self-respect, he wanted me to go to Scotland and marry without William's consent. And I," her face, now trailed with tears, raised to Elizabeth, "I agreed! I was such a fool! A silly, romantic fool."

"You did not go, however." Elizabeth moved closer and put her arm around Georgiana's shoulders as the girl reached for her handkerchief.

"N-no, I did not. Only because William came unexpectedly to visit me. I found I could not deceive him, and when he found out about Mr. Wickham, he stopped the plan at once. He let Mr. Wickham call on me as had been planned, and then William confronted him. He told Mr. Wickham he would never see a penny of my dowry, and that man, the man who had told me he would marry me if I had nothing, laughed at me and said, 'Nothing ventured, nothing gained'."

Georgiana's head drooped. Elizabeth held her until her sobs, more relief than regret, subsided. She said at last, "You were very fortunate that William arrived when he did. It must have been a terrible experience to have Mr. Wickham revealed for the villain he is, but at least you were not married to such a horrible man." She tipped Georgiana's head up with a gentle gesture to look into her tear-starred eyes. "Why did you need to tell me this story? Did you think I would blame you for believing a deceiver?"

"I...I did not know, but I did not want you to accept me as a sister without knowing how weak I have been."

"Not weak, Georgie, just young and trusting. And I could never reject you as my sister, any more than I could reject one of my own sisters by blood. Mr. Wickham is in the past, and he needs to be put aside as a lesson learned. Come," Elizabeth rose and drew Georgiana to her feet. "Let us go in before we take a chill. I do not want to sniffle all through my wedding."

Georgiana smiled. "Yes, let us go in. I would dearly like a nice hot cup of tea."

On the evening before her wedding, Elizabeth retired early, knowing she was unlikely to get much sleep, and fatigued by the effort to keep up a calm demeanor with so many thoughts pummeling her brain. In her room, she occupied her favorite position in the window seat, the ghost of her image in the glass hovering over the dark night outside. By this time tomorrow, she would be Mrs. Darcy, and likely be with her husband, where she would be initiated into the mysteries of marital intimacy. While she was not entirely unaware of animal husbandry, since stockbreeding was a common topic among estate owners, she knew very little of the mechanics of human sexual relations. They were far more complex, of course, than with animals, based on emotion and not instinct, but the object was still procreation, especially the producing of an heir.

The light tap on her door made her swing her legs down and turn as she called, "Come in."

Elizabeth fully expected to see Jane. Instead, her mother's almost furtive entrance made her uneasy, despite the fact she anticipated the purpose of the visit. Mrs. Bennet closed the door behind her and took several steps into the room. Her face was set, almost grim. Elizabeth felt her pulse begin to beat rapidly. Trying to keep her countenance, she indicated a chair. "Will you sit down, Mama?"

"No, Lizzy, thank you. I have come because it is time for me to give you certain information you will require tomorrow night."

Elizabeth drew a shaky breath and said, "Yes, Mama."

Mrs. Bennet clasped her hands before her and did not meet her daughter's eyes. "You know I have had reservations about you marrying Mr. Darcy. Men of his station may seem like characters from a fairy tale, but they are not always kind or trustworthy. They are used to power, over people as well as other things. I hope you do not regret your choice."

Feeling vexed at such a description of Mr. Darcy, Elizabeth said defensively, "I am sure I will not, Mama."

Mrs. Bennet nodded. "You have always been headstrong. Well, so be it. As to the duties of a wife, your first and most important is to submit to your husband. When you are alone for the first time, he will touch you in ways and in places you have never been touched, and this will arouse feelings in you that you cannot anticipate." She drew a breath and explained briefly and with some hesitation the act of intimacy. "I hope he asks no more of you," Mrs. Bennet finished, "but whatever he requires you to do, you will do. That is the way of marriage, especially to members of the *ton*."

At a loss for words and blushing fiercely, Elizabeth felt it was best to end the interview. "Thank you, Mama. I am certain I will be fine."

"I hope so, Lizzy. Good night."

Mrs. Bennet escaped, and Elizabeth sat back, leaning her cheek against the chill glass of the window. She trusted Mr. Darcy. The thought of him harming her was ludicrous. She put aside her mother's foreboding as due to her disapprobation of the match. Suddenly Elizabeth had a vivid image of an incident that had occurred several days before. She and Mr. Darcy had walked out in the garden, and he had asked what the gardens on the far side of the house were like. Smiling, Elizabeth too him along a narrow flagged path and through a gate.

Lavender and verbena filled the beds between the walkway and an old stone wall. Near the front of the structure, a rose arbor arched above a rustic bench, its gray branches twined and twisted; a few faded pink petals hung forlornly, the last remnants of bounty.

"This is one of my favorite places at Longbourn. Jane and I have used this arbor since we were children as a place to exchange secrets without fear of being seen or overheard."

Darcy glanced up. The only windows overlooking the area were on the second story. When the roses were in full bloom, anyone inside the arbor would be invisible. "I can understand why. It is very private."

Something in his voice made her look up at him. His dark eyes held a fire she had seen briefly at other times when he looked at her; now it consumed her, drawing her to him inexorably. Elizabeth thought as he took her in his arms that he had never before attempted any of the liberties some betrothed couples took. Uncertainty fought with curiosity; given Elizabeth's natural fearlessness, she did not resist, only keeping her head lowered. After a moment, she became aware of the strength of his arms and the power inherent in his body. Her breathing quickened. Like the day in the morning room, Darcy cupped her face in his hands and brought his mouth to hers, pressing her lips in a firm kiss. Intrigued, Elizabeth returned the pressure. She felt him hesitate and then run the tip of his tongue over her lower lip.

A sudden sensation in the center of her body, startling, imperative, caused her to instinctively arch against him. Her lips parted. He began to explore her mouth, his hands caressing her back. Emotions shivered through her. Heat filled her from head to foot. Darcy released her suddenly. His breathing sounded heavy and harsh. He lowered his face to her hair, murmuring her name. Elizabeth felt his embrace ease; she found she did not want him to let her go. She felt so enfolded, so safe in his arms.

Elizabeth stopped his apology by pressing her fingers lightly to his lips. "You did nothing wrong, Mr. Darcy," she said, her voice a little uncertain. "I could have stopped you had I chosen to."

"I sincerely hope that is true," Darcy replied. He breathed in deeply several times. "I believe we should return to the house now, while I still retain a measure of self-control."

The experience had been enlightening and quite pleasant in a disturbing way. She had learned over the time of their acquaintance that he was a passionate man in many ways. Perhaps her mother's misgivings were based on her perception of the same quality, though she had interpreted that quality differently. There was truly no knowing what any man was like until you lived with him, Elizabeth acknowledged, and after tomorrow she was bound to Mr. Darcy for the rest of her life. Despite her belief in her betrothed's goodness, a small shadow of uncertainty remained, firmly suppressed.

The day of the wedding was clear. Pale sunlight turned the landscape to a patchwork quilt of golds, browns, and grays interrupted by sharp greens. Elizabeth asked for a tray in her room rather than go downstairs to break her fast. Annie brought her tea, and toast with raspberry jam, encouraged her to eat, and began to lay out her garments for the wedding. She had just finished when Mrs. Bennet put her head in the door and ordered Annie to attend Jane. Elizabeth smiled at the maid, and with a quick bob, Annie left her.

Elizabeth had rather be alone. She would have gone to Jane, but she knew their mother would hover over her sister until it was time for Mrs. Bennet herself to make ready. The sisters might have a quick word before they left, but the days and nights of companionship and sharing all they thought, dreamed, and hoped for were over. It was the saddest part of marrying. Although they would always retain that unconditional love and care for one another, their new families would become their priorities. Elizabeth found herself hoping the promise of such a relationship with Mr. Darcy was not an illusion. As much as she discounted her mother's foreboding, she knew it required time to form deep attachments of the mind and spirit. What she felt for him boded well. She wanted to be certain of what he felt for her, but she was realist enough to know that the feelings of a lover and a husband might not be the same.

Annie's services were usually shared by the Bennet women, but today Miss Darcy had very thoughtfully sent her maid, Millie, to help with the wedding preparations. Mrs. Bennet seized upon the girl's expertise in fashion and sent her directly to Jane, leaving Annie to help Elizabeth dress and to style her hair. Elizabeth wore the pearls Mr. Darcy had given her, her dark curls swept up in a mass of braids and ringlets. She saw herself in the glass and caught her breath.

"Oh, Annie, how grand it looks. Thank you."

"Yes, miss. Those are the most beautiful pearls I ever saw."

"They belonged to Mr. Darcy's mother. They will go well with the gown."

"Very well, miss."

Mrs. Bennet came in to give Elizabeth a final perusal and nodded reluctantly. "The pearls are a bit extravagant, Lizzy, but as they are the most expensive of gems and as Mr. Darcy gave them to you, it is wise of you to wear them."

After that, there was only a quick meeting in the downstairs hallway with Jane while they waited for their mother to descend the stairs. They held each other's hands tightly; tears starred their eyes as they acknowledged that this was a parting for them as well as a new beginning. Mr. Bennet found them there, smiled, and called up the stairs for his wife. He looked grave as he escorted his family to the carriage. Mrs. Bennet fussed and fretted as they drove the short distance to the church, exhorting Jane not to wrinkle her dress and twitching the fabric this way and that. Elizabeth almost laughed when she caught her father's ironic eye. Some things, he seemed to say, never change.

The church was already full when Mrs. Bennet and three of her five daughters took their places in the family pew after a triumphant march down the aisle. Lord and Lady Matlock and Georgiana were seated with Colonel Fitzwilliam and the Hursts in the front. They were the subject of much buzzing in the congregation. The wood of the old church glowed a mellow umber, brilliant shards of light from the stained-glass windows shivering over the assembled townspeople. Seeing that the principals had arrived, the deacon went to summon the bridegrooms. The pastor took his place, the two young men stood before the altar, and the doors of the porch opened to reveal Mr. Bennet with one daughter on each arm.

Mr. Bennet walked his two daughters down the aisle of the little church, a gray, dignified figure. Jane's pale blue gown was more elaborate than she might have wished but less extravagant than her mother wanted. It boasted a demi-train, Belgian lace trim on the hem, on the sleeves, under the bodice, and inset into the neckline. The skirt was split over a full lace petticoat. The only redeeming factor was the single color rather than the darker stripes her mother had favored. She was so incredibly beautiful her groom felt light-headed, looking at her throughout the ceremony.

Elizabeth's new ball gown was indeed suitable for her wedding, a simply cut pale-cream silk, the bodice heavily embroidered with fernlike swirls of green set off with seed pearls. Mr. Darcy's wedding gift fit as beautifully with the gown as if he had seen it. Neither bride wore a wedding bonnet. A stiffened piece of the lace on her gown covered Jane's pale gold hair. Elizabeth's pearl clips shone with every movement of her head. Darcy's heartbeat quickened as she reached him. Mr. Bennet put each daughter's hand in the minister's as the question was asked, "Who giveth this woman to be married to this man?"

He spoke the reply, "I do," in a husky voice.

The minister then put each woman's hand in her groom's. Mr. Bennet held each daughter's gaze for a moment before he retreated to the family pew, where Mrs. Bennet sat in state and beamed at the crowded audience.

"With this ring, I thee wed. With my body, I thee worship, and with all my worldly goods, I thee endow."

The words in Darcy's dark, vibrant voice repeated in Elizabeth's head as their traveling coach proceeded along the road from Hertfordshire to London. Her husband sat next to her now instead of across the narrow aisle between the seats. Darcy had greeted the wedding breakfast guests at her side and made an effort to speak with the friends and neighbors who attended. Elizabeth was grateful he had undertaken the courtesy, knowing it was for her sake.

Darcy had tucked a single blanket over both their legs; a heated brick under Elizabeth's half boots warmed them. Her russet-wool traveling dress was warm enough, but she welcomed the comforting body of Darcy close to her. She shifted her position a little when he circled her with his arm. He raised the curtain on the window next to them, and insubstantial light filtered into the coach, dulling polished wood and leather. The hazy sunshine muted the countryside so that Elizabeth thought it was like traveling through a dream, the familiar strange and somehow unreal. The heavily sprung coach made little of the irregularities in the roadway, and its sway was more soothing than uncomfortable.

Elizabeth's bonnet lay on the seat across from her. Her new husband's hat sat next to hers. His dark curls tempted Elizabeth. She drew off her glove, reached up, and stroked them back from his temple, running her fingers through them. Darcy captured her hand at once and pressed his lips to her palm. Elizabeth drew his head down and pressed her lips to his. His response sent fire surging through her body. Shaken, she leaned against him and felt him trembling. Darcy said in a low voice, "We shall be alone together soon, my beloved. Until then, why do you not rest?"

Elizabeth colored. Yes, they would be alone together when they reached Darcy House. She said, "I did not mean to provoke you, Mr. Darcy."

"My dearest Elizabeth, your lightest touch sets me on fire. You do not know what you do to me."

"I wonder," she replied, settling into the hollow of his shoulder, "if it is anything like what I felt when you kissed me in the rose arbor?"

Remembering her response, Darcy's arm tightened. "I hope it is, Elizabeth. And why do you still call me 'Mr. Darcy'? Are we to proceed like those couples who never seem to speak one another's given names?"

"You speak mine often enough, sir." Elizabeth looked up at him with an arch smile. "What shall I call you, then? Fitzwilliam?"

"It is my name, but my family calls me William."

"Does no one ever call you Fitz?"

"My cousin Richard has been known to do so, when he wishes to vex me."

Elizabeth relaxed against him. "I would not want to vex you. So I shall call you William, William."

Darcy chuckled, pulled the blanket higher over their laps, and put his head back. He knew when she fell asleep by her slow, even breathing. His wife! His Elizabeth slept pressed against his body. He had dreamed so often of holding her that the reality seemed almost dreamlike. Darcy shifted his position carefully to cradle her even closer, and pulled the blanket higher over her sleeping form. She was completely at ease with him now. He prayed her trust would continue into their marriage and that he would be everything to her she might hope for. He cherished her love, but he wanted more; he wanted her friendship, her companionship, her understanding. He wanted her to be his completion, as he believed only she was capable of being. Darcy closed his eyes, tightened his hold on Elizabeth, and slept.

The sky darkened as they approached the city, and the wind became fitful, blowing in gusts that bent and shook the trees along the road and buffeted the sides of the equipage. A storm was advancing on them. He lowered the curtain, shutting out the heaviest drafts, and continued to doze as they progressed into London. As always when he traveled, his senses were aware of his surroundings. When the noise of inbound traffic began to infiltrate the coach, he straightened and spoke gently to his bride.

"We are entering London, my dearest. It is about half an hour to Darcy House."

Elizabeth sat upright. Her hands reached up automatically to ensure her hair was not askew. It would not do for the mistress to enter her new home looking untidy. As she straightened her skirts, she heard rain begin to tap at the coach. Darcy pulled the curtain aside enough to look out. As he did so, streetlamps ran orange fingers of light along the window frame. The air did not have the clear, green smell of country rain. The damp permeating the coach had more the odor of a wet chimney.

Darcy released the leather curtain and sat back. "We are in for a storm," he said. "I hope we reach Darcy House before it became a deluge."

Despite his hopes, it was beginning to rain in earnest by the time they reached Mayfair. At Darcy House, a footman came out with an umbrella to hold over them as soon as the coach halted. Steves had jumped down before the wheels stopped rolling to lower the steps and open the door. Darcy got out, turned, and handed Elizabeth out. She kept close to him as they entered the door, held open by a formal Mr. Burgess. He bowed to them both, shut the door, and they were home.

Home, Elizabeth thought. She was suddenly aware that this was now her home, not Longbourn. Their home. And the estate, Pemberley, in time would also be their home. The realization brought a swift pang of uncertainty but no regret. She was Mrs. Fitzwilliam Darcy now. She must grow accustomed to being mistress of this house, not just a dweller in it as she had been at her family home. Elizabeth refused to be intimidated. However, a small qualm of disquiet remained.

Servants took Elizabeth's spencer, bonnet, and gloves and Darcy's hat, gloves, and greatcoat with smooth efficiency. The senior staff members were drawn up in the entry hall. Darcy introduced the butler and his wife, the house-keeper, and the cook, Mrs. Bunne. Elizabeth's smile at the name was perhaps a trifle too broad, but the cook, a short, plump woman with gray-peppered hair and merry brown eyes, seemed to understand. Elizabeth also met Martin, Darcy's valet, and the two senior footmen besides Steves. Last, Mrs. Burgess indicated a pretty girl a little older than Elizabeth.

"Mrs. Darcy, this is Clara. She is an upstairs maid, but I have assigned her to act as your abigail until you are able to make whatever arrangements you wish for a permanent lady's maid. She has had some experience but is not formally trained."

She said in a soft soprano, "I will try to please you, madam."

"I am sure you will do just fine." Elizabeth smiled at the girl, who had curt-sied nervously when introduced.

"Mr. Darcy," Mr. Burgess went on as the staff returned to their duties, "Mrs. Bunne has planned a light supper to be served whenever you are ready. I thought you might wish to use the breakfast parlor this evening rather than the formal dining room."

"Thank you, Mr. Burgess. That will do admirably. In an hour?"

He looked at Elizabeth, who nodded.

"Very good, sir. Madam. Shall I have Mrs. Burgess show Mrs. Darcy to her rooms?"

Darcy said, "No, thank you. I will take her myself."

He offered Elizabeth his arm. As they climbed the main staircase, she looked up at him and said with a raised eyebrow, "Mrs. Bunne? You could not have warned me?"

Darcy grinned. "You handled the situation quite successfully, my dearest. Although if you had laughed, she would have taken no offense. She is resigned to her name."

Mrs. Bunne's name did not, apparently, affect her culinary skills, Elizabeth thought two hours later as they finished the excellent meal in the breakfast parlor, which could easily have held the Longbourn breakfast room and half the morning room. Wall sconces gleamed on oil paintings in gilded frames, pastoral landscapes, and still lifes of flowers and fruits. The table was set with two places at the master's end. Silver candlesticks shimmered with the clear light of beeswax candles, surrounded by decorations of white chrysanthemums and masses of elaborate white satin ribbon bows. The fine china was painted with yellow roses and wreathes of greenery entwined in lavender ribbons. Everything from the snowy linens to the flatware and crystal sparkled. It was like a fairy banquet. And this was how she would live from now on, Elizabeth thought. Surrounded by luxury, served by people whose only purpose was to make her happy. It was heady and a little frightening. She hoped she lived up to expectations, not only those of her husband but also those of everyone who mattered to him.

Neither of them did justice to the food. When the pudding course was cleared, Darcy waved the footman away and rose. "Our compliments to Mrs. Bunne," he said to Mr. Burgess.

Elizabeth took his arm, and they went out onto the first-floor landing. She hesitated, unwilling to take the initiative as to what their next activity would be. Darcy smiled down at her.

"I will take you on a tour of the house tomorrow, my love, but I can say that in addition to the breakfast parlor, this floor holds your private sitting room, the game room, and some guest quarters. The formal rooms are, of course, on the ground floor, along with the music room, the library, and my study. The second floor holds more guest quarters, the nursery, and Georgiana's sitting room. Our rooms and family quarters are on the third floor. Is there anything you wish to ask me?"

"Not now." Elizabeth smiled at him. "As it is early, would you like me to play for you?"

"Very much."

Darcy took her downstairs to the music room, which held a magnificent pianoforte as well as Georgiana's harp, several comfortable chairs, and a settee. Darcy led her to the instrument. While Elizabeth settled herself on the bench, he sorted through sheet music and selected several pieces he particularly liked. For the next hour, Elizabeth played and sang light airs and undemanding works that soothed her gathering disquiet.

When she finished, she ventured without looking at Darcy, who sat nearby, "I believe I will retire now."

Noting that she was beginning to show signs of nervousness, her husband rose. "Of course. I will take you to your rooms. Clara will have everything ready for you by now."

When they reached the third-floor landing, Darcy opened a carved and paneled door to the left. The bedroom was twice the size of her bedroom at Longbourn. Two simpler doors led to other rooms. It was furnished with a large half-tester, four-poster bed of walnut, and a white Adam fireplace where low flames snapped and crackled. The windows were draped, and the bed curtains had been drawn back. Both fabrics were obviously new, as was all the linen. The room was spotless but had not been redecorated for many years. As she looked around, Elizabeth decided it must not have been occupied since Darcy's mother was alive. She doubted Lady Anne de Bourgh had ever occupied these chambers.

As if reading her mind, Darcy said softly, "I did not have anything done to your rooms except for new linens and drapes. You will want to make them your own, as I doubt my mother's tastes and yours are similar."

"They are most spacious," Elizabeth replied. "Later, perhaps, I will think of having them redecorated, but for now, they are more than adequate."

"Then I will leave you for now." Darcy kissed her forehead, "All will be well, Elizabeth."

The door closed softly behind him. Elizabeth looked around the room. To her delight, she found there was a window seat, as well as two chairs before the fireplace. Elizabeth wondered what her mother would say when she saw Darcy House. It was so like her stories of the Cheshire estate. Would Mrs. Bennet be even more resentful that Elizabeth was living as she herself had intended to live?

Clara came in from the dressing room, effectively ending Elizabeth's contemplation.

"I've drawn your bath, madam," the maid said. "The house is very modern, and Mr. Darcy had a new copper tub put in a fortnight ago."

Suddenly feeling the need of a bath to wash away more than any lingering road dust, Elizabeth followed her into the dressing room. The tub in its tiled corner was capacious, the water was hot, and there was lavender-scented soap. Half an hour later, clean, dry, and in the nightdress and dressing gown gifted her by her aunt Gardiner for this night, Elizabeth sat at her dressing table while Clara brushed out her hair.

"Shall I plait it for you, madam?"

Elizabeth looked in the mirror and thought of Darcy's hands touching her hair. "No, thank you, Clara. I believe Mr. Darcy prefers it down." She rose. "You may go now. I will call for you in the morning when I want you. Good night."

With a curtsy and a good-night, Clara left her. Elizabeth looked at the door she now knew led to Darcy's bed chamber. He would come through it shortly, through this dressing room, and into her bedroom. And then…

Elizabeth returned to her bedchamber, chiding herself for cowardice. Every woman who married experienced what she was about to; she would survive. She loved Darcy with all her heart. She believed he would be as gentle as possible. Even her mother had said that, after the first time, there was little or no pain. Looking for temporary distraction, she walked around the room. A vase on a small table held a bouquet of ferns and bronze dahlias. Elizabeth trailed her fingers over the petals, layered, she mused, as were her emotions: love, anticipation, uncertainty. And something deeper and more elemental she had begun to realize was physical desire.

Darcy knocked softly at the door of Elizabeth's dressing room. Bathed and freshly shaved, he wondered if Elizabeth would welcome him, or if she had the fears of most brides that he would have to overcome. Receiving no response, he opened the door quietly.

Elizabeth?"

She sat on the window seat, her gaze on the streaming glass panes, lost in thought. He reached her before she became aware of him, causing her to rise so abruptly that she grasped his shoulders for support. He chuckled, folding her in his arms.

"I have you, my love," he murmured into her hair. "You are safe with me."

Elizabeth lifted her face to find his eyes full of dark fire. "I will always be safe with you, my dearest husband."

Darcy touched her lips with his, carefully. Her response amazed and thrilled him. When at last she rested against his drumming heart, he stroked her back slowly, knowing this night was to be all he had dreamed it might be.

"Do you wish to stay here, beloved, or will you share my bed, as I have long hoped?"

Elizabeth leaned back to smile up at him. "I will share your bed and your life, for as long as we both shall live."

Darcy closed his eyes for a heartbeat. Then he picked her up and carried her through her dressing room and into his own bedchamber. "Here, beloved," he whispered, as he put her down in the middle of his vast bed. "Only here, with me, for all our lives."

Elizabeth woke to the deep whisper of heavy rain against the windows. Thunder grumbled in the near distance with a sound of barrels rolling over cobblestones. The drapes and bed curtains were drawn, and she was warm, snuggled against Darcy's side. She had risen once in the night to use the commode in its alcove off her dressing room and to clean herself. The fires were out, and it was cold, but Elizabeth did not resume her discarded nightdress, preferring the feel of Darcy's skin against her own.

How wanton I have become in a night, Elizabeth thought, settling carefully so she did not wake her sleeping husband. *Nothing I feared came to pass, except for a little pain, and it was not so bad as my mother implied.*

Darcy had made love to her twice. The first time stroking and kissing her until the strange impulses Elizabeth felt before they married became clear to her. He had, indeed, touched her in places and ways that she had never imagined, and the result had been a transcendent pleasure and a desperate need. Her body heated under his hands, his mouth, tasting her, stroking her, stimulating her secret places until she was lost in a paroxysm of sensation.

"I wish I did not have to hurt you," he whispered against her neck as he moved over her, "but there is no choice."

Elizabeth's response, her mind and body hazed with ecstasy, was to tighten her arms around him. The pain was brief, and then the building momentum of her climax shut out all other sensations. The second time had been deep in the dark hours when he woke to find her stroking his chest.

Elizabeth had said only, "Come to me, my husband."

Now she lay quietly, waiting for the dawn and her new life. There were bound to be conflicts of one kind or another. He was not a man who would attempt to dominate her, and she was not a woman to submit to domination. They would have children, God willing. They would live out their lives together, loving, arguing, compromising, talking, sharing, trusting; knowing a joy in one another her parents had never experienced. It was all Elizabeth might have dreamed of or hoped for. Neither was a perfect being, but together they would build a life as near to perfect as any human had a right to live.

Elizabeth closed her eyes and drifted off to the liquid music of the rain.

Chapter 12

$\mathscr{G}$eorge Wickham carefully trimmed his beard with the sewing scissors he had stolen from his former landlady. He did not look beyond his hands in the mirror. To see his face brought crashing back the memory of his disfigurement; the searing pain as Husk's knife slashed down his cheek while he twisted and writhed to free himself from the two brutes holding him. He had not taken Colonel Fitzwilliam's advice to leave London with the remains of Slade's money. Instead, he attempted to increase his funds in a card game. Husk had walked in just as he lost everything but a few pounds on a hand he had thought was unbeatable.

Wickham was about to call out the winner for cheating when Husk's men seized him and dragged him into the alley next to the gambling hall. Husk followed, sneering as Wickham tried ineffectually to escape. Husk, real name unknown, was a moneylender, fence, and landlord with interests in several brothels and gambling establishments. He was not a patient man, and Wickham owed him a large enough sum to make collecting it important to Husk's reputation.

"Thought you'd bubble me, eh, George? Find a little pelting village and live high until a new widow comes along? You think I'm totty-headed, Georgie? You owe me two hundred yellow boys. You think I'd let you track on me?"

Stammering, Wickham tried to explain his bad luck. That he had been cheated out of the money he meant to pay Husk. But the hulking bully refused to listen. Gathering Wickham's coat in one huge fist, he drew a knife that looked a foot long to Wickham's terror-distorted vision. He heard over the sniggers of the men holding him his own voice wailing that he would pay, just give him another few days, a week at most, and he would deliver the money. Husk stared into Wickham's white face. His own was a cold mask that showed no mercy. He nodded to one of the men, who patted Wickham's pockets, removed his pocketbook, and took out the contents.

"Twenty pound, Mr. Husk."

"I'll have more in a day or two," Wickham gabbled. "Give me that much time. I'll pay you, I swear!"

Husk grinned like a death's-head. "I've heard your lies for the last time. You fancy yourself a top diver, eh, Georgie? One for the ladies, eh?" Husk put the tip of the blade under Wickham's chin and pressed until blood trickled into his soiled cravat. "I could slit your gutter lane, but that won't get me my two hundred pound or discourage other fools from trying to foist me."

Wickham saw the blade flash as pain ripped down his cheek. He screamed, writhing in the grip of Husk's bullies. Husk nodded, and the men threw Wickham to the ground. As Husk looked on with a satisfied smirk, they kicked and beat Wickham while he curled like an unearthed worm in the filth underfoot, crying and begging.

"One week, Georgie," Husk declared as he waved his men off. "Or next time it'll be your whirligigs you lose."

Laughing, the three men left the alley. Wickham lay groaning for several minutes before he crawled to the nearest building wall and pulled himself to his knees. Leaning on the blackened bricks, he vomited up the remainder of the cheap whiskey he had drunk. When the spasms passed, Wickham tore off his cravat and pressed it to the streaming wound on his face. After a time, he was able to drag himself to his feet. He left the alley and staggered back to his room above a local alehouse. The prostitute he was sharing it with took one look at him and went out. She returned in a quarter hour with the local "doctor", a man of questionable credentials who sewed up and physicked the denizens of the area, when he was sober enough to see what he was doing.

His efforts to close the wound on Wickham's face were as successful as any he made. The prostitute had brought along a bottle of cheap gin. To the sound of Wickham's screeching cries and curses, the doctor doused the wound with it.

"Don't know why," he said over the injured man's sobbing moans, "but alcohol keeps a wound from going bad. Most of the time, anyways."

The prostitute had left a few coins on the dresser before she departed. She did not return. It was several days before Wickham was strong enough to leave the room. When he was, he collected the ten pounds he had hidden away for an emergency and took a post chaise out of London to the north. He knew Husk was as good as his word, and in addition, Wickham had a score to settle.

In his shabby room, Wickham chanced a glance in the small gray mirror and quickly looked away. The room was little more than a bed closet—dirty, dingy, and smelling of stale bodies, cheap spirits, and despair. His newly grown beard covered the lower portion of his face, but the livid scar, with its small rows of marks where the stitches had been, ran from his cheekbone to the corner of his upper lip. The disfigurement had left his face drawn into a permanent sneer. To the curious, he explained it away as a wound from the war in France. The lie was good for a free drink once or twice but no more than that. There was an overabundance of wounded and maimed soldiers roaming England, and liquor cost coin. The worst was that women no longer looked at him with pleasure in their eyes. He was marked for life, any chance of marrying a wealthy wife gone.

This is Darcy's fault, Wickham thought with a snarl. He had money enough to pay the price of his little sister's stupidity. Wickham could have lived well on the five thousand pounds and gotten another five thousand from Slade. Instead, Annie Young was out of reach, and if he ever showed his face in London again, Husk would kill him. He tied his cravat and straightened the ill-fitting coat, glancing at a week-old newspaper lying on the scabrous dresser. Darcy was married, to a young and no doubt beautiful and rich wife. Everything Wickham should have enjoyed. Well, he thought as he left the room, Darcy will not enjoy her for long.

Lady Matlock brought Georgiana to Darcy House on the Monday following the wedding. Elizabeth had sent an invitation to tea, and the party arrived in good time in spite of the rain that still washed the streets and buildings of London. Elizabeth met them in the entry hall, embraced Georgiana warmly and curtsied to Darcy's aunt.

"I am so happy to have you home, Georgiana," she said as she led them to the drawing room; her tone and smile were so genuine that Lady Matlock also smiled. "William is at a meeting with his accountants, but he should be home in time for dinner."

As they took their seats, and Elizabeth rang for tea, Lady Matlock noted Elizabeth's carriage and movements. *I can well believe*, she thought, *Darcy's statement that she is a very accomplished dancer. She moves with grace and poise. In time, perhaps my nephew will actually learn to like dancing.*

"Have you decided when you will remove to Pemberley?" Lady Matlock asked as Elizabeth poured out the tea.

Georgiana was all attention for the answer, but Elizabeth hesitated before replying. "We have not discussed it, but I know William is anxious to return to the estate before winter sets in. I would suppose no later than a week from now." She looked at the older woman. "Although I will not have assumed all my duties as mistress by Christmas, I wish to make the holiday as joyous as possible. Do you think you and Lord Matlock will be able to join us, at least for part of the time?"

"Thank you, my dear," Lady Matlock replied. "The holidays at Pemberley have been conducted quietly for some years. I should very much like to see a holiday season like those I remember from years ago."

"I will do my best to make that happen," Elizabeth promised.

"Have you had any dresses made, Elizabeth?" Georgiana ventured. "And there are other items you will need, heavier shifts and nightdresses."

Elizabeth shook her head, her face pink. "I am afraid I have not left the house since we arrived. I was hoping you might go with me to shop for what I will need."

Smiling widely, Georgiana glanced at her aunt. "We could all go shopping tomorrow, if you have nothing else planned, Aunt."

Knowing her niece's love of shopping, Lady Matlock smiled. "I think that is an excellent idea. I am sure our modiste can have enough gowns for the present ready in a week. We can purchase the other items at the same time. If there is anything you require later, there is a competent mantua-maker in Matlock and a lady in Lambton who has sewn dresses for Georgiana on occasion. There is also a milliner in the village and several merchants in Matlock who can supply your needs."

Elizabeth felt tears start in her eyes. "Thank you, Lady Matlock. I appreciate your help and concern greatly."

"You are my niece now," the lady replied with a smile. "Please call me Aunt Madeleine, and I shall call you Elizabeth."

The trip to Pemberley took nearly three full days, the company twice stopping at inns for the night. The weather turned colder the farther north they traveled, while rain slid into sleet and then snow. Elizabeth was glad she had worn a new traveling ensemble, as the one she had worn after the wedding was too light for the climate. She found the landscape very different from the rolling hills and farmland of Hertfordshire. Rugged and at times stark, the high, sharp mountains and frequently heavily wooded terrain stimulated her imagination. Elizabeth felt as if she were traveling back in time to an era when castles brooded over their surroundings, with villages clustered like frightened animals at their feet.

The coach turned into the drive at the gatehouse just as the dimmed light of the sun disappeared over the western peaks. Torches were lit along the full half mile of the driveway, and the house blazed with lights. They crossed a little hump-backed stone bridge over a large stream running through the park into a lake. Looking eagerly out the window, Elizabeth caught her breath. Pemberley House was lit like one of those old fortresses; orange fire struck off its white limestone exterior, spilling over the gardens nearest the four story structure. It was magnificent. The most stately, perfectly proportioned building she had ever seen. It was not imposed on the setting, but seemed to grow out of it naturally. Elizabeth was only able to see the irregular bulk of the high, wooded ridge behind it, or guess at the extent of its famed gardens.

"It is wonderful." Elizabeth turned a glowing face to her husband. "I can hardly wait to see it by daylight."

"You may have to wait until the snow abates a little to really appreciate the view," Darcy told her with a smile, "but the result is worth it."

So it was. Elizabeth spent an idyllic week exploring the house and grounds with her husband before her natural sense of responsibility caused her to engage

Mrs. Reynolds in a plan for teaching her the duties of the mistress of Pemberley. Elizabeth was already familiar with the household accounts for Longbourn, and had a firm grasp of the nature of responsibilities at Darcy House. However, the size and scope of Darcy's estate left her wondering how she would ever learn everything. Mrs. Reynolds took her measure and smiled to herself.

"We can begin with the simpler duties," she reassured Elizabeth, "and go on to more complex matters whenever you are ready. It is not as hard as it looks, and you have knowledge of household accounts in general as well as those at the town house, so handling those of Pemberley will not be as difficult as if you had never done such before."

They determined to meet on a daily basis until Elizabeth was familiar with the general outline of what she would be responsible for, and then they would meet several times a week as she gradually took over management of the household. They were in Elizabeth's private sitting room, engaged in their third meeting, when Mr. Niles knocked at the open door and brought in a salver with three visiting cards. Elizabeth looked at them and then read the names aloud to Mrs. Reynolds. "Mrs. Courtland, Mrs. Ellington, and Lady Walker-Price."

"Mrs. Courtland's husband has an estate that borders Pemberley to the south for a short distance. Mrs. Ellington's husband is a longtime friend of Mr. Darcy. They were at university together. Lady Walker-Price," the housekeeper hesitated and shot a swift glance at Mr. Niles, "requires careful handling. Her mother married a baronet, and the lady sees herself as a social force in the neighborhood."

Elizabeth raised an eyebrow. "I see. Thank you, Mrs. Reynolds. Please show the ladies up, Mr. Niles. We will require tea as well."

Mr. Niles announced the visitors formally, beginning with Lady Walker-Price. She was a middle-aged woman with a carriage upright to the point of stiffness. An air of superiority preceded her like a waft of perfume. She was dressed in a fashion more suited to London than the country, expensive and mildly over-decorated. A large diamond brooch pinned to the lapel of her short jacket sparkled in the light. Elizabeth immediately identified Mrs. Courtland as a follower; she was timid. and uncertain of her place with the older woman. She had brown hair, brown eyes, and an extremely modest brown wool visiting dress with long sleeves and a high neckline. She resembled a rather unassuming sparrow. It was Mrs. Ellington who took Elizabeth's full attention. She nearly gasped as the lady curtsied, and she returned the gesture. Mrs. Ellington's classic features and golden hair were so like Jane's that Elizabeth felt a moment of intense longing for her sister.

She indicated chairs and resumed her own seat. Mrs. Reynolds had removed the ledgers, leaving only Elizabeth's workbox. She smiled at her visitors and said, "Welcome to Pemberley. How kind of you to call."

"I had intended to visit," Mrs. Ellington replied in a lovely contralto, "as soon as you had a chance to settle in. Mrs. Courtland was coming with me when Lady Walker-Price arrived, and we decided to come together."

"I am pleased you did." Elizabeth caught the very slight emphasis on the "we" and remembered Mrs. Reynolds's veiled warning. "I have not had an opportunity to meet any of our neighbors yet, so your call is most welcome."

Tea arrived, accompanied by raspberry tarts, little sugar cakes, and fresh fruit from the Pemberley glasshouses. Elizabeth noted the tea was strong, and there was plenty of sugar, another subtle hint of her abilities as hostess. As she served the ladies, Mrs. Walker-Price watched her every movement as if she were a new maid of uncertain skills. Never one to be intimidated, Elizabeth waited until the visitors had helped themselves to the sweets before initiating what she hoped would be a conventional conversation. "I understand, Mrs. Ellington, that your husband and mine were at university together?"

"Yes. Theodore and Mr. Darcy have been friends for years. I am afraid we have not seen as much of him as we would like for the past several years, but I am sure that will change now."

Her smile was genuine, and Elizabeth responded in kind. She was startled to hear Lady Walker-Price's sharp voice cut in. "Yes, we rather thought we should see you at Sunday service in Lambton. It is a usual way to meet one's neighbors."

"Mr. Darcy wished to attend services at the Pemberley chapel," Elizabeth answered. "I am sure we will attend services in Lambton as well."

"Hmm. Your cook makes the tea quite strong."

"I can send for another pot if it is not to your liking, Lady Walker-Price," Elizabeth offered, silently gritting her teeth. A social force locally, indeed.

"I find a good strong cup of tea bracing in this cold weather," Mrs. Ellington said. "Have you plans for the holidays, Mrs. Darcy?"

"Mr. Darcy's uncle and aunt, Lord and Lady Matlock, are arriving several days before Christmas for a short stay. My own uncle and aunt will be coming from London next week with their children for a month's visit."

"And your own family?" Lady Walker-Price inquired with another stare.

"Will not be able to join us this year, I am afraid."

"A large family, is it not?"

"I have four sisters."

"No brothers?"

"No, no brothers. More tea?"

Mrs. Courtland ventured her first comment at that point. "I have a brother. He is in the merchant marine. I think having sisters would be lovely."

Elizabeth smiled at her encouragingly. "It is, although there are the inevitable disagreements. My eldest sister, Jane, was recently wed. In fact, we were married in a double ceremony. She married Mr. Darcy's best friend, Mr. Bingley."

"How romantic," Mrs. Courtland murmured.

"And a great financial saving for your father, I presume," Lady Walker-Price sniffed.

You presume far too much, Elizabeth thought as she controlled her urge to utter a sharp reply. "It was a far greater saving for my mother's nerves. We were the first to wed."

Mrs. Ellington laughed. She had a sweet laugh, low and without artifice. "Two weddings to plan at once might overset any woman's nerves," she said.

"I suppose so, if she is given to such things." Lady Walker-Price set her cup down with something like purpose and straightened her spine even more. "I understand yours was a very short courtship, which would give her little time to prepare."

"Short?" Elizabeth set her own cup aside. "I do not have the honor of understanding you, Lady Walker-Price."

"I have it on good authority that you and Mr. Darcy were only acquainted for a matter of several weeks when he…ah…precipitously proposed."

Mrs. Ellington shot the other woman a look that combined shock and disapprobation in equal measure. "Surely, Lady Hazel, that is not…."

For a moment, the similarity to Caroline Bingley's attack at Netherfield held Elizabeth frozen. Then her eyebrow arched, and her chin came up. She said, still calmly, "May I inquire as to the source of your information?"

"My mother, Lady Sybil Braithwaite, is a great friend of Mr. Darcy's aunt Lady Catherine de Bourgh, who is also the mother of his late wife." Her tone implied that Lady Catherine's word was not to be disputed.

"I see. I am aware of who Lady Catherine de Bourgh is. As is often the case with Lady Catherine, she is sadly misinformed. I have known Mr. Darcy for some time. Mr. Bingley's estate borders my father's in Hertfordshire, and Mr. Darcy was a frequent visitor."

"It is quite common for people to meet through mutual friends," Mrs. Ellington put in firmly. "That is how I met my husband. My cousin and his elder brother were friends. We met at a weekend party at his aunt's home."

"Mrs. Ellington is from Nottinghamshire," Lady Walker-Price replied, "not so very far from here. We all expected Mr. Darcy to marry one of the local young ladies he has known for years when he remarried. Hertfordshire seems so very far away."

Suppressing a desire to respond by asking Lady Walker-Price to leave her home, Elizabeth kept her countenance. She was fully aware an angry reaction was exactly what the other woman wanted. She said as pleasantly as she could manage, "If Mr. Darcy did not choose to marry a local young lady, all of whom I am sure are very worthy, then one must assume, having known them for years, he did not wish to marry one of them."

Mrs. Courtland's eyes grew very large. Mrs. Ellington coughed into her handkerchief, but her eyes sparkled above the delicately embroidered edge. For several moments, Lady Walker-Price sat frozen, unable or unwilling to respond. Into the silence, a light step sounded in the hall, and Georgiana entered the room. She halted abruptly, as her eyes flicked over the assembled women. "Oh, Elizabeth, I did not know you were entertaining."

Elizabeth drew a breath and smiled warmly at the girl. "Come in, Georgiana. These ladies were kind enough to call on me, and we have just been having a most interesting conversation."

Georgiana curtsied to the ladies and took a chair next to her new sister. Mrs. Ellington, recovered from her temporary indisposition, took another cup of tea. She admired the service, a dark-green pattern on gold-edged white porcelain. The action reminded Elizabeth again of Jane's propensity to change the subject when a conversation grew tense.

"Royal Worcester, I believe? It is lovely, Mrs. Darcy."

"Rather too old fashioned for my taste." Lady Walker-Price glanced at her cup and set it down. "My mother has a service for fifty of Wedgewood, a pattern called Absalom's Pillar. It is not new, but I like it very much. It is so dignified."

"Oh!" Elizabeth smiled with a twinkle in her eye her husband would have recognized instantly. "I, too, like some old things. Especially those that are truly dignified."

Her slight emphasis on the words "some" and "truly" caused Mrs. Ellington to hastily say, "I am having a small dinner party next Tuesday. If you have nothing planned for that evening, I hope you and Mr. Darcy will attend? I have not sent out the invitations yet."

"I do not believe we have any engagements that day. Thank you, Mrs. Ellington."

Their eyes met in perfect understanding. Elizabeth knew certainly as the discussion moved to general matters in deference, she thought, to Georgiana's presence, that she had made her first friend in Derbyshire. She would have been interested to hear some of what was said in Lady Walker-Price's capacious carriage as she returned the two other ladies to Mrs. Ellington's home.

"I should not connect myself too closely with Mrs. Darcy," she stated repressively to Mrs. Ellington. "It is apparent to me she has an impertinent streak and a tendency to speak slightingly of her betters."

Mrs. Ellington replied briskly, "Oh, nonsense, my dear Lady Hazel. I like Mrs. Darcy, and I saw enough of Lady de Bourgh one afternoon in Lambton to believe the lady is more arrogant than aristocratic."

"Really? How so?" Lady Walker-Price, for all her airs, was never above a bit of gossip.

"I had encountered Nancy Sandhurst at Tarkinson's Millinery, and after shopping for an hour, we decided to have tea and a snack at the Lambton Inn. Lady de Bourgh was on her way from Pemberley, this was not long after Mr. Darcy and Lady Anne were married. Apparently one of her coach horses threw a shoe. While the beast was being seen to, she came into the inn. She marched into the dining room, stared around as if it were some second-class coaching inn, and sat down quite near us. She demanded immediate service, although she could plainly see the maid was serving another table. When the poor girl attended her, Lady de Bourgh began abusing her for being slow and practically shouted for tea."

Mrs. Courtland had one gloved hand to her mouth; she was able to imagine the maid's humiliation perfectly well. She had suffered years of mortification and worse at her husband's hands. Lady Walker-Price sniffed. "Some of those girls are barely competent, but one should not make a spectacle in public."

Ignoring her, Mrs. Ellington went on. "When the tea and cake came, she instantly declared the tea cold and the cake inedible. Nancy and I had just had the same cake, and it was delicious. Lady de Bourgh called for the innkeeper. Mr. Holcomb was not available, and when Mrs. Holcomb arrived, Lady de Bourgh upbraided her for everything from the food to the weather. You know Mrs. Holcomb is the soul of politeness, and she simply stood there and let her guest rant. At last, she brought another pot of tea and some biscuits herself and refused any payment. I think we were all relieved when Lady de Bourgh's footman came to the door and indicated they might proceed. I am afraid I would be inclined to give little credence to anything Lady de Bourgh said," she finished. "Especially considering that Lord and Lady Matlock are staying with the Darcys for Christmas, which tells me *they* approve of the match."

"I like her," Mrs. Courtland almost whispered. "And Mr. Darcy is a very important man. It would not do to offend him."

"Hmm." Lady Walker-Price considered the information with a sniff. "Nonetheless, I shall reserve my judgment for the time being."

Well, Mrs. Ellington thought wryly, *there is a first time for everything.*

When the callers had gone, Elizabeth noted that Georgiana was fiddling with her skirts, an unconscious trait when she was uncertain or disturbed about something. Elizabeth laid a hand on the girl's arm and smiled reassuringly at her. "What is the trouble, Georgie?"

Georgiana shook her bright head. "I am so sorry, Elizabeth. I heard the names of your visitors from the doorway of the music room, and when Mr. Niles announced Mrs. Walker-Price, I went back inside. I'm such a coward! I never know how to act with her or what to say. She always seems to be criticizing things, as if nothing is ever up to her standards." Georgiana looked up with tears in her eyes. "I should not have left you alone to face her, though. William would not be proud of me."

"You will meet other Mrs. Walker-Prices in your lifetime," Elizabeth said kindly. "If you do not want them to intimidate you, you must learn to deal with them. Most take themselves far more seriously than anyone else takes them. They like to feel important, and they do that by making others feel less important. It is not a pleasant character, but if you know who you are, you will not allow their criticisms to hurt your feelings or influence you. Unless they become really offensive, it is better to disagree politely or change the subject."

Georgiana raised her head. "Our aunt has that same china she was speaking of. It is a scene of a *tomb*, for heaven's sake! And there is so much of a design in dark blue, when one is served on it, one can hardly tell where the pattern leaves off and the food begins. She reminds me of Lady Catherine."

Surprised that Georgiana had expressed such a strong opinion on such a mundane subject, after a moment's reflection Elizabeth realized it was a criticism of the woman rather than the china. She could not openly criticize her aunt, and she was too well bred to speak badly of her elders.

Elizabeth said slowly, "Yes, I can see the resemblance. But she is not related to you and has no influence on your life."

"I am glad William was not here." Georgiana looked into Elizabeth's eyes. "I do not believe you have ever seen him really angry. His whole face darkens, and his voice grows soft and so cold. I know him to be a very good man, but it is still frightening."

Intrigued, Elizabeth leaned a little toward the girl. "When have you seen William so angry?"

"Last…last summer. And when Lady Catherine came to visit Pemberley. It was right after William and Lady Anne were married. He was out with Mr. Standish, and she…she came in unannounced and began berating Anne for everything she could think of. The house, the servants, her clothing, her manners. It was terrible! I did not know what to do. She treated Mrs. Reynolds like an untrained maid and called Mr. Niles incompetent. Anne nearly swooned, and I was in tears when William came home. When he saw Lady Catherine, his face changed until I hardly knew him. He asked me to take Anne to her rooms to rest, and then he shut the drawing room door behind us." Georgiana shivered. "You could hear Lady Catherine to the second landing. I never heard William's voice, but half an hour later, Lady Catherine left, and she never returned."

"Did she not come for Lady Anne's funeral? I am sure she would have been allowed to attend if she insisted."

Georgiana shook her head. "William wrote her, but she did not respond."

"I think," Elizabeth said softly, "Lady Catherine is far more destructive than Lady Walker-Price. Now, let us talk of something else. Do you know anything about household accounts?"

"No. Mrs. Reynolds has been doing the accounts, with William's approval."

Elizabeth met her new sister's inquiring gaze. "Would you like to learn? One day you will have a household of your own to manage, and the household accounts will be part of your responsibilities. Mrs. Reynolds is teaching me about the various Pemberley accounts. If you wish to, I will let her show you the simpler ones as well."

Georgiana's bright smile lit her face. "Oh, I would love to learn anything that will help me be a good wife when I do marry."

"Excellent. Then we will meet with her tomorrow after dinner."

Elizabeth waited until she and Darcy went to their rooms that night before discussing the visit with her husband. She found him sitting before the fire in their bedchamber, his long legs stretched out to the fading blaze, one arm along the back of the sofa. She ran her hand across his shoulders and came around to face him. He reached up for her and drew her down beside him. He sat straighter when Elizabeth remained upright rather than snuggling against him, as was her habit. Her serious expression warned him something was not right, and he was instantly focused on her. "What is it, love? What has happened?"

Elizabeth drew a breath and said, "I had my first visitors this afternoon. Mrs. Ellington, Mrs. Courtland, and Lady Walker-Price."

At the last name, Darcy frowned slightly. "Was it a pleasant visit?"

"Not entirely. Mrs. Courtland seems a timid soul, easily influenced. I like Mrs. Ellington very much. Lady Walker-Price, however, is a different matter. I am perfectly well enough versed in country society to deal with the Lady Walker-Prices, and Mrs. Reynolds put me on my guard when Mr. Niles brought their cards up by indicating the lady sees herself as a social arbiter. Apparently she sees herself as a moral one as well."

Darcy's dark eyes held Elizabeth's gaze intently. "Has she insulted you?"

"Not exactly. It appears her mother is a friend of Lady Catherine. Your aunt is apparently putting out the old story that we had barely been introduced when you suddenly proposed. She is spreading the idea that our marriage was a hastily patched-up affair, with the usual implication. I gave Lady Walker-Price to understand the truth without going into detail, which is none of her business. But I thought you should know. If Lady Catherine is putting out these stories among her friends in London, there is a chance someone else in the neighborhood may hear of it. I did not want you to be blindsided if it was mentioned."

Elizabeth was treated to a modified version of the Darcy glower. "No one who values his well-being would dare suggest such a thing to me. As for Lady Walker-Price, her husband is a fool who lets his wife behave however she pleases because it is easier than attempting to control her, but he is not invulnerable to pressure. I will not have you maligned by that woman or anyone else!"

"I am sure no one who knows you would believe you so naïve as to be drawn in by a scheming country fortune hunter."

It was intended as a jest, but Darcy's reaction was to grip Elizabeth's shoulders and say in a hard voice, "This is your home. These will be your neighbors, our friends. You know enough of gossip to understand how damaging it can be in a small community. I will not have you subjected to speculation and whispers of impropriety or worse. It is intolerable!"

Startled, Elizabeth repressed her first instinct to pull away and tell her husband it was not a matter of such overwhelming importance, when the realization possessed her that it was, indeed, important, to Darcy as much as to herself. Not only did he have a position of standing in the community, but he was also her husband. He had not only a right but also a duty to protect her, physically and emotionally. And she did understand the power of gossip to ruin the reputation of a woman; indeed, her whole family. There was Georgiana to think of as well. The firelight washed them, bringing out the cleanly molded bones of his face and reddening his dark curls. Elizabeth raised a hand and gently stroked his cheek. "If you act directly to silence Lady Walker-Price, may it not be taken as a sign that what she says has a basis in truth?"

Darcy closed his eyes briefly. His hands stroked down her arms, a sign he was no longer gripped by his first outrage. "What am I to do, then? This cannot continue, Elizabeth."

"Of course it cannot. However, I imagine Lady Walker-Price's reputation for malicious gossip must be well known in the area. Mrs. Courtland was appalled, and Mrs. Ellington started to reprove Lady Walker-Price, who continued as if she did not exist, a very vexing and rude behavior. Surely, much of what she relates is taken with at least a grain of salt?"

Darcy had grown calmer, although anger still simmered beneath the surface. "She has the reputation of jumping to conclusions, many, if not most, erroneous. But her title carries enough weight to make her believed by those to whom such things matter."

"I doubt they are particular friends of yours." Elizabeth caught his hands, which immediately enclosed her own. "Mrs. Ellington has invited us to a dinner party next Tuesday evening. I apologize for not consulting you before I accepted, but I thought it might be a way for me to meet some of our neighbors and for them to meet me. She indicated that you knew her husband well. It seemed an excellent place to begin socializing with people you know."

He nodded. "I have known Theo Ellington since university. He is a decent man, and his wife is a fine woman. She is very much involved in charity work with a local orphanage, and other assistance to the poor. Our closest neighbors will certainly be there. It is a good idea to go. Once they have met you, no one will believe anything but good of you. And you are in charge of our social engagements. You do not need to consult me, unless you have some question or concern about an event."

"Really?" Elizabeth smiled teasingly in the way he loved. "You will not mind going to a ball a month and any other party I choose?"

"So long as you are happy, my beloved, I will be happy. The Ellington dinner party will do for a start."

"I shall have to be on my best behavior, then."

Darcy leaned toward her and whispered, "So long as you are not on your best behavior tonight."

Giggling, Elizabeth wrapped her arms around his neck and kissed him. His arms enfolded her. Darcy rose, picked her up, and carried her to bed. She did not know, and Darcy did not tell her, that he had resolved to speak to Lord Matlock at Christmas about Lady Catherine's continued attempts to blacken Elizabeth's name and disrupt their lives. Darcy was determined that something would be done to stop her, whether by concerted effort or by his actions alone.

Chapter 13

*T*hat same night, another married couple sat talking in the mistress's bed-chamber of Fiddler's Croft, the Ellingtons' home. Lily Ellington plaited her hair while her husband watched lazily from a chair by the fire. He never ceased to wonder at his wife's golden beauty or his luck at securing her hand in marriage. She was not only stunning, but she was also an intelligent partner, something few men of his acquaintance could say of their wives. She finished and rose, smiling at him. He held out his hand, and Lily came to take it, rubbing her fingers over its firm surface.

"I called on Mrs. Darcy today," she said as she sat in the companion chair, still holding her husband's hand. "I was going with Millie Courtland when we were appropriated by Lady Hazel Walker-Price, but I decided to go anyway."

"What is she like, the new Mrs. Darcy?"

His dark, dry voice thrilled her as it always did, although Lily knew he was less interested in her reply than in studying her face. "Lovely. Dark hair and eyes, small. She must not stand much above Mr. Darcy's shoulder. Not only that, she is intelligent witty, and a countrywoman like myself. I like her. And she is the first person I have ever known to leave Lady Hazel with not a word to say for at least one whole minute."

"My God, a paragon!"

Lily smiled mischievously. "It was all I could do not to laugh out loud at Lady W-P's face. She was being so rude, I am afraid if it had been me, I would have asked her to leave. But Mrs. Darcy turned her innuendo back on her very neatly. She was insinuating Mrs. Darcy had somehow trapped Mr. Darcy into marrying her, on the basis of her mother's old friend Lady Catherine de Bourgh telling some such tale."

"That one. Bah! She did not even bother to come here for her own daughter's funeral." Theodore Ellington stared at the fire for a moment. "Lady W-P is getting entirely out of hand. It's a wonder the woman's spit does not poison her. I cannot think Darcy will take kindly to his wife being defamed if he comes to hear of it. We should do something to bring Mrs. Darcy into local society."

"I have already done so. I personally invited them to our dinner party next week. I sent a formal invitation this afternoon as I meant to do anyway, but I thought asking her while I was there sent a clearer message."

"A good thought. Darcy is one of my oldest friends. We will do everything we can for his wife."

Ellington raised Lily's hand to his lips. He smiled at her softly, and then turned her hand over to place a lingering kiss on the palm. Lily reached out and ran her fingers into his hair where it curled at the nape, a trait he disliked and she loved. In the firelight, his profile reminded her of the face on an ancient coin she had seen once, imperious and serene. He raised his head as if aware of her scrutiny.

"You are a paragon yourself, my love."

Lily rose, her eyes darkening with passion. "Come to bed, Theo, and prove your words to me."

The night of the dinner party at Fiddler's Croft was clear and cold. There had been a light snow that morning, but by afternoon, a chill set in to freeze the countryside into glittering ice fields. The Darcy coach deposited Darcy and Elizabeth under the portecochere, where a footman stood to hold the door for guests. Inside, a fireplace carved with sheaves of wheat and wide ribbon swags centered by a medallion of fruit and flowers warmed the large hall. Another footman took their outerwear, Darcy's greatcoat and Elizabeth's russet pelisse. Theodore and Lily Ellington waited on the first landing to welcome them. Theo shook hands cordially with Darcy and bowed to Elizabeth as they were introduced. She wore a deep-green velvet dinner gown in the new fashion; a wide, black satin ribbon under the bodice trailed nearly to the hem. When Elizabeth entered her rooms earlier to dress, she found a box covered in blue velvet on her dressing table. Inside was a necklace of gold lace set with pearls and square-cut emeralds, and a pair of matching earrings. They sparkled in the lamplight as Elizabeth put out a tentative finger to touch them.

"Mr. Darcy asked me what you were wearing tonight, madam, and brought these for you. Are they not beautiful?"

"They take my breath," Elizabeth murmured with tears in her eyes. "They look very old."

"They belonged to his great-grandmother, he said."

Lily noticed them immediately. "You necklace is beautiful. Is it Spanish?"

On the way to the dinner, Darcy had answered Elizabeth's questions about the necklace. Now she responded. "Italian. The set dates from the Renaissance. Mr. Darcy's great-grandfather brought them back from his grand tour and gave them to his fiancée, Mr. Darcy's great-grandmother."

"Thus blending history, culture, and romance," Theodore said with a smile. "One can hardly do better."

Other guests were arriving, and the Darcys passed on to the drawing room. As they approached the doorway, Lady Walker-Price's voice could be heard declaiming, although the words were indistinct. Another voice answered her, but the arrival of Darcy and Elizabeth engendered a sudden quiet among those gathered in the large room. Then conversation picked up too quickly, creating the impression of voices babbling over one another. Darcy held his temper with an effort. Elizabeth felt the muscles of his arm tighten under her hand, and pressed her arm briefly against his side. Lady Walker-Price glanced at them and pointedly took her glass of sherry to a chair at the far side of the room. Her husband, a stout, rubicund fellow with the face of a placid sheep, trailed after her.

Darcy let his gaze move around the room. At once, a woman detached herself from a small group and came across to them. "Mr. Darcy, I am very happy to see you here."

"Mrs. Arbuthnot." Darcy bowed. "May I present my wife, Mrs. Elizabeth Darcy? Elizabeth, this is Mrs. Arbuthnot, the wife of the vicar of Lambton church."

The ladies exchanged curtsies and greetings. Mrs. Arbuthnot was gray, middle-aged, angular, and looked as if she would be more at home in a country manor than a vicarage. It was her voice, Elizabeth realized, they had heard answering Lady Walker-Price. A footman brought a tray of drinks, and Elizabeth accepted a glass of sherry. Darcy declined a drink; Elizabeth realized he was still angry, although his face revealed nothing but his usual reserve.

"Come and meet some of your neighbors." Mrs. Arbuthnot drew Elizabeth along with her. "I am sure Mr. Darcy will want to renew acquaintance with his fellows. Now, I believe you have not met Mrs. Weyland?"

The two ladies exchanged pleasantries, while Mrs. Arbuthnot caught the attention of another lady, who came forward with a smile. Elizabeth was introduced to Ruth Legere, wife of a landowner whose estate was closer to the border with Nottinghamshire. A plump, plain woman, Mrs. Legere had a bright smile and a sweet voice. Other arriving guests joined them. All were curious to meet the new Mrs. Darcy, and then stayed as they apprehended she was a lively conversationalist who engaged in give-and-take rather than try to dominate the circle. By the time Theodore and Lily Ellington were ready to take their guests in to dinner, Elizabeth was the center of a laughing group of ladies and several gentlemen. Theodore looked at his wife and shook his head slightly in admiration. She only gave him a serene smile and approached Darcy, who offered her his arm.

Lily had seated Elizabeth on her husband's right, with Mrs. Arbuthnot on his left. Darcy sat at Lily's right. Clive Kingman was seated across from him. The two men had known each other for years, and they fell easily into conversation.

After several minutes, Kingman lowered his soup spoon and said, "I understand Mrs. Darcy is from Hertfordshire."

"Yes," Darcy replied, sure enough of Kingman to expect nothing offensive from the man.

"I had no idea there were such ladies in the south. I must make a trip there soon. Perhaps I may have the same luck finding a wife."

"I wish you well," Darcy replied, "but I am afraid Mrs. Darcy is unique."

"Perhaps you should look closer to home, Clive," Lily said archly. "I am sure Lady Walker-Price would be most happy to assist you."

Kingman grimaced, and they all laughed. Darcy glanced down the table. Elizabeth was engaged in charming Theo Ellington, as well as Mrs. Arbuthnot and Viscount Frederick Truitt-Wayne, who sat on her right. Darcy knew by the tilt of her dark head that she was listening intently to something the viscount was relating. The story ended suddenly in a burst of mirth and Elizabeth's silvery laugh came to his ears. Darcy suddenly felt enormous pride in his wife, not for the first time. She was indeed unique.

Mrs. Arbuthnot had drawn the short straw of Mr. Walker-Price as a dinner companion. Mr. Walker-Price's idea of conversation was limited to the weather, the crops, his disgust with the insufficient work ethic of his tenants, and the outrageous cost of everything from seed to satin. By the fourth course, his voice was growing a bit slurred, and when the dessert course was cleared, he was well on his way to inebriation. Mrs. Arbuthnot knew his propensities well and kept her countenance in spite of the landowner's constant complaints. The lady to his other side was, unfortunately, left to bear the burden of his bleating.

The meal progressed amiably until the middle of the third course. Near the center of the table, Lady Walker-Price was holding forth to an older woman of distinguished appearance on the lack of propriety of the younger generation. After a few minutes of this monologue, the lady stared down her aristocratic nose at Lady Walker-Price with an expression of distaste. "It is all very well, Hazel," she said clearly with the familiarity of long acquaintance, "to belabor the probity of young people today, but you should remember that we were no angels at that age."

"I am sure I do not know what you mean," Lady Walker-Price returned sharply. "I have always observed the proprieties."

"Really?" The other woman raised a silver eyebrow. "I remember an incident at Vauxhall Gardens one night involving Freddie Truitt-Wayne and that scamp Musgrave."

Lady Walker-Price's face lost color rapidly. "Really, Eleanor," she hissed. "That was a misunderstanding, nothing more."

"Oh? I seem to recall the matter differently."

Lady Eleanor Truitt-Wayne looked down the table at her husband, who made her a courtly little bow of his head. Turning to the gentleman next to her, she asked after his mother, effectively closing the conversation with Lady Walker-Price and the subject in general.

Darcy found Lily Ellington observing the exchange with a smile of satisfaction. "That," she murmured, picking up her fork, "will be that."

She was almost correct. When the ladies withdrew to the drawing room, Mrs. Arbuthnot approached her as she was pouring out tea. "I am sorry Josiah could not attend tonight, but old Mr. Simpson is very bad and sent for him." Noting Mrs. Walker-Price nearby, she continued, "Josiah has been troubled in his about some of the rumors circulating in the community of late regarding Mr. Simpson's housekeeper and others. I believe he plans to deliver a sermon on the text, 'Let him among you who is without sin cast the first stone.' Josiah is rather strong on loving thy neighbor."

"That will be most instructive," Lily replied. "Tea or coffee?"

Elizabeth accepted a cup of tea. As she sipped it, she contemplated the other ladies in the room. "Mrs. Courtland is not here tonight," she said quietly to Lily.

"No." Lily's hand halted holding the teapot before she set it down on the tray. "Mrs. Courtland is not allowed to attend any gathering except church and the ladies' sewing circle at the vicarage. Her husband…is not social, and he does not allow her to be."

Elizabeth met her new friend's gaze, seeing anger beneath the calm demeanor. "She has no family nearby?" she asked obliquely.

"Only her brother, and he is at sea most of the time. Her parents are deceased. Mr. Courtland has no family. He was an only child."

Another lady came up for tea, and Lily turned away. Elizabeth took her tea to where Mrs. Arbuthnot was standing with Mrs. Legere. As she listened to their conversation, she understood what Lily Ellington had not said. The subject would not be discussed in public, or in private except among intimate friends. Often not even then. Mrs. Courtland was maltreated by her husband. It might encompass no more than keeping her isolated from other people, or it might mean she was physically abused. Whatever the case, Elizabeth inwardly resolved to do anything she was able to offer aid to Millie Courtland.

When their guests had gone, Theo and Lily retired to their chambers to prepare for bed. Theo stepped into his wife's dressing room as her maid was leaving. She sat at her dressing table, yawning, her hair still hanging loosely around her shoulders.

"I just wanted to say good night, my love. It was a very good dinner party. Do you not think so?"

"You seemed to be enjoying it particularly," she replied with a smile.

"Mrs. Darcy is quite remarkable. She is more educated than I would expect for a country lady, and witty into the bargain. I think Darcy has done extremely well for himself."

Theo was aware her response was distracted. She finished her night plait and said, "How did Mrs. Arbuthnot respond to her?"

"By the fish course, they were talking like old friends. Mrs. Darcy asked about charity efforts for Christmas, and you know Clothilde Arbuthnot's passion for charity. It was genuine, too. There's no artifice in the lady."

Lily nodded. She rose slowly and came to her husband, not looking at him. Theo put his arms loosely around her waist and pressed his lips to her forehead. "What is troubling you, my love?"

For a moment, she did not respond. When she spoke, her voice had an edge that caused him growing apprehension. "Dr. Morrow told me Amalia Hayworth has had a baby girl. Both are well. Mrs. Truesdale had her second child two months ago. Both of them were married after we were."

His arms tightened; he knew all too well what was coming. "We have a bright, healthy boy. I am perfectly satisfied with Forrest and you."

"Theo." Lily raised a face streaked with tears. "I want another child! I recovered fully after Forrest was born. Dr. Morrow said there was no reason I could not have another baby. Why do I not increase? By the time she was my age, my cousin Claire had three children."

"Need I remind you that you are not your cousin?"

His attempt to lighten the situation failed. Lily shook her head sharply. "Every Sunday I pray for a baby, and every month my courses come. Why am I denied this one thing I want so badly?"

Theo looked into his wife's beautiful face. The shadow of desperation in her eyes disturbed him deeply. "Lily, there is no answer to that. If God grants us another child, it will come in its own time. We make the effort. That is all we can do."

Slowly she lowered her head and pressed her cheek to his chest, she felt the strong beat of his heart against her skin. Theo held her for some time, gently stroking her back, his chin rested on her hair. At last he said, "It has been a tiring day for you, my dearest wife. You need to rest."

Lily drew back reluctantly. She was suddenly completely weary, drained of emotion. "Yes."

Theo smoothed wisps of hair from her temple and kissed her very gently. "Good night, my darling. Sleep well."

She nodded. When he returned to his own chambers, she removed her dressing gown, blew out the candle lamp, and got into bed. Lily knew her husband spoke out of love for her; he remembered all too well what she had endured at the birth of their son. She had suffered from severe morning sickness for nearly the first four months. When that abated, she was prey to spells of dizziness, and twice fainted, once near the top of the main staircase. After weeks of continued back pain and badly swollen feet, she had gone into labor for all of one night and most of the next day. When the baby finally emerged, Lily was so weak from pain, exertion, and loss of blood that Dr. Morrow despaired of her life. She lived despite it all, and she recovered. Her only comfort after the ordeal was Dr. Morrow's statement that first births were often the most difficult, and that she was not physically damaged and could bear another child.

Lily turned restlessly in the lavender-scented sheets. She adored their son, but how was she to explain to Theo her need for another child? He had a brother and three sisters. How was he ever to really understand what it was like to be raised as the only child in a family? As a child, Lily had had a nurse, governesses, tutors, cousins who visited occasionally, and a number of friends, but there had been no one to share the days with. No one to confide in, laugh with, no one to ease the small griefs of life. She did not want Forrest to grow up like that, loved but always alone.

She must, she *would* have another child. Determination filled her. She told the obscura of the canopy overhead fiercely, "Whatever I have to do, I will do it to have another child!"

In spite of her exhaustion, gray light already pressed against the draped windows when at last sleep came.

Chapter 14

*L*ord and Lady Matlock arrived two days before Christmas to find Pemberley decorated from front hall to kitchen and drawing room to servants' quarters. Holly and pine boughs, ribbons, candles in small metal holders, and mistletoe adorned the home. Strings of berries, paper lace, gingerbread men, and orange pomanders hung from the massive tree situated in a corner of the large drawing room, in the new German fashion. Red velvet draped its base liberally covered with wrapped gifts. Footmen added the presents the Matlocks brought. They were greeted by a smiling Darcy, a happy Elizabeth, and an unusually enthusiastic Georgiana. Dinner that evening was festive in keeping with the season; Mrs. Ames prepared several brace of partridge along with roast beef and mutton chops, any number of side dishes, and pies, tarts, trifle, and fruitcake for the dessert course.

Normally, there being only two gentlemen, the sexes would not have separated after dinner, but Darcy wanted to speak to his uncle privately, so the gentlemen adjourned to the study, while the ladies went on to the drawing room. A small fire had been started in the study fireplace and the lamps turned low, as no use of the room had been anticipated. The dim corners enclosed them in the quiet seclusion of that masculine retreat; the atmosphere matched Darcy's mood. He poured two brandies and sat with Lord Henry before the hearth. They drank in silence for several minutes before the earl turned his gaze on his nephew. "Well, my boy, what is the trouble? Everything here is the best I have seen it since your dear mother was alive."

"It is not Pemberley, Uncle." Darcy drew his thoughts together, took a deep breath, and said, "It is Lady Catherine."

Lord Henry took another sip of his brandy. "What has she done now?"

Darcy's face darkened in a way Lord Henry knew all too well; he had seen it on the late George Darcy's face before. "Lady Catherine has apparently been using her friends in London to spread the story that Elizabeth coerced me into marrying her by seducing me. The mother of one of the local gossips is a friend of Lady Catherine. The woman paid a courtesy call with two other local ladies, Theodore Ellington's wife and a Mrs. Courtland. At the first opportunity, she referred to the supposed haste of our marriage, making the usual implication."

"And? Did Elizabeth defend herself?"

"She is an old head on young shoulders. Elizabeth related several facts and changed the subject. Mrs. Ellington was so disturbed by the woman's rudeness she immediately invited us to a dinner party she was hosting the following week. She and Elizabeth have become quite friendly. However, that does not excuse Lady Catherine's actions. The tale may well turn up somewhere else. Uncle, I will not have this persecution go on. Something must be done, and I freely admit to you I have no idea of what will stop her -- short of forcibly locking her away somewhere."

"Catherine likes her own way. She can be extremely unpleasant when she does not achieve it, but this is an outrage." Lord Henry finished his brandy and set the glass aside. The glow of the lamps restored to his silver hair the pale gold sheen of his youth. He said slowly, "I am not adverse to that solution, but it would probably only cause more talk. I cannot think why she wants Rosings in any event. Even when Anne was there, the two of them rattled around in that huge house like two beans in a barrel. The dower house is much more manageable. With a small staff, she could be quite comfortable there."

Slowly Darcy said, "I do not think it is the house she wants."

"What then?"

"The contents." Darcy put his glass down on the small table between the chairs. He closed his eyes briefly before continuing. "I believe she wants anything that can be sold off easily."

His uncle leaned forward to study Darcy's face. "Catherine has more than enough income to live comfortably from the trust de Bourgh left her. She has a life interest in the dower house, and I understand Anne wanted her to have access to the house in town as well. Why should she need more money?"

"For a man."

Stunned, Lord Henry stared openmouthed for several heartbeats before reiterating, "A man? What man?"

"Her former steward, Mr. Rhymes. When I took over control of the estate, I had reason to believe he was taking money from the estate profits beyond his salary, but rather than make an issue of it and possibly harm Anne, I dismissed him and put my own man in. I have since learned he stays at the London house and spends a good deal of time at Rosings, and that certain items of moderate value are no longer in the inventory. That does not include any jewelry or other personal belongings of Lady Catherine."

Lord Henry shook his head again. "I can scarcely believe it. How old is this fellow?"

"Early forties, I should guess. He gambles. I believe Lady Catherine is subsidizing his gaming. With full access to Rosings, she would be able to sell off anything she wished. She knows full well she would never be brought to book for it."

"Can we go after the man for theft?"

"It would require proof, and I have none. She would, no doubt, swear it was all her doing, and indeed, if he is clever enough, that would be the truth."

The room grew silent. Lord Henry knew of a solution, but he also knew Darcy's agreement was unlikely. He said after a long silence, "How much are the Rosings chattels worth?"

"Furniture, fixtures, housewares, china, silver, paintings, objets d'art—approximately twenty thousand pounds. Many of the furnishings in the house are outdated or in poor repair."

Still cautious, Lord Henry said slowly, "I cannot imagine you have any intention of occupying the property?"

"No. I have been considering leasing or even selling it. The money could be set aside for a second son or for some other purpose, perhaps to enlarge a dowry if necessary. I have no interest in managing two estates. Pemberley already takes up enough of my time, and now, with Elizabeth here and the potential for a family, I do not want to spend my waking hours constantly immersed in estate business."

"I can understand that." His uncle nodded, hiding a smile. "Well, I can only say this. If you were to sell whatever of the contents of Rosings you have no wish to keep or otherwise dispose of, the money could be put into the de Bourgh trust. That would about double Catherine's income, and it would only be available to her in quarterly interest payments. I know." He raised a restraining hand at Darcy's look. "I am not fond of the idea of rewarding her actions in any way, but if she understands it is the best she can hope for and that, if this business continues, I will restrict her funds to a pittance -- which as trustee, I can do if I choose -- she will either have to agree or lose any chance of continuing this madness she has entered into."

For a time the two men sat in silence. Lord Henry watched emotions flicker in his nephew's dark eyes, unable to read exactly the course of Darcy's thoughts. At last, the younger man met his uncle's gaze.

"I offered her a similar solution before our marriage. One-third of the profits from the estate paid quarterly, as long as no other items belonging to the estate were removed and she agreed to live in the dower house. She never responded, which I took as a rejection. Let me talk the matter over with Elizabeth, as she is deeply involved in all of this. I will give you an answer before you leave."

The earl nodded. "If you decide to follow this course, we will speak to Catherine together. I want her to understand that, one way or another, I will not tolerate her actions. She knows me well enough to know I will follow through on any decision I take. Now," Lord Henry rose, "shall we join the ladies?"

Lady Matlock had sent a glance after her husband as he and Darcy left the dining room and entered the study. She knew her nephew well enough to see that he had been making an effort to focus on the dinner conversation. This indicated to her there was some matter of weight occupying his mind. She was not in the habit of interfering in other people's affairs, but it troubled her. Whenever he looked at his wife, his face softened in a way that told her he was very much in love and very happy. In any case, he would hardly discuss his personal life with his uncle. Well, Lady Madeleine thought with a sigh, whatever it is, Henry will tell me about it when we retire for the night.

When they were seated and Elizabeth had rung for tea and coffee, Lady Madeleine said, "It is a shame Mr. and Mrs. Gardiner were unable to arrive when they planned, but at least they will reach you in time for Christmas."

"Yes, happily. My uncle tries to keep his business interests and his family separated, but occasionally the one will intrude on the other."

Elizabeth knew there was no need to explain that the holidays were one of the busiest times of year for Gardiner Imports. Modistes and mantua-makers wanted his superior fabrics for their clients' gowns and pelisses. Any trouble at a warehouse at this time of year could not only significantly reduce profits but also pose the threat of damage to Mr. Gardiner's reputation. Luckily the problem had not been a fire; warehouse fires were disastrous; they often forced the owner out of business.

"I was sorry Colonel Fitzwilliam could not accompany you," Elizabeth said as she poured out tea. "I know William was looking forward to seeing him."

"We had expected him at Matlock several days ago, but some last-minute business at the War Office kept him in town. He will try to join us later."

As they drank tea and listened to Georgiana's happy chatter, Elizabeth was struck by how natural her actions felt. Her worries that she would be inadequate to her duties as mistress of Pemberley faded day by day. There was a great deal to learn, and Elizabeth knew it would be months before she was truly competent to take over all the aspects of her responsibilities. And yet she no longer feared that when the time came, she would fail either herself or Darcy. His belief in her was part of her confidence; more important was her belief in herself.

"You seem happy, my dear," Lady Madeleine said quietly. "And I have never seen my nephew look more content."

Elizabeth colored. "I am happy here. I know it can be difficult for a second wife to live up to her predecessor, but I believe Lady Anne would not resent my presence."

Glancing at Georgiana, Lady Madeleine said, "It was an...unusual sort of marriage. Both of them knew from the beginning that her time was short. Darcy was very protective of her, and he was fond of her, but in the end, she was as much his ward as his wife. I am very glad my nephew has found true happiness with you, my dear. He has had very little in his life for some time." Sipping her tea, she went on. "Have you met many of your neighbors yet?"

The conversation went on to the Ellingtons' dinner party and Elizabeth's involvement in Mrs. Arbuthnot's charitable efforts. Half an hour passed before Darcy and Lord Henry joined them. After a few minutes, they adjourned to the music room, where Georgiana played Christmas carols and sang a duet they had been practicing with Elizabeth. The Matlocks retired early, both fatigued from their trip. Georgiana followed them a short time later. Darcy and Elizabeth went upstairs together, but with her acute awareness of her husband, Elizabeth knew his conversation with his uncle had not been entirely satisfactory.

Darcy hesitated outside the door of Elizabeth's chambers. She laid a hand on his arm, studying his expression. "What is it, William? Can you tell me?"

He was silent for a moment and then said, "I would prefer to settle things in my mind before we talk. Tomorrow...."

"If you prefer."

He caught the small echo of pique in her tone, and for a second, his old habit of keeping everything to himself rose.

Before Darcy said something he would regret, he looked into her beloved face and sighed. "Forgive me. It is just that my uncle has proposed a compromise that goes against a basic tenet of mine -- to never reward bad behavior. Why do we not prepare for bed, and then we can discuss this?"

Elizabeth smiled. "As long as we do discuss it."

"I imagine Darcy did not care for your suggestion."

Lady Madeleine sat back on the chaise in her bedroom and pulled her feet up under the hem of her dressing gown. Her husband sat stiffly in a nearby chair, both hands on his knees in a posture of unrest.

"I did not expect him to. Damn it, Maddy, what am I to do? I could commit Catherine to a private facility, but she is not really out of her senses. She is angry and wants her own way, and she will go to any lengths to achieve it. She knows full well that she can strike at Darcy much more effectively by striking at Elizabeth. And all because of this…this Rhymes fellow! At her age!"

Madeleine tried not to smile. "If it were a man ensnared by a younger woman, would you be so surprised?"

Lord Henry looked at his wife's still-attractive countenance and shook his head. "No, my dear, I suppose not. But that does not solve the problem. Sending Catherine away would be bound to cause talk eventually, and if it were discovered where she was and why, you know what sort of scandal it would engender. Giving her sufficient resources to fund the villain will take her mind off Rosings and stop her campaign against Elizabeth."

"What about paying off Mr. Rhymes?"

The earl shook his head. "That sort always wants more. He would be back in six months with new demands, and the threat of scandal if he was not paid. Eventually he will tire of the game and move on. Let Catherine deal with his ultimate defection."

When the silence stretched out for long moments, Madeleine said, "Was anything decided?"

"He wants to talk it over with Elizabeth."

This time, his wife did smile. "Ah, Darcy is domesticating nicely."

"You make him sound like that stray cat the cook took in as a ratter," he growled.

"And a fine ratter he is." Lady Matlock lowered her feet to the floor and stood gracefully. "Do not worry, my dear. Darcy is nothing if not rational. He will see there is no other viable choice."

"I damn well hope so."

The earl sat quietly for a time contemplating his wife's dear face. He knew her features better than his own; the small laughter lines at the corners of her eyes and mouth, the curve of her lips, and her winged eyebrows. Her dark hair had hardly grayed, just a few strands here and there like silver filigree. His lover, his wife, the mother of his children, his partner; kind, intelligent, tolerant and steadfast. The lodestone of his life, always keeping him on course. Perhaps that was why he understood what Darcy felt for Elizabeth. He, too, had rejected the brittle beauties of the *ton* to marry a woman of impeccable lineage but with no social ambitions or pretentions.

Lord Henry also stood, leaned and kissed his wife's forehead. "Good night, Maddy."

"Good night, my love."

The door to the adjacent room closed behind her husband, and Lady Matlock slowly removed her dressing gown, blew out the candle lamp beside the bed, lay down, pulling the covers up. She did not know Elizabeth Darcy well yet, but she hoped a solution would be reached soon, for all their sakes. If Elizabeth refused to consider what was, in effect, paying Lady Catherine blackmail to stop her persecution, she doubted if Darcy would agree to the plan. Sighing, she closed her eyes and tried to sleep.

In the master bedchamber, Darcy and Elizabeth sat facing one another on the sofa before the fire. Elizabeth knew her husband was deeply troubled; she could tell his interview with Lord Henry must not have gone as well as she had hoped. She could scarcely believe the earl had refused to do anything about Lady Catherine, but whatever the outcome, the problem had to be faced and a solution of some kind found. Not only for her own benefit but for Darcy and their family.

Elizabeth said softly, "Can you tell me what has occurred?"

Darcy raised his head with a sudden gesture that reminded Elizabeth of an angry horse. "I suppose I should not have expected anything to come of it, but I hoped my uncle might have a useful suggestion."

"And he did not?"

"Oh, it was useful, I suppose, and practical after a fashion, but it goes sorely against the grain."

The bitterness in his voice wrung her heart. Elizabeth said, "What did he propose? He does not want you to give her Rosings?"

"No. He wants me to sell off whatever of the inventory I do not wish to otherwise dispose of and put the money into her trust, thereby giving her enough income to continue subsidizing Mr. Rhymes."

Carefully, Elizabeth said, "And you feel Lord Henry is asking you to give in to her demands in that way, rather than forcing her to stop her actions."

"Blackmail." Darcy bit the word off as if it burned his mouth.

"Are there any alternatives?"

He ran both hands through his hair. At last Elizabeth reached out and stroked his cheek with her fingers, knowing he would accept the gesture. He caught her hand and held it against his lips, not speaking. Elizabeth understood how a man of such unbreakable honor and principle would be racked by self-disgust at being forced to accept the earl's solution. Her practical nature was more sanguine, and yet she also felt the shame of bowing to Lady Catherine's will.

"Can you not work on the man, this Mr. Rhymes?"

"Pay him off? He would only return when the money ran out and demand more. I dealt with another like him for most of my life. Men like Rhymes are never satisfied." He drew a breath. "I suppose I should not balk at the idea. I offered her something of the sort myself before I left London."

Elizabeth moved closer to Darcy, her eyes meeting his. "Are the chattels worth a great deal?"

"Not enough to represent a major loss. I have no doubt some of the more valuable pieces are already gone. By the time the bulk of the contents were sold, it might amount to perhaps twenty thousand pounds. You know it is not the money, Elizabeth."

"Yes, I know. You have just given me the reason. It is being forced to make concessions that violate your strongest beliefs because of a man who reminds you of Mr. Wickham."

Darcy looked at her for the first time, his eyes very dark. Elizabeth was afraid she had said too much, but at last he drew her into his arms and held her tightly. They sat that way while the fire slipped into pulsing coals. His voice almost startled her when he finally spoke, and she raised her head to look up at him.

"I will speak to my uncle in the morning. There will be strictures on the funds. They will be paid out as part of the regular interest, not in a lump sum. She will have to move to the dower house, or the London house if she prefers. And I will not agree unless she retracts everything she has said about you."

Elizabeth laid her head against his shoulder, her body pressed into his. "I know this situation is not of my making, but I still feel guilt I have been used to hurt you."

"No, my love. The only guilt in the matter is Lady Catherine's. Her impropriety created the situation, and her malevolence fueled it. In the end, she is the one who will suffer for it." Darcy rose and drew Elizabeth to her feet. "Come, beloved, it has been a long day. Let us go to bed."

Before their holiday guests arrived, Elizabeth and Georgiana delivered the Christmas baskets to the Pemberley tenants. She had consulted with Mrs. Reynolds before the baskets were made up to find out what each family could best use, besides the generous amounts of food given. Clothing predominated, especially children's clothing and baby things, including small blankets. Elizabeth also insisted that toys for the children be included. When everything was prepared, she and Georgiana, accompanied by a footman, were driven to the various tenant cottages to deliver the gifts.

Elizabeth's research allowed her to greet each family as if she already knew them, and the tenants took from their first exposure to the new mistress of Pemberley the impression of a warm, kind lady who cared deeply for their welfare. Watching her new sister, Georgiana began to understand how important it was for the mistress of an estate to know her dependents. Her respect and admiration for Elizabeth grew with every visit, and when they returned to Pemberley House, she could hardly wait to tell her brother of their day.

Elizabeth also wished to speak to Darcy but not about the tenants. When they had finished dinner and Georgiana went to the music room to practice, she drew him into the morning room. Darcy immediately sensed that she was troubled and led her to sit on a sofa near the fireplace where they could speak quietly.

"Was there a problem today, dearest?"

Elizabeth shook her head but still remained silent. Darcy took her hands and waited. At last Elizabeth smiled ruefully and said, "You know my opinion of gossip, but something did occur today that has me troubled."

"Will you share it with me?"

"I share everything with you, my love." She drew a breath. "Our last basket was for the Lennarts. They live closest to Lambton, and Georgiana wanted to buy something in town after we left their cottage, so we drove into the village. As we were coming back along the branch road, I saw Lily Ellington coming out of a small dwelling at the edge of the woods. She was alone, and there was something…furtive about her behavior. It troubled me, but she had gone out of sight toward Lambton before I was able to decide if I should approach her."

Darcy frowned. "I believe the cottage you speak of belongs to an old woman whose real name is unknown. She goes by Hephzibah and is considered a hedge witch who dispenses remedies to the locals. I know no harm of her. Her potions are most likely old folk medicines. She also sells dried herbs. Our cook buys from her on occasion."

"But if Mrs. Ellington is ill, why would she not go to Dr. Morrow?"

Darcy shrugged. "Some women prefer to consult Hephzibah rather than the doctor for certain maladies."

Elizabeth closed her eyes briefly and nodded. "Yes, I see. Well, then, I shall think no more on it."

Nor did she, until two months later, when the memory was suddenly and violently forced upon her.

The Gardiners and their four children arrived at Pemberley the day before Christmas, to the delight of the young Gardiners and the satisfaction of the adults. Snow fell lightly, frosting the shrubs and leaving a gleaming crystal finish on the ground. Mrs. Reynolds took Elizabeth's uncle and aunt to their suite, and Elizabeth led her nieces and nephews to the nursery and schoolroom, where they were to be accommodated. The two older children would have beds in the small bedrooms assigned to former young Darcys, and the two younger would sleep in the nursery, with their nanny in the adjoining nurse's room. In preparation, the rooms had been cleaned and toys brought down from storage in the attic box rooms. A hobbyhorse had been painted anew with hemp mane and tail replaced. A number of other toys were available, as well as children's books and games. While the children enjoyed a special nursery tea, the Gardiners, refreshed from the dust of travel, joined Elizabeth, Darcy, Georgiana, and Lord and Lady Matlock in the drawing room for tea and conversation.

"It is good to hear children's voices and laughter here again," Lady Matlock said at one point. "I well remember when Darcy was a child, how he looked forward to Christmas, not so much for the gifts as his cousins' arrival and the holiday visits of friends with their children."

"I remember very well," Darcy agreed. "I was allowed to greet our guests beside my mother. Father had a sleigh and driver to take us on rides around the park. The last year we celebrated in that way was when I was thirteen."

Elizabeth heard the wistful note beneath his words and smiled with delight. "We shall have such festivities next year," Elizabeth promised. "As for this year, Mrs. Ellington and Mrs. Arbuthnot are holding a Christmas party tomorrow after services for the children at the orphanage. Mrs. Adams is making some of the treats for the children. We are to take them to the vicarage when we go to church tomorrow."

She thought, but did not say, that one day it would be their children who ran and laughed and filled Pemberley with joy.

"Elizabeth found a trunk of toys put away in the attic," Georgiana continued brightly. "Our head gardener, Peters, and his son repainted and refurbished them. My maid, Daisy, and Elizabeth's maid, Clara, sewed clothes for the dolls from scrap fabric. There should be toys for all the orphans."

Lady Matlock and Mrs. Gardiner exchanged a look that said they both recognized Elizabeth's influence on Georgiana and on the community. "That was well done. So many orphanages do not have the funds to hold Christmas parties for the children. I am happy to find the local one has support from ladies of the area."

"I did not know how hard it is to grow up with no family," Georgiana said softly, "but Daisy grew up in an orphanage, and she was very happy to help with the dolls."

The talk moved to other subjects. Darcy felt pride for Elizabeth swell his heart. His wife had not been raised to take over the management of a complex household such as Pemberley, and yet she stepped into the role with grace, enthusiasm, and intelligence. She had not used her position or wealth to impose herself into Derbyshire society. The natural warmth and caring of her character drew people to her. She was a natural leader. He had not deceived himself in his belief that she was a perfect mistress for Pemberley, but neither had he realized how right he would be proved. Darcy resolved that even though it meant giving in to his aunt's perfidy, he would protect Elizabeth from any further attacks.

Elizabeth looked thoughtful at Georgiana's words. A vague idea had formed in the back of her mind, but she put it aside to focus on her guests. There would be time enough later to pursue it. The next morning they took the food and toys by the vicarage to find Mrs. Ellington had a small handcart already loaded with clothing gathered by Mrs. Arbuthnot, as well as more treats for the party. She thanked Elizabeth sincerely, exclaiming over the renewed toys and dolls with tears in her eyes. Elizabeth assured her it was her pleasure to be able to offer the children at the orphanage the means for a happy Christmas.

"I have been thinking that perhaps next year we might engage some of the other local ladies in the orphanage party. I am sure there are enough who have an interest in the welfare of the children to offer their services. Surely there are other attics with unused toys that could be refurbished."

"Oh, Mrs. Darcy!" Impulsively, Lily seized Elizabeth's hand. "That is such a wonderful idea! I know of several ladies who have older children, and I am sure they would be happy to see any toys they retain reused in such a worthy cause. Most of the local gentry give money to support the orphanage as well as subscriptions for the schoolmaster, Mr. Binner, but this is another way they can help. Will you call on them with me?"

"Certainly," Elizabeth said warmly. "Mr. Darcy and I are going to London in February for several months. We can meet after our return to discuss it, if that is acceptable? And, if you will, please call me Elizabeth."

Mrs. Ellington smiled. "And you shall call me Lily."

They said a warm good-bye, and the Darcys departed for church.

Chapter 15

"Mrs. Darcy, you wished to see me?"

Mrs. Reynolds entered the old nursery to find Elizabeth standing in the center of the room, a faint color in her cheeks. The old housekeeper smiled to herself but kept a neutral face. The room had been thoroughly cleaned for the arrival at Christmas of the mistress's young cousins, but the rudiments were as they had been since Miss Darcy was a child. Elizabeth turned to the woman she considered a friend as well as a very valuable employee and indicated their surroundings.

"As you know, Mr. Darcy, Miss Darcy, and I will be traveling to London in a few days for a three-month stay. While we are gone, there are renovations I want made to the nursery suite. At present, I do not want Mr. Darcy to know of them. You will know the local people to use for whatever our own men cannot do."

"Yes, ma'am. I believe I am to congratulate you and the master?"

Elizabeth's blush deepened. "The baby has not quickened yet, but I am fairly certain. William does not know yet. I intend to tell him after we reach London. He is sure to realize from the purchases I will be making if I do not."

Mrs. Reynolds smiled openly then. "He will be so happy. The master is very fond of Mr. and Mrs. Gardiner's children, and he raised Miss Georgiana practically alone. He will make a wonderful father."

"I have no doubt he will," Elizabeth agreed. She turned to the room, "I want all the walls in this room painted cream with white woodwork, including the wainscoting, and the same in the nurse's bedroom. The floors are to be sanded and varnished. The nurse's bed has woodworm. It is to be replaced along with the mattress. The other furniture is to be painted or refinished as necessary. I have located a cradle in the attic. I would like it to be repainted white as well. I may have some things moved from other rooms, but I will buy the mattresses, rugs, material for curtains, and any other soft goods in town."

The housekeeper did not need to make a list, nor did Elizabeth have any doubts that, when they returned to Pemberley, everything she had indicated would be done. She intended to buy a new coverlet for the nurse's bed as well as bed curtains and a rug. Smiling, Elizabeth left Mrs. Reynolds and went down to the library to read for an hour before luncheon. She saw the door to Darcy's study closed, and hesitated. He was most likely working on estate matters; she did not want to disturb him and continued on to the dark solitude of her second-favorite room in the house.

While she sought a book, Elizabeth remembered what William said when he first introduced her to this room. "My mother was the first one who inspired in me the desire to read. She read to me from my earliest years, not just stories for children but poetry, history, and literature. By the time I was ready for a tutor, I read quite well. My father was very proud of this library and used it constantly. When he allowed me full access to it, I felt as if he had given me the most wonderful gift in the world. He told me I now had the entire world within my reach—all the history, philosophy, and literature that humankind had created was contained in books, and it was mine for nothing more than the effort of reading, which was a pleasure for him and for me."

And for me as well, Elizabeth thought, *thanks to my own father's joy in books and willingness to share that love with me.*

Smiling, she selected a volume of poetry and sat down to enjoy her time.

An associate had once said to Wickham when he escaped capture by a hair, "The devil takes care of his own." Well, he was having the devil's own luck today. Perhaps his revenge on Darcy was meant to be. He had made it to the Lambton area with no one the wiser, and although he was avoiding any place where old acquaintances might recognize him, he believed the changes in his appearance were enough to allow him to escape casual notice. Now he kept to the shadows of a large shed behind the mercantile, unseen by the merchant and a worker helping load a wagon with a week of staples.

It was a Pemberley wagon, Wickham knew. It was well kept, the paint bright, and the two great shire horses sleekly groomed. The driver wore serviceable clothing, but he had the comfortable, well-fed look of Darcy's employees. Unlike many wealthy gentlemen, Darcy had never dressed his house servants in livery, disliking the elaborate costumes employed by many of the gentry. He preferred his footmen wear dark-green coats and fawn breeches with white shirts and neckcloths. It was a uniform look without being a formal uniform. The outside workers wore sturdy garments in deference to their duties.

The men finished loading and threw a canvas over the wagon, and the workman disappeared back into the store premises. Wickham held his breath. The driver and the merchant moved beyond the wagon in friendly conversation. The merchant produced a bill of lading, which the driver perused casually. Wickham gathered himself and made a scuttling run for the wagon's rear. He caught the tailboard, heaved himself up, and slid under the cover into the wagon bed. For a tense moment, he froze as the horses stamped and shuffled at the unexpected movement of the wagon, but there was no response from the men, and he relaxed. Moving as carefully as he was able, Wickham insinuated himself behind two large hogsheads. One held molasses, the other flour. Both were clearly labeled. There were more large barrels and a number of smaller containers of salt and sugar, as well as other dry goods. Pemberley used large amounts of foodstuffs to feed its people, over and above what was produced on the estate. Darcy was always generous, Wickham thought with a sneer. Except to his boyhood friend.

He felt the wagon rock as the driver climbed to the seat. With a slap of the reins and a call to the horses, the wagon jerked forward and they were in motion. In his cramped position, the trip seemed to Wickham to take hours. The jarring as they drove at a trot left his muscles stiff, but he dared not change his position for fear the driver would feel the movement. When at last he heard the driver exchange a greeting with the gatekeeper, he risked shifting enough to lift the edge of the canvas and peer out. The vista of woods and water that he knew so well greeted him. This should have been his. Old Darcy should have left him some part of it, Wickham thought as he settled back. If he had he managed to wed Georgiana Darcy, he would have found a way to get rid of her brother and take control of Pemberley. Another plan destroyed by his enemy. No matter. After tonight, all the old scores would be settled in full.

The wagon rolled over the gravel drive, turned right in a slow curve, and stopped, then backed carefully to a halt. The driver jumped down and called to someone farther away. Wickham slid to the rear of the wagon box and raised the canvas enough to look around. The main entrance to the cellars made a wide, dark mouth ten feet away, the doors already left open. He took a deep breath, pushed his way from under the cover, and went over the tailboard. He landed in a crouch, his nerves taut the first shout of discovery. When none came, Wickham ran to the opening and jumped down the shallow steps to the brick floor. He continued at a fast walk, passed the stairs to the half floor where the kitchens were located, and continued along the corridor until he reached a door as old as Pemberley itself. The arch of time-blackened oak was as hard as the iron hinges and lock plate. Wickham tried the door. It swung quietly out, and he entered the wine room, laughing silently as he closed the door behind him. Who but Darcy would leave his wine room unlocked?

Wickham found a thick candle in an iron holder by the door, with a flint and steel on a small shelf below. He lit it and looked around. The room was unchanged from the last time he had occupied it. Rows of wooden wine racks held bottle after bottle. They stretched back for at least fifty feet and for twenty feet to either side. He went down the five steps to the stone floor, no longer afraid of being found out. After selecting a bottle at random, Wickham sat on the steps and took a knife from his coat pocket. He worked the cork out with some effort, tipped up the bottle, and drank deeply. He knew he could not stay here. There was too much risk that the butler would come down to select wine for dinner, but it would do until the wagon was unloaded.

Taking another long swig of the wine, Wickham leaned back against the door. It was a pity that sweet little Georgiana had to die with the others, but there was no way to save her. If Darcy had not stopped the elopement, she would be his wife, with her dowry to finance the life he should be living. After a year or two, Wickham have seen to it that Darcy met with a fatal accident.

Then he would have taken over Pemberley in his wife's name. That had been such a lovely plan, he thought bitterly, but this is almost as satisfying. He drank again and laughed softly. A quick visit to his ladylove would be in order before the night's activities. Georgiana had enough jewelry in her rooms to set him on his way out of the country. Anything else was a bonus.

Once Wickham was as certain as he could be that the activity of the area was centered in the kitchens, he made his way to the servants' stairs and climbed stealthily to the third floor. He still had the devil's luck. The stairs were empty, and he remained undiscovered. He did not draw an easy breath, however, until the door of the old nursery closed behind him. This was the one place in the house no one ever visited. As Wickham looked around the moderately sized room, he became aware the windows were uncurtained, showing a view of the wooded ridge behind the house and gardens. He stepped into the nurse's room, noting that the bed had been dismantled and stacked against a wall. The mattress had been left on the floor to be taken away. Both rooms had the bare look of chambers in the process of renovation.

Well, well. Wickham turned in a circle, his lips stretched in a lupine grin. So the nursery was to be put to use once more. What a pity it would never happen. After tonight, there would be no more Darcy and no more Darcys. His laugh echoed, soft and evil, through the quiet space.

The time passed slowly in memories of his life at Pemberley; of old Mr. Darcy, so easy for his charming godson to gull, of university, with its myriad opportunities for pleasures of the bottle and the bed. He thought of his subsequent life in London, using Darcy's payment in lieu of the living at Kympton until the money ran out. A new appeal met with the denial of the living or any further assistance from his boyhood friend and unknowing rival. That was when the scheme to engage Georgiana's affections and elope with her had been born between him and his longtime lover, Annie Younge. After being shown a few forged references and a practiced face of gentility, Darcy and his cousin the colonel had fallen into the trap.

Wickham consulted his pocket watch: three in the morning, the dead time of night. The best time for his purpose. He made his stealthy way to the other wing through deserted halls, always on guard against the appearance of a night footman. He made it to the corridor where the family rooms were situated without raising an alarm. The doors were unsecured, and no footman patrolled the hallway. Swiftly Wickham gathered several lamps from the empty rooms and began to soak the doors and floors with the oil they contained, noting with a smirk that the efficient servants had kept them filled. At last he shoved the empty lamps out of sight in the alcove leading to the servants' stairs, and went to the last door on the left, Georgiana's dressing room.

The drapes were open when he entered Georgiana's bedroom, and the bed curtains drawn back. Moonlight lay like a benison on her sleeping face as Wickham stood and looked down at her. She looked like a child; the child he remembered leading on her pony around the grounds of the estate, the child who had trusted him, the child he had betrayed. For a moment, some frayed thread of compassion stirred in Wickham's tattered soul. What a wife she would have made him—rich, beautiful, and innocent. Then the thread broke and drifted away, and darkness descended on the core of his being. Shaking himself, Wickham took a handkerchief from his coat pocket along with curtain cords cut from the drapes in her dressing room, and leaned over her.

Georgiana woke with the sensation of smothering, instinctively struggling to rise. The bedclothes hampered her. She felt strong hands grip her wrists and wrap something thick around them. Georgiana tried to scream, kicking and lashing her head. The obstruction in her mouth prevented anything but a moan. The man threw back the bedcovers and tied her ankles. Georgiana felt terror claw at her chest. The man's face, as revealed by the moonlight, was a gargoyle mask, leering at her. He ran his hand along her exposed leg, stopping at the knee. A *frisson* of terror left her faint. But with a shake of his head, he tossed the bedclothes carelessly back over her and lit her bedside lamp, revealing the awful face of George Wickham. Stifled with fear and lack of oxygen, Georgiana stared with dilated eyes at the scar disfiguring his face. He looked down at her, and after a heartbeat, his remembered voice whispered in a terrifying travesty of intimacy. "Lovely Georgie. What a pity, my dear, that you are at home tonight. I am afraid you must die with the others. It is all your brother's fault, you know. If he had acceded to my perfectly reasonable request for the Kympton living, none of this would be necessary."

He stared at her for a second longer, while Georgiana felt the room spin and darken, and then, taking the lamp, he left her. Returning to her dressing room, Wickham went quickly through her jewelry cabinet, selecting items that could be pawned for more than enough to allow him to travel to Scotland. From there, he would find a ship to take him to the Continent, far from the vengeance of the Fitzwilliams. Wickham shoved the jewelry into his inner coat pocket, took up the lamp on the dressing table, and moved silently to the hall door.

Elizabeth became aware she was awakening, her mind muzzy with sleep. Her head rested on her husband's shoulder, his warm skin under her cheek. The smell of him filled her nostrils; faint spice; his natural, clean odor, and beneath it, the scent of their lovemaking. She smiled and nestled closer. They were to depart for London in the morning, and there she would find the best way to tell Darcy he was to be a father. Elizabeth closed her eyes to return to sleep, but at the edge of consciousness, she felt an unease. Her sleep had been disturbed because something was not right.

She raised her head and concentrated on the space around her. It was deep in the night or early in the morning. The bedside candle had guttered out, and the fire in the hearth made only a faint glow in the room. The only illumination came from the drawn drapes, where indirect moonglow spilled onto the floor.

Fire. Candle. Lamp oil. Elizabeth drew air into her lungs and sat up. A faint but distinct smell of lamp oil permeated the room. At her side, Darcy roused and reached for her. His hand brushed her hip as she got out of bed, grabbed her dressing gown from where it had been thrown over a chair, and donned her slippers. As she moved toward the door, Darcy's voice stopped her. "What is wrong, Lizzy?"

"Smell," she responded. "Lamp oil. It's too strong. Mrs. Reynolds adds a spice to it to repel insects, lemongrass. My uncle imports it from India."

She was speaking rapidly and still heading for the hall door. Darcy's feet hit the floor, he snatched up his dressing gown and shoved his feet into house slippers. "Wait!" He drew air into his lungs. His nostrils flared. "You are right.

Something is amiss." He caught up to her and put a hand on her shoulder. "I want you to lock both doors. Do not open to anyone but me. It may be nothing of import, but I need to make sure of that."

Elizabeth hesitated. She wanted to protest, but suddenly she thought of the child in her womb and nodded. "Please take care, my darling."

He bent and brushed her lips with his. She watched him disappear through the connecting door to her dressing room, and turned the key in the lock. Chilled by fear, her hands trembling, Elizabeth went to stand by the hall door and wait. She knew William was alarmed in spite of his assurances, and inevitably, the idea of fire filled her mind. There were servants' stairs at both ends of the hallway, but that fact gave her no comfort. Fire consumed everything. Even if she reached the stairs, there was no certainty of safety.

If she opened the hall doorway just a crack, she thought, she might hear something to tell her what was happening. She silently opened the heavy panel several inches. Tension stiffened her body. After what seemed an hour, Elizabeth heard a vague commotion somewhere at the far end of the hallway, and Darcy's raised voice shouting one word: "*Intruder!*" Terror thickened her breath. Unable to stand by when her beloved might be in mortal danger, she opened the door and stepped into the dark space. Instantly Elizabeth became aware that the night lamp by the stairs was no longer burning. She felt her slippers squelch in something wet. The light, citrusy odor of lamp oil assaulted her senses, magnified a dozen times. The carpeting was soaked in it. Oil dripped from the woodwork, the doors, the stair rails. She looked toward the noise and saw two men silhouetted against the dark height of the end window, locked together in combat. A lamp on the table beneath the window rocked between them. Darcy reached them as one of the men gave a sharp cry, and the two bodies separated.

The man who had cried out slumped against the wall. Blood glistened on the front of his coat. Darcy's weight struck the other man hard enough to send him a staggering step backward. Darcy was a large man, strong and fit, but Wickham possessed the superhuman strength of madness. Light darted on heaving bodies. The stained blade of Wickham's knife threw red splatters of blood onto his frayed sleeve.

Feet pounded on the stairs from below. Men shouted. Darcy's left hand grasped Wickham's right wrist. In the blind force of the fight, Darcy's only thought was to save Elizabeth and the others in his keeping. With a supreme effort, his right hand forced Wickham's left wrist up to keep the knife glittering in that hand away from his face. Straining against the crazed strength of the other man, Darcy pushed Wickham inexorably backward toward the alcove entrance to the servants' stairs. As they neared the window, Darcy's feet slipped on the oil-drenched carpet. He slid sideways, turning Wickham with him as they grunted and swayed in a desperate struggle.

They grappled, the two bodies locked together. Elizabeth ran toward them, her only thought she must reach Darcy. She slipped in the oil underfoot, struck the wall hard enough to elicit a gasp of pain. As she righted herself, she saw the intruder tear his arm free of Darcy's grip in a last frenzied effort, saw him snatch up the lamp and fling it into the air with a shriek of triumph. As the light jerked from one face to the other, her step faltered. The man's features were distorted to a maniacal mask, his teeth bared in a rictus of pure hate. Unaware she had cried out, Elizabeth flung herself toward the struggle.

The momentum sent both men backward into the table. It overturned as the lamp arced up and then fell like a burning star. Darcy saw the flare of light from the corner of his eye. In that tiny instant he knew he could not catch the lamp. There was only one alternative; he struck out at it with all the strength of his arm and shoulder. His hand hit the base of the lamp as it descended, pain shot into his wrist and up his arm. The lamp smashed through the window just as Wickham spun toward the escape of the alcove and the servants' stairs, but the fight had left him disoriented. Wickham stumbled on the trodden, oil-soaked carpet, his boots sliding in pooled oil. He flung out both arms to regain his balance, struck the fallen table, and with a terrible cry hurled backward into the broken window.

The panes, already shattered by the lamp, broke free of the frame. Glass sprayed out in a glittering fan. Darcy made a grab for Wickham. His momentum threw him sliding toward the jagged gap in the wall. He grabbed wildly at the window frame as Elizabeth reached him and threw both of her arms around his waist. Together they swayed and then straightened, the image of lamp and man falling through black space before them. A long scream ended in a sickening sound of impact on the stone walk three stories below, amid a shower of little flames as the lamp flared and went out. Cold wind flowed over them. Darcy turned with Elizabeth in his arms, he buried his face in her hair. The sound of his harsh, ragged breathing filled the space while she held him to her, trembling with shock.

At once, men surrounded them. The whole episode had taken barely five minutes. Mr. Niles came up to them in a dressing gown, his fine hair ruffled, looking as discomposed as anyone would ever see him. Darcy left Elizabeth and knelt by the man who had fallen. Steves looked up at Darcy; blood soaked the front of his coat, his breathing sounded strained in the sudden quiet. "Sorry, sir," he muttered. "Almost…had him."

"There's nothing to be sorry about," Darcy told him quietly. "It was Wickham, and he will trouble no one any longer." He motioned to the footmen. "Take him to the nearest bedroom. Mr. Niles, send for Dr. Morrow at once, and get Mrs. Reynolds."

He turned to speak to Elizabeth when sudden fear gripped his chest. Why had Georgiana not heard the commotion and at least tried to find out the source? Darcy leaped to his feet and crossed to the door of his sister's rooms in two strides, Elizabeth a step behind him. As he reached for the doorknob, the panel opened, and Mrs. Annesley stood before them, her face blanched by shock and fear. "Mr. Darcy, help me. It's Miss Darcy!"

They ran after her across the dressing room, hearts pounding painfully. In the bedroom, Georgiana sat propped against a chair, rocking herself back and forth. Cut lengths of drapery tiebacks were strewn around her, along with a crumpled handkerchief. Darcy fell to his knees at his sister's side and gathered her in his arms. For several minutes he held her tightly and crooned wordlessly to her, as he had when she suffered nightmares as a child. She did not cry but made small mewling sounds.

Mrs. Annesley turned to Elizabeth, who watched the two before her with fear and pain in her eyes. The older woman's voice penetrated her shock, and she looked aside as Georgiana's companion said, "I found her on the floor. She had somehow fallen out of bed. She was tied hand and foot, and that rag was in her mouth to keep her quiet. I think she was trying to get help, the poor child. Who would do such a wicked thing?"

"A wicked man," Elizabeth replied. "Please send for tea. Very hot. I will have Dr. Morrow attend her when he is finished with Steves."

Mrs. Annesley hurried away on her errand. Elizabeth stooped over her husband and Georgiana and said quietly, "William, let us take her to the chaise longue in her dressing room. She is too distressed to be put back to bed right now."

Darcy glanced up at his wife as if he had not heard her. Then he rose, picked Georgiana up in his arms, and carried her into the next room, settling her on the chaise while Elizabeth brought a blanket to wrap around her. The dressing room lamp was gone, but she found a candle lamp on the dressing table and lit it. Darcy sat beside his sister and held her against him. She had quieted, and as Elizabeth drew a chair up to sit by her, she raised her head and shuddered. "It was *him*. He said…he said I was g-going to die!"

"He is gone for good," Darcy assured her in a low voice. "He is dead, Georgie. He fell from the end window. He will never come back, he will never harm you or anyone again."

Elizabeth reached out and took the girl's hand, squeezing it comfortingly. "You have had a terrible experience, dearest, but it is over, and only those who love you are with you now."

Slowly Georgiana nodded. Elizabeth found a handkerchief and gave it to her. The girl wiped her eyes and held it tightly in both hands. Darcy looked at Elizabeth, hesitated, and then said very softly to his sister, "Georgie, did he harm you in any way? Tell me, please, dearest. Whatever happened, we will make it right."

She shook her head. "No, Brother. He just tied me. I think he…he was insane. He hardly looked human."

Mrs. Annesley returned with the tea and Daisy in her wake. Her open face was very pale but composed. She made Georgiana a cup of the strong tea with enough sugar to almost qualify it as syrup. She gave the cup to Elizabeth and prepared another cup, not quite so sweet, for Pemberley's mistress. Elizabeth drank it gratefully, aware all at once that she was shaking, shocked by the night's events. Darcy looked at her and rose, letting Mrs. Annesley take his place. The companion spoke as she settled by her charge and took the girl's hand. "I woke and heard some noise I could not identify and came to see if Miss Darcy was all right. That was when I found her. I wish I had wakened earlier."

Elizabeth said, "If you had, you would have been in grave danger. Georgiana is right. I believe the man was quite mad."

With the comfort of Elizabeth's presence and her brother's gentle words, Georgiana calmed enough to drink the tea. She would recover. She was a Darcy at her core. Wickham's actions would not scar her, especially now that any danger from him was gone forever.

"There is no danger now, my dearest," Darcy said, echoing her thoughts. "So long as you are unharmed, all will be well."

Darcy leaned over and kissed Georgiana's cheek. When he returned to the hall, Mr. Niles appeared with Mrs. Reynolds. The butler said, some of his usual aplomb having returned, "A groom is riding for the doctor. It will take a bit to clean up all this oil, but I will have it set right as soon as possible. I have also instructed the groom to summon the magistrate. Shall I have the...the body moved to a cellar room or left where it is until he arrives?"

"Move it," Darcy responded shortly. As he turned to enter the room where Steves had been taken, he saw several lamps from the rooms along the hall shoved carelessly into the alcove. "I will await the magistrate, but I want that... carrion off Pemberley property as soon as possible."

"Yes, sir." Mr. Niles was obviously in agreement.

Darcy found Steves in Mrs. Reynolds's capable care. She looked up as he approached the bed and said, "The wound is shallow. His coat absorbed much of the blow. There has been considerable bleeding, but there seems to be no damage to the lungs or other organs, just a broken rib."

"He...meant to...burn the house down," Steves said. "I was up early to... see to loading the coaches, and...I heard something. No time...to raise the alarm. Had a knife."

"Do not concern yourself," Darcy said. "It is quite clear what his intention was. He did not succeed, thanks to you. Rest until the doctor arrives. I will speak with you later."

Darcy returned to his sister's rooms to find Mrs. Annesley speaking quietly to Georgiana. He saw her maid, Daisy, was attending her, and Elizabeth had prepared another cup of hot, sweet tea. She looked up, still pale, and Darcy repressed a shudder. What if Wickham had succeeded? They might all be dead.

"I am afraid," Elizabeth said shakily, "my slippers are ruined."

As he watched, she suddenly dissolved in tears.

Darcy took her in his arms. "If you had not become aware of the odor of the lamp oil, my dearest, we should not have been warned, and Wickham would have done what he intended." *Not only would all of us have died,* Darcy thought silently, *but the maids in the attic bedrooms, with no possible way of escape.* "I will not scold you for not obeying me and leaving our rooms. You steadied me when I nearly followed Wickham out of the window. Now, come back to your chamber, and I will call Clara if she is not already waiting for you. There is still much to be done, but I want you to rest." He bent and kissed his sister's forehead. "You also, dearest."

Her maid said, "I'll see to her, Mr. Darcy."

He nodded. Drawing Elizabeth to his side, he walked with her to the door of her bedchamber. Clara stood in the open doorway, pale but calm. Elizabeth gazed up at her husband, seeing the love and concern in his eyes, and smiled faintly. "Come to me when you can, William. I have something I want to tell you."

The trip from Pemberley to London tired Elizabeth more than she expected, even though they took an extra day on the road. It was late afternoon when they reached Darcy House. Darcy suggested Elizabeth rest for the remainder of the day. Her ready compliance left him grateful, if slightly disturbed. He resolved to have Elizabeth seen by Sir Laurence Covent, the foremost expert on childbirth in the country. Many of the most successful *accoucheurs* had trained with the specialist, and Darcy wanted to be as certain as possible that all was well with Elizabeth and the baby. She had not yet shared news of her condition with anyone else, although he was certain Mrs. Reynolds was aware of it and undoubtedly had been even before Elizabeth realized the truth herself. He had no doubt Clara suspected her mistress' condition as well.

"I will write Jane and my father after we reach London," she told Darcy on the morning of their departure. "My father will fail to reply, and Mama will pen several pages of superfluous advice and admonitions."

She spoke lightly, but Darcy heard the echo of sadness beneath the words. "I am sure she means well," he said soothingly.

"Yes," Elizabeth agreed neutrally, and no more was said.

Elizabeth took a tray in her chambers their first night at Darcy House and slept until morning. Breakfast was the first time the three of them had been together in nearly twenty-four hours. Elizabeth looked rested, Darcy noted gratefully. She wore a day dress in fine wool of deep gold that Clara had let out at the bosom with lace insertions, and she showed no sign of being with child. As they ate, Georgiana chatted about visiting her favorite bookshop for the latest sheet music of Herr Beethoven and a new novel by "A Lady" that she wished to read. Elizabeth looked at Darcy with a mischievous upturn to her lips that lifted his heart. She said, "Would you like to go shopping with me today, Georgie? I have some special purchases to make. My Aaunt Gardiner and Aunt Madeleine are joining me."

Georgie sat up even straighter in her chair. "Oh yes, Elizabeth, thank you! I should love to go. What are you shopping for?"

"Oh," Elizabeth sipped her tea, "a new bed, mattress, coverlet, material for curtains, two rugs."

Georgiana's eyes widened. "Are you redecorating your chambers?"

"Not at present. These are for Pemberley. Also a crib, and bedding for that and a basinet."

For a moment, as the import of the words penetrated Georgiana's consciousness, she was silent, but her eyes grew wider and wider. At last she squealed, clapped both hands over her mouth, and jumped to her feet. She hurried around the table, leaned over, and hugged Elizabeth, her face aglow with a huge smile. Dropping into the empty chair next to her sister, she said breathlessly, "When? When is the baby to be born?"

"Sometime in late August, by the best of my reckoning."

"I can hardly wait!" Georgiana's eyes sparkled with tears. She brushed them away and said, "I am so happy for you, dearest Elizabeth, and for you, Brother. I shall be an aunt. Oh, this is wonderful news! Does anyone else know?"

"William," Elizabeth teased. "I am going to write my family this morning. I will tell my aunts Gardiner and Madeleine when they arrive. William is meeting with Lord Henry on business, so we will have the day to ourselves until dinner."

The two aunts' responses to Elizabeth's news were filled with all of the joy and love that might be expected. The ladies took the Darcy town coach, with two footmen in attendance. Steves remained at Pemberley to recover from his wound, but when they returned, he would take up his new position as special attendant to the Darcy ladies.

Elizabeth knew the nature of the "business" her husband and Lord Henry were undertaking and suspected Lady Matlock did as well, but she refused to allow it to darken her pleasure in the expedition. Mr. Gardiner's warehouses produced the perfect curtain material for the nursery and nurse's rooms, and Elizabeth found all of the bedding she required at a shop recommended by Mrs. Gardiner. The day was passing quickly, and Elizabeth found herself tiring, so they decided to let the search for the rugs and bed wait until another day. A tea shop near the bookstore Georgiana wanted to visit offered half an hour's rest. While Georgiana went off, with a footman accompanying her, Elizabeth and her aunt took a table near a window and ordered tea and cakes.

Watching her niece, Mrs. Gardiner said with a smile, "Do not fret, Lizzy, if you fatigue more easily than before. Your body is working even when you are sitting still."

"I know," Elizabeth replied ruefully. "I just dislike not being unable to do whatever I want without having to rest."

"In time," Lady Matlock said, "you will be grateful for all the rest you can get. It is part of the process. Once the baby comes and you recover, you will return to normal."

Elizabeth nodded. She looked past Lady Matlock at a woman of some years who was staring at her offensively. She had been speaking to the serving girl, who scuttled away quickly with a glance at their table. The woman was thin and bony, the lines of her face sharp, and the planes flat. Her hair under an elaborate hat was too dark and lacked the gloss of natural color. She was dressed expensively in dark colors that succeeded in draining any natural color from her sallow skin and emphasizing the bright spots of rouge on her cheeks. The color rose in Elizabeth's face, and she looked away.

"Lizzy," Mrs. Gardiner asked quickly, "is something wrong?"

"That lady in the corner, in the large hat, who is she? She seems to dislike me intensely, and she reminds me of someone, but I do not know her."

Lady Matlock turned deliberately in her chair to gaze at the woman, who immediately looked away. As she turned back, she said, "That is Lady Sybil Braithwaite. Her husband is Sir Percival Braithwaite, Bart."

"That explains her behavior." Elizabeth shook her head. "I have met her daughter, Lady Hazel Walker-Price."

"Has she caused you trouble?"

"She has tried, without success. I will explain when we return to Darcy House."

Lady Sybil rose and gathered her things. As she passed their table, she sniffed loudly but did not pause. Lady Matlock chuckled. "You need have no concern for Lady Braithwaite's opinions, my dear. Even with the *ton*'s unquenchable love of scandal, she has antagonized some important people. She is a toothless tiger, hardly welcome anywhere. Her daughter is a copy of the mother."

Mrs. Gardiner patted Elizabeth's hand soothingly. "You have so much to be happy about, Lizzy. Do not let someone like Lady Braithwaite cause you distress." She nodded to the doorway. "I see Miss Darcy returning. From her ecstatic expression, I believe she has obtained the music she wanted."

Chapter 16

"**I**s Elizabeth joining us?"

Darcy shook his head. "She feels her presence would incline Lady Catherine to refuse our offer. She is to go shopping with Georgie, Aunt Madeleine, and her aunt Gardiner."

The two men sat in Lord Henry's study while they waited for his carriage to be brought around. Darcy's carriage was available, but his uncle felt the Fitzwilliam crest was a more valuable factor when dealing with Lady Catherine.

A grin Darcy could not repress lit his face. Lord Matlock regarded him closely and then said, with a twinkle in his eyes, "Shopping amuses you?"

Darcy's grin widened. "It is what she is shopping for. Elizabeth is with child."

A smile of real delight spread across the earl's face. He reached out and slapped his nephew's shoulder. "Congratulations, my boy! What wonderful news. When is the baby due to arrive?"

"Elizabeth believes in late August. She has asked Mrs. Reynolds to use our men, and any local craftsmen who can supplement their skills, to renovate the nursery and nurse's room."

"You married a wise woman, William. The local craftsmen will be proud to be involved in preparing for Pemberley's heir. She is well, I hope."

"I want her to see a specialist while we are in town, but Elizabeth claims she feels fine and has no concerns about the birth. She reminds me that her mother had five children in eleven years without a single problem. I remind her, although it is hardly necessary, that she is *not* her mother."

Lord Henry said, "A wise precaution in any case. You have not made an announcement yet?"

"Elizabeth wrote her sister and father after we arrived. We will stop in Hertfordshire on our way back to Pemberley and stay with Bingley and Jane for a few days. I am sure her mother will have a great deal of advice, which Elizabeth is certain to ignore."

Lord Henry chuckled. He rose and poured two small brandies, handing one to his nephew. "To the next generation of distinguished Darcy men -- or women." They touched glasses and drank. Darcy rose to his feet as his uncle said, "Well, William, shall we call on your aunt? I did not request an interview. I felt it better to arrive unannounced. We are more likely to find her at home that way."

They talked little on the short trip to the de Bourgh town house. Both men understood that this was the final confrontation with Lady Catherine; either she would agree to their plan, or she would face the threat of being confined in a private facility for "nervous disorders", no doubt with persons suffering from dire conditions. Now that there was a babe on the way, her persecution had to cease. Darcy refused to have Elizabeth harried, especially while she was with child, no matter how strong her nature.

Lady Catherine's butler admitted them without comment and showed them into the drawing room. It was upwards of ten minutes before the mistress herself entered the room. Her appearance shocked her brother and nephew; her sallow skin was pale and her expression pinched. She appeared to suffer from some internal malady. Lady Catherine took her usual chair and sat stiff and unmoving while Lord Henry and Darcy found seats across from her. She did not offer refreshments, and neither man would have accepted had she done so. They all realized this was not a social call.

"I know why you are here," Lady Catherine said at last. Her voice sounded as strained as her manner.

"I expect you do," her brother replied. "We have come to try and resolve the matter of your demand to be given Rosings."

"Demand? It is mine by right." Her voice was bitter. "I earned it!"

Lord Henry drew a steadying breath. Beside him, Darcy sat almost as rigid as his aunt. "Whatever your opinion on the subject, let me state at once that Darcy will not deed Rosings to you. However, we all know the building is not what you want. It is the items of value contained in Rosings, whatever of them is left, that you wish to obtain. With the money from their sale you can continue to subsidize Mr. Rhymes."

Lady Catherine's hands were clasped tightly in her lap. Darcy noted that her morning gown looked as if she had worn it for twenty-four hours. The lines in her face deepened, and she looked at her brother with something near hate in her eyes. "What I do with my property or my life is none of your affair, Henry."

"It is if the scandal touches the family. You have attacked Mrs. Darcy and attempted blackmail, all because of an obsession with a man young enough to be your son."

Lady Catherine came half out of her chair. Passion twisted her face, she hissed, "You fool! You stupid, blind fool! Mr. Rhymes *is my son!*"

Darcy gripped the arms of his chair; the words struck him like a blow to the midsection. For a moment he could not draw breath. Lord Henry was in an even worse state. He sat as stiff as wood, staring at his sister in shock. Darcy saw his aunt sink back in her massive chair. It was as if some reservoir inside her had been drained. She looked old and worn out, and he could not help but feel pity for her.

"Your son," Lord Henry repeated at last in a near whisper.

"Yes." Lady Catherine bent forward a little, her eyes on her clenched hands. "That is why Sir Lewis left his entire estate to Anne. He hated me for giving another man what I could not give him. Sir Lewis wanted an heir, but he...he was not always...capable. He drank and caroused with his friends and spent much of his time in London with his mistresses. I was young and lonely. We had house parties in those days, hunting and shooting parties for his cronies. One of them took a fancy to me. Sir Lewis rarely exercised his husbandly rights, and there was little danger of discovery. It was brief, but Milton was the result." She let out an audible breath, almost a sigh. "Do you remember the summer I went away to Scotland for a rest cure? I found a family to care for my son there after he was born. I did not see or hear from them again, although I paid them until he was grown. Four years ago, he came to Rosings. His foster mother had died, and on her deathbed, she told him everything. He had known he was not her natural son, but that was all. He wanted to be near me, but he knew we could never acknowledge the relationship, so I hired him to replace my old steward. We were happy...until Anne died, and Darcy took over the estate." For a moment, anger flared again in her expression, then died away.

Darcy said quietly, "That was why he was taking money from the estate profits above his salary and living here when you were in town."

"Of course. I could not openly give him money, but I allowed him to supplement his salary from the estate. I ran Rosings for over twenty years. It was mine to give."

Darcy did not argue with her. Lord Henry, who had recovered his composure, said, "Why did you not come to me when this all began, Cathy? We could have made some arrangement for him."

"You were newly made Earl of Matlock. Your heir was an infant. Would you have been so charitable then to my bastard son? I could not take the chance. Sir Lewis might have divorced me, but he knew how you would react to that decision, so he kept me and never let me forget what I had done until the day he died. I can honestly say I was never so relieved in my life as at the moment the doctor pronounced my husband dead!"

Lord Henry was silent. Darcy said slowly, "Lord Henry and I came to offer you one-third of the profits from Rosings on a quarterly basis. I will sell off the furnishings and add twenty thousand pounds to your trust. Together, the interest will be enough to allow you and...your son to live comfortably in the dower house, or here in London if you prefer." He hesitated before adding, "My wife is with child. I will no longer have her threatened, by you or anyone else."

"So there will be another generation of Darcys." She almost sneered. Her eyes closed for a moment. She looked weary and defeated. Straightening her shoulders, Lady Catherine said, "It is of small matter now. After I disposed of my jewelry, I sold off the more valuable pieces from the house because Milton is...dying. He has lived a hard life, sometimes a dissolute life. Because of that, he has contracted consumption. The doctors give him only a short time to live. I wanted the funds from whatever of value is left so that I can take him to one of the European spas that treat consumptive patients. It might postpone the end for a while."

Lord Henry looked at Darcy and saw his own reaction reflected in the younger man's eyes. "I will see to it, Cathy. I can have funds transferred to a bank on the Continent where you will have access to whatever you need. I am sure whoever has been treating him can recommend the best facility. If you wish me to make the arrangements, I will do so. You need worry about nothing."

"It is too little too late," Lady Catherine replied without rancor, "but that is my fault, not yours. Thank you, Henry." She met Darcy's eyes at last. "I...am sorry I was forced to use my connections in the *ton* to pressure you, but I saw no alternative."

Darcy doubted Lady Catherine was truly repentant but did not question the statement. They left her shortly thereafter. Uncle and nephew rode in silence. The usual clamor of London traffic was no more than a distant surf barely invading their thoughts. At last Lord Henry said, "All these years, she has carried that burden. No wonder she hated Anne. It was not right, but at least I understand her motives."

"Yes," Darcy agreed. "Raising the child of a man she hated while strangers raised her own child. An exemplary case of the sins of the fathers. I cannot condone her actions in any way, but they are finally comprehensible."

Darcy did not stay at Matlock House. He returned home almost immediately to find Elizabeth and Georgiana enjoying tea and talking of their purchases, some of which were laid out on the table between them. Darcy leaned over and kissed his wife's brow. As he straightened, he became acutely aware of several tiny dresses and a small, intricately patterned blanket in shades of green, yellow, and blue. Something Darcy had never experienced before rose in his chest. It gripped him with an emotion so powerful that it momentarily overwhelmed him. He turned away, his eyes stinging with tears he fought to control. *Our child will wear those garments*, he thought. *The life my Elizabeth and I have made together.*

Only the years of rigid self-control allowed him to retain a semblance of composure. He became aware that Elizabeth was speaking to him, and turned to her.

"William? What is wrong? Do you not like what we have purchased for the baby?"

He smiled a little. "They are perfect. They are just...so *small*."

Elizabeth chuckled. "Babies are small, my love." She reached out and took his hand.

Georgiana, her eyes resolutely on the blanket, rose and said, "If you will excuse me, I will see to our purchases."

"Yes." Elizabeth still watched her husband. "Thank you, Georgie."

Gathering the blanket and dresses, Georgiana hastily left the room. Elizabeth studied Darcy's face as he sat in the chair beside her. She knew he was troubled, but whether by something to do with her condition or by his interview with Lady Catherine she had yet to discover.

"Will you tell me what is wrong, William?"

Darcy closed his eyes briefly, still holding Elizabeth's hand. In terse sentences, he related what he and Lord Matlock had learned from Lady Catherine. Elizabeth caught her breath at the revelation of Mr. Rhymes' relationship to the rigidly proper noblewoman. When he finished speaking, she looked down for a few moments, struggling to define what she felt. Now that she was to become a mother herself, she had some inkling of what Lady Catherine had suffered.

"We must forgive her, William," Elizabeth said softly at last. "Her actions were wrong, but she must have been in constant pain. I know society shuns a woman who has an illegitimate child and vilifies the child, who had no choice in the matter. But a mother does not feel that way. She must have loved the father as well, or why would giving up her son have tortured her as it has? This is the child of her body, however he was born."

"So was Anne," Darcy said with a lingering bitterness. Then he sighed. "I suppose you are right. Legitimacy is more a matter of property inheritance than morals. Lady Catherine was forced into a marriage with a man she neither liked nor respected, and by her own admission, the affair was her doing. In the end, it ruined three lives."

"And now that her son has returned to her, he is dying. Some might say that is a judgment of God, but I do not believe in a creator who would take such a mean revenge."

"No more do I," Darcy agreed. "Her sin has become its own punishment. I only hope she can find some peace in the rest of her life." Elizabeth smiled as he raised her hand to his lips to place a lingering kiss on the back. "I am a very fortunate man, my loveliest, most wonderful Lizzy."

The weeks passed quickly from spring into early summer. As the heat and mephitic air of London worsened, Darcy and Elizabeth began preparing to repair to Pemberley. They would not return for the little season as their baby would be too young to travel at that time, and neither regretted the fact. Georgiana, who would not come out for two years, preferred life at Pemberley to the city and was eager to be at the only place she really considered home.

On a particularly humid morning two days prior to their departure, Darcy was surprised when Mr. Burgess announced Charles Bingley. The two men shook hands warmly, and Darcy indicated a chair while he went to the sidebar and poured two modest brandies.

"I had no idea you would be in town," Darcy said, He handed Bingley his drink and sat in the companion chair. "No trouble, I hope?"

"I had to come into the City on business," Bingley replied. "But I am glad to find you here. Congratulations on the happy news. Jane almost danced when she received Elizabeth's letter. We are hoping for the same news soon."

Darcy thanked him, aware of an undertone of tension in Bingley's inevitably cheerful demeanor. He said, "I think there is something more to this visit than to offer congratulations."

"Yes." Bingley drank slowly with his eyes on the glass. When he raised his head, Darcy saw that the younger man looked paler than usual. "It is Jane. Or, rather, her mother. Mrs. Bennet visits constantly. When she is at Netherfield she comments and suggests, orders the servants about, and generally behaves as if it were her home rather than ours. It is affecting Jane badly and getting worse. She loves her mother, and I like Mrs. Bennet, but the lady cannot admit that Jane is not only a grown woman but also a married one. I am afraid we cannot stay at Netherfield Park indefinitely."

He finished his drink as Darcy contemplated the situation. "Have you made any decision about where you wish to relocate?"

Bingley sat forward. "We would like to be closer to you and Elizabeth. Jane misses her sister very much, especially now. I have spent the morning with my accountants. My financial situation is solid and actually better than I expected. I can afford to buy a modest estate, which is all I desire. If not in Derbyshire, perhaps in a neighboring county."

"I do not know of any properties in the area currently for sale," Darcy said slowly, "but I shall watch for anything I believe will suit you."

Bingley's face wore its first genuine smile of the day. "If it is in good repair and profitable, I am certainly interested. My thanks, Brother."

Darcy smiled in return. "You will have stormy weather when Mrs. Bennet finds out you are leaving, but you can get through that. And Derbyshire, as I am well aware, is too far for daily or even monthly visits."

Three weeks after the Darcys' return from London, Mrs. Arbuthnot approached Elizabeth as she stood and chatted to several local ladies after services. To Elizabeth's surprise, her first words were, "Do you knit, Mrs. Darcy?"

"Adequately. Not nearly as well as my mother or my sister Kitty. Why do you ask?"

"I believe you know that I host a sewing circle every other Wednesday at the vicarage. A number of the local ladies meet as they are able, and we make clothes and other items for the families living on the parish, and for tenant families who are not doing well or whose landlords are less than charitable. At present we are knitting children's jumpers and baby things for next winter. If you are able, I would love to have you join us. Mrs. Ellington," she nodded at Lily who stood with her husband and the vicar, "is a member."

Elizabeth smiled. "Certainly I will come. Have you enough yarn? I can bring extra if it will help."

"Most of the ladies provide their own, but additional materials are always welcome. Thank you, Mrs. Darcy."

With her own baby on her mind, Elizabeth felt a stirring of an idea that presently refused to come out and be recognized. It was one she realized she had felt before. She attended the next sewing circle. The women who came for the circle were from the local gentry, and several from the lesser nobility who had homes in the area. Elizabeth had met Lady Truitt-Wayne at the Ellingtons' dinner party. Most of the other families had been known to her husband for years. They were welcoming, and Elizabeth felt comfortable with them in spite of her deprecation of her skills. In fact, she was as accomplished at knitting as most women. As she worked and chatted, she felt Lady Walker-Price's gaze on her. She looked aside suddenly, surprising a glare so hostile that Elizabeth instinctively stiffened. Noting her sudden discomfort, Lily glanced at Lady Walker-Price and inclined her head to Elizabeth.

Murmuring so only Elizabeth heard, she said, "The queen bee looks displeased. I believe she thinks all her worker bees have deserted her."

Elizabeth smiled and continued with her work. Had she looked at Lady Walker-Price once more, she might have felt something approaching fear.

When the group broke up, Elizabeth took Lily aside and approached Mrs. Arbuthnot. The vicar's wife smiled as they came up to her. Satisfaction lighted her homely face. "Well, ladies, I think we accomplished a fair amount today. Mrs. Toddy will be very glad to have the baby things. She has not been well since the birth of her latest."

"I am sorry to hear it," Lily said.

Elizabeth found the reticence in her friend's voice odd, but she drew herself up and spoke to Mrs. Arbuthnot. "I understand there is a school here for the boys of the town and the tenants' sons. Are the local girls schooled in any way?"

Mrs. Arbuthnot seemed taken aback by the question. "Their mothers teach them household skills, and if they can read and write, they teach their daughters what they can. I am sure you know the tenants' daughters are not expected to need more than that as they usually marry. The wives of shopkeepers and craftsmen instruct their daughters in running a household or helping in the shop, including enough ciphering to assist customers. Occasionally a merchant has ambitions to rise in society and will send his sons to a public school and his daughters to a ladies' school. However, not many in Lambton do so. Why do you ask?"

Mrs. Arbuthnot's face showed a keen interest in the answer, and Lily Ellington moved closer to Elizabeth, her face alight with interest,

Elizabeth replied slowly, "And the children at the orphanage?"

Lily gave a small gasp.

Mrs. Arbuthnot said, "Mrs. Moore does what she can, but she has much to do just running the orphanage. The boys go to the town school until they are old enough to work. She does teach the girls to read simple texts, so they can study the Bible, and encourages them to read suitable books as they can."

"It is in my mind that classes to teach the girls reading, writing, and simple ciphers would allow them to run a household more competently and to find employment if they do not marry. They could also learn simple cooking, sewing, and knitting. Such skills might make the difference one day between employment as a drudge or as a housemaid or shop assistant. Miss Darcy's maid, Daisy, was raised in an orphanage. It would also make them more desirable as wives to men of some substance."

Mrs. Arbuthnot was nodding. Enthusiasm glowed in Lily's face. She said, "Oh, Elizabeth, what is a wonderful idea! We should meet to discuss it, if you agree, Clothilde?"

"Indeed," Mrs. Arbuthnot replied. "I do not have the sewing circle next Wednesday. Does that suit, ladies?"

Agreement was reached, and the ladies met at Pemberley on the appointed day. Elizabeth noted that Lily looked somewhat downcast and wondered if she was ill. They gathered in Elizabeth's private sitting room to discuss the matter and form a general plan for the proposal.

"I visited the orphanage shortly after the holidays," Elizabeth related as she poured out tea in her private sitting room, "to inquire if they needed anything the Christmas gifts had not provided. Mrs. Moore was very informative. I like her."

"She is adept at making bricks without straw," Mrs. Arbuthnot commented wryly. "I am sure she will support your proposal, Mrs. Darcy. She cares deeply about the children's welfare."

Lily looked thoughtful as she sipped her tea. "I do not think there is enough room at the orphanage to hold a class separate from the daily work. Clothilde, is there not a small building behind the vicarage that used to be used for storage?"

"There is, and it is just about the right size. We will need benches or chairs, and the place will have to be thoroughly cleaned. A coat of paint would not go amiss, either."

Elizabeth had started a list. After a few minutes, she looked up. "What about a teacher? Can you think of anyone suitable?"

Mrs. Arbuthnot considered. "There is a Mrs. Davenport, she used to be a governess. She lives with her sister on the other side of Lambton. She may be willing to supplement her pension by instructing several days a week. I believe she worked for the Mastersons at one time. Their daughters turned out very well."

"Yes," Lily agreed. She seemed to momentarily search for words and made a little fluttering motion with her hand. "I…I went to seminary with Lucinda Masterson. She was very well prepared."

"As for cooking skills," Mrs. Arbuthnot continued, "some of the older girls help in the orphanage kitchen. I am sure we could find a way to use that to teach them meal preparation."

As they talked, Elizabeth noticed that Lily looked more and more ill at ease. They discussed the preparations for a few more minutes before both women noticed that Lily has grown very quiet. Elizabeth saw Lily's face was flushed and drawn as if in pain. Mrs. Arbuthnot also noticed the young woman's condition. She gave Elizabeth a significant look.

"Lily?" Elizabeth reached out to touch her friend's hand. "Are you well?"

Lily stammered, "I am…just a little…dizzy."

She half rose and then slid to her knees; Elizabeth sprang forward to support her. Mrs. Arbuthnot quickly rang for the butler, then helped Elizabeth raise Lily back into the chair. As she took Lily's wrist, she felt the pulse hammering at her fingers. Mrs. Arbuthnot peered into the young woman's face. Her eyes were half open, the pupils dilated.

The vicar's wife said in a strained voice, "Lizzy, you must call Dr. Morrow at once. Mrs. Ellington is very ill."

Mr. Niles came in with a quick knock at the door. Elizabeth indicated Lily. "Please send for Dr. Morrow at once."

Mr. Niles said, "Yes, madam."

He retreated on his errand and between them, Mrs. Arbuthnot and Elizabeth lifted Lily to her feet. They supported her down the hall to the blue guest suite, the nearest one on that floor. Once they had eased her onto the bed, the women removed her dress, petticoat and stays, and covered her with the bedclothes. Elizabeth summoned Clara and sent her for Mrs. Reynolds. She also asked cold water and cloths be brought to bathe her friend's face. When Clara returned with the housekeeper, Mrs. Reynolds had her medicine case with her. She quickly examined Lily and straightened with a grim expression that sent a chill of fear through the two women.

"I do not think I should give her anything, Mrs. Darcy. I have seen these symptoms once before. Certain plants such as foxglove, can cause them if eaten. Do you know if Mrs. Ellington suffers from any maladies?"

"She has never mentioned any," Elizabeth said. "But we are not on such intimate terms that she would confide in me." She looked to Mrs. Arbuthnot.

Mrs. Arbuthnot shook her head. "Her husband should be notified. Until the doctor arrives, she needs to be kept quiet."

"Mr. Darcy should also be apprised of this," Elizabeth said. "He rode out to the Sims' to speak to Mr. Sims about a problem with his well."

"I will send someone to both gentlemen right away, Mrs. Darcy." Mrs. Reynolds picked up her medicine case and left them.

Elizabeth drew a chair near the bed and sat where she could watch her friend as Clara changed the cold cloths on Lily's forehead. She looked very young, like a sick child. Mrs. Arbuthnot had also pulled up a chair on the far side of the bed. She contemplated the two women, Mrs. Darcy and Mrs. Ellington. The vicar's wife recognized as she had immediately upon meeting the former, that she was a woman of character and strength. *It is a pity the two ladies are not better acquainted*, she thought. *Mrs. Darcy might now have a better understanding of whatever is affecting Mrs. Ellington.*

Lily moaned and began to stir. She tried to roll onto her side. Elizabeth leaned over to help her; Clara ran into the dressing room and returned with a basin just as Lily gave a small cry and emptied the contents of her stomach. Elizabeth supported Lily until she eased. Mrs. Arbuthnot handed her a towel wrung out of cold water, and she gently wiped Lily's face. They helped her to lie down again. Elizabeth turned to Clara as she started to leave the room, stopping her. "I think we had best let Dr. Morrow examine that."

"Yes, ma'am."

Clara retreated into the dressing room, and the two ladies resumed putting cold compresses on Lily's forehead. She seemed barely conscious, moaning now and then but not speaking.

"She is a little cooler," Mrs. Arbuthnot noted after some minutes. "Whatever could be the matter?"

Elizabeth shook her head. "I have no idea. She seems healthy and has never mentioned any afflictions. I do not know if she might be with child, but this does not seem like anything I have ever heard about such a state."

"No," Mrs. Arbuthnot said. "It is as if she ingested some kind of poison or drug."

The memory of Lily hurrying furtively away from the cottage by the woods suddenly came back vividly. Elizabeth caught her breath and stared at her friend. At Mrs. Arbuthnot's raised brows, she briefly told her of the incident.

"I think you should tell Dr. Morrow of this as soon as he arrives," the older woman said with a frown. "It may be very important."

Elizabeth nodded. They waited in growing tension for another half hour until the sound of voices from the stairs and feet in the hall alerted them to the doctor's arrival. Mr. Niles knocked and opened the door to admit the physician, who went immediately to the bed. When he had briefly examined the patient, he turned to the two women. "How long has she been in this state?"

Elizabeth answered, "We were meeting to discuss a project of mutual interest when she suddenly collapsed. I had noticed she seemed somewhat distracted, but I did not think it was physical until then." She hesitated and then continued. "There is something else I must tell you, Dr. Morrow."

When Elizabeth had related the incident near Lambton, Dr. Morrow only nodded. He went into the dressing room to examine the vomitus; on his return, he turned to Mrs. Reynolds, who had remained in the room. She had waited in the event she should be needed.

"Please crack open a window, Mrs. Reynolds. The room needs to be cooler. I do not know what she has ingested, except that it has opiate properties, but the fever must be addressed first."

The doctor began to speak to Lily with quiet authority until her eyes fluttered and opened. She started, her expression fearful and confused. Elizabeth immediately soothed her, assuring her she was safe and with friends.

"What did you take, Lily?" the doctor asked. "Was it something Hephzibah gave you?"

After a moment, she nodded weakly. "Baby."

Firmly, Dr. Morrow persisted. "Did you take it as she instructed you?"

Lily closed her eyes. Slowly she shook her head. "More...often. Did...not help."

Dr. Morrow nodded. He turned to Mrs. Reynolds once more. "Bathe her with cold water, with ice in it. Also get as much water down her as she will take. All we can do for the moment is try to lower her fever and flush whatever she has taken from her body. I will visit Hephzibah after I leave here and find out exactly what is in the tonic she gave Mrs. Ellington." He turned to Elizabeth. "She must be carefully watched until the fever lessens."

Mrs. Reynolds had already sent Clara for the ice water and drawn a chair to the bed. Elizabeth knew Lily could not be in better hands. She and Mrs. Arbuthnot followed the doctor into the hallway when there was a commotion in the entry hall. They heard a raised voice and then boots pounding up the stairs. Theodore Ellington took the steps three at a time. He halted abruptly at the sight of Dr. Morrow and the two ladies. "Where is Lily? What has happened to her? For God's sake, Doctor, tell me she is not...."

"Calm yourself, Ellington," Dr. Morrow advised. "Lily is resting. She took some sort of concoction she obtained from Hephzibah. I believe it has to do with her desire for a baby."

Normally the doctor would not have been so explicit in front of Elizabeth and Mrs. Arbuthnot, but Theodore Ellington's face was white with fear and shock. He pulled a small brown bottle from his coat pocket and thrust it at the physician. "This! This is what she has been taking. When they told me she was taken ill, her maid became frightened and showed me where she kept it. If that damned witch has harmed Lily with her poisons, I'll see her hang for it!"

Elizabeth stepped forward and said firmly, "Mr. Ellington, Doctor, I am sure this disruption will not do Lily any good. Please accompany me to my sitting room so we may confer in private."

Without waiting for agreement, she led the way to her sitting room. For a second, the quiet space seemed almost alien. The papers Lily's collapse had disarranged still lay scattered on the floor. Elizabeth indicated chairs as she retrieved the papers and rang for tea. Mrs. Arbuthnot chose a chair near

Elizabeth. Dr. Morrow uncorked the little bottle and sniffed the contents. He tipped it to obtain a drop on his finger and tasted it. Recorking the bottle, he put it into his medical bag. Tea came, and Elizabeth gave everyone a cup before resuming her seat. Mr. Ellington set his aside without tasting it. His eyes never left the physician. Dr. Morrow took a swallow of tea and considered the distrait man. "First, Ellington, I believe your wife is not in any immediate danger. She has a fever, but it is not dangerously high, and it is being treated. Normally, I would not ask such a personal question in company, but these ladies have been instrumental in caring for Mrs. Ellington, and they were present when she told me what she had done. Sir, is your wife trying to conceive a child?"

Ellington closed his eyes as if in pain. After several moments, he said in a low voice, "She desperately wants another child. I have told her more than once that I am happy with her and Forrest, but she will not rest until she is with child again."

"Apparently she went to Hephzibah seeking some remedy to aid conception. I venture to guess the concoction has a bit of mandrake in it. That is an old folk remedy for barrenness in the Mediterranean area where Hephzibah comes from. Mandrake root has opiate properties. No doubt the concoction has other herbs and plant material in it. If taken as directed, it should have been harmless. I have never known Hephzibah's potions to harm anyone, and some of them are no doubt beneficial. However, Mrs. Ellington indicated she has taken more than instructed. The cumulative effect has made her ill. It is well she was here when she collapsed, for now we can see to it that she ceases taking the mixture. I will also have a word with her regarding the dangers of attempting to force her body to do what it does not wish to do."

"When can I take her home?" Ellington asked. His expression had relaxed a little, and color was returning to his face.

"Not for a day or two. I am sure Mrs. Darcy will not mind Mrs. Ellington staying at Pemberley."

"I will be most happy to have her remain as long as Dr. Morrow feels appropriate." Elizabeth smiled at Lily's husband. "If you wish to remain here as well, I will have the adjoining room prepared. Lily is my friend, and I want only the best for her."

Theodore Ellington rose. "Thank you, Mrs. Darcy. I will accept your kind offer. I am most deeply in your debt for taking care of Lily. Doctor, may I sit with her for a time?"

"If you do not wake her or discuss the matter if she wakes. She requires quiet at present."

"Of course."

Elizabeth conducted him back to the blue suite and advised Mrs. Reynolds that Mr. Ellington would sit with his wife. When she came back to her sitting room, she found Mrs. Arbuthnot and the doctor in a discussion of folk remedies.

"You can hardly expect country people," Dr. Morrow said mildly, "not to use the remedies their parents and grandparents used. It's all well and good, as long as the remedy is not worse than the disease."

"I believe," Mrs. Arbuthnot replied, "that the same could be said of a good many medicinals. Laudanum, for example."

What the doctor answered escaped Elizabeth. Hearing a familiar tread on the stairs, she waited in the hallway until Darcy appeared. His face was concerned but not as she knew it would have been if she was the one taken ill.

"Elizabeth, what has happened? Niles said Mrs. Ellington collapsed."

"I will explain later. She is better now, and Mr. Ellington is sitting with her. He will be staying with us for a day or two until she can return home."

Darcy followed her into the sitting room and greeted the doctor and Mrs. Arbuthnot.

Dr. Morrow spoke to Elizabeth. "Please instruct Mrs. Reynolds when Mrs. Ellington feels better she should take some chamomile tea, and dry toast if she is able."

"Certainly, Doctor."

"She should be all right now, but call me if there is any change."

Elizabeth agreed, and he took his leave shortly after. When he had gone, Elizabeth informed her husband of the morning's events. "I am glad I saw her leaving the cottage that day. The doctor might have spent far more time determining what was wrong. I hope this will convince her to allow further children to arrive when they are ready rather than forcing the issue."

Mrs. Arbuthnot said thoughtfully, "Lily Ellington's mother is delicate. I believe Lily is her only child."

Darcy nodded. "That would explain why she takes such an interest in the orphanage and wants another child. Growing up as the only child in a household can be difficult for a sensitive character, as I have found with Georgiana. Mrs. Ellington may not want her son to experience the inevitable loneliness."

"I believe you are right," Elizabeth agreed. "I shall try to talk with her when she is recovered, perhaps as we all work together on the project to educate girls from the orphanage. That will serve to take her mind off of her need for another child for the time being."

Elizabeth had discussed the idea of teaching the orphanage girls some domestic skills to help them make better lives for themselves and found her husband in full agreement. As she walked with Mrs. Arbuthnot to the front hall, she did not see Darcy's dark eyes studying her with undisguised love and admiration. *Mrs. Ellington will not be the only one,* Mrs. Arbuthnot thought with a secret smile, *to increase more than once.*

Chapter 17

The next time Lily opened her eyes, her first sight was her husband with a chair drawn up to the bed, holding her hand in both of his. Mrs. Reynolds had left them alone for the time being, although she meant to return to check on Mrs. Ellington's progress. Lily tried to speak, but he hushed her. He sat without speaking and stroked her hand.

"Theo," she whispered, "dearest Theo. I am...so sorry."

"You need to rest, my dearest. Dr. Morrow said not to speak of this yet."

"I must speak." Her voice was faint. "It is my fault, Theo. My fault. I wanted a baby so badly. I went to Hephzibah. She told me to wait, that my body was not ready yet, but I insisted. I took too much of the tonic." Her eyes closed, and Theodore thought she was asleep again. But after a minute she murmured, "Sorry. So sorry."

"All is well," he reassured her, not certain if she could hear him. "Dr. Morrow says you will be fine." His low voice took on a fierceness. "I do not know what I would have done if I had lost you. Promise me, *promise me* you will never do something like this again."

Tears gathered and rolled down her cheeks. "I promise."

He wiped them away with his thumb and brought her hand to his lips. "Sleep, my darling. I will be here. I will always be here."

A fortnight after Lily's illness, the Darcys stood in the sunlight washing over the church in Lambton after Sunday services, talking to Mr. Arbuthnot and his wife. Elizabeth was telling Mrs. Arbuthnot that she had spoken to Lily and had arranged for her to call at Pemberley on Wednesday next so they might go together to the sewing circle. As they spoke, Elizabeth noticed Mrs. Courtland standing with Lady Walker-Price. She wore her usual high-necked, long-sleeved dress despite the heat of the morning. Her head was bowed and her shoulders slumped, as if she were being scolded for something. Her mouth tightening, Elizabeth started to look away, when Mrs. Courtland suddenly left her companion and walked to join them, her hands clasped nervously before her. Lily smiled at her friend, unaware of what had transpired. They exchanged the conventional greetings. Mrs. Courtland seemed on the verge of speaking when a gig rolled at a fast trot along the road and pulled up sharply. Lyle Courtland's voice shouted roughly, "Millie, get over here! You've done your praying for the week. We're goin' home."

Mrs. Courtland cringed. Her cheeks flushed and then turned pale. Elizabeth saw a look of terror flicker across her face before she turned and scurried toward the vehicle. Lady Walker-Price approached the gig before Mrs. Courtland reached it and leaned forward to speak to Mr. Courtland. Elizabeth wondered if she meant to reprimand him for his treatment of his wife, but the brief conversation showed no signs of contention. Courtland reached down as his wife came up to the side of the gig, caught her arm, and jerked her up to the seat. He gave the group a sneering look just as Darcy came up. Darcy's face darkened, and he stared at Courtland with open contempt. For a moment, their gazes locked, and then Courtland whipped up his horse so suddenly that the beast leaped forward, almost throwing Mrs. Courtland out of the gig.

Mrs. Arbuthnot was still watching the retreating gig. "Drunk on the Sabbath. And at this time in the morning!" she said sharply. "And that is not the worst of his transgressions. That man ought to be horsewhipped!"

"I have tried to speak to him," her husband said with a sad shake of his head. "But he refuses to talk to me. Unfortunately, there is nothing material I can do."

They moved away to speak to other parishioners. Darcy put his arm behind Elizabeth's back, not quite touching her but making her aware of his support.

"It is a shame the law cannot do something about men like Courtland," Darcy said grimly.

Theodore Ellington nodded. "He hates me because of a piece of land my father purchased from his father. He claims they were cheated. It was boggy ground, and the elder Mr. Courtland did not want to spend the money to drain it. We gave more for it than it was worth, but it is now a small lake with output to a stream that drains into the Derwent. During the season, it has some of the best shooting in the county, as you know, Darcy."

Darcy nodded. "I do indeed." He turned to Elizabeth. "Shall we go home, Mrs. Darcy?"

She gathered her pelisse around her and took his arm with a brief feeling of gratitude. "Certainly, Mr. Darcy."

He began to walk toward their carriage. Elizabeth raised her head to find Darcy's eyes sparking with anger. Uncertain of the cause, Elizabeth asked, "What is it, William? What has Mr. Courtland done?"

"Nothing the law can call him to account for, more's the pity."

"But what?" she insisted.

Darcy drew in a calming breath. In a low voice he answered, "It is common knowledge that he abuses his wife. She has never complained, but Mrs. Arbuthnot and others have seen the evidence. That is why she wears dresses that cover her arms and neck."

Elizabeth stopped abruptly. "Mrs. Ellington implied something of the sort the night of the dinner party, but no one talks about it. People *know*, but no one *does* anything to stop him!"

"There is nothing to be done," Darcy responded harshly. Modifying his tone, he said, "A wife is her husband's property. The law does not recognize a husband's abuse of his wife as assault unless she is severely injured or killed. Even then, the punishment is usually too lenient."

Darcy handed Elizabeth into the carriage for the trip to Pemberley. They said nothing more about the situation of Millicent Courtland. Elizabeth knew such things occurred. They were not discussed publicly, or even privately by most people. Woman sometimes talked about such things among themselves, and no doubt men did the same. Oher than talk, nothing happened to stop the abuse until the death of either husband or wife. William's willingness to speak of it to her was a measure of his respect for her as a partner in life.

Elizabeth remained silent as they drove home, except for a few words about the projects of the sewing circle. She noted that William seemed pleased by her participation. Elizabeth knew he thought, but did not say, that at her present stage of pregnancy he wished her to rest more than was her wont. Rest was something Elizabeth was reluctant to do. She insisted on carrying on her household duties and had barely consented to confining her walks to the Pemberley gardens and immediate grounds. In spite of Dr. Morrow's assurance that Elizabeth was healthy, Darcy could not completely put aside the stories of his mother's near death at his birth, and his memories of her passing so shortly after Georgiana was born.

Despite his misgivings, Darcy was proud that his lovely Elizabeth was becoming an integral part of the community in the best possible way. She was taking her place with the ladies who constituted their neighbors and friends. Darcy could not have hoped for better. Lady Catherine's efforts to discredit her seemed to have failed. He had received a letter from his uncle informing him that Lady Catherine and Mr. Rhymes had departed for the Continent on their way to Switzerland. She had left no forwarding direction, but he had transferred funds to a bank in Zurich. Lord Henry seemed to be stepping away from the entire situation except for the financial arrangements. Darcy did not blame him, but he felt some passing empathy for his aunt's suffering.

Wednesday morning was clear and cool with a brisk north wind blowing down from the peaks. Lily Ellington was to call for Elizabeth at twelve thirty, as the sewing circle met from one to three. This gave the ladies time to return home and prepare for dinner. Elizabeth had gathered the materials she was to take, and sat in the drawing room to await Mrs. Ellington's arrival. When she heard a carriage in the drive, she rose in happy expectation of her friend's entrance. But when Mr. Niles announced her guest, Elizabeth took one look at Lily's face and hurried to take her hand. She led Lily to a sofa and sat beside her. "Lily, what has happened? What's wrong? Are you ill?"

The other woman groped in her pocket, withdrew a note, and pushed it at Elizabeth with a shaking hand. Alarmed, Elizabeth opened the paper and read it.

My dear Lily,

My husband has forbidden me to see you again. Lady W-P told him that your illness was because you had taken an overdose of laudanum. I do not believe it, but I dare not disobey him. Forgive me.

MC

Stunned, Elizabeth gazed at her friend, the paper still held in her trembling fingers. Anger rapidly overtook her shock. Elizabeth said, "How dare she? This is outrageous! To even think, much less say, such a thing is beyond anything I have ever heard. Are you going to take the matter to Mr. Ellington?"

Lily sat hunched forward, trying to maintain a semblance of composure. She looked near to fainting; even her lips were colorless. "Theodore has gone to Matlock on business. He will not be home until tomorrow." She raised her head. "Is Mr. Darcy here?"

"He rode out with Mr. Standish, our steward, to settle some tenant dispute that required his personal attention." Elizabeth rose, went to the sidebar, and poured a small amount of brandy into a glass. She brought the glass back and put it in Lily's hands. "Drink that, slowly."

Lily sipped, coughed, and set the glass aside. She looked up at Elizabeth, her large blue eyes, so like Jane's, wide and dark. "What am I to do? Once this rumor is general knowledge, even if my friends do not believe it, it will damage not only me but Theo and Forrest. Does she really hate me that much? Why?"

Elizabeth resumed her seat. She took Lily's hands and said quietly, "Whatever the reason, we must stop this at once. You know village gossip as well as I do. It takes on a life of its own. Usually it is harmless, just information about the goings-on in the neighborhood. Even when it takes on a malicious character, the results rarely last beyond the next little scandal. This is different."

"But how am I to stop it? If she told Mr. Courtland, she has told others. Oh God! How could this happen?"

Elizabeth sat in thought for several moments. Darcy would have instantly recognized the lift of her chin and the look in her eyes. She said, "Does Lady Walker-Price attend the sewing circle?"

"When she is not in town, she usually comes, although what she produces is a mystery."

Encouraged by the faint irony in Lily's voice, Elizabeth said, "We are going today. If she is there, you must confront her. You must not let her spread this lie to the other ladies, as she is sure to do." She rose. "Come. I have everything ready. She believes no one will stand up to her, but that is just what is necessary. It is the only way to fight this attack."

Lily closed her eyes briefly. Then she rose and nodded. "You are right, Elizabeth. If I do nothing, she will use that as evidence the story is true. I do not know what Theodore will do when he finds out, but I cannot wait. Let us go."

The trip to the vicarage was made in silence. Elizabeth realized how difficult this was for her friend, and she offered the support of her presence. When they reached their destination, Elizabeth had the footman carry the extra yarn and her sewing basket so she could walk unencumbered at Lily's side. As they approached the vicarage, Elizabeth noticed Dr. Morrow's gig parked in the shade of a small grove of oaks to one side. Its patient horse nibbled grass as it waited. Several other conveyances stood nearby, their drivers talking idly in the shade. Briefly she hoped that one of the Arbuthnots was not ill, but her mind was too occupied with the confrontation ahead to dwell on the thought.

The vicarage parlor was spacious enough to easily hold more than the half dozen ladies seated in a loose circle in the center of the room. Mrs. Arbuthnot was not present, but several members of the circle were already at work on garments. The others sat in various attitudes of attention to Lady Walker-Price, who was speaking in a low voice with an expression compounded of secrecy and superiority. At Lily and Elizabeth's entrance, a sudden distinct silence fell over the room. Lady Walker-Price looked up, and her mouth pruned as if the two women were contaminated.

Lily raised her head and crossed to stand directly in front of her enemy. She said in a quiet tone that was clear enough to be heard by all of the assembled ladies, "Lady Walker-Price, is there anything you wish to say to my face, instead of spreading vicious untruths behind my back?"

The older woman gawked at her for several seconds before coming to her feet in a state of outrage. "How dare you?"

"How dare *you?*" Lily cut her off, her own anger rising. "I am a Christian woman. I would never even contemplate the terrible sin you accuse me of. I do not know your motive for this malicious attack, but it sickens me to think anyone would contemplate, much less repeat, such an outrageous lie."

"I suppose it is a lie that Dr. Morrow's housekeeper says your husband produced your bottle of 'medicine'. What could that be but laudanum? And your maid had to show him where you had hidden it." Lady Walker-Price sneered at Lily triumphantly.

"I thought better of Dr. Morrow's servant than not only to repeat but to completely misrepresent the facts."

"Not when you represent yourself as a prominent member of this community. Your reprehensible behavior is everyone's business. Perhaps if you did not associate with ladies of questionable virtue, this would not have happened."

Her glare at Elizabeth left no doubt of whom she was speaking. One of the women rose to her feet in protest, but Dr. Morrow's strong voice cut through the tension with the calm precision of a scalpel. "Perhaps it would help if I cleared up this nonsense once and for all. Sorry, Lily. I do not usually talk of my patients' concerns, but in this case, I feel it is justified." He came into the room and faced the three women. Mrs. Arbuthnot was a step behind him, her face set in lines of disgust. "Mrs. Ellington," he went on, "felt the need of a tonic and went to old Hephzibah, something I am sure more than one lady in this room has done. Lord knows what she puts in her concoctions, but I have never known them to harm anyone. However, she always instructs the purchaser how much and when to take her potions. Mrs. Ellington, feeling the tonic was not acting as well or as quickly as she wished, took extra doses. The result was a brief illness of no serious nature, from which she recovered in several days." Dr. Morrow stared directly at Lady Walker-Price. "In addition, allow me to correct your medical ignorance. Laudanum is an opiate. An overdose would produce, if not death, an illness that would require several weeks in bed. It would require several months to recover completely. And that, I am sure, will be the end of this malignant claptrap."

Lady Walker-Price, for once at a loss for words, seemed reluctant to contradict the doctor in spite of her obvious humiliation. Before she came up with a response, Mrs. Arbuthnot said firmly, "Thank you, Doctor. I am sure we are now all better informed. Lady Walker-Price, we will not require your attendance at the sewing circle today. I will see you to the door."

"Do not bother." Lady Walker-Price picked up her untouched sewing basket. "I know my way out." She shot one furious look at Elizabeth. "This is your doing. You will regret it."

Elizabeth chose not to respond, and Lady Walker-Price stalked from the room. She left left a silence into which the drop of a pin would have been deafening. Mrs. Arbuthnot drew herself up, smiled at the ladies, and said, "I believe I shall order tea a bit early."

She went out. Dr. Morrow murmured to Lily, "I am glad I was here to consult with Mr. Arbuthnot about a medical matter. I shall have a word with my housekeeper, you may be certain of it."

With that, he followed Mrs. Arbuthnot out.

The lady who had risen, Mrs. Wildemot, smiled. Her expression told Elizabeth that, at some time, she had been the object of Lady Walker-Price's strictures. She indicated the chairs next to hers. "Come and sit with me, ladies. I think this will be a very productive afternoon."

Darcy arrived home just before dinner and did not bother to change as it was only the two of them. When he came downstairs from washing off the dust of the day, Elizabeth met him at the door of the small dining parlor. Her face told him instantly that something had happened. He followed her to the table and took his seat at the head. The footman held Elizabeth's chair and then served the first course, after which Darcy waved him from the room.

"What is it, Elizabeth? Something has upset you."

She placed her napkin carefully on her lap before meeting his steady gaze. In concise sentences, she told him what had occurred. She began with Lily Ellington's arrival at Pemberley, and concluded with her own return to the house less than an hour before. She expected Darcy's approbation of her actions. The gravity of his expression when she relayed the encounter with Lady Walker-Price surprised and unsettled her.

With a slight frown, Elizabeth said, "Do you believe what we did was wrong?"

Slowly Darcy replied, "Why did not Mrs. Ellington take the matter to her husband?"

"Mr. Ellington was in Matlock on business. He is not expected home until tomorrow. We would have asked you, but you were out. You know at least as well as I do, William," Elizabeth added, trying to suppress the annoyance she was beginning to feel, "the immeasurable damage such a story can do to a family. I thank God that Dr. Morrow happened to be at the vicarage and overheard Lady Walker-Price. His word in such matters has the effect of law, and Lady Walker-Price did not attempt to contradict him."

"She would not," Darcy replied. "To do so would only weaken her position." He drank a little of his wine before he met her eyes. "I shall call on Ellington as soon as I may. This affair has gone beyond gossip. It needs to be addressed where it begins --with Mr. Walker-Price. Once he realizes it is not just Ellington but both of us, and potentially others, who have had their fill of his wife's outrageous behavior, he will have to control her or suffer the consequences. I do not think he would relish being shunned by his neighbors."

"No, I imagine not. I have only met him once, but he seemed oblivious to his wife's actions."

"He takes the path of least resistance. Never a good choice."

Elizabeth smiled teasingly. "One you would never make."

Darcy reached out and laid his hand over hers on the snowy linen tablecloth. "I shall have to find you a suit of armor and a lance so you can slay dragons properly."

"I do not think," Elizabeth said, "I would find armor comfortable, and as for a lance, my tongue is sharp enough to serve."

Darcy's chuckle was followed by a brief but promising kiss to her hand.

The next morning, Darcy was preparing to ride to Fiddler's Croft when Mr. Niles announced Theodore Ellington. The two men shook hands, and Darcy led his friend to his study, closing the door behind them. Ellington's face was set in hard lines. Darcy wondered if he was angry because Elizabeth had encouraged his wife to confront Lady Walker-Price. His first words, however, dispelled that idea. "I would like to personally thank Mrs. Darcy for assisting my wife in stopping the rumor that she had tried to harm herself. It was a godsend that Dr. Morrow was at the vicarage, but even Mrs. Ellington facing down Lady Walker-Price would have left doubt in people's minds."

"You may, of course, see Mrs. Darcy," her husband replied, "but the problem is larger and more dangerous than one rumor or one family."

"Indeed. Lady Walker-Price has caused trouble in this community for far too long, and it has gone far beyond village tittle-tattle. Involving Courtland was sheer malice. If she is not stopped, eventually someone will be irreparably harmed."

Darcy poured two small brandies and brought one to his friend. "I was going to call on you this morning for the express purpose of discussing the matter. I believe we need to see Mr. Walker-Price. He allows this to go on, and in my view, he is as culpable as his wife. I am sure we can engage a number of local gentlemen to withdraw their society from the Walker-Prices if he does not stop Lady Walker-Price from continuing her attacks."

"I had something of the same notion." Ellington sipped his brandy. "Legally, of course, he is responsible for any significant property or financial damage she causes, but no person of sense would try to prosecute defamation. The scandal would be worse than the original offense. Even if her stories are proved false, it is a matter of too little too late."

"Then we had best attack the problem at its source."

"Can you go now, Darcy?"

Darcy nodded. "I will have Mr. Niles find Mrs. Darcy, if you will wait in the drawing room until I have my horse brought around."

The two men reached Greenwood Hall a little before noon. When the butler answered the door, he hesitated to take their cards. His expression was polite but guarded. "Mr. Walker-Price is not at home, gentlemen. I shall leave your cards if you like."

Ellington stared the man down. "Mr. Walker-Price will see Mr. Darcy and me, or he will be called on by a committee of his neighbors. I do not think he will relish what they have to say."

The butler bowed and ushered them into the drawing room. It was an overly elaborate room full of satins and silks in a variety of colors and patterns in the currently fashionable Egyptian mode. The furniture was extensively carved and gilded, and sphinx heads decorated the finials of a large curio cabinet. An elaborate French gilt clock ticked importantly on the heavily carved mantel. *No doubt,* Darcy thought as they waited, *everything is in the latest fashion and obviously expensive, but it has been chosen without taste or restraint.* Ellington seemed to echo his thoughts. His face registered distaste as he looked around. They did not have long to observe the room, however, as the butler returned shortly and led them to Mr. Walker-Price's study.

It was similarly over-decorated but in slightly more masculine colors and materials. Mr. Walker-Price did not rise from behind his cluttered desk. He stared at his visitors with an assumed belligerence that deceived no one, least of all Mr. Walker-Price.

"Why have you come, gentlemen, and what is this threat of a committee calling on me?"

"I think you know the reason for our being here, sir," Ellington responded coolly. "My wife was recently ill for several days from perfectly natural causes. Lady Walker-Price disseminated false information that Mrs. Ellington had attempted to harm herself, a falsehood that Dr. Morrow himself contradicted. You must be aware of the harm such a vicious rumor could do my family. Consider yourself fortunate that Darcy has not accompanied me as my second."

At that, Mr. Walker-Price paled. He blustered for a moment and then rose and poured himself a healthy portion of brandy, downing the liquor in two swallows. Belatedly he indicated the sidebar to the two men, both of whom declined. The brandy was replaced before Mr. Walker-Price resumed his seat. He waved the other men to chairs. "Sit down, gentlemen." He drank a less generous amount of brandy and rested his glass on the desktop, shoving aside a stack of invoices. "Say what you have come to say."

"This community," Ellington replied firmly, "cannot allow Lady Walker-Price's behavior to continue. If you cannot control her actions, we will see to it you are shunned by as many of your neighbors as choose to do so, and I have to believe that will be most, if not all, of the gentry. You are responsible for her behavior, sir. She will not be allowed to continue as she has done."

Mr. Walker-Price finished his brandy without responding. At last he said wearily, "I suppose I ought to have put a stop to it long ago. But Lady Walker-Price is a strong-willed woman, and it has been simpler to let he do as she pleased rather than confront her and live in a household of perpetual contention." He shuffled the papers on his desk around without looking up. "I am, you see, a poor manager. I really do not like country living, but here, Lady Walker-Price is the center of the local society, and in London, she is only one more member of the minor nobility. I honestly did not realize how threatened she felt by Mrs. Darcy—no offense meant, Darcy—until she came home from her sewing circle nearly hysterical." He sighed and went on slowly. "I think it is time we returned to town. The season is over, but there are other entertainments before the little season begins. She will have to content herself with that."

Ellington suppressed a scowl of disgust at the man's open admission of his inability to stop his wife's depredations. Mr. Walker-Price, however, was already on his way to inebriation. Ellington recognized that Mr. Walker-Price was the sort of man who, in his cups, was likely to bemoan his fate in lachrymose self-pity.

"Perhaps," Darcy ventured carefully, "Lady Walker-Price would benefit from the services of a specialist in nervous conditions?"

"I can try," Mr. Walker-Price said without much conviction. "I will, at the least, remove her from the neighborhood. I have been thinking of selling out and purchasing something closer to town." He rose, and Darcy and Ellington stood. "I will see to your concerns, gentlemen," he said as he walked them to the study door. "Good day to you."

As the two men rode out of the drive leading from Greenwood Hall, Ellington shook his head. "Removing her will only make her someone else's problem. I suppose it is the best we can do, though."

"You cannot make a lapdog into a mastiff," Darcy replied and kicked his horse into a smart canter.

Darcy and Ellington had barely ridden away when Lady Walker-Price barged into her husband's study with barely a perfunctory tap on the door. "What did they want?" she demanded.

Mr. Walker-Price turned on her. His tone, for once, was hard rather than placating. "What in God's name possessed you to say that Mrs. Ellington tried to do away with herself?"

Taken aback, his wife's eyes narrowed, and her voice, never dulcet, grew sharp. "I said no more than what Dr. Morrow's housekeeper told Cook when she went to get more salve for her rheumatics. That Mrs. Ellington took too much of her 'medicine' and made herself ill. What was I to think but that she had overdosed herself on laudanum?"

"Whatever you thought, you should have kept silent. Good God! Ellington could have called me out over it!"

Mr. Walker-Price resorted to the brandy bottle again. His wife snorted. "Nonsense. Do not be so weak."

"Yes," Mr. Walker-Price responded, waving his glass dangerously. "I have been weak. But I've finally had enough. Get Tilda to pack your trunks. We are returning to London."

"Town? Now? You are foxed or crazy. I am not leaving until this is settled with that upstart Mrs. Darcy. I have no doubt she is behind all of it. She is trying to take my place with the ladies of the neighborhood."

Mr. Walker-Price drank deeply. Like many who imbibed quantities of liquor over a period of time, he was able to function adequately in spite of the amount he had taken. "I see. You expect me to stand quietly under the latest hornets' nest you have stirred up? Perhaps I should get a stick and hit it a few more times!"

He did not sound as if a hornets' nest was what he wanted to hit. His wife turned away to exit the room; Mr. Walker-Price rang for his butler. Lady Walker-Price halted to watch him. When the butler knocked and entered, his master said, "Please ask Mrs. Lang to have Tilda pack Lady Walker-Price's trunks and then make preparations for a journey to London. Lady Walker-Price and I are leaving tomorrow."

"Very good, sir."

The butler left with alacrity before Lady Walker-Price regained her voice, which had progressed from sharp to shrill. "How dare you? I said...."

"You say entirely too much. Your malice has offended too many people. If we remain, the entire neighborhood is ready to turn against us. And pray do not say 'nonsense.' Darcy and Ellington have made the statement that we will be shunned, and they do not lie. Now, get out of my study, and next time you enter it, knock properly first."

Mr. Walker-Price turned his back on his wife, who stomped out of the study. He made his way to a chair before the fire, glass in hand. He had no doubt he would hear about this endlessly, not only from his wife but from her mother. Nonetheless, it felt good for the moment to be master of his household. Sell out, he thought, and buy something closer to town. The country bored him; his steward did all the planning and management of the crops and dealt with the tenants. He only agreed to everything. There was no social life to his taste. A little shooting, a little hunting, a few dinners, a harvest festival, and the Twelfth Night balls. Nothing to rival a play, a good pantomime in town, a boxing exhibition, or a race meet at Newmarket. Yes, that was the idea. Move away from here and all the trouble his wife had caused.

Mr. Walker-Price finished his brandy, leaned back in the chair, and slowly nodded off.

Chapter 18

Millie Courtland stood in the front parlor of her home and stared at the ashes of the blotter she had just burned. Her shoulder ached where her husband had gripped it when he ordered her to write Mrs. Ellington and Mrs. Arbuthnot to withdraw from their friendship. She knew he had read the blotter in a mirror once before when she made some remark in a note that she was not allowed to attend a gathering. The insult he had perceived cost her still another beating. Tears formed in her eyes. He had seemed so kind, so caring when they were courting. She did not realize until they had been married for nearly a year that he could be so cruel when in drink, or that his drinking was to eventually grow from the usual port and whiskey of all gentlemen to a daily routine that began in the morning and did not end until he collapsed in bed or reached a state of nearly insane anger.

Shivering, Millie wondered if he had gone out. She thought to ask the butler, but as she turned, Lyle Courtland appeared in the doorway. He held an open decanter of port in one hand. As he swayed, it slopped a little onto the floorcloth. "There you are. Did you write those cows like I told you?" Courtland's voice slurred.

"Yes," Millie replied softly. She recognized he was already well on his way to inebriation. "Yesterday."

"Nobody else? Maybe somebody you sneak off to see at Ellington's place?"

"No." She lowered her eyes as he approached. Cold filled her. It was so early in the day! "There is no one," she replied hopelessly. "You know that."

"I don't know nothin' of the kind. Ellington would do anything to get back at me for callin' his father a cheat."

Millie drew a shaking breath. "Mrs. Ellington would never countenance such behavior. Why do you accuse me of such license when you know it is not true?"

Courtland grabbed her arm and shoved her out of the way. "Liar!" He advanced to the fireplace and stared into the ashes. The remains of the blotter lay blackened amid the coals. He spun around. "You damned liar! It doesn't matter anyway. You're finished sneakin' off to the Ellingtons' to meet your lover. You think I don't know, but I'm not blind! Give the bastard the son you won't give me!"

"Lyle, please," Millie said wearily. "There is no one else. There has never been anyone but you. You know that. I would never betray my vows. I do not know why you torture yourself and me with groundless accusations."

Courtland strode back until he stood nearly toe-to-toe with his wife. "Groun'less? You think I don' see other men look at you? Who is he? A gen'leman? A groom? A bloody footman? Who!"

He grabbed her sore shoulder with his free hand and shook her. Millie put her hands up, pressed against his chest. Pain twisted her face. "No one. There is no one! Please, Lyle, you are hurting me!"

Courtland slapped her hard enough to dislodge her hair on one side. Her cheek and temple went numb and then hot with a ferocious pain. He raised his hand again, but she pushed him away as hard as she was able, and he stumbled back.

"Stop it, stop it!' she yelled. "I've done nothing to you!"

Her husband straightened. His teeth were bared like a wild animal. "Hit your husband? That what you learn from Ellington's cow?"

Desperately, Millie said, "I did not hit you. I just tried to stop you from hitting me again. You beat me all the time. I do not deserve such treatment!" Millie retreated another step. "Why, Lyle, why? I have tried to be a good wife to you. You used to say you loved me, but now I am nothing to you but someone you can abuse. Why?"

"Because," he took another awkward pull directly from the decanter in his hand, "you're a trull. A light-skirts. A dirty lil' wh—"

Millie felt the pain not only of her body but her soul. The beatings, the humiliation, the abandonment, the constant fear of the last years rose in her chest until she could barely breathe. Something within her broke in a hot flood. She stepped close to her husband, no longer in control of herself. And she slapped him full in the face. "I hate you," she heard herself hiss. "I hate you! I hate...."

Courtland's face went white and then an ugly purple. He took a step backward, no longer in control of his fury. *This woman dares to strike me?* The outrage of it consumed his brain, destroying whatever reason remained *She dares to condemn me when she is the one to blame for my troubles? Damn the bitch!* Courtland became aware of the weight of the crystal decanter in his hand. He slammed it into the side of his wife's head with the full force of his drunken rage. The delicate glass struck her over the ear, where the bones are thinnest. Millie staggered back. He struck her again; the neck of the decanter broke with the blow. Blood sprayed over his hand and arm, he dropped the ruined decanter and stared in horror at what he had done.

This time the pain was different. It exploded inside Millie's head and filled her sight with fiery birds that flew in all directions. She did not feel her lacerated scalp as blood and wine soaked into her hair and gown. She did not feel the impact when she fell, bleeding heavily, to the floor. She did not hear the butler's horrified cry or Courtland's anguished shouting of her name as he picked her up and laid her on the sofa. Millicent Courtland was no longer in pain. She had passed into eternity.

The day after Darcy and Theodore Ellington confronted Mr. Walker-Price, Elizabeth was in the nursery when Mr. Niles informed her that Mrs. Arbuthnot waited in the drawing room. Surprised and pleased, Elizabeth said, "Will you ask her if she would like to see the nursery please, Mr. Niles?"

Several minutes later, Mrs. Arbuthnot joined her. She was delighted with the room, but Elizabeth knew by her manner that she was troubled. Leading the way to her private sitting room, Elizabeth indicated a chair and was about to ring for tea when the minister's wife stopped her. "I have not come on a strictly social call, Elizabeth." She bit her lip and continued. "I received a note from Millie Courtland resigning from the sewing circle. She did not come to church Sunday, as you know, and I am beginning to fear something is wrong. She may be -- ill. I would not put it past Mr. Courtland to deny her Dr. Morrow's assistance. I wish to call on her to ascertain her condition."

Slowly Elizabeth said, "Mr. Courtland will not be pleased, if he is at home."

"I do not care a fig for Mr. Courtland's approbation. It is my Christian duty to see to the welfare of my friend. However, I thought if you wished to come with me, two might be more successful than one. I realize in your condition the trip, although relatively short, may not be comfortable, but if you cannot go, perhaps Mr. Darcy might accompany me?"

"He has taken a new hunter out to assess its abilities. He will be home shortly. How did you arrive?"

"I drove the gig."

Elizabeth closed her eyes briefly. "If you can wait for a few minutes, I will have the carriage brought around. I promised William I would not stir from the grounds without either him or Steves in attendance, and I believe the three of us would have a problem sharing a gig."

For the first time since her arrival, Mrs. Arbuthnot smiled. "It is quite an image. Very well. Of course, I will wait. Perhaps Mr. Darcy will have returned by then."

He did not, however, and twenty minutes later the two women entered the Darcy carriage and departed, with Steves occupying his customary position at the rear. As usual, he was armed with a pistol hidden under his coat in the event of any trouble his size was insufficient to overcome. They had been gone about a quarter hour when Darcy rode in on the hunter, a large, handsome sorrel he had purchased from a local breeder. He entered the house smiling to be met by Mr. Niles, a worried frown on his usually impassive face. "Mr. Darcy, I am glad you have returned, sir. Mrs. Darcy has accompanied Mrs. Arbuthnot to the Courtlands' home. She took the carriage, and Steves went with them, but considering…everything, including Mr. Courtland's reputation, I wanted you to know immediately."

Darcy's face grew dark. "How long have they been gone?"

"A quarter hour or a little more."

"Thank you, Mr. Niles."

Darcy spun on his heel and returned to the stables. He saddled Sultan without waiting for a groom and rode out at a fast canter along the driveway. At the road leading past the Courtland property, he realized it would take him considerably less time to go overland. Taking a low hedge with ease, he headed the big stallion across the fields. He was reassured that Elizabeth had taken Steves on the trip to her friend's, and with Mrs. Arbuthnot there, it was unlikely Courtland would do anything worse than refuse to let them see his wife. Anger flamed in Darcy's mind. Why were men like Courtland allowed to mistreat the women of whom they should be most protective? Courtland was a bully, and Darcy hated bullies. He had known others in his life who looked on their wives as slaves, using the law to intimidate and suppress them. Those women lived miserable lives, always in fear. Only in the case of murder or serious injury were the husbands punished, and the punishments were frequently less severe than if they had killed or injured a valuable animal.

This has to change, Darcy though as Sultan cleared a fence and headed across a pasture that led to the Courtlands' park. Unfortunately, it was going to take either some horrendous act or a general alteration in the attitude of society to accomplish that.

The Darcy carriage pulled up in front of Courtland House. Steves jumped down, placed the step, and helped Mrs. Arbuthnot and Elizabeth to descend. They followed him to the front door, which stood ajar. As soon as they reached the porch, they heard a sound that sent gooseflesh down Elizabeth's back. It was a thin wailing that rose and fell, the sound of someone in unbearable pain. Steves leaped forward and pushed the door fully open. Mrs. Arbuthnot caught her breath, and Elizabeth gave a low cry, pressing both hands to her mouth. A middle-aged woman she judged to be the housekeeper stood in the middle of the entry hall. Her eyes were closed, her lined face contorted, both hands twisted in her apron. It was her voice keening.

Mrs. Arbuthnot went to the woman, took her by the shoulders, and shook her gently. "Mrs. Denton, what has happened?"

The housekeeper swallowed hard and tried to regain some semblance of composure. "Mrs. Courtland...in there." She pointed a shaking hand at the parlor door. "Oh, my dear God!"

Before either woman could move, Steves strode to the parlor door, looked in, and turned back. His face strained, he said, "Please, ladies, you must return to the carriage."

Grimly, Mrs. Arbuthnot demanded, "What is it?"

She started purposely for the parlor only to have Steves' large frame implacably block her path. "Please, madam, you cannot go in there. You do not want to see. Please let me escort you to the carriage."

Mrs. Arbuthnot turned purposefully to the housekeeper. "What has happened here? Answer me!"

"He," Mrs. Denton gulped and twisted her apron in both hands, "Mr. Courtland has killed Mrs. Courtland! Mr. Everton saw it all!"

At the end of her endurance, Mrs. Denton collapsed onto the floor sobbing heavily. Elizabeth seemed to come out of a trance. She said to Steves, "Find a footman or a groom to go for Dr. Morrow and the magistrate. Hurry."

"There is no need, madam." The elderly voice was shaken but controlled. A slightly stooped man with thinning gray hair came into the entry and bowed to the ladies. "I am Mr. Everton, the butler. I have already sent a groom for both the doctor and constable. If you will allow me?"

He stepped past Steves, who had moved a pace into the entry, and firmly shut the parlor door. Mrs. Arbuthnot almost protested but turned instead to Elizabeth. For the first time since their arrival, she remembered that Mrs. Darcy was with child and should not be in such a situation. She said, "Steves is right, Elizabeth. You must go home. There is nothing we can do here."

"We cannot just leave her," Elizabeth protested. "Someone should stay with her until...until the doctor arrives."

No one in the entry heard the sound of a horse pulling up sharply in the drive or the pounding of boots as Darcy crossed the porch and halted on the threshold. He took in the scene in a second and reached his wife in two strides. Elizabeth felt his arm circle her protectively. He held her against his solid strength, and at last, tears gathered and fell down her cheeks.

"Millie Courtland is dead," Mrs. Arbuthnot told him grimly. "Killed by her drunken husband." She turned to the butler. "Where is that poor excuse for a man?"

The butler looked from Steves' imposing bulk to the two women and Darcy's masterful presence. Years of formality did not desert him, even in crisis. "Mr. Courtland was in his study when I came down the hall. He was writing something at his desk."

Darcy leaned down and spoke quietly to Elizabeth. "Please return to Pemberley, Elizabeth. I will deal with the situation here. There is nothing you can do, and you have more than yourself to think of."

Elizabeth shivered and nodded. Steves stepped forward. He expected to accompany both women, but Mrs. Arbuthnot remained firmly rooted to the entry hall. "I will stay, Mr. Darcy. Millie Courtland was one of our parishioners. I will not leave her until the doctor arrives."

"Very well," Darcy agreed, recognizing her determination. His chief purpose was to get Elizabeth back to Pemberley, where she could be cared for when the inevitable reaction set in. "Steves, take Mrs. Darcy home. I will tell the magistrate he can speak to her later if he needs to. Then send the carriage back for Mrs. Arbuthnot."

Steves said, "Yes, Mr. Darcy." There was a note of gratitude in his voice.

He waited for Elizabeth to exit the house. She looked up at her husband, her eyes dark with grief and pain. Darcy touched her face gently, and without further words Elizabeth accompanied the footman outside. His face stony, Darcy strode down the hallway. This time Courtland would answer for his actions. It was only tragic that his wife had to die to achieve justice. He heard the butler shuffle along the polished boards behind him.

Darcy said without turning, "Is there any room in the house where Mr. Courtland can be detained until the law arrives?"

"Yes, sir," the butler began. "The wine—"

The sound of a pistol shot from ahead halted both men midstride. Darcy ran to the open door of the study. Courtland lay slumped over his desk. A sheet of paper lay under his left hand; his right arm hung to the floor. A pistol still dangled from his fingers. The smell of gunpowder and blood stained the air. The side of Courtland's head, just over the right ear, had been shattered by a bullet.

Darcy went to the desk and looked at the sheet of paper half under Courtland's free hand. It had escaped all but a few spots of blood. The scrawled writing was just legible, and he leaned over to look at it. Darcy read the note and straightened. He felt almost physically ill. The dead man had called his wife's death an accident, he condemned the Ellingtons and the Arbuthnots for leading her astray, and excused himself from guilt because his wife's desertion had driven him to drink. Disgusted to his soul, Darcy went back to Mrs. Arbuthnot, who had seated herself on the second tread of the stairs.

They waited in silence until the magistrate arrived with Dr. Morrow. The two officials went into the parlor. When Dr. Morrow returned, anger filled his usually calm face. "I'll see Courtland hang for this if it's the last thing I do," he told them.

Darcy indicated the hallway. "You will find him in the study. He has escaped human justice. I expect the justice he faces now will be impartial, unlike a human jury."

Dr. Morrow stalked down the hall without a word. Mrs. Arbuthnot accepted Darcy's hand to rise, and sighed. "I will return to the church as soon as I may and inform Josiah of what has happened. He will need to make funeral arrangements for Millie. I believe her only relative is a brother in the merchant marine, but I do not know his name or the name of his ship. There may be some information in her papers."

"Let the magistrate sort it out," Darcy advised.

They waited together in silence until the carriage returned from Pemberley. Darcy handed the vicar's wife in and stood until the driver turned onto the main road. He spoke briefly with the magistrate, who arrived half an hour later. After a brief consultation, Darcy mounted Sultan and rode back the way he had come across country. After reading Courtland's note, the magistrate agreed it should be entered into the record at the inquest but not made public. There were enough facts to support a verdict of suicide and willful murder without involving anyone else.

Darcy reached home to find Elizabeth waiting for him in her sitting room with Georgiana. His sister undoubtedly knew of Mrs. Courtland's death. Darcy saw that she was shaken by the tragedy, however her focus was on Elizabeth rather than herself. Darcy went to Elizabeth immediately, sitting beside her and taking her hand. She raised a pale face to his, but Darcy read her well enough to know she was not in danger from the events of the morning.

"Have they arrested him?" she asked.

Darcy hesitated. "No. He took the matter into his own hands. There is nothing more except for the legalities."

Elizabeth squeezed her eyes shut and leaned her head on her husband's shoulder. After a time she straightened, squared her shoulders, and breathed in deeply. "Clothilde did not come in. I suppose she thought the news would be too shocking after...what had already happened. There will need to be preparations for Mrs. Courtland's...funeral, and I am sure she will need help. I will write a note to Lily Ellington tomorrow when she is aware of the situation, and we will do whatever is necessary."

Darcy opened his mouth to protest that Elizabeth needed to think of herself first, but a look and a slight shake of the head from Georgiana stopped him. Elizabeth's influence was bringing his sister from girlhood to womanhood with grace and maturity. His wife would never be content to sit by and let others take the burdens of life. She would always step in and do whatever she was able to assist them. It was a part of her character Darcy found extremely admirable, among a host of others. He nodded slightly in return.

"As you will, my dearest wife. Just rest today. I promise you we will provide whatever assistance is required."

Elizabeth rose and touched his cheek lightly. "I shall go upstairs and rest until dinner. Will that suit?"

"Very well."

Darcy stood, took her hand, and kissed it lovingly. As she also stood, Georgiana said a little shakily, "I believe I will rest until dinner as well. Thank you, Brother."

Darcy watched the two most important women in his life leave, and he thought, not for the first time, that the day he had entered the Meryton assembly had been the luckiest day of his life.

The first social event Elizabeth was to attend after her lying-in and churching was the annual harvest festival. It was held at Lambton at the harvest moon in September. Clara was just buttoning her gown when Darcy knocked lightly and entered. He waved the maid away with a smile. "I'll do that."

Clara curtsied and left them, and Darcy moved behind his wife, his long fingers working at the tiny buttons.

"I have invited new neighbors to accompany us to the festival," he said as he bent his head and kissed the sweet curve of her neck. "The gentleman has purchased Greenwood Hall."

"I did not know it was sold."

Elizabeth studied her reflection in the full-length pier glass mirror. The empire style of the gown was better suited to her returning figure than a more detailed gown would have been. She smiled at their reflection; Darcy slipped his arms around her and drew her to rest against his body. "I will be glad when my body returns to its usual state. I still do not feel quite myself."

"You have never looked more beautiful, my dearest wife."

Darcy kissed her again. Elizabeth felt the heat that his touch always brought rise in her. "I am grateful that all went as well as it did. Our son is so beautiful, is he not?"

The sharp jolt of fear that the impending birth had engendered in him was gone. Darcy smiled. "The most beautiful baby in the world." He kissed her tenderly. "Come, let us go downstairs and greet our guests."

Elizabeth tucked her hand into the crook of his proffered arm. As they went down the main staircase to the second floor, she looked up at him. He wore the secretive, self-satisfied smile she recognized from whenever he gave her an unexpected gift.

"What are they like?"

"They remind me of a couple we are very fond of."

"Oh, I hope they are as pleasant as Theodore and Lily Ellington."

"I assure you, you will not be disappointed, my love."

They reached the door of the drawing room. Mr. Niles stood to one side to await orders. Darcy said, "Champagne, please, Mr. Niles," and the butler departed with a bow.

Darcy stepped behind Elizabeth as she turned to the doorway. Her chin was up, and she wore a bright, welcoming smile. As she stepped over the threshold, she stopped abruptly with a gasp. Then Jane's voice said, "Lizzy!"

The sisters ran to one another, they embraced amid the laughter of the other occupants of the room. Elizabeth released her sister but kept hold of her hand. Her eyes went to the two men who approached her with broad smiles. Georgiana, who had been seated next to Jane, was on her feet clapping with delight.

"Well, my Lizzy," Mr. Bennet said as she turned and hugged him tightly, "you look as you always have. I had thought motherhood might change you."

"Papa!" She laughed through the tears sparkling in her eyes. "Do not be concerned. It has only made me more joyous and even more thankful for every day." She glanced around the room. "Is Mama here?"

Bingley accepted a hug in his turn and shook his head. "She did not want to make the trip. I am afraid she is most unhappy with us for removing so far from Meryton."

"My son-in-law wisely asked me to accompany him," Mr. Bennet said with his familiar ironic smile. "He felt he could not manage the move without the constant admonitions and advice of at least one Bennet."

Mr. Niles arrived at that moment with the champagne, which he expertly opened and swiftly served. When everyone had a flute, Darcy raised his glass. "To old friends and new neighbors, to family, and to my wonderful wife, Elizabeth."

When they had drunk, Elizabeth raised her own glass and said, "To my husband, Fitzwilliam Darcy, the best man I have ever known."

The rocking chair moved backward and forward easily, soothing both the mother and babe who occupied it. The only sound was a soft, crooning lullaby, barely audible. Elizabeth Darcy watched the sleeping infant in her arms with a sense of wonder and a love that filled her body and soul with joy. The risk, the pain were forgotten. Bennet William Darcy slept in his mother's arms, unaware that he was heir to a vast estate and fortune, beloved by his family, and destined to live his life in rapidly changing and frequently challenging times. The dark curls that covered his head rested against Elizabeth's breast. His rosebud mouth moved a little in his slumber, and his dark-blue eyes were closed. They would turn to a darker brown in time.

Around her, the nursery radiated security, peace, and serenity. It was a reflection of her life. Its soft greens, yellows, and blues were in gentle contrast to the cream and white of painted woodwork. Elizabeth had elected to nurse her son herself rather than employ a wet nurse. At present his regular nurse was at supper, giving Elizabeth a chance to be alone with her son. She spent as much time as possible with him, as did his father. Darcy was determined that their son not be shunted off with nurses and tutors. His father and mother had always given him their time as well as their love, and he wanted his children to have the same experience.

Jane and Bingley were settled at Greenwood Hall. They were barely an hour's drive from Pemberley, which added another layer to Elizabeth's happiness. Jane was due to have her first child in four months. By then, Elizabeth believed she would be able to take Ben with her to stay for her beloved sister's lying-in. Their children would grow up together, forming a bond as strong as any family might boast. Their mother had taken the move of her eldest daughter to Derbyshire badly, but with their father's assistance, she finally accepted that her influence over Jane was at an end. Both parents and the three younger sisters were to visit in the spring. Elizabeth viewed the prospect with both anticipation and some consternation. William did not seem to have any concerns about the visit, so perhaps it would all work out well. Her father would bury himself in the library, her mother would be awed by the grandeur of the house and estate, and her three sisters would find common ground with Georgiana to occupy their time.

The lessons for the girls from the orphanage were progressing well. The shed behind the vicarage was renovated. A stove, benches, and a desk for Mrs. Davenport had been added. Darcy, Theodore Ellington, and Charles Bingley had financed the improvements, and several of the local ladies provided supplies. Mrs. Arbuthnot had helped Elizabeth set up the classroom, since Lily Ellington was too near the birth of her daughter, Bethany. She had not suffered as she had with her son's birth, and the baby was healthy and robust. The annual party at the orphanage in December had gone well, including the attendance of Mrs. Davenport, who declared a number of the girls to be promising students.

With a little tactful persuasion, Mr. Bennet had been able to use the funds made available by the marriages of his two eldest daughters for investments Darcy recommended, thereby increasing the amounts of his remaining daughters' dowries. Darcy also promised Elizabeth he would add to the amounts if required so that her sisters might make appropriate marriages.

In something like awe, Elizabeth contemplated what her life had become, all because of the unwavering love and devotion of one man. It was a love that wrapped their lives around, and it would bind them until death, and, if God willed, continue beyond. Her William. Smiling down at her sleeping son, Elizabeth rocked softly on.

21379715R00149

Printed in Great Britain
by Amazon